PADMAVATI

SUTAPA BASU

Readomania

Readomania Publishing
A division of Kurious Kind Media Private Limited
466, DDA SFS Apartments, Pocket 1, Sector 22, Dwarka,
New Delhi – 110077
books.readomania.com
email: support@readomania.com
Facebook: facebook.com/iamreadomania
Twitter: twitter.com/iamreadomania

Reprinted in 2025
First Published in 2017 by Readomania

ISBN: 978-93-858545-6-9

Typeset in Palatino Linotype By Shine Graphics
Printed in Delhi

For

the love of my life,

Stavya

Cast of Chief Characters

Mrinalini Rao is a senior journalist with a national daily who is researching the life of Rani Padmini of Chittor.

Uma is a local village girl whom Mrinalini meets in Chittorgarh.

Gandharava Sena is the King of Singhaldweep, and Padmavati's father.

Champavati is the Queen of Singhaldweep, and Padmavati's mother.

Padmavati is the Princess of Singaldweep, only daughter of King Gandharava Sena and Queen Champavati.

Ginni is a parrot of the Hiraman species who can speak like a human being and is Padmavati's childhood friend.

Ambika is daughter of Padmavati's nursemaid, born on the same day as the princess. She is Padmavati's childhood friend.

Kunwar Ratan Singh is the Prince of Chittor, adopted son of Rawal Samar Singh. He becomes the Rawal of Chittor around CE 1302.

Rawal Samar Singh is the Rawal of Chittor and adoptive father of his sister's son, Ratan Singh.

Prabhavati is Ratan Singh's senior-most wife.

Kunwar Vir Bhan is the son of Ratan Singh and Prabhavati, presumptive heir to the throne.

Raghav Chetna is an artist and small-time courtier at Chittorgarh.

Ba is Ratan Singh's natural mother and the sister of Rawal Samar Singh. She lives in the royal palace in Chittorgarh.

Prince Gora Rajsinha is Champavati's younger brother and Padmavati's guardian in Chittor.

Prince Badal Rajsinha is the motherless teenaged son of Prince Gora Rajsinha.

Alauddin Khalji is the second Khalji ruler of the Delhi Sultanate. He ruled from CE 1296 to 1313. After taking the throne by rebelling against his mentor and uncle, he is on a campaign to bring all of North India under his rule.

Prologue

The New Queen had decided.

It had been raining steadily for two days. Stormy winds had twisted trees and felled massive branches. Filled with sloshing, muddy water, the deep trapezium-like shaft, spread over a thousand square yards and referred to as the *Kund* or sacrificial fire cavity, could not be used for the pyre. Yet, any further delay would be disastrous. The sand in the hourglass trickled down steadily and the enemy was hammering at the gates.

The subterranean cavern would have to do, she had said. Bullock carts loaded with bundles of hay, wood-chips and numerous pots of clarified butter began drawing up to the mouth of the dark underground tunnel. Men, whose tears mingled with the rain, carried grist and fuel for the conflagration into the centre of the wide cave.

The queens, along with their ladies, maids and young girls, bathed and attired themselves from head to toe in gorgeous garments, jewels and ornaments. Married women bedecked themselves in their crimson-and-gold wedding finery. Some women held baby girls in their arms who smiled beatifically, unaware of their fate. After offering veneration to the deity and consuming a sacred meal that included a drink of whey and basil mildly laced with marijuana, the women began to approach the cavern. Men lined the path, hands folded, heads bowed in salutation to the *satis*. Husbands and brothers, fathers and sons, unmindful of the rain, were each searching for a beloved face.

In the enclosed space, the air was becoming scarce as the women surrounded a rude platform erected amidst mountains of hay and wood, liberally doused in clarified butter. The temple priests, having completed the rituals, stood by, chanting verses from the Vedas. Everyone waited for the senior queen to lead, but she seemed to falter. The New Queen gently slipped past her and ascended the platform. She sat down in the centre and folded her palms. Instead of closing her eyes, she looked ahead calmly. The other royal ladies clambered up to sit in a semicircle around her. Some had to be helped up by their maids because they were infirm or they were trembling with terror. The girls, maids, noblewomen and their female attendants stood behind the seated ladies, facing the priests. The babies in their arms looked around curiously, as if this was a new game.

The chief priest held up a flaming torch. Calling out, '*Jai! Ek Linghji Ki Jai,*' he lit the pyre.

Whoosh!! The hay, wood and butter sprang into a wavering pillar of fire. The priests ran pell-mell to the cave opening to escape the brute firestorm. The flames spread quickly, encircling the platform, sucking out whatever little air there was in the cave. The women clutched at their throats, desperate mouths agape. Shrill screams echoing down the tunnel were abruptly choked off. Some mothers smothered their children to save them from the agony of burning. A few girl infants escaped the laps of mothers who were already alight. Tiny limbs spewing flames, they ran around, shrieking at their unexpected torment.

Other women clutching babies, young girls and maidens attempted to jump off the burning platform. Though they had voluntarily embraced the idea of grace through fire, their instinct for survival rejected the terrible death facing them. But their leaps for freedom landed them right into fiery, blazing, scarlet hands that enveloped them lovingly. Burning bodies rolled on the rocky floor, already dead. Orange and blue tongues licked greedily at human skin, making the royal ladies screech uncontrollably. Some jumped up, beating their burning garments with bare hands in vain. Flames whirled around them until each became a separate bonfire reaching out to ignite more panicked women. All of it turned into an inferno of figures gyrating in agony. The roar of combustion growled within the cave, punctured by the hiss of sizzling skin and the sharp cracking of bones. A nauseating smell of burnt hair rose with clouds of thick grey smoke.

Once the pyre was burning merrily, the conflagration began to seek more air. Bellowing like an animal, the fire squeezed left and right through the narrow tunnel towards openings on both sides. The weeping men, still gathered just outside, were swept back as flames burst out of the tunnel.

In the centre of all the chaos, only one figure remained serene and motionless. As the gold, saffron and blue blaze made rings around her, rising higher and higher, slowly enclosing the New Queen, she was like a sculpture, absolutely still. Nothing seemed to touch her; not the torment, not the grief, not the fear. It defied all principles of logic. Where did a girl find such strength, not garnered even by the meditation of ascetics, to tolerate the torture of being burnt alive? Her dark silhouette, in lotus pose, palms folded, was a sublime sight. When the great white heat reached the core, her body exploded in a shower of sparks. The tremendous blast ricocheted against the red, hot rocky walls sending horrific echoes floating out to the listeners.

The *jauhar* took hardly a few minutes to extinguish Padmavati's living mortality but gifted her with indelible immortality; a significant niche in the history of India. Time could not dim her charisma nor age wither her stunning beauty. For centuries to come, the supreme sacrifice of this legendary Queen of Chittor would attain a place of undying pride and honour in the hearts of all her country's people.

1

Mrinalini Rao was a tall, slender, attractive woman. But her winsome looks in no way detracted from her skills as an intrinsic news-hound working with a lead national newspaper, *The Daily Express*. She had a curious knack of worming her way through layers of deception to expose the gory truth behind seemingly banal events. Investigative reporting was her forté and her peers joked about what they called Mrinalini's nose for the scent of a scoop. But right then, Mrinalini was unable to see anything other than what lay just beyond her nose. Sighing, she sat down on the warm stones.

Mrinalini was at Chittorgarh, a fort whose very name conjures up the most romantic tales and myths. Built on an isolated plateau of the Aravalli range, the fort overlooks the countryside from a height of nearly six hundred feet. Her eyes took in the panoramic view of plains criss-crossed by furrows of cultivated fields, cleaved by the Gambhiri River and broken by scrub and infrequent thorny acacias. As far as the eye could see, the cloudless sky melded with the brown-green patchwork. Rushing wings and loud shrieks turned her eyes upwards. Throngs of black specks were wheeling overhead against the orange and rose tints of the evening. *Playing their last games before heading home for the night*, mused Mrinalini. Entranced, her feet traced tiny circles round and round as she tilted her head to the winged multitudes making their circular flights. They spun around in ever-maddening circles and she spun with them until she felt that she was spinning up, up, up; rising to the birds...the heaviness of her body left behind, her spirit winging away with them.

Flying is freedom...I feel no time and no space. I am flying with the birds...they are flying with me. They are calling me...telling me there are no beginnings and endings here, only infinity...only timelessness that reaches out to touch the timeless in me.

Mrinalini closed her eyes to savour the perpetuity and instantly lost her buoyancy.

When she opened her eyes again, there was a slight queasiness in the pit of her stomach as if she had been in a lift that had descended too fast. She looked around. She was still in the garden, a short distance from *Ram Pol,* the massive gate through which she had entered the fort about thirty minutes ago. Overhead, black dots were still in motion, though the flocks had gone. And she noticed that none of the birds had come to settle inside the fort. *Come to think of it, I haven't heard a single bird call from the trees here since I have entered,* she thought, looking at the several tropical evergreens with well-endowed canopies that dotted the gardens. *Probably not enough worms, with tourists stampeding through the grounds.*

Well, I haven't found a worm, either. She gave a tiny shrug. *This entire expedition has been a colossal waste of time. All because of Sisodia. Oooh! I could kill him.* But she could not, for he was her boss. Bosses exist to be insufferable and obeyed without question.

Mrinalini was the senior reporter with the broadsheet and Mr Pratap Sisodia was its Chief of Bureau. Usually, he was quite amenable to her suggestions about stories worth following up or rejecting. But when the controversy over the film on Padmini, the Rajput queen, blew up, he was like the proverbial bull aggravated by a red shirt. The more he read of people commenting that Padmini was only a figment of a poet's imagination with no place in the annals of history, the more he snorted and pawed the dust.

Mrinalini had never seen her cool, pragmatic boss so emotionally strung up. Eventually, he had asked his senior reporter to depute her ongoing stories to a junior, drop everything, and dash off to Chittorgarh town to extricate the facts about the renowned queen. Sisodia's obvious angst about the entire furore transmitted to Mrinalini that her real objective in this investigation was to unearth evidence to prove the historicity of Padmini, rather than the truth. She had never seen her boss so obsessed with a story.

While reading up on the history of Mewar, she had found mention of its Sisodia dynasty. The name had jumped out at her...the same as her boss' family name! *Was there a connection?* Mrinalini had shrugged. *Whatever it was, Boss had behaved like ants were crawling through his pants.*

As a professional journalist, Mrinalini had diligently followed process, looking up online sources and visiting physical authorities such as museum archives as well as academic references before actually visiting the location. After two weeks of sifting through information, she had realized that seeking evidence for Rani Padmini's existence was like walking on quicksand. There were mentions of her by historians but no validation other than in the poetry of bards such as Jayasi's *Padamavat* or Labdodhya's *Padmini Charitra Chaupai* or paintings by artists inspired by her myths. Certainly, one of the queens of Chittor during the 13th century had been a lady named Padmini, but whether she was actually the legend who is venerated for her beauty and sacrifice all over Rajasthan could not be authenticated.

Beginning the probe, Mrinalini had found it difficult to drum up enthusiasm for it. She had felt more like a piece of chamois leather being used to polish Sisodia's ego but as she gradually fell into one black hole after another in her search for facts about Padmini, her natural curiosity was piqued. *Why this silence about her? Why have most historians dithered to authenticate her existence?* If anyone had mentioned her in their account of Chittorgarh's history, they carefully referred their source to local legends or songs by bards. *Why is this so? Did such a peerless beauty, an unimaginable fantasy of a woman exist or not?* After touring museums, libraries and resources in Delhi, Jaipur, Udaipur and even in the small Chittorgarh town, the last port of call was Chittorgarh itself, the fort where Rani Padmini had lived and died.

However, by now Mrinalini was intrigued by quite a different aspect of the Queen's life...rather her death. The archives or literary renditions about the said Padmini differed on various matters but they all agreed on one point. Padmini died by committing *jauhar*...voluntary death by burning. The very idea held Mrinalini by the throat.

It was a personal hang up. Since childhood, fire had been her bogeyman. Even a tiny flame of a matchstick would make her scream with terror. Her puzzled parents had tried to reason with her, even taken her to consultants, but to no avail. She could not be rid of her terror. So... no Diwali crackers, no birthday candles and no cooking on a flame for Mrinalini.

As Mrinalini had read accounts of Padmini's death, the picture of the *jauhar* began to come alive in her mind, painted in technicolour. So much so, that just the name, 'Padmini' brought forth the visual of a young girl walking into a crackling fire and made Mrinalini actually gasp, as panic strangled her. She would see the fire coming closer and closer, feel the hair on her bare skin singe, and the sharp stinging pain of the first flames licking at her. She would force herself to close her eyes and shake her head vigorously to rid her mind of the horrifying images.

How could somebody want to take on such a terrible torture? Death by any other means is far easier than burning alive. Knowingly letting your body suffer such horrible agony...how could she? Was she human? Was she made of the same stuff as us? Who was she? Who was this Padmini?

A few weeks of this and the mythical queen had revealed a completely different dimension to Mrinalini.

Now it was her own quest, a personal endeavour to discover the real woman behind the legend of Padmini. *What was the truth? Was she for real?* Till now, she had failed to unravel the mystery. Her last hope was this monument. *Would it reveal the secret of Padmini's reality to her?*

Mrinalini saw the imposing fort, abruptly rising from the plains and straddling the skyline, much before she had entered the Chittorgarh town. She had been updating herself online with the fort facts while her cab had been speeding down the dusty roads. Apparently, the origins of the fort were misty with myths. Chittorgarh, wherein *garh* means fort, was originally called Chitrakut and had been built by the local Maurya rulers.

She was reading aloud from her tablet, as her taxi approached the fort,

'Roughly in the shape of a fish, the fort has a circumference of 13 km and covers an area of 700 acres. The fort complex comprises sixty-five historic structures, among them four palace complexes, nineteen main temples and four memorials. The fort had once boasted of 84 water bodies but only 22 of them remain now. These water bodies are fed by natural catchment and rainfall, and have a combined storage of four billion litres that could meet the water needs of a population of fifty thousand souls for upto four years. These water bodies are in the form of ponds, wells and step wells. The fort has seven gates, each gate is called *Pol* in the local language, namely the *Padam Pol, Bhairon Pol, Hanuman Pol, Ganesh Pol, Jodla Pol, Laxman Pol* and the main gate, named the *Ram Pol,* leading into the fort. All the gateways to the fort are massive stone structures with secure fortifications for military defence. The doors of each gate have wicked, pointed arches reinforced to fend off elephants and cannon shots. The top of the gates and the adjacent fort walls have notched parapets and slits for archers to shoot at the enemy army. As one passes through all the seven gates, a circular road within the fort provides access to the numerous monuments.

Chittor fort was constructed in two major phases. The escarpments of the hill have been cleverly used as the fort walls and are an integral part of its fortifications. The first hill fort was established in the 5th century and successively fortified until the 12th century. The second, more significant defensive structure, fortified with seven gates was constructed in the 15th century during the reign of the Sisodia Rajputs...'

There...again, Sisodia Rajputs...the journalist had noted.

After crossing the stone bridge over the Gambhiri River; more of a brook, the cab wound its way up through the seven gates. Twisting and turning for more than a kilometre, Mrinalini had spied the massive *Ram Pol* ahead.

'Stop! Stop!' Mrinalini had instructed, scrambling down from the cab. The huge, arched gate was bulwarked on either side by squat and stunted hexagonal pillars with intricate bas relief at the base. Bending down to examine them, she had traced the detailed elephant carvings with her finger. Climbing back into the cab, the journalist had entered *Ram Pol*.

Driving further inwards, her vehicle had halted by a building. Mrinalini had descended and grimaced at the ugly modern office. *Completely spoils the retro ambience...* but that was where she got the ninety-rupee entry slip.

Then Mrinalini had exchanged phone numbers with the driver, promising to give him a call when she would be ready to leave the fort. In turn, the driver assured her that he would be parked in the Chittorgarh town. Then he had reversed and left. Hitching her backpack, she had paused, trying to decide which way to go. A decrepit, elderly man had approached her. From his faded khaki shirt and trousers, she gathered he was a guard or gatekeeper employed by the Rajasthan Tourist Department that maintained the fort.

'*Namaste* Madam*ji*! You better be quick. It will be sundown soon and you will not be able to see all the monuments before leaving the *garh*,' he had advised Mrinalini in his quaint, accented local dialect of Hindi.

'Why? Does the *garh* have a closing time?' She had scrutinized the walls of the office searching for timing alerts and found none.

'Nooo,' replied the codger, 'but nobody stays here after dark.'

'And why is that so?' Mrinalini had asked casually, hitching her backpack up.

'Well...you know...they say...people say...that spirits roam the grounds.'

'Spirits?' laughed Mrinalini. 'Whose spirits?'

'Madam, don't laugh,' he had quavered in an injured tone. 'This fort has seen a lot of bloodshed. Thousands of soldiers have died defending it, countless women have sacrificed themselves here to protect the honour of their families. Haven't you heard of the *satis* and *jauhars*?' When Mrinalini had nodded, he continued, 'This is the fort where they lived and died. Where will their spirits go? They roam the *garh*. After all, it is their right to stay here.' His compassion for the disembodied denizens of the fort had made Mrinalini arrange her face into a grave expression to show her empathy.

'Thank you for letting me know about the spirits who live here. In fact, I have come to talk to them,' she remarked, tongue in cheek. The gate keeper's jaw had dropped and his eyes goggled, but she quickly walked away before he could respond. The old man had slowly turned around to stare at the receding back of this peculiar girl from the city, and shaken his head.

Mrinalini had come upon a stretch of green lawns spread around some ruins. She entered the garden and scrambled up the broken structure. Looking down the other side, she had gasped. Some feet below her was a green and sedate pool of still waters reflecting the azure sky. *This must be one of the twenty-two tanks,* she told herself, *so calm and serene!* Outside, a paved avenue went past the garden. *And that must be the circular road that links all the palaces and temples. Later…later I will walk on it to access each of the structures.*

For the moment, Mrinalini wanted to take in the historic ambience of the fort. So she had sat down on the pink stones and waited, breathing deeply, to let Chittorgarh work its magic.

A breeze wafted past bringing with it the coolness of the evening. Mrinalini giggled as she recalled the old man's words. *How can ghosts trouble me in this tranquil place?* In any case, Mrinalini was too much of a realist to believe in floating wraiths. She only believed in concrete phenomena that could be proved by reason and logic. Besides, nothing scared her easily, other than…fire. *Okay, my fear of fire is illogical but spirits, ghosts, spectres…no way!* Gradually, the placidity of the surroundings seeped into her and Mrinalini relaxed. *If this garh is unable to tell me the truth about Padmini, nothing else can. But what* is *the truth?*

Was it possible that a woman of such extravagant beauty actually existed? A woman whose body was so fragrant with the scent of flowers that bees hummed around her, mistaking her body for a bouquet? Or was it just a myth created by the imagination of poets? What kind of a woman was she that a Sultan who ruled over nearly all of India was besotted with her even before he saw her?

Lulled by her meditative mood, Mrinalini watched the western sky deepen with the approach of twilight. The hush around her, devoid of even the natural bird chirps and insect sounds, perfectly matched the peace pervading her being.

2

An impulse made Mrinalini turn around.

'Khamaghani!'

She was startled. A figure stood just beyond the ruined structure in the dappling shadows. Her dress and lithe form made Mrinalini assume she was a girl. Garbed in a plainly-styled deep yellow *salwar* and *kameez*, her head was swathed in a matching *dupatta.* Though it looked translucent, the *dupatta*'s edge was pulled over her forehead in such a way that its edges hid her face quite adequately. She bent low from the waist, both palms pressed together at her chest in the traditional Rajasthani greeting.

'Khamaghani.' The girl said again, following it up with more common,*'Namaste!'*

The garden was fast filling with the gloom of the descending eventide and Mrinalini could not clearly see the girl's face, as she bent downwards. Her low and musical voice sounded friendly.

'Hi!' said Mrinalini. 'So are you another late visitor?' The girl nodded. Mrinalini stood up and jumped down from the ruins to land beside her, the backpack bouncing on her back.

'But you are not late, *bhayeli*. You are right on time,' the girl remarked.

'Uhh?' Mrinalini was nonplussed. 'What's your name?'

'I am Uma,' she said simply, and turned to look towards the ramparts.

Mrinalini was not one to accept matters at face value. *Who is she? Certainly seems to be from around here. . .speaks the lingo, alright.*

'Hi Uma! I am Mrinalini Rao and I am a journo.' She extended a hand.

Ignoring the gesture, the girl took a few steps ahead to stand with her hands resting on the sandstone ruins. Mrinalini narrowed her eyes. She noticed that the girl's arms were covered by the long sleeves of her *kameez* and ended in a cluster of bangles that twinkled in the fading light and fell onto her outstretched hands in such a way that only the slender fingers were faintly visible in the gathering darkness. *Who wears so many bangles anymore?*

Mrinalini tried again. 'Have you come a long way to visit Chittorgarh?'

Uma shook her head. 'I live close by. *Mharo dhaani*, my village is inside the *garh*, just beyond the *sarovar*. I come here often.'

Bingo! Bullseye! She is a local, Mrinalini gave herself a mental pat. 'Then you must know everything about this fort.'

'Yes, I do,' Uma agreed. After a moment's silence, she said, 'Chittorgarh has many tales of the *Rangro*. But the most beautiful is the legend of Padmavati.'

'Padmavati? Who is she? You mean Rani Padmini?' A familiar thrill began rising from the pit of Mrinalini's stomach...the thrill of anticipation that a long hunt could be drawing to a close. *Maybe this village girl knows something. If I can keep her talking...she may just give me some useful information about the real Padmini.*

'Yes. Her name was Padmavati,' the girl insisted.

'But why?' Mrinalini hurried to clarify. 'I mean why is Padmini...Padmavati's story the most beautiful? There have been many other famous queens...well-known in history...whose stories are buried in Chittorgarh.'

'Growing up here, I have heard many tales and myths about Padmavati. But when I came to know that Padmavati's real story was buried while she still lived here, I knew there was something significant in it. And I wanted to dig it out...I felt...it was time that the world knew her *sacch*...a reality that has been sleeping, waiting for the right moment of *jagran*.' Passionate undertones laced her soft words.

Mrinalini's heart began to thud violently. *What does she mean? What is she saying? What does she know? Is it possible that this village girl seriously knows something that others don't?*

'Hey! That's great news because I want to do the same thing. You know...reveal the truth,' she exclaimed. Her analytical antennae constantly buzzed warnings. 'But... but...is there some proof? How can I be sure it is the truth?'

Uma was quiet. Mrinalini waited. For some unknown reason, she felt that she was going to hear something momentous.

'Have you heard of the *Padma-wali*?'

Mrinalini knit her brows. '*Padma-wali*? What's that?' She shook her head. 'Never heard of anything like that.' Uma was silent, so she continued. 'I have gone through the archives at the Udaipur museum and the National Archives at Delhi. I have studied the references from texts written about Padmi...I mean, Padmavati by Jayasi and Tod, in *Padmini Charitra Choupai* and *Khoman Raso*... even some translated manuscript by Amir Khusrao. Of course, I couldn't read any original writings but enough translated stuff to understand the historicity of her story. But nowhere did I find even a hint about anything called *Padma-wali*. What is it?'

By then darkness had completely shrouded the garden. The only light was from the moon, a thin slice missing from its face, peeping through the branches of the trees. Uma turned around. Sighing deeply, she said, 'How will you hear about the *Wali* when it was hidden?'

'Hidden? Who hid it?'

'Who would want to hide but the writer herself?' Uma began walking towards the paved path.

Agitated, Mrinalini strode after her, catching the one word that that hit her like a stone. 'Herself?'

'*Aavjo*.' Uma stood on the avenue and beckoned Mrinalini. As Mrinalini looked down to circumvent the bushes, the girl replied, 'Yes. Padmavati, herself.'

When Mrinalini came abreast, Uma turned left and began to walk down the road. Involuntarily, Mrinalini stepped alongside, speaking slowly, 'You mean, Padmavati wrote the *Padma-wali* herself, and then hid it somewhere and nobody knows about it because nobody found it?'

Even as she spoke, she realized that they should have gone straight ahead and crossed the road. In fact, she remembered seeing an arrow-shaped board pointing ahead. Though it was too dark to read, Mrinalini was sure the arrow said, 'This way'. But they were going along another path.

'Are you sure we are walking in the right direction?' Mrinalini asked.

'You want to know about Padmavati, not the entire history of Chittor, don't you?' Uma sounded amused.

'Yeees. That's right,' Mrinalini said slowly, her mind grappling with other matters. 'Just a sec. If nobody knows about *Padma-wali*, how do you?'

'Because I have read it...'

'What?!' croaked Mrinalini. *Did I hear that right?*

'Yes. I found the *Wali* and read it.'

'How? Where? Who are you?' Mrinalini stood still in utter astonishment.

Uma took two steps ahead and turned to look back at her. The journalist still could not see the girl's face covered under the pulled-down veil. Yet, Mrinalini felt there was a smile on Uma's lips as she said, 'It is a little complicated, *bhayeli*. *Aavno!* Come, let's go on.'

'Of course, it's complicated,' Mrinalini quipped. 'And I am not going another step until you tell me.'

'Okay,' Uma sighed. 'Please be patient. Can you do that?'

'Yes, yes. I am all ears,' said Mrinalini, thinking, *it better be good or I'll shoot you.*

'*Aachho.* Legends about this queen of Chittor have always been floating around here, but our family had a special link to her. You see, one of my *badhera,* long, long ago, happened to be part of Padmavati's troupe of palace maids. She was not known to the Queen; there were hundreds of maids serving her. But my ancestor, then a young, inquisitive girl, was infatuated with the beautiful queen and would seek opportunities to observe her. It was by chance that she had peeped through a palace *jharoka* and saw Padmavati and her companion bent over a low desk in her *shringar kaksha.* She was intrigued and so watched them for a while. She saw that they were dipping quills in a pot of black liquid, like *kajal* and making marks on a yellow cloth. Something like a *phad* painting but these marks were black squiggly characters.'

'You mean they were writing?' Mrinalini was now listening with rapt attention.

'Yes. That is what my great-great-great...grand ancestor suspected. She did not know to read or write. In those days, most people, even from wealthy families, could not read or write. Only the priests could, or...people who knew magic. My *badhera* was badly scared. The queen was not a priest. Then was she a sorceress? She returned home and told her mother. Obviously, her mother warned her to keep silent and not do foolish things like spying on the queen. But, it was such a strange story...especially after what happened to Padmavati. In our family, this story has been passed down through generations. But we have always been told it is a family secret and must not be spoken of beyond the *parivar.*'

'Is that all? That Padmavati could write? How does that prove that she wrote the *Wali*?' Mrinalini felt let down.

'There is more. Though my *badhera* decided to keep away from the queen, her curiosity took her back to the *jharoka*. This time, she not only saw them write and then fold the long stiff piece of cloth, she even heard Padmavati tell her friend, "This is the truth. You must keep it hidden till it is time. Promise me that you will do as I say."

Her friend held her hand and said, "I promise, Princess."

Maybe my *badhera* made a slight noise but something made the queen look towards the *jharoka*. Instantly, my ancestor had fled, afraid of the consequences of being caught.'

'Okay, then?' Mrinalini asked, impatiently.

'Then...? Nothing. For centuries, it remained a family secret. My father told me the story when I was a child. He is a school teacher and teaches Sanskrit at the village school. I was also studying there till last year. As children, my friends and I would come here to play. As I grew older, our family story would keep cropping up in my head whenever I came to these ruins. Slowly the idea of this manuscript made me crazy. I wanted to know, what was the truth of it...was there really a story written by the queen? What did Padmavati mean when she said that it should be hidden? I became convinced that it *had* been hidden, long, long ago, somewhere in the fort. When I told my father about it, he told me I was mad. He said it was only a story. But I retorted that I would find it one day and prove that I was right.' She fell silent.

'What happened after that? Did you find it?' Mrinalini was getting irritated. *What a long story! Maybe is it a just a fable or is it....?*

'Yes,' replied Uma simply.

'Oh!' Mrinalini was suddenly speechless. Then she asked, 'Where is it now?'

Face obscured by the thin *dupatta,* Uma half-turned to her. 'Where it should be...in its hideout.'

Mrinalini stared at her. On her left loomed the fortified walls and moonlight cast long shadows on the avenue.

The journalist could not help stressing each word. 'You. Put. It. Back. In. Hiding. Why?'

'Because it wasn't time for the truth to come out,' Uma uttered this wildly audacious reason in a matter-of-fact tone.

'Can...can...I...umm...I...see it?' Mrinalini asked softly, expecting an excuse.

She was stunned when Uma said, 'Why not?'

Mrinalini was still trying to grasp the idea, as the girl went on softly, 'But before you see it, I could tell you what is written in the *Wali*. Would you like to hear the story written in the *Padma-wali*?'

'You mean...you read it?' Mrinalini was astonished.

'Yes, I did,' she said casually. 'It is written in an archaic language, but it is quite like Sanskrit. Now that is a language that I have learnt from my father since childhood, so I could understand much of it. But sometimes, I had to find my own meanings into the events written by her. Sometimes I imagined the way the people around Padmavati would have responded to her, while at other times, I had to take my father's help to clarify what she wanted to say. But I read it so many times and thought so much about it that now her whole story is as clear as glass to me.'

That's a little too much, thought Mrinalini. *Something's not quite right*...but before she could grill her like a true-blue journo, Uma spoke up again, 'Tell me, *bhayeli*. Do you want to hear Padmavati's story as she told it?'

Mrinalini was in two minds. *Should she allow Uma to carry on with what was likely to be a cock-and-bull story or should she stop it all right here?* She looked up at the bright moon. *It must be late evening, now.* Right then, in the darkness, it was not really possible to investigate anything. Exploring the fort will have to be done the next day, in daylight. *Sleeping is going to be impossible tonight, so why not listen to this girl's fairy-tale or maybe it will be the truth....?*

Mrinalini smiled at Uma who was again looking across the fort walls and said, 'Yes, please.'

'*Aachho*.'

So, leaning against the dark crumbling stones of the ramparts, washed in a silvery glow that left her profile in shadows, Uma began the tale.

'Padmavati embarks on the *Padma-wali,* a title she has herself given to the manuscript, with a large *Om*. Then come the usual salutations to the pantheon of gods with a special couplet to her *Ishta Devata* or cherished divinity, the ultimate misanthrope, Mahayogi Shiva...'

3

An oval emerald, snugly nestling in tiers of frothy white lace, floated in the crushed silk of turquoise seas. It was the enchanted island of Singhaldweep, off the eastern coast of Bharatdesh. A land that entices you into such a magical spell that you wonder how you existed without experiencing such a paradise.

Encouraged by temperate climes and sea breezes, the fertile land grew a crown of tropical woodlands, spiked by the fiery flame of the forest, inked by purple jacarandas and highlighted by the bright yellow laburnums. It was criss-crossed by gurgling crystal streams, while fruit trees burdened with ambrosial mangoes, oranges and jack fruits bent their branches to the ground, inviting themselves to be plucked. The cool forests were scented by jasmine, magnolia and *mahua* flowers. Animals and birds, lulled into placidity by the natural harmony, co-existed in peace.

Ponds, lakes, lagoons abounded all over, speckled by temples and monasteries springing up on their banks. Devotees swarmed them, meditating, praying and offering obeisance to the gods. Hymns and chants to the Trinity of Brahma, Vishnu, Shiva resonated in their precincts. Picturesque hamlets and villages reflected in the serene pools and rivers.

Unique, too, were the inhabitants of Singhaldweep. Men were tall, strong with striking features, almost god-like in appearance. Women were like flowers; supple of body, graceful and well-endowed. Their moon-like faces showed off dark, coquettish eyes while black clouds of hair fell from head to knees. They spoke in the sweet tone of *koels* and cuckoos. Each one seemed to belong to a breed of padminis.

They called themselves 'Singhas' after their national emblem, the lion. But there could not be more good-natured, amiable lions than these Singhas. Food, shelter and security easily taken care of, people here were absorbed in intellectual and cultural pursuits. Most knew to read and write. Art, sculpture and literary discourse were common pastimes. Simplicity was a way of life. Meals consisted of the abundant fruits and vegetables overflowing in the jungles and markets, supplemented by fish leaping in the streams and the sea.

Men and women wore similar cotton sarongs, preferring white or pastel colours. Only the women sported a long piece of cloth flung over their right shoulders, covering their bosoms and tucked into the waistband of the sarong with a frilly end. Embroidered bustiers and bodices matched sarongs. Men went about mostly bare-chested. Only during special occasions would they add on jackets, thickly encrusted with gold braids and jewels. Contentment and tranquillity exuded from the masses and cocooned the island.

Singhaldweep was ruled by the powerful Raja Gandharava Sena, whose lineage could be traced back to the ancient Kamboja Kshatriyas mentioned in the Mahabharata. In search of adventure, the Kambojas had sailed around the southernmost tip of Bharatdesh and come upon Singhaldweep. The island fascinated them so much that they had stayed on. A credit to his ancestral glory, Gandharava Sena's majesty was displayed in the hundreds of thousands of soldiers arrayed under commanders in charge of forts that secured the country. His stalls were filled with more than sixteen thousand of the best Arabian steeds while seven thousand Singha elephants, each an image of the mighty Airavat, belonged to him. When the elephants bowed to him, he looked as magnificent as Indra, the king of gods. He was a universal monarch and everyone deferred to him. No one dared to emulate him.

Gandharava Sena, while being the titular head of the kingdom, governed through laws and administrative decisions taken in consultation with his Council of ministers. The Council, a remnant of the traditional Kamboj *Gana–Parishad,* an assembly of senior and respectable elders, had always been Gandharava Sena's mainstay.

Unable to take our gaze away from this haven, we see on its pristine white sands two men walking. They were powerful men at the royal court; the Chief Minister and the Head of the Council. Garbed in simple white sarongs and cotton sleeveless jackets, no trappings of power were displayed...not even an escort for security. Only a bird fluttered above their heads but they did not notice it. Both greybeards were habituated to a pre-dawn stroll on the beach when the mist was still rising from the depths of the ocean. Often they would meet to talk of either state affairs or of the dazzling wonder of the orb ascending from the waters.

Pressing his beard down with a hand, the Minister asked, 'So, how did His Majesty, King Gandharava Sena deal with the problem of the upstart, Maharaja Tejasvini?'

'Oh, him?' said the Council Head. 'Amicably settled.'

'Really, is there a wiser ruler than our King?' It was a rhetorical question. The Head knew and did not bother to reply. The Chief Minister went on, 'As far as I know, there is no kingdom, far and wide, who is not our ally. Our Gandharava Sena's foresight is worthy of acclaim!'

'Well, you know his policy. He believes that real power lies in winning hearts and not lands. That is the reason we are always so busy drawing up treaties and agreements,' declared the Head.

'Just observe how he has persuaded Tejasvini! Everyone warned him of the man's anger and arrogance. But no! Our King sent him countless gifts and finally when they met, the man was wet clay in our king's hands. Worth learning, his skill of parley. Even at my age,' laughed the Minister.

'You see, he needs love...of the people around him just like we hunger for food. In fact, the more love he receives the stronger, healthier and happier he grows. We are blessed to have such a monarch, but after him...'

His reflections were interrupted by a third voice,

'We are all blessed, Sire, to have a King and Queen like our rulers.' With a flash of white teeth, a dark suntanned face smiled up at them. He was a fisherman gathering nets full of the silver bounty of the seas, whom the two old men had stopped to watch. He went on, 'See how we prosper. Our fields, orchards, ponds and lakes yield more than our needs. We have peaceful trade with our neighbours. All of Singhaldweep loves Their Majesties and blesses them in return.'

'Truly said, my man,' nodded the Minister. They ambled on.

Champavati, the queen of Singhaldweep, was a beauteous damsel, princess of a coastal kingdom from Bharatdesh. His eye being habituated to the padminis of his island, Gandharava Sena had been quite finicky in his choice of wife. Finally, he had settled on the ravishingly gorgeous Princess Champavati, whose skin was as soft and velvety as the champak or frangipani flowers that grew in such profusion on the island. In due course, they had a daughter. As a baby, her even features and large, luminous eyes, rosebud mouth and adorably dimpled arms and legs held forth promise of extravagant beauty later. As she grew older, her allure captivated even her parents. Sometimes, even they were astonished that they had given birth to such a bewitching child. Her skin as delicately translucent as the petals of a lotus, inspired her doting father to name her 'Padmavati'.

As no more children were born to the royal couple after Padmavati, the princess became the sun, moon and the stars in the King's and Queen's universe. The King even began to toy with the idea of handing over the reins of his kingdom to his daughter. He reasoned with Champavati, 'Is a daughter any less than a son?'

'But the Council has to agree, my dear,' said Champavati, as usual, going to the core of the matter.

'I will bring up my proposal to the Council only when my garden blooms. Now is the time to sow the seeds, cultivate the plants and let them grow to their full potential.' It was a fitting example, for the Singhas were mainly occupied in farming.

Champavati nodded genially. More pragmatic of the two, she was used to her husband's flights of fancy which may or may not come to fruition.

Gandharava Sena began to bring up his daughter like the son he would never have. From an early age, Padmavati's days were filled with lessons; training in use of weapons, warfare, horse riding, elephant battles and statecraft as well as classes in studying the ancient Vedas, painting, sculpture and literary arts. Not only did the King personally select her teachers but he would take regular reports of her progress from them. The little princess hardly had any leisure for all the carefree and artless activities that children rejoice in. She had no friends other than two companions. One was Ambika, the daughter of her nursemaid, who was coincidently born on the same day as Padmavati and the other was a talking Hiraman parrot called Ginni. Ambika was her shadow and Ginni was her soul. He was also the princess' advisor and talebearer. She came to know of everything that was happening on the island from him.

Often, in the evenings when her studies were done and the palace was lit up by lamps, Padmavati and Ambika would sit in one of the several palace courtyards, on a circular platform built around flowering trees that sprinkled it with fallen blossoms. Ginni would perch next to them. And a delightful conversation would ensue among the friends.

This evening was like several other evenings, when Ginni began his tale by saying, 'You won't believe what I saw today…'

Young Padmavati interrupted, 'Ginni, do you see unbelievable things every day? *That* is unbelievable.'

'Okay. So you don't believe me, do you? What do you know with your nose stuck forever in ancient, dusty books? Adventures happen in real life, not in books,' Ginni declared, miffed.

'But Ginni, the princess doesn't only read. She is so skilful with her sword. Today she defeated Guru Tarak's son, Anshuvat in a duel,' chipped in Ambika.

Ginni snorted. 'There she goes…Padmavati's trumpet. Ambika, when will you have something original to say? Anyway, since you girls are not interested, I won't tell you what I saw.'

Both girls instantly began to mollify the parrot's ruffled feathers. 'No, no, Ginni. Please tell us. What did you see? We believe you…every word. Pleeease, Ginni.'

Ginni preened himself and began, 'Today, I decided to visit the northern coast of Singhaldweep and I saw a strange sight. Fishermen on a boat were throwing fish back into the sea…'

'You must have made a mistake,' cut in Padmavati. 'Fishermen take fish out of the ocean and not put them into seas.'

'Yes, Ginni…a mistake,' repeated Ambika. She really was the Princess' echo.

'No, I did not make a mistake,' Ginni said emphatically. 'The fishermen were throwing fish back into the sea. So I dived down to the mast of the boat. I was curious to know the reason.' And he stopped to build the suspense up.

Ambika was the first to give in. 'Oh Ginni! Please go on.' Padmavati only nodded, her lovely eyes wide open.

'Do you know what the fishermen were saying?' The girls shook their heads. Ginni preened some more and went on. 'They were saying that it was the King's orders. If they caught more fish than people need or buy, they must throw the extra fish, while they were still alive, back into the sea. That was the way to respect the Sea God's gift.'

'That's a good rule,' said Padmavati, thoughtfully. 'We must not waste our resources.'

'What a wise king we have!' intoned Ambika.

Ginni would hop from one claw to the other and say, 'Would you have known this if I did not go out into the world and bring you the news?'

'No...,' admitted the girls as Ginni flew around them, cackling with glee.

Consequently, Princess Padmavati may have been tutored and coached by great instructors of distinction in their fields, but her sensibilities were being honed by Ginni's pragmatic philosophies.

Everything blossomed early in Singhaldweep and Padmavati was no exception. She had grown into a peerless beauty with poets and bards frequently singing her praises. Lyrics would be penned to her eyes comparing them to vivacious bumblebees or to her sculpted lips or to her swan-like neck. Gandharava Sena was proud of his daughter. She was beautiful not just in appearance. She was deeply conscious of honour and righteousness. Her personality displayed integrity, moral strength and ethical honesty.

Yet, at times, in the seclusion of their bedchamber he would sigh, 'Champa, do we *have* to get our Padmavati married?'

His pretty wife would pick up her gold scissors to snip the thread off the tapestry she was embroidering and say, 'That is the custom, my dear.'

'But why can't she be married and still live with us?' He would ask.

'Do you think a man who would be willing live in his wife's home would be worthy to be our daughter's husband?' Tradition had been the backbone of the queen's family and she found difficult to accept Gandharava Sena's unconventional notions. Usually, she went along for the sake of being cordial but sometimes she could not help protesting.

'That's not the point. I doubt if there exists a man who is worthy of my Padmavati. Who can hold a torch to her knowledge, her principles and her abilities?' The king would retort irritably.

'Are you not being too biased, my dear? Perfection is not a human attribute,' she reminded him.

Nevertheless, he remained his daughter's ardent patron; after all he was the gardener who had nurtured the lotus to bloom so that its scent intoxicated everyone. He built Padmavati her own palace on a high rock overlooking the ocean whose songs had been her lullaby. A palace of seven spires, it sprawled over a good many acres with courtyards, arches and gardens. Here Padmavati began to reside with a huge household of ladies, maids, servants, guards and soldiers. Yet, even with such a large retinue, her devoted companions remained Ambika and Ginni. The princess was now old enough to enjoy her learning whether it was her skills with the sword and bow or art and literature. She was inclined towards poetry and would be often found reciting verses from the great epics or her own creations in the terraces overlooking the sea. The constant crash of the breaking surf provided music to her mellifluous voice. She was supremely content with the way her life was going on and never even dreamed that she may have to give it all up.

On an auspicious day, the King broached his dearest wish to his Council that Princess Padmavati be made the Crown Princess. For a few minutes, there was complete silence and then rose a buzz of mutterings. Gandharava Sena was aghast. *Was there going to be dissent?*

Seeing his reaction, the elderly Chief Minister stood up and waved his hands to calm the assembly. He spoke with his usual dignity,

'O great King! You have constantly ruled Singhaldweep with the utmost of prudence and wisdom. So I appeal to the same sense of judgement when I say that our people will never accept a woman on the throne of this kingdom.' He paused as the others murmured in agreement. 'Instead, I have a suggestion. Why don't we get the Princess married to a suitable man...?' And as the King vigorously shook his head, he hastened to add, 'And invite him to be the Crown Prince? Then Princess Padmavati will become the Crown Princess, just as Your Majesty desires. After you, both will rule Singhaldweep together.' He smiled at Gandharava Sena, whose father he had served, and then him, ever since he had ascended the throne.

The King stared at him as the suggestion sank in. 'You mean we look for a husband for the Princess who will also stay back in Singhaldweep as its Crown Prince. Will any upright man, prince or not, agree to such an undignified condition?'

'Why not, Your Majesty?' chimed in another greybeard, 'To be the Crown Prince of Singhaldweep is a matter of great honour.' Gandharava Sena looked around the room. All the ministers were nodding. Though a little unconvinced, he gave in to the decision that a search begin for a suitable husband for the Princess rather than bequeath her the status of his direct successor.

The evening of the meeting, when the three friends gathered for their usual chat, Ginni seemed unusually downcast. His green feathers, usually fluffed up, were limp. Even his blood-red hooked beak seemed faded. He was unable to participate in all the chaffing with the girls but refused to give a reason for his despondency. Only when Padmavati had prodded and poked him mercilessly, did he divulge the news of the King's meeting with the Council and their decision. He had been perched outside a window of the Council chamber, as he often did, to eavesdrop on meetings.

Padmavati was stunned at the fate decided for her. *How could they take such an important decision about my life without asking my views on it? And my father expects me to rule the country...how can I do that if I can't rule my own life?* For a moment, a bolt of rage flashed through her. But it subsided as soon as it had sprung up. Her guru constantly warned her that inviting anger was bidding farewell to wisdom. Quietly, she asked Ginni, 'What should I do, now?'

Ambika looked from the bird to her beloved friend's face. *Do even the noblest women have to bend to the caprices of men?* She mused sadly.

Ginni's unblinking eyes stared up at the yellow moon that had risen from the glittering waters. 'A man who would agree to be bribed by a throne to stay at his wife's home will not be a man of much self-respect,' he said thoughtfully.

'That is exactly what I was thinking, too, I will not marry such a man,' said Padmavati and whispered, 'In fact, I do not want to marry at all.' Ambika nodded her head.

'Once your father invites proposals for your hand, there would be hundreds, nay thousands. How do we sift the chaff from the grain?' Ginni was thinking out aloud. The girls waited. 'What if...what if we held a contest? Maybe a duel with a champion as a test of the man's prowess' Ginni said slowly.

'How will that help?' Ambika wanted to know.

'Silly girl, don't you see? If a man can beat the best champion of Singhaldweep, we can assume that he is a great warrior and warriors usually have oodles of manly self-respect. His ego will not allow him to agree to live in his bride's home. Then the King and the Council cannot marry you to him. See?' Ginni fluttered his feathers.

'And as long as the champion is not defeated by a contestant, I cannot be married either,' Padmavati added with a shrug.

'So, in both cases, you will not have to marry,' crowed the parrot.

'How clever you are, Ginni!' Ambika clapped her hands. Ginni hopped about, humming a little song.

The very next day, Princess Padmavati was called to meet her parents. It was in the private boudoir of Queen Champavati that Gandharava Sena chose to break the Council's decision to his daughter. He was not very proud of it and believed a mother's love would soften the harshness of the decree. When he had finished speaking to Padmavati, who sat with her mother's arm around her shoulders, the silence in the room boomed like thunder. Every muscle taut, the King waited for the storm to break. But nothing like that happened. A bewildered Gandharava Sena looked at his wife's face, which displayed some puzzlement too.

Padmavati removed her mother's arm and stood up. She looked at once slender and vulnerable, as well as strong and determined, as she began speaking to her parents, 'O my esteemed father and my compassionate mother! You have brought me up with love and indulgence because you believed it to be your parental duty. Today it is my turn to return your affection by carrying out my filial duty. My father, the King of Singhaldweep, has decided I must marry and so I shall. I lay my obedience at his feet.'

Both the parents released their breath in a long sigh of satisfaction, visibly relaxing as they thought exactly the same thing—*Thank God for our daughter's sense and wisdom.* So when Padmavati continued in a soft voice, they hardly heard her.

'I have only one condition. The man whom you select as a suitable groom for me will have to pass a trial before I marry him. He must defeat a champion of my choice at a sword duel.'

When she had finished, her parents stared at her in dismay. 'You mean, it will be a *swayamvara,* like the bride choosing her groom?' Champavati asked anxiously.

'Well...sort of. Only that my choice will depend on his prowess against my champion,' pointed out Padmavati.

Gandharava Sena frowned. But he had always found it difficult to find fault with his daughter. Slowly, he nodded his head. 'She is right,' he said. 'How else will we know if the boy is as good as our daughter, at least, at swordplay?'

Champavati shook her head but didn't argue. She knew from past experience that she could never win when both father and daughter were allied against her.

As Gandharava Sena walked away from the Queen's chambers, he mused, *how did Padmavati get this idea of a contest? Could it become an obstacle in my plans?* Then he shrugged indulgently, *if my little Padmavati wants it, I will go along.*

4

Gandharava Sena was fuming. His ears were red, and almost smoking in anger. 'How dare he? How DARE he?' He muttered, striding to and fro in Champavati's boudoir.

'Who, dear?' The queen asked in a mild tone. The best way to calm her husband, she knew, was to act as if the reason for his rage was insignificant and not worth losing his temper over. Gradually, the idea got through to him and he began to cool off.

'That...that bird!' The king spluttered.

'Bird?' Champavati was genuinely puzzled.

'The parrot...Padmavati's parrot. What's his name? Kinni? Pinni?'

'Ginni,' prompted the queen. 'What has Ginni done? He is Padmavati's best friend.'

'Hardly,' exploded the king. 'Do you know where our daughter got this idea of a contest for her *swayamvara*?' Champavati shook her head as he went on. 'From Ginni! Imagine!'

'Ginni gave her the idea? Is he really so clever?' Champavati wondered.

'Clever, my golden slipper! He is a traitor...turning a daughter against her father's wishes...putting ideas into her head! I will...I will...have him chopped into tiny pieces and eat him for my lunch, today.' Champavati grimaced at her mental vision of the little bird being chopped. Still retaining her principle of calmness, she asked the king, 'Are you sure that Ginni has done it?'

'Yes, yes. Guru Tarak's son, Anshuvat has heard Ginni and Padmavati discussing this.'

The King smote his fist into his palm making Champavati jump.

'I refuse to tolerate it. People will laugh...a powerful king like me trumped by a silly parrot. No, no. I must have him for my lunch, fried and curried.'

Gandharava Sena strode out of the room, calling to his guards.

These words sent a chill down the tiny avian spine of Ginni who was pecking at ripe grapes from the vine just outside the boudoir window. He had gone pale with fear and his little heart thudded. Instantly, Ginni decided to flee from the palace.

Not far from the palace walls was a bamboo grove, and Ginni wormed his way into the centre of the tangle. For nearly five days, he lay there in the darkness, without food and water. He missed his friends, Padmavati and Ambika, and wondered what they must thinking about his sudden disappearance. He wished he had taken some time out to bid them farewell. But none of it was possible now. Finally, hunger made Ginni crawl out and make for the forests. On a tree nearby, he spied a luscious mango. Flying up, he perched on the branch and began pecking at it to suck the juice. As the sweet liquid trickled down his dry throat, Ginni closed his eyes in sheer pleasure. He had just drunk his fill when something clattered. Ginni opened his eyes and saw the world through a wire mesh. He had been trapped in the net of a bird hunter.

Ginni was petrified, thinking that he would be taken to the palace and the King would have him chopped to pieces. Nearly unconscious, he swung like a ball at the end of the net as the hunter walked through the forest paths. Gradually, Ginni realized that he was being taken elsewhere. Sure enough, soon he smelled the sea, so he opened one eye to try and get some bearings. From the cacophony around him, he identified the area as the docks of the island where ships were loaded and unloaded. The hunter seemed to be arguing.

'I will not take a piece less than ten gold coins.' That seemed like the hunter.

'Ten gold coins! That is too much for a bird.' Another man spoke. He was speaking in the island dialect but with a different accent. *Not a native, for sure,* deduced Ginni, understanding that the two were haggling about him.

'Bird? This is not a bird. This is a Hiraman parrot. See this dark line around his neck...it is his identity that he is a genuine Hiraman parrot. Do you know what's that? It is a parrot that speaks like a human being. It is very valuable. Kings and Queens die to own a Hiraman parrot,' said the hunter.

Not King Gandharava Sena, thought Ginni sadly, *he wants to chop me up instead.* And a tear rolled down his red beak.

'Still, ten gold coins? Take eight and give me the parrot,' said the foreigner.

'Alright,' agreed the hunter, holding out the net. The foreigner brought out an empty bird cage and the hunter rolled Ginni, who pretended to be unconscious, into the cage and shut its tiny door. Gold exchanged hands. Ginni's new owner walked away with long strides, swinging the cage from side to side as Ginni held on to its bars for dear life.

Soon, Ginni came to know where he was being taken... on-board a ship. His owner was a sailor and hung his cage from a hook on the ship's deck. Once the cage stopped moving so nauseatingly, Ginni got up on his feet, shook his feathers and took a look around. His worst fears were confirmed. The ship was in the process of leaving Singhaldweep. Ginni was being taken away from his home and friends. He was sure he would never see them again. Grief settled on the little bird and Ginni tucked his head under the wing and cried silently.

Back in the palace, when Ginni did not join them in the evening, Padmavati and Ambika searched for him; in the palace rooms, out in the garden and even in the fruit orchards surrounding the palace. When they did not find him, they looked for him in the rooms of King's palace, his offices, in the underground storerooms, in the kitchens, in the gardens, everywhere; but there was no sign of Ginni. Ambika did notice that the palace guards also accompanied them on this hunt but she did not know their real orders from the King. To cut it short, Ginni was not found. After tearful days and nights, Padmavati concluded sadly that a cat must have got her friend. She fell into acute depression and nothing revived her; neither learning nor poetry nor Ambika's jokes. Ginni was more than a childhood friend. He was the princess' life; the proverbial creature in whom Padmavati's breath resided. She became listless, lost her appetite and did not have the energy for either her favourite books or for swordplay and archery.

Her parents were worried sick, the Council members were troubled, palace servers were sad and Ambika, who loved her blindly, was frantic. Nobody had realized how deeply Padmavati was attached to Ginni.

One day, Ambika said, 'Princess, let's go for the evening *aarti* and prayers at the Mahadev temple where, in the glow of thousands of lamps, the chants resound in one's heart.'

'No, Ambi. I don't feel like going anywhere. You go. It's Monday and your day of obeisance to the Mahadev.' From a tender age, Ambika had been an ardent devotee of Mahadev Shiva and fasted every Monday in his honour.

'Please, dear Princess, just for today. Please come,' Ambika insisted softly. Padmavati reluctantly agreed.

The magnificent temple had been decorated with rows and rows of dazzling oil lamps. Padmavati gaped at the majestic sight, while Ambika observed her carefully. When prayers commenced and the head priest venerated the great ascetic god by encircling his image seven times with the ten-tiered splendidly-lit lamp, she could see her mistress was entranced.

'It was so beautiful, Ambi. Thank you for taking me along,' Padmavati told her friend on the way back. Silently from her heart, Ambika thanked the great Lord Mahadev for showing the way.

Soon, Padmavati began visiting the Mahadev temple nearly every day. It was built on the edge of the sea and after prayer service, Padmavati would sit on its winding staircase and gaze endlessly at the waves undulating the blue. Ambika was glad that she had been able to divert her beloved friend while the King, Queen and others heaved a sigh of relief.

Once again the Chief Minister was walking the white sands with the Council Head. They had come to a consensus on an important administrative issue when the Council Head remarked, 'It is so strange that no serious contender has come forward for the Princess' *swayamvara*. It has been. . .how many days. . .nearly six months since we announced it.'

'No. I don't find it strange, at all,' said the Chief Minister. 'Fighting the royal champion! Is that an easy feat? Everyone knows the reputation of our soldiers. Who would want to suffer a humiliating defeat?'

'But I did hear that a youth had risked the duel,' the Council Head ventured.

'Oh yes. Not one, but four foolish boys. But they were thoroughly trounced just a few minutes into the duel. Namby-pamby. . .these princes of our neighbouring nations!' He laughed and added, 'It's easy to admire from afar and write love paeans to a lady but to fight for your love—now that needs both courage and skill...sadly lacking in young men, today.'

'I heard that the princess' champion is always dressed in white and is masked. Is that so?' The Council Head asked curiously.

'Oh yes,' confirmed the Chief Minister and explained, 'White is the princess' favourite colour, don't you know?'

'Oh! I see,' said the Council Head, adding, 'Anyway, the princess doesn't seem particularly bothered about the lack of contestants.'

'Yes. She is perfectly happy studying, training with weapons and writing poetry,' chuckled the Chief Minister.

'I have also heard that she has a new pastime... meditation,' remarked the Council Head.

'Hmm...so have I. So have I,' agreed his companion.

While Padmavati pined for her soulmate, Ginni found himself in a village on the banks of the great Ganges river in Bharatdesh. For a few days, Ginni's cage was hung up outside the dark, one-room hut where the sailor's family lived. Ginni was half-starved, for he was not used to eating dry gram and a few green peppers, but that was all he received as his daily meal. Besides, grief was eating into him. He would lie all curled up in a corner, unless the village boys decided to poke him with sticks. Then he would hop around trying to avoid their poking. And he never spoke a word. The sailor would comment, 'That wily hunter cheated me. This is no Hiraman parrot. He took eight gold coins for an ordinary bird.'

So when a wandering mendicant wanted to buy the parrot, he gave it away almost for nothing. Again, Ginni was bumping along in his cage, hung from a long bamboo pole held on the mendicant's shoulder. There were times when, resting under a tree at night, the man would ask,

'Hey Parrot! What's your name? Can you speak?' or 'Say *Namaskar*...say *Salaam Alekiem*. What about saying *Pranam Maharaj*?' But Ginni did not bother to make even one squawk. In fact, sometimes he wondered if he had lost his voice...it had been so long since he had heard himself speak. At least the man did not treat him cruelly, but Ginni had to still survive on a diet of gram and peppers. Miserably, he would think, *don't they grow fruit in this vast Bharatdesh?*

One day, after a long, hot, dusty walk through sandy tracts, they reached a rocky plateau. The mendicant shaded his head against the bright sunlight to look towards its peak. Ginni also squinted upwards. He saw a kind of citadel whose walls crawled all along the uneven rocky surface of the table-top mountain. It looked like a huge fort. After an hour or so, they were approaching a tall, arched gate. The mendicant had a long conversation with the guards and then they were let inside the fort. They spent the night under one of the many *chattris* or canopies dotting the fort grounds. The next day, the mendicant bathed in an open tank inside the fort, said his prayers at a nearby Shiv temple and dressed in a clean tunic-*dhoti*. He had also washed the cage and bathed Ginni, who enjoyed the feel of water pouring over him after so many months. From the temple, he smeared vermilion on his own forehead and between Ginni's eyes. *No doubt, the mendicant had plans for something special.*

Ginni did not need to do much guesswork, as they joined a queue entering a grand palace. It moved slowly and after nearly two whole hours, the mendicant holding Ginni's cage was ushered in by a turbaned and whiskered guard into a vast room. Ginni perked up and looked around him, hoping against hope that they were back in Gandharava Sena's throne room. The furnishings were rich and it was filled with men dressed in silks and jewels. There was a throne, too. In fact, two thrones but none of the men sprawling on them were Gandharava Sena. One was thin and elderly with a flowing white beard and the other was a tall man in his late twenties, with high cheekbones, long thin nose, deep-set brown eyes that glinted sharply and a slight furrow between his brows as if he was always squinting against the bright sun reflecting off the desert sands. He looked like he spent most of his day in the saddle. The muscles rippling under his gem-studded tunic hinted he was happier wielding a sword or mace against an opponent than sitting amidst this opulence. For no reason at all, he reminded Ginni of Padmavati. Not knowing what he was doing, Ginni suddenly called out,

'O Prince! You are brave, noble and bold.
Many lives in your hands you will hold.
When cut down by the very honour you rely on,
Only love shall redeem you. That is a tale foregone.'

A stunned silence hummed through the assemblage as the echoes of his words reverberating in the vast chamber died down. The first to recover was the mendicant, who whispered to Ginni, 'So you *can* speak? And how!' Then, turning to the older of the regal men, he bowed almost to the ground. Humbly, he said, 'Forgive me, *Annadaata*! This silly bird does not know when to speak and when not to. He did not mean to insult you by addressing the young Kunwar. Forgive me, my lord.'

Rawal Samar Singh gazed at the parrot for a long time. Everyone in the room held their breath, not knowing which way the situation would go. After all, this was the Rawal of Chittor, the bastion of Mewar's honour. Ginni's unblinking eyes stared back at the old man. Then the lips above the white beard curved into a smile and his eyes twinkled. An audible sigh went around the room as lungs released air collectively.

'Get up. Get up, Fakir,' said the Rawal to the mendicant, still kneeling on the floor. 'The bird is amazing. How did he know that Ratan Singh is my son and the Prince of the realm? He is astoundingly clever!'

The mendicant scrambled up, saying, 'Yes, my lord. He is a Hiraman parrot...very clever...speaks very well. That is the reason I dared to bring him to you, my lord.'

'Hmmm...how much do you want for it? I want it for my son,' said the Rawal.

The wily mendicant's eyes sparkled. 'You will buy it, my lord?' He asked.

'Yes, I will,' replied the Rawal. 'Isn't that the reason you brought him here?'

'I am only a poor man...,' began the mendicant, wringing his hands.

'Lakshman Singh!' called the Rawal to a burly man to his right. 'Give him as much as gold as he wants.' Instantly, Rana Lakshman Singh, his son's relative by marriage and principal advisor, slipped out a cloth bag that jingled when he dropped it into the cupped palms of the mendicant. Instantly, the mendicant went up to the throne and knelt at its foot. He placed Ginni's cage at the Rawal's feet. With his knees still bent and hands folded in gratitude, the man backed out of the room.

The Rawal picked up the cage and observed Ginni for a few moments before calling out, 'Ratan!' When his son came forward and bowed, he extended his arm with the cage saying, 'This is an extraordinary bird. Keep him safely.'

Placing a hand on his heart as he knelt before his father, Ratan Singh said, 'Your wish is my command, Father.' It was then that Ginni saw the thin white line that ran from the hairline down the left side of Ratan Singh's face, curving into his short dark beard. Probably a sword cut. *He is a fighting man*, Ginni surmised. A court servant took the cage out of the room and passed it to Ratan Singh's servant.

Thus it was that Ginni reached the fort of Chittor, thousands of miles away from Singhaldweep.

5

'That is a fantastic tale,' Mrinalini exclaimed when Uma stopped speaking. 'And you found all this written in the *Padma-wali*?'

'Most of it.' Uma seemed disinclined to waste words unnecessarily.

'And this Singhaldweep...where is it?' Mrinalini was on her fact-checking binge.

'I don't know,' said Uma.

'I mean...where is it located now? Well...you know, is it the island that we call Sri Lanka now?'

'I don't know,' came back Uma.

'Well...Malik Mohammad Jayasi mentions Lanka as the name of Padmavati's land in his famous poem *Padamavat*. So, it could be the present-day Sri Lanka, isn't it?

'I don't know.'

'What *do* you know, Uma?' said Mrinalini, exasperated.

'Only what Padmavati wrote in the *Wali*, and the legends passed down over time,' reiterated Uma. 'What I am saying about Singhaldweep is what she has written. Whether the island is Sri Lanka today or not, I can't tell you. All she writes is that the Singhaldweep flag showed a lion with a raised paw against a golden rising sun.'

'But there are many flags that have the lion as its central motif,' complained Mrinalini.

'Does it really matter where Singhaldweep is located today?' Uma's tone smacked of restrained impatience.

'Noo...not really,' agreed Mrinalini, uneasily. She liked facts, tagged, labelled and slotted. 'By the way, do these parrots actually speak in human language?'

'I don't know. But I have heard tales that Hiraman parrots choose those who understand them.'

'Weird!' Mrinalini shook her head. Then she demanded, 'How did Padmavati write about Ginni's experience of the journey and Chittor? They were separated.'

'Isn't it obvious that Ginni would have prattled all of it to Padmavati at a later date?' Her tone made it clear that it was a rhetorical question.

'Umm...so...Ginni and Padmavati will meet again?' Mrinalini inferred.

'Maybe...,' murmured Uma.

Ambiguity made her uncomfortable, so Mrinalini shifted track 'But isn't it strange that after bringing up his daughter like a son and heir-apparent, Gandharava Sena succumbs to the archaic tradition of a son, even if it is a son-in-law, sitting on the throne?'

'No, it isn't,' said Uma, firmly. Suddenly, she seemed eager to explain, 'Being ruled by a man was the established tradition in those days and people went along with what was expected of them. What is unusual is his endeavour to change the tradition...that did require a lot of courage. But he realized that completely changing an accepted custom would invite criticism not only from other kings but also from within his own administration. Naturally he did not want to risk the reputation of his kingdom for a personal idiosyncrasy. His Chief Minister's suggestion in the circumstances seemed a good solution. It also tells us of his loyalty to duty towards his kingdom and its people.'

'Yes, I guess you are right. But I loved Ginni and Padmavati's cleverness. How they gauged male vanity! And made a brilliant plan to truss up her would-be admirers with their own arrogance...,' Mrinalini laughed. 'She was a very smart girl.'

'Yes. That she was. Now should I continue?' Uma asked.

'Yes...no, no wait. One more thing...why did you say that the women of Singhaldweep belonged to a breed of padminis? What is "a breed of padminis"?' Mrinalini knit her brows looking sideways at Uma.

From behind her veil, Uma replied, 'Our scriptures have classified women into four types. The highest class were the *Padminis,* most cherished for their physical, mental and emotional attributes. Next were the *Chitarinis* who are maternal in nature, then the mediocre *Hastinis* while the worst and last are the *Sankhinis,* who are ugly in all respects. The women of Singhaldweep were famed for their padmini characteristics and many old epics and poems praise them.'

'Oh! I didn't know that 'padmini' referred to certain feminine attributes. Trust our hoary chauvinist gurus to classify women that way,' sneered Mrinalini.

'Actually the scriptures also classified men into four types...,' commented Uma, 'but let's not deviate from Padmavati's tale...'

'Yes, yes,' acquiesced Mrinalini. Actually, they had not proceeded very far from the garden. The journalist looked up and was instantly arrested by the dark shadows on her right. Moonlight was blotted out by the solid darkness of several domed edifices. A ramp led up to a small door inset into a high wall. Latticed windows and arched balconies on the upper part of the wall were hazily visible were moonbeams slanted.

Mrinalini pointed to the door. 'What's that? Looks like an important part of the *garh.*'

'That is the Rana Kumbha Palace. Not only is it a significant part of the fort, it has been built over an older palace. Probably the oldest here,' explained Uma.

'Oh yes...the Rana Kumbha Palace. James Tod wrote about it in his '*Annals of Mewar.*' Apparently he tried to enter the underground rooms of this palace but the noxious air and reptiles discouraged him. Besides, many of Chittor's famous incidents took place in this palace, isn't it?'

'All the royal families of Chittor lived in this palace, but not Padmavati. She had her own palace to the south. The old palace on which this Rana Kumbha palace is erected was built on the rocks of the plateau. Instead of removing the rocks, the recesses between the rocks were converted into underground rooms and tunnels.' In contrast to the enthusiasm with which she had discussed the traditions of Singhaldweep, Uma's voice was flat, as if she was chanting from a history book.

'Can we take a look around?' Mrinalini persisted.

'No.' Uma said flatly. Then she softened the harsh retort by adding, 'We will come back later. For now, let's walk to the palace where Padmavati lived. But before we reach there, don't you want to know how she came to Chittor?'

'Yes, of course,' Mrinalini hastily agreed. She hurried after Uma who had begun to walk away. She was too good a journalist to annoy and lose this intriguing source of information.

'Then listen to what the clever Ginni did and later recounted it with relish to Padmavati.'

6

One warm evening, Ginni was bathing in one of the numerous fountains that gushed in Kunwar Ratan Singh's palace. As he fluttered his wings and fluffed up his feathers to dry them, he wondered, *Is it never pleasant here? What a land! During the day, hot winds howl and blow sand through the palaces while at night the stone walls are chilled by icy breezes. How I wish I was back in Singhaldweep!* At that moment, Ratan Singh rushed past him. Ginni flew behind him noiselessly. The Kunwar's sun-burned face was dark with anger as he strode through the palace corridors, one hand on his sword. When he entered his bed chamber, he flung himself on his couch, an arm across his eyes. The servers in the room bowed asking whether he would like some wine or food.

Lifting his arm, he said through gritted teeth, 'Get out!' Immediately, they scuttled away. Ginni settled on a low stool beside the bed and began to hum softly. Soon the chamber was filled with a sweet, low melody. The parrot noticed Ratan Singh's limbs gradually lose their stiffness and relax. He opened his eyes and observed the bird.

'Ginni?'

The Hiraman parrot stopped humming.

'Ginni?' Ratan Singh called again.

'Yes, my Kunwar?' Ginni turned his beady eyes towards Ratan Singh.

'You have travelled to many places, haven't you?'

'Yes, Sire.'

'Have you ever heard of the padmini women?'

'I may have, Sire. What makes you ask?'

Ratan Singh sighed deeply. 'Nothing. . .it is Prabhavati. . . her tongue is like a sharp knife.'

Ginni remained silent.

Prabhavati was Ratan Singh's senior-most queen. They had been married when he was still a boy and she dominated him as though he was still one. Besides, she was the first of his fourteen wives and concubines and considered herself the real contender for the title of the Rani of Chittor when Kunwar Ratan Singh succeeded Rawal Samar Singh.

With another sigh, the Mewari warrior continued, 'I was taking lunch in her palace. She cooks well but today the *gatta ka sabzi* tasted salt-less. I had only made a casual remark about it and she lashed out at me like a venomous snake. She has the arrogance to tell me if I don't like her cooking, never to come for meals to her palace... tells me if I have such big ego to go get myself a padmini! Imagine! That woman is too much...women must know their place...,' he railed at his absent wife. Ginni was still silent. Ratan Singh went on 'In a fit of temper, I shouted back at her...' And he stopped.

'What did you tell her, Sire?'

A little shamefaced, he replied, 'I told her I will leave, and never come back to Chittorgarh until I get a padmini. I know, it was impetuous of me but she is such a shrew. Now that I have taken the challenge, my honour is at stake. Where do I get a padmini? Is there such a thing as a padmini at all?' Ratan Singh looked at the bird. 'What do I do now, Ginni?'

'Get a padmini,' Ginni quipped.

'Get a padmini, you say,' Ratan Singh mimed the bird's tone. 'From where?

'From Singhaldweep.'

'Wait, what? You mean padminis actually exist?' Ratan Singh sat up, astonished.

'Yes, they do...many of them. But you have to travel across the land to the sea. Then sail to Singhaldweep. Can you do that?' Ginni asked.

'Of course, I can,' Ratan Singh affirmed staunchly. 'What do I have to do?'

'If you believe you can brave the mighty ocean, let me tell you about the ultimate padmini,' said Ginni, and out poured the magical tale of Padmavati and her land triggered by his pent-up homesickness and longing for his friend. As he described the charms of the serene, verdant, contented Singhaldweep, Ratan Singh was lulled out of his nasty mood. When Ginni mentioned its elegant men and bewitching women, its graceful palaces, temples and lakes, its generous and just rulers, Ratan Singh was transfixed.

Slowly, gradually, building suspense like a master story teller, Ginni brought his narrative around to Padmavati. Once there, he could not remain detached. Months of yearning for his soulmate bloomed forth in poetry

She is a lyric on a poet's lips.
She is a dream an artist paints.
She is a muse a sculptor chips at.
No more wondrous creature than this exists
Just a glimpse of her is sheer bliss.

Dark grey eyes below winged brows,
Limpid and deeply serene.
Without bias, they view the world
To her, it is a precious pearl.

Thickly-meshed tangled eyelashes,
Whether they sweep down or flutter,
Like tipsy bumblebees trampling a flower,
They ignite hearts, such is their power.

Moulded with tender fingers
Her nose is a delicate flute.
Each nostril, so pretty
Seats diamonds that wink in vanity.

Her lips are soft rose petals
Like Kamdeva's bow, they tease.
Pouting, quivering at times
In a passing wayward breeze.

Rounded pretty pink shells...
Are those her dainty ears?
Embellished with gemmed gold,
Peep shyly through wisps of hair.

Framed by dark curls
Beauteous portrayal,
Of a heart-shaped visage
Budding on a graceful neck.

She blooms, a perfumed bouquet,
Her heady scent tantalises bees
To weave circles around her
Crazed by deluded fancies.

Ah! How can I describe her complexion?
Luminous as the moon...
Peaches squeezed in cream,
Soft as lotus skin.

Cloaked in rain clouds of dark hair,
Her thick mane nets sunbeams
And falls to her ankles,
In fragrant gleams.

Graceful dignity in every line,
She steps forth like a goddess.
Tall, sculpted, elegant,
Poised mien wholly flawless.

Enthralling is my Padmavati.
For the substance of her magic
Arises from the love and wisdom,
Ensconced in her heart.

Immortality will certainly pursue her destiny,
When mortal agony transcends to divine ecstasy.

Not content to describe her beauty, Ginni went on to speak of her strong character, her astute wisdom, her love of justice and honour, her skills at warfare, statecraft and the sublime arts of literature, philosophy and painting.

At first, Ratan Singh could hardly believe that such a fascinating creature was not a figment of imagination. *Can a living being be so perfect?* Every evening, he would ask Ginni to tell him more about Padmavati. Listening to his tales cast such a powerful spell that Ratan Singh would hurry to his bedchamber after dinner every night. He forgot meal engagements with wives and assignations with concubines. Soon they began to send spies to scour his palace and question his attendants. They wanted to discover their husband's latest allurement and were puzzled to know that a parrot's chatter had captivated him. They could not make head or tail of it and went back to the petty politics and jealousies of lives spent within the narrow walls of their palaces where the outside world hardly ever encroached.

Ginni narrated to him all the thrilling adventures that the princess, Ambika and he had undertaken in Singhaldweep. Every night, as he listened, it seemed to Ratan Singh that he was actually observing the three friends together. Padmavati became, for him, a living entity with whom he loved spending time in his imagination. He loved her clever ideas, her unique thoughts, the amusing games she played with Ginni and Ambika, her laughter, her sorrows, her aspirations. Unawares, Ratan Singh fell desperately in love with the Padmavati of Ginni's stories. As Ginni had expected, before long, the Rawal's son was eager to see Singhaldweep with his own eyes and meet the fascinating Padmavati.

The Hiraman parrot instantly changed course by telling Ratan Singh how impossible it was to fulfil his wish. He informed the warrior of all the dangers and difficulties he would have to face while crossing the fearful seas. Cleverly, Ginni instigated Ratan Singh to prove his macho audacity. At the same time, he continued with his chronicles of Padmavati, fanning Ratan Singh's fiery ardour. Ginni desperately wanted to see his princess again and cunningly used Ratan Singh to achieve this goal.

Rawal Samar Singh was upset when Ratan Singh expressed his desire to visit Singhaldweep. After all, the Rawal had adopted Ratan Singh, son of Bhanumati Devi, his dearest widowed sister, as heir. Ratan Singh had been just a babe when his natural father, a Rana of a small constituency of Mewar, was killed in battle. Samar Singh had brought his sister and her baby boy to Chittor. Since Samar Singh had no son, despite having several wives, he decided to adopt his sister's boy as the Kunwar or Prince of Chittor. Ever since, Ratan Singh had been groomed to take over the reign of Chittor that was the seat of Mewar's power and glory. All the Ranas, Thakurs and Jagirdars who headed clans and constituencies of the realm of Mewar had sworn allegiance to the powerful Rawal Samar Singh. Together, these heads formed a Council and advised the Rawal on the administration of Mewar. But much of their advice was divisive and each ruler was only interested in furthering the interests of his own constituency. Samar Singh was aware that there were rumblings of dissent in Chittor itself. The Rawal wanted to keep his heir, Ratan Singh beside him at Chittor to control these unruly clan chiefs.

'Why, my son, do you want to go this mythical island?' The old man asked.

'*Maro Bapji*, Singhaldweep is not a mythical island. It exists beyond the South-east coast of Bharatdesh. I can reach it by sailing across the seas for a few days. Let me go, *hukum*. I am keen to see the world before I'm too old to do so.'

'Ratan *balyo,* I understand your restlessness. Lolling around inside the palaces of Chittor is tedious for a warrior like you. You want to be on the battlefields; hear the clash of swords; smell the blood. But my son, is this a time to go so far away from home? Do not forget that the eyes of the vulture are on Chittor. That Turk, Khalji is waiting... waiting to spot a tiny chink in Chittor's strength and the moment he does so, he will swoop down to attack. The warriors of Mewar are loyal and brave. They will defend Chittor to the last drop of blood but I am old. If you stay away from Chittor too long, it is inviting trouble. Not just from the external enemy but internal foes too.'

'*Hukum,* I won't be gone long. I will return in a few months,' Ratan Singh pleaded.

'*Balyo,* I love you too much to deny you. But think well on your decision,' said Rawal Samar Singh, muttering, 'I don't understand your sudden wish to visit this faraway place.'

'*Bapji,* I will bring you a daughter-in-law from Singhaldweep,' declared Ratan Singh.

The Rawal sat up, astounded. 'What?' he exclaimed, 'You are going to Singhaldweep for a woman? You have fourteen wives and yet you want one more? Why?'

'Because none of them is a padmini,' explained his son, his eyes gazing into the distance as though he could see something on the far horizon that his father could not.

The Rawal stared at Ratan Singh. His hawk-like profile was etched against the bright, hot sunshine pouring in through the open *jharoka,* but the sharp lines of his face were diffused with an emotion the Rawal had never seen before in his warrior son. He knew it was useless to dissuade Ratan Singh; go to Singhaldweep, he would.

'Go if you must, but don't go alone. Take Raghav Chetna with you,' was all the Rawal said with a wave of his hand and a sigh.

Oh, oh...that's not a good idea, thought Ginni, listening from the ledge of the *jharoka. Raghav Chetna is a crafty man, too devious for a simple soul like my Ratan. Well, I will have to manage...*Ginni shrugged. Raghav Chetna was a hanger-on at the Rawal's court. He was an artist who painted portraits of the Rawal and other courtiers for a fee. It was rumoured that he also had a penchant for sorcery. Mainly, Chetna was a young man who lived by his wits.

But Ratan Singh was beaming. He had got his way.

'Yes, *Bapji,* yes. I will take Raghav with me but nobody else.' He went on to explain, 'I want to travel incognito. I will be safer if nobody knew I am the future Rawal of Chittor. Besides, Khalji's spies will not even realize that I have left the fort. I will leave by the *Chota Pol.*'

'Yes. That is a good idea,' said the old Rawal. 'But speak to your *Ba* before you leave. Ask your mother if she agrees with your foolhardy ideas.' And he sighed again... deeply. *They were not good, the portents...*

Ba, Ratan Singh's mother, only observed her son's glowing face as he described Singhaldweep and his purpose to journey there. She knew it was no use speaking about her fears of a future that she could only half-glimpse in the mist. She blessed her son, praying for his success, as she had always done.

7

When the two young men stepped over the edge of the wooden dhow and waded through the waist-length surf to the wet sandy beach, hardly anybody gave them a second look. Wearing dirty white *dhotis* pulled up to the knees, bare-chested, limbs and face bronzed to a coppery shade by months spent outdoors under the tropical sun, they were hardly distinguishable from the sailors around them. But those who chose to look closely would notice first the white cloth ropes wound around their heads into a sort of turban, a style not seen in these parts and next, the scabbards strapped across their chests holding short daggers at the waist.

On their part, the pair could hardly believe the sight of wildly luxurious frondescence that met their eyes. Ginni squawked excitedly, flying ahead to dive into the foliage. *I have missed the scent of my land,* he thought, gulping hungrily at the florally fragrant warm breeze. Kunwar Ratan Singh and Raghav Chetna followed the sailors to a beachside tavern. They had boarded the fishing vessel at Kutch. It had taken them months to sail around the peninsula of Bharatdesh and reach this island. After meals of dried vegetables and stale water, they were dying for fresh food and drink. They sat on wooden tables and benches laid out on the sand. The sunshine was mellow and the breeze cool. The burning heat of the desert sun was missing here. Both the men looked around them curiously. In a distance, under the canopy of trees, they observed a village. Simple but elegant, spacious villas surrounded a common pond. Even from afar, they could see its inhabitants going about their daily tasks; busy but unhurried. Children were playing merrily under shady trees.

Ratan Singh turned to the sailor beside him and asked, 'Who is the ruler here?'

For an answer, the sailor pointed above the forest. Ratan Singh saw a distant flag flapping in the breeze. Obviously, it was flying from the tower of a tall building screened by the trees. Squinting, Ratan Singh made out a black lion against a golden sun whose rays fanned out from a semicircle. *Yes, it was a rising sun and. . .and the lion had one paw raised.*

'The lion and the sun?' he said slowly.

'Yes. King Gandharava Sena belongs to the Suryavanshi lineage,' the sailor explained.

Ratan Singh and Raghav Chetna exchanged glances.

'You mean his ancestors are from the Raghuvanshi line?' asked Raghav.

'I suppose so,' he shrugged. 'But his family line is of hardly any significance here. Actually, Gandharava Sena himself commands great love and respect in these parts. Rulers of the neighbouring kingdoms consider him their leader. His inclination for justice, laws, good governance and respect for people's rights makes Singhaldweep a rich and strong country of contented, happy citizens.'

'People's rights?' Chetna wrinkled his brow. 'What's that?'

An old woman in a grey sarong had begun to serve the diners one by one. The Kutchhi sailor leaned back and began to spell it out.

'Here the people have the right to follow any religion, pray to any God, take up the occupation of their desire, not necessarily the one followed by their father, marry according to their wishes and have access to courts of justice. Nobody, rich or poor, is above the law and all children, boy or girl, are enrolled in national schools. Everybody is literate. Women have more liberty here than in Bharatdesh and are highly respected.'

Ratan Singh, trying to absorb these new notions, absent-mindedly bit into a mango slice from the fruit platter placed before him. Suddenly, his mouth overflowed with sweet juice that dribbled down his chin to his bare chest. Startled by the sticky shower his face contorted comically making his table companions laugh out loudly. Chetna bit into the fruit cautiously but it was so juicy that it leaked from the corners of his lips. Both men focused on delving into the delicious assortment of fruits that was evidently the first course. Never had they eaten such luscious pineapples, papayas, mangoes, lychees and other unknown fruits before.

The next course was platters of pearl-white steaming rice with a variety of lentils and vegetables. Each dish was lightly flavoured with spices and tasted delectable. At the next table, Ratan Singh noticed men were gorging on fish curry. He realized that the hosts had been sensitive enough to ensure that their vegetarian tastes were not offended by seating them separately from the fish eaters. Instantly, he gauged that the people of this island were a few rungs above those in his native Mewar when it came to interpreting and respecting human perspectives that may differ from their own. He wondered, *is this empathy a natural consequence of liberal thinking, whatever that is?*

The men had just scooped out the last of the mouth-watering rice pudding and were licking it off their fingers when Ginni perched on Ratan Singh's shoulder. Golden flesh from his fruit lunch sticking to his red beak, he came closer to the Mewari's ears whispering, 'Hurry up! Have you finished? If you fill your belly so much, you will be too sleepy to see the sights of Singhaldweep.'

Playfully, Ratan Singh slapped at the cheeky little parrot that fluttered just out of his reach, squawking indignantly. But he touched Chetna on the shoulder and stood up, waving farewell to his belching companions.

Soon, Ratan Singh and Chetna were wending their way through a forest, following Ginni, who flew excitedly ahead. They reached the main gates of the fortress of Singhaldweep, where the guards registered them as traders from Bharatdesh. As they walked through the massive stone gates, the two men halted in amazement. Facing them was an architectural fairy-tale wonder that rose in series of rounded turrets, domes of various sizes, hanging balconies and stylish arches. At various levels, its golden roofs sparkled in the sunshine, while white walls dazzled the eye. Spread over acres of woodland and landscaped gardens dotted with fountains and natural lotus ponds, paved paths lined with gay flowers meandered in and out of a cluster of elegant palaces. From each rooftop flew the royal pennant; the lion with a raised paw against a golden rising sun.

'How beautiful!' gasped Chetna, his aesthetic fancies thrilled.

'It is very appealing,' agreed Ratan Singh. 'Why don't we build something like this in Chittor?'

Chetna gave him a withering look. 'Only when Chittor is finished with its petty internal politics, can you even begin to think innovatively.'

Ratan Singh glared at him.

'Who will buy my scented garlands? I have rose, jasmine, marigold bands.' Lilting, a melody floated to the men still standing before the massive guarded gates. Together, they turned to their right and stared again. A woman sat on a stone bench under a tree weaving strings of flowers from a laden basket. Never had they seen such a lovely girl. Fair of face, slender yet voluptuous of form, her loose hair like a black silk veil, nimble fingers busy, she seemed to have stepped out of a painter's imagination.

For a few minutes, they could not tear their eyes away. Besides, the girl was unveiled. Her face, dimpled arms, neck and feet were open to public gaze. Both men, who were habituated to the shrouded women of Mewar, just drank in the sight. Gradually, they became aware that amused looks were coming their way. Soon, they realized why. Most of the women among the swarms roaming the streets, even the mature matrons, were as attractive as the flower girl. In fact, some were stunning.

'Ah, the padminis!' exclaimed Ratan Singh softly.

Right then Ginni landed on his shoulder. 'Stop gawking like a schoolboy. You are the future Rawal of Chittor, remember? Not an ordinary mortal to drool over girls like Chetna is doing,' he scolded.

Ratan Singh instantly straightened his turban and smoothed his up-turned moustache with finger tips. *Yesss,* he thought and looked around.

Singhaldweep was a land of villages. The only town on the island grew haphazardly around the royal palace. Its avenues were lined with stores selling things from edibles to clothes to utensils to jewellery and open stalls with shelves stocked with vegetables and fruit; lush and fresh. Vendors sold flowers, toys and knick-knacks. The bazaar petered off into homes and villas edged by gardens and a pond or two. Strangely, Ratan Singh could see no fences or walls to demarcate where one owner's land ended and the other's began. Yet all the properties were organised and roads were clean and well-kept. *What kind of people are these? Aren't they afraid that their land will be stolen?* Ratan Singh wondered. He looked closely at the throngs around him and suddenly noticed that the men, too, were specimens of virile masculinity. He reacted by pulling his shoulders back, thrusting out his chest and standing as tall as he could.

Observing his immediate surroundings, Ratan Singh was amazed once again. Despite being a bazaar, there was none of raucousness around him as would be the case in Chittor. Here, people spoke in low, courteous voices, exchanging pleasantries while buying and selling. The goodwill in the air was palpable and it gave Ratan Singh a clue as to why the Singhaldweep citizens were careless about securing their belongings. Sufficiency and complacency kills envy and hatred; it brings out the best in people. Singhaldweep was a living analogy of social harmony where its citizens followed the principles of generosity and amiability.

Ginni broke into Ratan Singh's musings by squawking loudly in his ear. As the Mewari shook his head to clear his ringing ears, Ginni asked, 'Do you want to see Padmavati's palace or not?'

'Yes. Yes. Of course,' Ratan Singh snapped out of his trance. He remembered the true purpose of his visit to Singhaldweep. 'Chetna, come this way.'

The two men began to follow Ginni, who hopped from tree to tree. They were walking along a broad avenue that led them back to the massive iron gates of the royal palace. The gates were emblazoned with the lion-sun emblem. Between the thick grills, the view of the expansive formal gardens was splendid; symmetrical beds of roses, sunflowers, lilies and other rare and unique blooms, rippling fountains, some with music, trilling birds and small animals cavorting. While there were platoons of guards around the gates both inside and out, Ratan Singh could not help wondering at the casual approach to security here compared to the gates of Chittor where it was a much more serious business.

But Ginni did not go towards the gates. He began to follow the line of trees that marched down the avenue encircling the palace grounds. Both men hastened to follow him as they would lose their way otherwise in this strange but fantastic place. The palace walls were too high for them to glimpse anything inside. Only Ginni could do that, as he was flying parallel to the wall. After a steady trot of nearly an hour, the three of them had come around to what they assumed was the rear of the grounds. Here the wall ended at a cliff that rose right from the sea. At least three miles across the curve of the cliff, the wall and avenue began again, probably back towards the palace gates.

The sheer steep face of the cliff here, slick with seaweeds and dampened by the continuous crashing waves, was a better defence than any wall.

Ginni swooped down to perch on Ratan Singh's shoulder. 'Look up!' he whispered.

Obediently, Ratan Singh tilted his head and looked up the rocky walls and then couldn't look away. His jaw dropped. The grey-green cliff had a crown of gold and purple. Clinging to the high rock's craggy head was a palazzo; walls painted sparkling gold topped with conical purple roofs, round turrets and square towers rose like slender fingers to touch the sky, wide grilled terraces and lovers' balconies hung precariously over bubbling waves. This dainty palace seemed straight out of a child's fairy-tale.

'That is Princess Padmavati's palace,' Ginni said in Ratan Singh's ear.

'Is she an *apsara* to live so high in the sky?' whispered Ratan Singh, not wanting Chetna to hear. He had not divulged to the artist the real reason for his visit here. Chetna could not decipher Ginni's words. For him they were bird calls. But Ratan Singh had no such problem. What people do not know is Hiraman parrots choose when and who could understand them.

'Well, she happens to be the ultimate padmini,' Ginni whispered back.

'How will I know until I see her?' Ratan Singh despaired.

'Don't you worry. It will happen soon enough,' Ginni chuckled.

Ratan Singh turned his head to frown at Ginni who regarded him with beady eyes. 'Do you know something that I don't?'

'Yes and no,' Ginni said, and merrily cackled.

Chetna, who had not noticed the palace yet, was squinting into the distance where the sea reflected the rosy trails left by the sunken sun in the waves. Turning towards Ratan Singh and Ginni, he asked with a smile, 'What is the silly parrot saying?'

Ginni gave him an angry look.

Chetna's aesthetic inclinations were revelling in the enchanting charms of the island. He was already planning to begin a series of paintings and sketches to immortalize the different aspects of Singhaldweep.

Ratan Singh did not answer. He was also looking to the horizon, but his mind was occupied by thoughts of how he could get a glimpse of the princess.

Evening leached light from the sky as the three of them walked back the way they had come. They had to search for lodgings to spend the night. Ratan Singh looked back at the purple turrets flying the royal pennant against the darkening sky. *I will return. I will see her.*

8

'I don't believe a word of it,' Mrinalini exploded. 'It is like a child's tale. It cannot be true.'

Uma, who was walking a little ahead of the journalist, stopped for a bit and then continued on her way. Her words flung over the shoulder were quite cool, 'That's up to you. I am telling you what I have read in the *Wali* because you wanted to hear it. I don't have to tell you what I have read. To see if it's true, read it yourself.'

'Exactly! That is what I want to do. Let me see what she actually wrote. It's possible that....'

'...I have made up all that Ratan Singh and Chetna encountered?' finished Uma. 'Isn't it possible that Ratan Singh would have narrated everything to her?'

'Possible...when they meet, which you certainly seem to be taking your own sweet time in getting to,' countered the sceptical journalist. 'Show me where you have hidden the *Wali* and I will read it myself,' Mrinalini took long strides trying to catch up with Uma.

'That's where I am taking you,' Uma's tone had soothing inflections compared to Mrinalini's agitated one.

'Oh! Are we going there?' Excited anticipation erased her rudeness.

'Yes. After all it is all yours...' Her brows furrowed at this enigmatic remark but Mrinalini focused on catching up with the girl, who added, '...but you are not interested in hearing me...'

'No. No. That is not what I said.' Mrinalini interrupted. 'It's just that this Singhaldweep place is just too perfect to be real.'

Uma did not reply. She halted and waved her hand upwards in an arc, saying, 'This looks perfect too. But are you sure it is?'

Mrinalini looked up at the dark velvet vault overhead. It curved from east to west, north to south pierced by glittering silver pin pricks; a sight distinct to the open spaces here. Moonlight lent a magical cadence to the fortress walls, ordinary rocks and clefts. *Well, yes. It does look very enchanting now but something creepy like a snake or a poisonous lizard could be hidden under any one of these rocks.*

'Besides,' continued Uma, 'Perfection is like putting your eye to the tiny hole in a magic toy camera that you get in the *mela*. When you shake the coloured glass pieces in the cardboard cylinder, you see beautiful patterns, because your eye is far from them. But if your eye is closer, all you will see are bits of broken glass bangles. Since you are centuries away in time from what is taking place in the *Wali*, don't look closely at it and judge it against the perceptions of the present day. Just sink into the story and try to sense the emotions...and eventually the truth will come to you.'

Mrinalini frowned, trying to understand what Uma was telling her. Her reference to being far from the time zone of the *Padma-wali* reminded Mrinalini of the sudden feeling of timelessness that she had sensed earlier in the garden. Yet, she had an uncomfortable feeling that she was missing a crucial point. There was a clue right in front of her nose and she could not see it. Her journo instincts were being deflected and she did not like it. Nevertheless, she bit back a tart retort because she wanted to get her hands on the *Wali*.

Uma's words came floating back in the night air.

9

Dawn was still hidden behind the pearl-grey skies, when Padmavati came through the billowing curtains onto the terrace of her palace. A sarong was wrapped around her bare body and tied casually above her bosom. She sat down cross-legged on a grass mat laid on the floor for her daily routine of meditation.

The princess' first visits to the temple of Mahadev had charmed her and she had become a daily devotee. Over months, she had begun to spend more and more time in worship. For hours, she would sit at the feet of the enormous idol of the great Mahadev, Mahakal, Mahamaya. Other devotees would come and go with their offerings; priests and priestesses would conduct daily prayers, but none of it touched the still figure of the young princess. She would be lost in her thoughts of the Mahayogi. Her royal parents, who were waiting for the ultimate warrior to defeat the princess' champion and marry her, were anxious. *Was their daughter becoming a yogini? Would she reject marriage and join the sadhvis? Who would rule the kingdom, if she did not have a husband?* So they prevailed on the head priest of the temple to dissuade Padmavati's sudden predisposition towards meditation and prayers.

Under the guise of a philosophical discourse, the head priest tried to delve into the young princess' thoughts. He approached the girl sitting in solitude on the steps of the temple.

'Your Highness, what are you thinking so deeply?' he ventured.

Startled out of her contemplations, she took a few minutes to reply. 'O Wise One, I am wondering why men worry so much about the future. Look at the ocean, the birds, the clouds...in fact, all of nature. Do they worry about the past or the future? For them, Time is like a river. They flow with it, focused only on the role envisaged for them by the Creator.'

'True, Your Highness. But men have been gifted with the power to think. Thinking naturally leads to worries and anxieties of what may or may not happen.'

'But doing so wastes our precious time on Earth. We should embrace this life. You see, the future has already been defined for each of us. Thinking or worrying about it won't change what is predestined,' she countered.

Amazed at such an insight in the young girl, the priest tried to divert her, saying, 'Nobody really knows the truth, do they?'

Padmavati shook her head. 'I am not sure. I can only speak of my own experience.'

Very gently, the head priest asked, 'And what is that, Your Highness?'

'When I meditate, sometimes I leave my physical self behind. I see myself rising above it and floating wherever I want to go. I feel free of the burdens of life. My Consciousness sharpens and I float in a domain where there is no space and no time...' The girl's voice trailed off, as if she could see her visions. The priest found it difficult to accept that a few sessions of meditation had transcended the princess to the highest levels of Consciousness. Even after years of meditation, he had not been able to reach this stage of spirituality.

He probed, 'But isn't the concept of timelessness a myth?'

Smiling at the elderly man, Padmavati said softly, 'There are no myths, only beliefs. If we believe strongly in our essence...in our indestructible *atma*, we will be catapulted into timelessness. You see, what you call a myth is happening to us...to each of us all the time. Once we become aware of this ongoing phenomena, the truth is revealed to us.'

The priest could not say anything. Certainly, her words proved that she was spiritually more evolved than he was. And yet, she spoke so innocently of her profound ability. All of a sudden, the priest recalled his promise to the King. In a persuasive tone, he began, 'Your Highness, your ideas are indeed admirable...'

'In fact,' the girl-princess interrupted, 'I want to tell everyone about them. You see, it will help them to live life with tranquillity. Birth, death, joy and sorrow will not affect them. They will be free from fear, anxiety and pain.' She looked up into his face, pleading, 'O Wise one, will you initiate me into priesthood?'

'Your Highness, you know priests and priestesses in Singhaldweep have to forsake all earthly ties, including marriage and royal titles to take the vows. If you do that, what will happen to your commitment to your royal duties? What of your responsibilities to your subjects and kingdom? What of your promises to your parents that you will carry on their good work?'

Padmavati was silent...for a long, long time. The priest did not speak any more. He had already planted the seed. Distant and golden, the orb slowly sank into the waves and gulls screamed overhead. The princess kept sitting on the temple steps till lamps lit up the temple and the evening chants flowed around her. Then she quietly walked away.

Having been schooled from a young age to be loyal to her duties and commitments, Padmavati realized that it would be highly selfish of her to follow her own wishes. Therefore, she gave up her aspirations of priesthood but not her worship of the Mahadev. She still visited the temple and practised meditation, for it brought her immense peace and joy. However, she went back to her books, poetry, weapons-practice and long chats with Ambika.

This morning, the sea breeze gently lifted wisps of the princess' loose, long hair. It was crisp and cool on the terrace after the last few days of balmy weather. Padmavati closed her eyes and composed herself in the lotus pose. In hardly any time, she easily passed into the trance. As usual, she felt herself levitating and then slid out of her earthly body. Her immortal core, variously called spirit, soul, *aatma, âme* or *rooh,* hovered above the still figure on the floor. However, it remained attached to its physical element by a bright, pulsating thread. As the princess tried to move upwards, she felt a tug. She looked across space and noticed a glowing smoky trail suspended a little distance away. Padmavati knew the trail represented the desire of another *aatma;* a desire that must have been born many, many eons ago. Yet, the strength of that desire was so strong that it was intact despite the march of Time. Its potency had survived several births and deaths. As she watched the trail, it twisted this way and that, long fingers moving lazily as if seeking something. The gentle pull she had experienced had been from these fingers. *Somebody is seeking me,* she thought, *and has been looking for me a long time...searching intensely...who could that be?* By and by, the princess returned to her physical form.

Till now, the figure in lotus pose on the terrace had been breathing quietly and steadily as if in deep sleep. Now she gave a small cough and opened her eyes. Tranquillity seeped through her. A slight smile played on her lips, as she slowly got to her feet, her hair unravelling down her shoulders. Gathering it in one hand, she wrapped it round and round her fingers knotting a soft, large chignon at her nape.

Orange stripes shot across the sky heralding the arrival of the sun. Twittering birds quarrelled in the foliage; sea gulls screamed and rode the waves to feast on shoals of sardines. Padmavati watched dolphins cavorting in the distant grey-green firth. They loved sardines too. Young dolphins leaped up, spinning in the air. Other dolphins followed, each one jumping higher and gyrating faster than the previous one. Padmavati laughed out loud at their sport. She held on to the balustrade and breathed deeply of the scented, crusty air. *How good to be alive on a day like this, dear God!*

All of a sudden, she glanced to her left. At the end of the paved path was a human figure. It was too far to see the face but the bare torso indicated he was male. Instantly, she turned and slipped through the curtains into her room. It was her habit to converse with Nature in the pre-dawn hours. Her family, friends, royal servers knew this was private time and nobody disturbed her. *Who was this man? Why was he watching her?* Her composure, wrought by meditation refused to be disrupted by these questions. Still, Padmavati was curious.

It had been a couple of weeks since Kunwar Ratan Singh and Chetna had found lodgings with an elderly couple. Their meals were prepared by the old lady who just added two more portions to their own simple meals while cooking. With generosity typical of the Singhas, the couple did not ask for any compensation for caring for them. On the second day, Ratan Singh went to the old man and respectfully kept a bag of gold coins at his feet.

The man was surprised and asked, 'What is this, my son?'

Ratan Singh folded his hands and replied, '*Baba,* when you have called me your son, it is my duty to support you. This is all I have now, so please keep it.'

The old man accepted the gold while his wife smiled, tenderly. They were childless.

Chetna did not bother about returning their caregivers' benevolence. He was in his element here, roaming all day long, a roll of thick cloth under his arm. Whenever something caught his eye—and a great deal did—he would unroll the cloth and with a few bold strokes of charcoal transfer a likeness on it. Later, he would use dyes to paint his sketches. He was busy with his pursuits and Ratan Singh was free to inquire about the royal princess. Of course, he was discreet because, as he soon discovered, even a slight supposed criticism of the royal family would rouse the indignation of the usually calm Singhas.

As Ginni had guessed, the princess continued to follow the policy that he had proposed. Even now, after so many months, she was waiting to marry a prospective suitor who would fulfil her condition by defeating her champion in a sword duel. Listening to gossip in the bazaar, Ratan Singh became aware of an undercurrent of anxiety in the kingdom. People were worried about who would sit on the throne after Gandharava Sena as the chances of the princess' marriage were becoming remote. They were afraid that once the surrounding rulers realized that Singhaldweep did not have an heir, they may pounce on it like vultures when the powerful Gandharava Sena left the world. What would then happen to their beautiful land? Will it be torn to pieces by the hungry jackals who would each want a piece of it?

Ratan Singh realized that Padmavati's marriage was more a matter of national security than a social necessity for Singhaldweep. Brought up to inherit Chittor, he empathized with the fears of the Singhas. Yet, he could not help a flash of tender ache run through him for Padmavati. For them, this exquisite girl was only a means of security. Her marriage would provide them a future king and defender. Nobody was bothered about her happiness or desires. *I will ensure she is happy,* he thought and then made a wry face. *You will have to defeat her champion first,* he reminded himself.

He was certainly going to attempt it. So each day, before darkness, he would go to a secluded part of the forest and practise his sword play. He had bought a good sword, strong, sharp, yet lithe, from the local armourer. Here, the practice was to craft elaborate decorative hilts with embedded gems but Ratan Singh, the desert warrior, preferred a simple hilt with a comfortable grasp. He slashed and swiped, leaped and twirled in a small clearing, exercising his already-skilled sword arm. The rabbits and deer would stare fascinated at the crazy human and then scamper away in horror. Only Ginni, who had been witness to Padmavati's own training under Guru Tarak, would be present, fluttering overhead and screaming instructions or critiques.

On his return, Ratan Singh would take a detour. Walking down the paved avenue, he would get the closest he could to the cliff on which Padmavati's castle hung, and stare at the empty terraces, wishing he could get a glimpse of the famed beauty.

One grey dawn, his wish was granted, or so he believed. A figure wrapped in white appeared at the balustrade of the highest terrace. Too far for any features to be discerned, all Ratan Singh saw was how the person gathered a mass of long, thick hair into a huge heavy knot behind her neck. From this he assumed she was a woman and maybe the padmini of his dreams.

Eventually, it had been Ginni who lost his patience and exclaimed, 'How much more do you need to practise?'

'Practice is important,' gasped Ratan Singh, breathing heavily after an especially vigorous series of leaps and lunges. 'See, I'm catching my breath. No opponent will give me the time to breathe and then attack him.'

'...or her...,' corrected Ginni. Ratan Singh looked at his friend quizzically, who went on, 'I believe you are as good with the sword as you can be. All these weeks of practice have helped to wipe off any rustiness due to the days of inactivity during the voyage.'

Ratan Singh did not comment, so Ginni kept talking. Emphasizing each syllable, he said, 'I think you should apply for the contest tomorrow itself.'

The Mewari warrior looked up at the blue patch of sky visible between the trees. An eagle wheeled high above tracing lazy circles. He looked down at Ginni and nodded his head.

Ginni beamed.

Ever since Ginni had come back to Singhaldweep, he had wanted to rush to his friends, Padmavati and Ambika. But he had been afraid of Gandharava Sena's ire. Often he would perch in a tree in the royal gardens, hiding himself in the leaves and observe his childhood playmates as they passed by. But he had a strong intuition...the same kind of perception that had made him spout greetings to Kunwar Ratan Singh, rather than the Rawal at Chittor. Now, it told him that if only Ratan Singh and Padmavati could be united, his safety was ensured. Obviously, he wanted the occasion to arrive sooner than later.

10

The next morning, yolk-yellow sunbeams shimmered in drops hanging on tips of leaves. It had rained the entire night. The world looked squeaky clean. Ratan Singh awoke with anticipation bubbling up inside. After a refreshing bath at the well behind the house, he offered up prayers to Lord Ganesha, Lord Surya. . .his family deity, Lord Shiva, Goddess Shakti and a pantheon of deities. Then he donned a simple saffron *dhoti* and yellow *angavastran* more suitable for a *yogi* than a warrior. Other than the *murkis* or gold rings in his earlobes that all Mewaris had, he wore no jewellery. The Kunwar of Mewar wanted to maintain his modest appearance through simple attire as part of his camouflage. He strapped his trusty sword on his waist and was ready.

According to the rules of the contest, Ratan Singh had already registered himself as a participant at the gates of the royal palace. He gave his identity as Ratan Singh, son of Samar Singh from Mewar. As no more duel contestants had come forward for a very long time, the King had let it be known that if anybody did show an inclination, he was not to be denied on any pretext. Not just the people, the King and the royal administrators were also desperate to acquire a bridegroom for the princess.

Ratan Singh went into the main room of the cottage and touched the feet of his caregivers. Ginni cocked his head from the window sill. Taking his parrot-friend's advice, Ratan Singh had finally divulged his plan to take part in the duel to the elderly couple and Raghav Chetna. The old man and woman blessed him deeply because they knew that a duel with the Princess's champion was not only arduous, it was risky. Chetna was excited that he would be able to enter the palace as Ratan Singh's companion.

Chetna walked into the room and then stopped short. He stared at Ratan Singh. 'Are you going to the grand royal palace wearing an old *dhoti* and *angavastaram?'*

Everybody else, including Ginni stared back at him. Raghav Chetna was dressed like a Singha nobleman. In red and white, his dhoti, pantaloons and waistcoat were intricately patterned and sewn with sequins.The hilt of a gold dagger protruded from a broad jewelled belt. Several pearl strings around his neck and heavy gold earrings completed the picture.

As the others looked him up and down, Chetna gave a sheepish look, 'What? After all, we don't go to King Gandharava Sena's palace every day. Shouldn't we dress for the occasion?'

Ratan Singh replied, 'Yes!' hiding his smile behind a hand. Ginni had no such qualms. He fluttered over Chetna's head cackling derisively. Chetna tried to swat at him, but Ginni just flew higher, chortling even more.

'That silly bird!' Chetna exploded, showing Ginni his fist. The elderly couple stopped gazing at Chetna and smiled at Ginni's antics.

The woman said, 'Sit down, boys. Let me get you some steamed yam and milk for breakfast.'

Chetna instantly sat down on the mat laid on the floor. But with butterflies fluttering from his stomach to his throat, Ratan Singh said, 'No *Amma*. I cannot eat now.'

'My son, I will not let you go without eating. So sit down and eat what you can.' Both the men ate the simple but freshly-prepared meal while Ginni pecked at orange slices.

Finally, the trio reached the palace gates. When the guards called for Ratan Singh, they were surprised to see that instead of the well-dressed gentleman, his muscular companion in simple saffron was the contestant. But on looking closely, they were intimidated by his hawk-like profile with the white scar. While Ginni flew unseen overhead, the two men were guided through the landscaped gardens on the left of the sprawling palace. Chetna looked longingly at the grand main building. He had so hoped to enter it and view its magnificence. The two uniformed officials led them into a copse of banyan trees. On reaching the place, they realized that trees encircled a large hall with a peripheral corridor of arches. Inside, spectator stands went up the four walls till the roof. Just above the main door was a large royal enclosure for the king, queen, princess, ministers and courtiers. The wooden floor of the hall was the contest arena. Ratan Singh and Raghav Chetna were made to sit on a dais opposite the royal enclosure. Already the stands were filling up as people entered through the other doors. It had been a long time since they had the chance to enjoy a duel and wanted to make most of it. The seats in the royal enclosure were empty. Ratan Singh realized that he would have to perform to an audience and sighed.

Then he looked up at the enclosure opposite that was bedecked with flowers and wondered...just as Chetna spoke out his thoughts, 'Will we see the renowned beauty today?'

It irritated him and he snapped back, 'Speak with respect. She is the Princess of the realm.'

'Yes. Yes,' Chetna was suitably abashed. 'It's just that the whole world has heard so much about Princess Padmavati... even here, people can't stop praising her virtues...that I am very curious to see this celebrated lady.'

'Well, you will finally get your wish,' Ratan Singh said shortly.

A flourish of trumpets sounded, and both men looked up expectantly at the royal enclosure. First, in marched guards who stood in double rows on either side of the thrones. They were followed by the ministers who stood beside their seats and finally, led in by the Chief Minister, the royal couple appeared. Gandharava Sena looked magnificent in the ornamental Singhaldweep dress, gems on the hilt of the dagger at his chest sparkling as much as those on his high crown. Keeping in step with him and not following him, Ratan Singh noted, was the resplendent Queen Champavati in a glittering sarong and bustier, jewels on her arms, neck, ears and head reflecting the sunlight streaming through the open windows high above the spectator stands. Perched on one of them was the irrepressible Ginni watching the proceedings below. As the royal couple settled on their thrones, Ratan Singh expectantly searched the space behind them for Princess Padmavati. A crowd of smiling fine lords and ladies of the court entered after the royal couple but there was no sign of the princess. Then it caught his attention that there had been only two, not three thrones. So the princess was not going join her parents. *Since the duel was a contest to decide her bridegroom, she must be too shy to be present here, and is decorously awaiting the result in the palace,* thought Ratan Singh, feeling dejected. He had so hoped to see her that this possibility had not occurred to him.

The main door opened to reveal a man in white. He was of medium height and slight stature, rather wiry, especially as he seemed to walk on the balls of his feet. The usual dhoti over pantaloons and a full-sleeved waistcoat were gleaming like fresh snow. No ornaments on his body, but he was wearing a white metal face mask with slits for eyes and nose. It extended up to his head, over it and behind it to the nape fitting the entire head snugly. It was like a metal helmet worn in battle but in this case it covered the face and protected it, too. This was the princess' champion, as became apparent by the resounding applause of the spectators and even of the royalty. Ratan Singh laid his *angavastran* on the seat and stood up, as the champion slowly walked to the centre of the hall. The Mewari closed the intervening distance and both the duellists stood facing each other. The mask prevented Ratan Singh from seeing the expression on the other's face; *was it arrogant, afraid or confident?* Keeping to the Mewari tradition, Ratan Singh held his sword in both hands at waist level and bowed deeply to his opponent. He was gratified to see the Champion return his bow in the same manner. The gesture was a display of respect to one's opponent and though Ratan Singh was amidst foreign rituals, it meant a lot to him. All at once, a man appeared at his elbow with a tray. On it was a similar face mask as the Champion was wearing. Obviously, he was being offered the same protection, but Ratan Singh waved it away. He did not like the constraint of a mask.

Both duellists took their positions, right hand holding the sword up in front of the face and left hand behind the back. The Chief Minister stood up and announced the rules of the contest. Other than the usual rules of a sword combat, basically in this duel if the sword touched the ground, it would spell the defeat of its owner. He concluded with the proclamation that if the Contestant defeated the Champion, the trophy he would win was the Princess Padmavati's hand. The trumpeters brought their instruments to their lips. Ratan Singh's fingers curled around the hilt in an easy but firm grasp so that he could use the full strength of his wrist to turn the blade anyway he wanted.

The trumpets sounded, '*Tooot-toot-toot-toooooo...*'

The Champion instantly leaped back and thrust towards Ratan Singh but the Mewari had already leaped to the side opposite to his sword arm. He advanced with short attacks forcing the Champion to retreat. Suddenly, the man jumped into air and twirled around, landing on Ratan Singh's unprotected left side and lunged. The Mewari warrior rolled on the ground and in one motion was back on his feet. His quick reflexes born of years of fighting battles saved him from a grievous wound, maybe death. But this action gave both duellists a clear idea of each other's skill with the blade. Ratan Singh realized that his opponent was as quick as lightening on his feet and he needed to be alert to counter his sudden movements. With short parries and thrusts, both opponents kept their guard and tried to find an opening in the other's defence.

The entire hall was hushed as the spectators silently followed each move. They realized that both were excellent swordsmen and well-matched. Ratan Singh performed a quick sequence pushing the Champion back and then took a combat stance; right leg in front with the toes pointed forward, knees slightly bent and left leg behind front leg with toes pointed straight left. In response, the Champion vaulted up, somersaulted in air and landed behind Ratan Singh's left leg. He did not even need to recover from this acrobatic manoeuvre as he slashed at Ratan Singh's left ankle. The Mewari was so stunned by his opponent vanishing from front of him and appearing at his rear that he could not parry and a thin line of blood was sketched at his ankle. He clenched his jaw in anger at being trapped this way by his opponent. *Damn it! Is he a swordsman or a dancer?*

Ratan Singh turned full circle in a trice and cut viciously at his opponent. But he missed. Advancing quickly, his sword caught the Champion's sword at the hilt and began to turn it around in a circle. He pressed down, taking full advantage of his greater weight and height. The lean Champion tried to move forward so that the blades would loosen and he could break Ratan Singh's hold, but the warrior held him in a vice. He maintained pressure and the Champion's sword kept turning towards the floor. If it touched the ground, all would be over for the princess' champion. In a sudden move, the shorter man kneeled on the floor and lowered his sword arm. Ratan Singh's blade released pressure and his opponent easily slipped out his sword. Instantly, he spun away and Ratan Singh lost his hold.

The spectators let out a gasp of relief.

But now Ratan Singh knew that his greater strength was his advantage. He went after the man and within a few moments, he had locked blades in an 'X' at the hilt. As is usually done, Ratan Singh's other hand thrust out to hold the wrist of the opponent's non-sword arm but he kept dancing out of reach. Therefore, Ratan Singh brought his whole weight to bear on his sword arm, pushing down the Champion's blade. He drove down with both hands on the hilt and bent his knees so that his opponent could not slip out from under his sword arm. Then he focused on exerting pressure on the blade under his sword. Gradually, the Champion's sword began to lower and despite a few attempts at up thrusts, the blade was undeniably getting closer and closer to the floor. Yet, Ratan Singh could detect the upward force of his opponent's sword tingle up the straining muscles of his own arm. The Champion would not let go, but neither would Ratan Singh. His arms felt as if they would be torn off his shoulders.

Would he be able to tolerate the pain as long as it would take? Ratan Singh was not sure and then he realized, *but isn't the champion waiting for me to break?* That thought gave him a little more strength, a little more resilience. *A little bit more...just a little more force and I can win,* the Mewari told himself. Never in all his life had he faced such a formidable opponent.

The tension in the room was so thick that it could be sawed into planks to build a house. Hundreds of pairs of eyes stared unblinkingly at the two gleaming blades locked in battle. Was this the end of their princess' contest? Will her champion be finally beaten? It certainly seemed that way with the white warrior's blade now inches from the floor. Even as they held their breath, an unmistakable clatter of metal hitting the wooden floor with great force announced the answer to the question that had been in every Singha's mind for the last few years.

Ratan Singh remained on bent knees, his sword trailing on the floor, staring at the other blade gleaming on the dark wood. He could hardly believe that it was over. Sweat streamed down his body. Some of it dropped into his eyes, stinging sharply. Slowly, he straightened. Nobody said a word. Nobody cheered the winner. The Mewari turned to his beaten opponent to express appreciation for his skill and was stunned. With both hands, the Champion tugged off the face mask. Misty, dark tresses unravelled falling like a cloak all the way to the ankles. Amidst this dark cloud was a bewitching face. Milky white skin, large dark eyes tilting at corners fringed by thick lashes, a patrician nose above finely-etched lips with an endearing pout in their centre. Ratan Singh blinked, then blinked again. *Was the sweat in his eyes making him so delirious that he was seeing mirages?*

Murmurs rippled across the stands '...the princess... the princess...' Ratan Singh stared at the vision in front of him, his mouth open like a stupid country oaf. *The princess? His opponent in this duel...was...the princess?*

'Padmavati?' roared a voice from above. He looked up.

Gandharava Sena was leaning on the rails of the royal enclosure, his face contorted with rage. 'What are you doing here? What is the meaning of all this?'

Princess Padmavati stepped past Ratan Singh. She stood below the royal seats, her palms together respectfully. 'Your Majesty, I must ask for your forgiveness because I kept certain aspects of the contest secret from you, my mother and my people.'

Gandharava Sena exploded, 'Why?'

The spectators were also whispering, obviously wanting to know the princess' reasons. With folded hands, she turned in each direction before walking to stand just below the royal enclosure. Now everybody could see her. Ratan Singh still stood in the same spot with his opponent's sword at his feet. The princess gracefully gestured him to take his seat on the dais, which he did.

Then she spoke.

'My royal parents and people of Singhaldweep, it has been two years since our great King proclaimed that the man who wins a sword duel with the royal champion can marry me. You accepted this condition because you knew that the man who married me will also become the ruler of the kingdom of Singhaldweep after my father.

You accepted this condition because you felt winning a tough duel would prove to some extent that the future ruler was worthy of ruling our land. In this way my parents and you felt assured of a good ruler.

Now I am the daughter of a king who places the security and well-being of Singhaldweep's people above his own child's happiness. Being that very daughter, I felt equally responsible that this mode of selecting the future ruler must not be flawed in any manner. The royal champion needed to ensure not just victory but also that the duel did not fall short of the highest standards of skill and ability. The intent to win must be driven by sincerity, zeal and dedication to the cause of the kingdom's welfare. Unstintingly, the champion I chose must put in due rigour. Now, who could more devotedly implement these ideals than the believer? Using a proxy to apply them was running a risk. I could not risk the future of our country. That is the reason I decided that I will be my own champion and fight the duel with the contestants.'

Her lovely face flushed with the passion of her words, the girl in white spread her hands in submission and asked, 'Tell me, Singhas, did I take the wrong decision?'

Muttering began in one corner and rapidly spread through the stands until in one voice, they roared, 'No, Princess Padmavati. You did right and we salute you.'

In the royal enclosure, Queen Champavati was wiping her eyes while King Gandharava Sena was trying not to show his emotions. He was so proud of this daughter of his! She should be ruling his land, not the man who had won the duel. And that thought made him glance at the winner.

Ratan Singh was sitting in his chair, staring at the princess. He looked dazed as a medley of thoughts spun through his mind. *Was this girl for real? Let alone a man, how could a woman take so much risk just for the security of her people? She is one in a million...in thousands of millions!* He was overwhelmed with her courage and wisdom. *I am fortunate to have just known about her.*

Right then, a bright green bird with a blood-red beak dropped to Ratan Singh's shoulder. Ginni felt this was the most propitious moment to make his presence known. Purring softly, he gently nipped the warrior's ear.

'GINNNNII!' screamed the princess, her dignified posture thrown to the winds in her wild excitement. Instantly, the bird fluttered across to her, whispering endearments. 'Ginni! Ginni! Where did you go? How could you leave me, my friend?' Holding him in cupped hands, Padmavati caressed him.

'PAARRROT?' roared the King. 'There he is! There he is! Guards! Catch him. Hold him. Net him! I must have that dratted bird for lunch.' Instantly, Ginni tried to worm his way into the princess' clothes to hide.

Padmavati patted her friend reassuringly and spoke to her father, 'No, Your Majesty. Ginni is my friend. You can't eat my friend, Sire, can you?' His daughter pleaded softly.

It took just one unbelievable millisecond for the King's fiery temper to melt... faster than butter in a hot pan. He swallowed, mumbling, 'Oh!...Alright...if you say so.' He took his place as Queen Champavati, the ministers and courtiers ventured to smile politely. The hall broke into loud cheers for the royal family.

Princess Padmavati bowed to her people, turned around and went out of the door, Ginni sitting triumphantly on her shoulder. Soon, she appeared in the royal enclosure. She spoke to her father who nodded. The King and Queen, each holding one of Padmavati's hands, turned to face the dais and the hall.

King Gandharava Sena announced, 'As proclaimed, the winner of this contest, Ratan Singh, son of Samar Singh of Chittor will marry my daughter, Princess Padmavati of Singhaldweep. The ceremony will take place in a week's time.'

As his sonorous voice died down, another one spoke up. Silent until now, Raghav Chetna stood up and said quietly,

'Your Majesty, the winner of this duel is a prince in his own right. May I introduce to you the future Rawal of Chittor, Kunwar Ratan Singh, son of Rawal Samar Singh?'

An excited clamour broke out in the hall, as people craned their necks to see Ratan Singh, still sitting calmly in his seat. The King and Queen were seen whispering with the Chief Minister. The princess intervened and so the King turned towards the dais and said, 'We proudly welcome the son of the illustrious Rawal of Chittor, whose Suryavanshi lineage matches that of Kambhojas and who is known as the Sun of the Hindu Dharma.' He extended both his arms and said, 'Kunwar Ratan Singh, forgive me for not proffering you a proper reception but I did not know. I invite you here. Your seat is with the royal family.'

Ratan Singh slowly got to his feet. His ankle was hurting. Folding his palms, he bowed his head and replied, 'Your Majesty, it is my great fortune to be in your presence. Please do not apologise. You are like my father and the fault is mine. I concealed my true lineage. I am humbled by your request to join you but I prefer to stay where I am. It is a Mewari tradition that I do not meet my bride until we are joined in holy matrimony before the sacred fire. I hope Your Majesty will forgive me.'

Queen Champavati smiled and King Gandharava nodded his head. In a few words, Ratan Singh had displayed respect for his elders, his bride-to-be and family traditions. He seemed a very suitable son-in-law and would probably make a good ruler.

The King went on, 'Well said, Kunwar! Now the other matter...by marrying my daughter, you accept the position of being the Crown Prince of Singhaldweep. But you are also heir to Mewar, so how will you manage both kingdoms?'

Everyone inside the hall held their breath.

'I accept with deep gratitude this position of great significance gifted to me by His Majesty of Singhaldweep.

I know my acceptance means that I may have to straddle two boats. But as of now, my father is the Rawal of Chittor and a worthy one. I…I wish to remain here after marriage to…learn about my duties. I believe we should let the future unfold by itself and tell us how we should proceed.'

The King, queen and the people of Singhaldweep only heard that Kunwar Ratan Singh had agreed to stay on the island after marrying their princess. They hardly heard the rest of his words.

Truth be told, Ratan Singh was overwhelmed by the speed with which his life in Singhaldweep had suddenly turned around from being one of a nondescript foreigner to that of a royal guest, even royalty. He still could not believe that he had achieved the right to marry the lady of his dreams and he did not want anything to become an obstacle to the wedding. He had no desire to become the Crown Prince but he had thought it best to accept and also agree to stay back. At the same time, he did not want to enter the sacred bond of marriage under false promises.

His confused thoughts went this way and that. *What should I do? Firstly, I need to know what this means…to be the Crown Prince of Singhaldweep. But of course, I have to return to Chittor someday. Maybe, I should seek a private discussion with King Gandharava Sena before the wedding. We could have an arrangement…if he agrees…whereby I could divide my time between the two kingdoms…*

Princess Padmavati had a quizzical look as she considered the man standing below her, his head bowed and his saffron *angavastran* fluttering in the slight breeze.

11

'How wonderful! What a perfectly romantic love story!' Mrinalini could not help exclaiming, despite being a confirmed cynic when it came to love stories.

'Not really,' countered Uma. 'Ratan Singh was captivated by the princess. But his emotions did not find an echo in Padmavati. She was not attracted to the Mewari other than having developed a deep admiration for his prowess with the sword.'

'Really? But why was that so?'

'Because Padmavati was a realist. Her approach to life was commonsensical. She was deeply spiritual and it made her view situations without being swayed by emotion. If anything, she was inclined to weigh things in their right perspective. According to her the most significant attributes in life were righteousness, integrity and highly ethical behaviour. Her thoughts and actions followed these principles,' elucidated Uma.

'I agree with her thinking. I am that kind of a person too,' nodded Mrinalini.

'I know,' muttered Uma.

Mrinalini gave her a surprised glance but went on with her analysis. 'What I find completely in discordance are Padmavati's ideals. My studies tell me that women during the 12th or 13th century were mostly kept in purdah; even Hindu women. I cannot imagine any of them thinking or even behaving as you say Padmavati did.'

'That is what makes Padmavati different.'

'Is this one of your own observations?' Mrinalini narrowed her eyes.

'Yes, of course. In the *Wali* Padmavati also speaks of her own beliefs and this is the impression that I got from reading about them. Besides, *bhayeli*, I believe you are referring to the women of our country. Don't forget that Padmavati was from Singhaldweep, not Bharatdesh. Also her father, Gandharava Sena had groomed her to sit on the throne. Possibly, it gave her a broader perception of the world and saved her from the pettiness that guided most feminine actions during those ages.'

Mrinalini's shrug was an eloquent expression of her incredulity. 'Maybe...'

'Also the spirituality integral to her personality maintained a balance between her emotions and reasoning. Possibly, her ability to transcend the physical world and loosen the shackles of time gave her perception objectivity.'

Mrinalini recalled, once again, her own inexplicable experience of infinite time. However, she wanted to make an unbiased evaluation of Uma's tale for the sake of veracity.

'Possibly...,' agreed the journalist, grudgingly. 'But, I want to read it all myself. Then I can judge the right or wrong of it. So where is the *Padma...Padma...*'

'*Padma-wali*?'

'Yes. I want to see it...I want to read it,' Mrinalini's tone was impetuous; though she was thinking, *hope I will be able to decode the Sanskrit in the text. Wish I had paid more attention to it in school...convoluted and confounding language that it was!*

Uma advanced briskly without replying.

'Hey!' called Mrinalini. 'I want the *Padma-wali*. Did you hear me?'

Uma's voice floated back. 'Come with me. I am taking you to it.'

'What a girl! All she says is "...taking you to it... taking you to it". When? Where?' muttered Mrinalini, exasperatedly running to catch up with Uma, who was fast vanishing into the night.

12

Queen Champavati was pacing up and down her boudoir. Ginni sat outside the window, hidden from view. He was contentedly sucking at a small juicy mango, but alert to the happenings inside. The Chief Minister had just left after meeting the queen. He had brought with him a detailed report on Ratan Singh; his family, reputation, *et al*. Nearly all of what she had heard made him appear to be an ideal spouse for her daughter, but there were two things that worried her. Firstly, that he was not Samar Singh's natural son. He was adopted and being well-versed in the throne politics of kingdoms, Champavati was afraid of envious aspirants plotting against him.

The second reason for her disquiet was the fact that Ratan Singh already had fourteen wives and numerous concubines. *What would be my daughter's position in the royal household of Chittor? The fifteenth wife? What about being a queen?* Padmavati would never be the chief queen when her husband attained the throne. That status would be given rightly to Ratan Singh's senior-most wife. *Then where was this marriage going to take my beloved daughter? Will it be to a hornet's nest where she will not be sure whether she is a wife or a concubine?*

Gandharava Sena came in briskly, saying, 'What is it, Champavati? I was at an important meeting.'

The Queen gently pushed him into a comfortable chair and said, 'Nothing is more important than our daughter. And anyway, you need a break from your ceaseless meetings. Here are some sweet tangerines, pineapples and a jug of cold grapefruit juice. Munch away and listen carefully to what I have to say.' Champavati gave her husband all the information the Chief Minister had brought and then conveyed her anxieties.

As it turned out, Kunwar Ratan Singh had already met the King a few days ago. Politely, he had thanked the King for his permission to marry his daughter and also for the gift of the royal position. At the same time, he had explained the situation at Mewar and how Khalji had been eying Chittor. When the King heard his proposal of dividing time between the two kingdoms, he welcomed it wholeheartedly. But he had a request: Padmavati would not accompany her husband to Chittor. Ratan Singh had acquiesced willingly. He did not want to subject a delicate flower like the princess to the travails of such long journeys. Both men had cheerfully shaken hands on this agreement. Ratan Singh was content that he had been true to his country and his commitments to his future bride. King Gandharava Sena had ruminated, *it's a fine agreement. Then my Padmavati can rule our kingdom as Queen and her husband can travel between Singhaldweep and Chittor. I like the idea.*

But he did not want to tell this to his dearest wife just yet. She was already too agitated. The King observed frown lines on her fair forehead. He leaned forward and smoothened them with tangerine-sticky fingers and said, 'My dear, you worry unnecessarily. Padmavati and Ratan Singh are going nowhere. As soon as they are married, I will begin the process of integrating them into the administrative system of the kingdom. You see, my dear, I plan to pass them the reins quite soon and then you and I can travel our kingdom and beyond as you always wanted to.'

Champavati sat down. Absent-mindedly wiping her forehead clean of tangerine juice, she said thoughtfully, 'Well, alright. I forgot that Padmavati will not go off to her husband's home like most brides.' However, she turned her eyes, dark with emotion, to her husband and exclaimed, 'But...the fifteenth wife...! Our Padmavati deserves to be the only wife, with complete sovereignty over her husband's heart...like...like me.' And a blush stole up Champavati's creamy cheeks.

Gandharava Sena leaned back with a smile. 'I don't think that is a problem. The boy is completely enamoured of our princess. . .rather love-sick, is the right word.'

'But for how long will it last?' countered Champavati. 'After all, it seems he is in the habit of flitting from flower to flower.'

'Don't forget that there is no other girl in the world as beautiful, as brilliant and as wise as our daughter. She is like the heavenly lotus. Remember the tale of the ardent bee which, seeking sweet nectar from the lotus' heart, becomes captive inside the bloom? Once Ratan Singh has fallen under Padmavati's spell, nothing can entice him away.' The King's tone was smug.

'Really?' Champavati was not easily swayed. 'How about the Rawalship of Chittor? Or his children by the other wives?'

Gandharava Sena sat up in the chair to argue with her just as Padmavati ambled in. She smiled at her parents, 'Oh! I didn't know you were in discussion with Father. I will come later, Mother.' She turned to go but the King and Queen spoke up together.

'Don't go, Padmavati.'

'We need to talk to you.'

So Padmavati sat down facing them and eagerly asked, 'Yes?'

Once again, the Queen spoke of the Chief Minister's report and added her own concerns. Gandharava Sena punctuated the narration with his comments from time to time. Patiently, wordlessly, Padmavati heard them both out. Then she went up to her mother and hugged her.

'Mother dearest, I understand you are anxious for me. But I am no longer your little girl. You and Father have brought me up with lots of love and care. You have tried to shelter me from all that's evil and unpalatable in the world. At the same time, you have also coached and trained me to fight for truth and justice and thus take my place in the world. Now it is time for me to step into that place. It is a place where I will have to take decisions and be responsible for the consequences of those decisions. You have fulfilled your parenting duties in an exemplary manner and now it is time for me to fulfil your expectations.

'As for my departure to Chittor, we know that after marriage, my husband will be anointed as the successor to Singhaldweep's throne. So, as of now, we can assume that I will not leave our island. But nobody has seen the future. I agree with you, Mother, if his country or duty calls, it is expected that my future husband will heed the call. How can he place a country received in dowry above his own motherland? Can anybody love their adopted country as much as their own? In fact, I would not trust a man or woman who can place their own interests above their duty to their motherland? And if my husband goes to Chittor, I go with him and accept whatever life has to offer me.'

'Well-said, my daughter,' Gandharava Sena's face was suffused with pride. Since he knew that between her father and husband, they had decided that she would not leave Singhaldweep, the King was not perturbed. *But listen to my daughter…how she proclaims these noble ideas. It only proves how well I have groomed her*, he thought.

The Queen still shook her head. 'No, my love, I cannot accept you as a man's fifteenth wife.'

'Mother,' said Padmavati, her eyes serious, 'I have come into this world with my destiny already written. Nobody can change it. If I am fated to be somebody's fifteenth wife, so be it.'

'But,' the Queen interrupted, 'we can refuse this match based on….'

'No we cannot, Mother.' Padmavati did not allow her mother to continue any further. 'The King of Singhaldweep had promised to wed me to anybody who would defeat the royal champion. He cannot dishonour his royal word by refusing to give his daughter's hand to the victor. As rulers of our land, it is our duty to adhere to the principles of truth, honour and ethics. I will marry Kunwar Ratan Singh, even if it may change my life altogether.'

Champavati stared at her daughter, her eyes welling up. Gandharava Sena sighed deeply and said, 'I agree with the princess. The honour of all Singhaldweep is implicit in keeping this royal promise. So we really have no option but go ahead with the wedding.' The king rose to his feet and patting Champavati on her shoulder, added, 'We have taught our daughter too well, my queen. Now we must be strong as she applies that learning. But, mark my words. One day, our Padmavati will do us proud. Not just us, but the whole world will know of her noble deeds. I am sure of that...I am sure....' And he turned to walk away briskly, ostensibly to his next meeting but actually to hide sudden tears of paternal pride springing up in his eyes.

Wedding morn dawned on a cool September day sparkling with mellow sunshine. The monsoon humidity had passed and the air had an autumnal nip to it. Ratan Singh, as was his habit, walked outside in his short dhoti to the well behind the cottage. He rotated the handle to let a bucket down the well. After it was filled with water, he pulled it up and upturned it on his head. He gave a short leap and gasped in shock as the icy water hit his body. Shrieks and cackles erupted overhead. Ratan Singh rubbed the water from his eyes to see Ginni fluttering, overcome with merriment at his actions. The muscular Mewari gave a wry smile and filled another bucket to pour over himself. After lathering himself well and rinsing it off with more buckets of water, he rubbed himself roughly down with a thick cloth. The crisp air carried to them the distant music of pipes and drums floating across the courtyard wall.

'What's that?' he asked Ginni.

'Must be some festival,' replied Ginni, preening himself on the wall.

Ratan Singh ignored the music, briskly wiping his shoulder-length hair. His stomach rumbled with hunger. He eagerly thought of the savoury yams being baked in the kitchen on the other side of the courtyard. His nostrils twitched at the appetizing whiffs floating in.

'*Amma*, I'm ready,' he called out to his foster mother before going inside to change into fresh clothes and complete his morning worship. Today, he particularly wanted to pray for divine benediction. Despite being married several times, Ratan Singh felt as if this was the first time that he was being bound to another in holy matrimony. All the earlier occasions he had gone through this event to acquiesce to the wishes of Rawal Samar Singh or fulfil a duty. But today, he was going to take the sacred vows from the depth of his heart and soul. He was to be married to the first and only love of his life and he wanted the Gods to bless this new phase of his life.

He was tying the knot on his dhoti when it seemed to him that the music outside sounded louder. It was coming closer and closer. Quickly, he pulled over his head a blue silk kurta, the only one he had bought for this special day, and walked out into the front room. Exactly then, a loud voice called, 'Kunwar Ratan Singh*ji*?' It came from outside the cottage.

Ratan Singh peeped through the window curtains. *What was this?* His mouth agape, he stared at the procession of horses, palanquins and musicians standing before the cottage gates.

'Oh my green chillies! They are wearing the royal crest.' That succinct observation was from Ginni who was perched on Ratan Singh's shoulder. The elderly couple and a half-dressed Chetna rushed into the room.

'What's happening?' Chetna wanted to know.

Ratan Singh shook his head when another bellow came from the gate. The old man quickly opened the door. Nobody kept the King's men waiting. Instantly, a portly man in an impressive uniform that prominently displayed the royal coat of arms entered. He ignored the elderly couple and looked from Ratan Singh to Chetna and back. He seemed confused between the two and murmured, 'Kunwar?'

Ratan Singh stepped forward, 'Yes?' and added politely, 'I am Kunwar of Chittor.'

Instantly, the man folded his palms on his chest and bowed so low that his hands nearly touched the Mewari's knees. Ratan Singh took a hasty step back and folding his own hands, said, '*Khamaghani*.'

His huge stomach nearly unbalanced the man who came back with difficulty to an erect position. Ingratiatingly, he announced, 'Today is a day of celebration for our country. The great Kunwar of Chittor will become the son-in-law of Singhaldweep. We are very fortunate, Your Highness.' He crossed both arms on his chest and bowed again.

Ratan Singh was not habituated to this kind of fulsome flattery, Mewaris being taciturn by nature. They do not indulge in unnecessary words and come to the point quickly. So he frowned, but did not want to be rude by asking outright the reason for the visit.

'I am Vishwasna, the major-domo of the King's household. Therefore, I have the singular honour of escorting the wedding gifts that the King has sent for you.'

Again, he bowed.

'Oh sure...wedding gifts...,' quipped Chetna, giving interested glances at the palanquins visible through the open gates. Ginni twittered.

'Ummh...there was no need for gifts,' said Ratan Singh, embarrassment audible in his voice. Then, thinking it sounded terribly discourteous, he instantly added, 'I am very grateful to the King, no doubt. It's just that his permission to marry Princess Padmavati was the greatest gift that I have ever received.' The sincerity of his words made the Major-domo smile.

'The great Kunwar is very unassuming, indeed. But our King knew that having just come to our island, you would be unaware of our customs, dress and traditions. So, he has sent with us your wedding dress, jewels, auspicious turmeric and basil along with other customary gifts. He has also sent a special horse for you to ride to the palace for the ceremony. If you permit me, I will arrange for the gifts to be brought in.'

Ratan Singh nodded his head. Immediately, the Major-domo clapped his hands.

Through the door, came a queue of men in the royal colours holding aloft trays covered with gold cloth. They began to lay the trays on the tables and chairs. Soon these surfaces were filled and more trays were coming in. In a few minutes, the people in the room were hemmed in by trays carpeting the floor in two layers.

Eventually all the gift palanquins were emptied. The major-domo bowed to Ratan Singh and said, 'Your Highness, to reach the palace in time for the ceremony, we will need to leave in about two hours' time. Till you are dressed and ready to leave, the ceremonial guard will wait at the gates with your horse and the palanquins for your guests.' A bemused Ratan Singh could only fold his palms in reply as the major-domo smartly marched outdoors to give his orders.

The four inmates of the cottage looked silently at each other, each one confined to the spot by the trays. Chetna was the first to recover. 'Hey! Let's look at these gifts.' And he began to uncover the trays, leaping from one to the other. The rich and magnificent gifts were numerous consisting of garments, jewels and ornamental daggers.

Chetna whooped excitedly, while the old man and his wife gasped. They had never seen so much wealth.

A large silver tray held the auspicious turmeric and basil along with a special ceremonial dress in yellow and purple, a huge gleaming sapphire turban pin as well as a dagger whose hilt and scabbard were encrusted with gems. 'This seems special,' murmured Ratan Singh.

'Yes,' replied his foster mother. 'It is the bridegroom's dress. You must wear it for the ceremony today.'

'But, this is the Singha dress. I have no idea how to arrange its accessories,' Ratan Singh rued.

'Don't worry. I'll help you,' said his foster mother, smiling.

So, the bridegroom went to dress in another room. His foster-father began to arrange the expensive gifts inside a cupboard. Chetna said, 'If you are planning to keep the gifts for yourself, you could pass me a few.'

The old man gave him a severe look. In these past months he had gauged Chetna's covetous nature well. He claimed kinship with the Kunwar but was always seeking ways of benefiting from the relationship. In fact, Ratan Singh was inclined to distance himself from the brash artist. The elderly couple had developed quite a dislike to Chetna and suspected he was not really related to the noble Kunwar. They endured his presence simply because he was Ratan Singh's companion.

Ratan Singh's foster father frostily replied, 'I am keeping these gifts safely so that they can be moved to Kunwar's palace after his marriage. After all, they are royal gifts and must go to the royal son-in-law.' He did not deign to comment on the last part of Chetna's suggestion.

Chetna grimaced and went off to primp himself, thinking, *this Singha crone is an idiot!* According to Chetna's greedy reasoning, Ratan Singh's family and friends had rights to all the Kunwar's wedding gifts. *And who is his closest associate in Singhaldweep other than I, Raghav Chetna? What was the harm in my taking a few baubles from so many? I could have picked up some things that caught my fancy but the stupid old man has locked them all up. He and his silly scruples!*

In less than two hours, Ratan Singh's guests were back in the room. Now they were all dressed in their best. After all, it was the wedding of the season. When Ratan Singh emerged from his room, all three stared in astonishment at the splendid figure. Wine-velvet narrow trousers emerged below a golden silk dhoti embroidered with dark yellow lions. It was knotted high in the island fashion, held in place by a decorative band. Thrust into it was the glittering dagger. The wine-coloured turban on his head, tied in the Singhaldweep way, was pinned by the large sapphire. Strings of pearls and rubies dangled across a matching jacket emblazoned with the royal crest.

Ratan Singh looked like a royal Singha bridegroom, every inch of him. After all he was the Kunwar of Mewar.

The beautiful white horse caparisoned with a silk saddle and harness in the royal colours pranced excitedly as Ratan Singh mounted it. His guests rode the palanquins. Ratan Singh noticed that the entire city, its streets, houses and buildings had been festooned with flower garlands and there were messages of felicitations for the royal event hung everywhere. The bridegroom's party proceeded to the palace on a road lined with wildly cheering citizens.

13

The palace gates and fences were entwined with floral garlands. Flags, banners and buntings in the royal colours were gaily fluttering on the roofs of the palace. The gates were open to receive numerous guests. When the bridegroom's procession drew up to the massive, ornate palace doors, it was greeted by conches and trumpets. Kunwar Ratan Singh descended from his horse and the rest of his party emerged from the palanquins. A large reception group of Singhaldweep's noblemen and ladies surged forward. Elegantly dressed, with jewels twinkling in the sunshine, they performed several pre-wedding rituals. Ratan Singh was anointed with sandalwood paste. Ladies holding salvers of lighted lamps, betel leaves, vermilion and other auspicious symbols orbited the bridegroom singing propitious marriage songs. Ratan folded his hands and bowed his head to receive the greetings courteously while his foster parents beamed. Raghav Chetna threw gracious smiles all around as if he was a royal relative to the bridegroom.

The Queen approached Ratan Singh, who bent reverently to touch her feet. She placed her hands on his head to bless him. Then raising him, Champavati slipped over his head a long, heavy necklace of braided gold chains; her wedding gift. The King came down the corridor. Ratan Singh touched his feet with both hands and then raised them to his head. The king blessed him. After greetings were over, Ratan Singh, flanked by the King and Queen of Singhaldweep, proceeded down the long corridor followed by the joyful, merry guests. Ginni, who had been reporting the morning's events to the princess had returned to perch on his usual grandstand view... Ratan Singh's shoulder.

The procession came upon a large open square. In the centre was a raised platform. Its corners were marked by four banana trees and floor inlaid with intricate patterns of rice powder and flower petals. From two opposite sides, paths lined with more rice-powder patterns led to the centre of the platform. On all four sides of it, seating had been arranged for guests. Four magnificent thrones faced its front.

'The stage is called the *Poruwa,*' whispered Ginni in Ratan Singh's ear. 'It is the venue where a traditional Singhaldweep wedding takes place.' *Nice to have Ginni explain things...all this is quite different from the rituals at home,* thought Ratan Singh, consciously keeping a genial expression on his face.

He was led to one of the thrones and as he sat down, the royal couple settled on thrones on either side. Across the *Poruwa,* through an arch facing him came strains of a melody sung by several female voices. A group of singers...well-dressed, bejewelled young ladies, led by Ambika emerged through the arch. They walked in two rows, holding carved ivory sticks that supported a long purple silk canopy. 'This is a popular wedding song,' Ginni explained to Ratan Singh. 'It is a paean to the beauty, sweet nature, and grace of the bride.'

The Mewari nodded but could not take his eyes off the parade. Coming through the arch was a mesmerizing sight. Right in the centre of the canopy walked an ethereal figure...Princess Padmavati in all her bridal splendour. Her white silk sarong and full-sleeved jacket was encrusted with tiny seed pearls strewn amongst delicate silver thread-work of lotus buds and leaves. A diaphanous lacy long scarf went over the right shoulder and was belted at the waist, forming frills. From her neck to her knees the traditional *mala hatha* of seven gold necklaces adorned her. The *karapati* or choker clasped around her neck was the first necklace. Its pendant was a diamond lotus with delicate open petals. Next came four chains of various lengths each with its lotus *paddakam* or pendant similar to the *karapati*. Below them hung the *paalaka* chain made of gold beads. Next was the *agasthi malaya*, a necklace of agate stones. The seventh necklace that reached to the princess' knees was the *pethi maala*, of diamond lotus petals. Her head and forehead was draped with the *nalalpatiya* or head ornament with a piece along the middle parting of her hair that ended in a large lotus pendant on her forehead. The *Ira Handa*, circular hair ornaments were pinned on either side of her hair parting. On one was engraved the sun and on the other was the moon.

'The sun and moon on her head symbolize the eternity of her married status,' helpfully commented Ginni. Ratan Singh hardly heard. He was too engrossed in drinking in this exquisite vision.

On her wrists were broad gold bangles, the *seli valalu* along with gold and agate circles. A large diamond lotus rested on the back of her hand with five chains attached to five finger rings. *Dimithi* ear ornaments were upside-down gold cups with pearl drops. Her tiny waist was encased in a gold belt sparkling with diamond lotuses.

But Ratan Singh was hardly aware of any of this elegant attire. Spellbound, he gazed at the dewy face of his bride. In tones of peaches and cream, her face glowed, the bright sunshine unable to expose a single blemish. Thick eyelashes fanned her cheeks as she demurely kept her sight downwards, concealing the lovely almond-shaped eyes, lustrous with perceptive wisdom. Below the dainty nose, the pair of finely etched lips were as tremulous as butterfly wings. Rose brushed her cheeks with a slight blush. The sword-wielding warrior of the duel was nowhere discernible in this captivating maiden. Ratan Singh fell once more in love with this uniquely entrancing person who had lived in his dreams for so long. In flesh and blood, she was even more breath-taking than in his dreams; she was almost celestial.

Ginni pecked gently at Ratan Singh's ear breaking into his trance. 'Wake up. They are calling for you.' The Mewari turned his head to see the King and Queen waiting, as an elderly priest beckoned to him. He understood that he must ascend the *Poruwa* from the right. Accompanied by his foster parents and Chetna, he began to walk in that direction and realized that his bride was standing on the left side of the platform with her parents. Both the groom and the bride climbed the couple of steps up to the *Poruwa* at the same time and met in the centre, facing each other. Behind them blazed the sacramental fire in a small brazier that would sanctify the union. They folded their hands and bowed to each other. Then the priest placed betel leaves in their hands, which they accepted and handed back to the priest. He offered them to the sacred fire.

The King stood beside the princess, holding her right hand in his. The priest, who stood between the couple, said to Ratan Singh, 'Bring forward your right hand, palm upwards.' He did so. The King placed his daughter's hand in Ratan Singh's signifying he had formally given her to the groom.

Chetna came forward with a tray of many sheaves of betel leaves tied together with a gold coin in each. The bride took each sheaf and dropped it on the floor. Ratan Singh was asked to do the same. After that, Ratan Singh's foster father came forward. Taking the Mewari's hand, he placed in it a gold chain and said, 'Clasp it around your bride's neck.' Ratan Singh looked at the old man in surprise. *Where did he get the gold chain?* But he silently carried out the instruction.

Now it was his foster mother's turn. A beautiful red and gold sarong folded in her outstretched arms, she came up to Ratan Singh. Gesturing to the princess, she offered it to him. Wordlessly and gratefully, Ratan Singh took it from her and held it out to Padmavati, who took it and turned to give it to her mother. It was a gift from a son-in-law to the bride's mother.

I know none of these customs but my kind, foster parents are familiar with them. So they had arranged for all these gifts without telling me. It must have cost them a great deal. Still they did it to make sure that I may retain my dignity and do not suffer any embarrassment on this significant occasion. How much they love me! Ratan Singh's heart filled with tenderness for the old people.

In the meanwhile, a distinguished-looking nobleman came up on the *Poruwa*. He took Ratan Singh's and Padmavati's right hands and wound a gold thread around their little fingers, tying them together. Then he poured water over the fingers. Later, he was introduced to Ratan Singh as Champavati's younger brother, Prince Gora Rajsinha. Once the fingers were tied, the ladies began chanting the verses from the Vedas. These were sacraments of matrimony ending with, ' *Yad etad hrdayam tava, tad astu hrydayam mama/yad idam hrdayam mama, tadastu hrdayam tava* (Wherever your heart lies, may my heart lie there. Wherever my heart lies, may yours be there, too.)'

When the chants died down, Ratan Singh's foster father came forward. Facing the congregation with the newly-married couple and their relatives behind him, he cracked a coconut on the *Poruwa* and sprinkled its water over everyone on the stage, the spectators and the holy fire to express his gratitude to the Almighty and to pray for divine blessings.

The *Poruwa* emptied with the wedding ceremony completed. Ratan Singh and Padmavati were husband and wife, bound in this life and for seven lives hereafter. The King and Queen with their new son-in-law and daughter led their relatives and guests to the sumptuous wedding banquet laid out in the great hall of the palace.

Consummating his various marriages and establishing conjugal relations had been a duty for Ratan Singh till now, with the purpose of begetting progeny to carry on the family line. He hardly knew his partners in the act and had never felt any desire to do so, either. But now, his feelings were completely contrary. His deeply sincere desire to fathom this delectable person who had become part of his life overpowered all other wishes. It was late night by the time the newly-married couple were finally alone in their bed chamber. Its walls had been hung with tapestries of flowers, the huge bed had a canopy of jasmine strings and rose petals thickly covered the counterpane. Bowls of fruit, sweetmeats and jugs of juices dotted the room. Her ladies had replaced the princess' bridal attire with a loose, soft cream sarong and a flowing tunic. A few flowers in her loose hair made her irresistibly alluring. Ratan Singh had been provided with similarly thin, cotton dhoti and kurta. Comfort was the key intent of this setting yet its innate intimacy made the couple extremely uncomfortable. A few moments alone with her and Ratan Singh became acutely aware of Padmavati's anxiety. *She is probably expecting the crude foreigner to pounce on her and claim his conjugal rights,* Ratan Singh thought wryly and decided, *I must take control of the situation or else I will never win her heart.*

He walked across the room to the door that led to a hanging balcony and opened it. 'They really have taken a lot of pains to make this room into a garden but so much floral perfume in an enclosed space can be overpowering, don't you think?' He said, turning to her with a friendly smile.

She seemed to relax, possibly due the physical distance he had created between them, and replied, 'Yes. That does happen.'

Ratan Singh went on easily, 'It has been a long and tumultuous day, both physically and emotionally. I don't know about you but I can hardly keep my eyes open.' He yawned to push the idea through. She was looking at him steadily, her large eyes getting larger, body rigidly still.

'I am a desert warrior and have spent most of my life outdoors. Without fresh air, I cannot sleep. I suggest that I curl up on a mat in this balcony while you, Princess, can snuggle down in the bed. That is, if you find space among all the flowers.' He laughed at his own joke.

Padmavati glanced at the bed and smiled back at him. The wall of ice between them had been crushed. The princess did not fail to notice his formal address to her which made it more than evident that he did not believe being on familiar terms with her came as a marital right.

Ratan Singh dragged a rug out on the balcony floor. He was about to close the intervening door when Padmavati came to it and held out a couple of pillows and a blanket. 'The sea breeze can turn chilly,' she said. The smile dimpling her cheeks reflected in her eyes. *The first barrier is breached,* mused Ratan Singh, thinking like a soldier.

He took her offerings with a soft, 'Thank you,' and shut the door with a definitive sound. Rolling himself in the blanket, he lay down on the marble floor. The salty zephyr played with his hair as Ratan Singh floated off on a cloud of sublime contentment.

The new couple soon moved into Padmavati's palace but for a couple of weeks, the same sleeping arrangements continued, though both carefully concealed it from everybody especially the princess' ladies and Ambika. In the meanwhile, other than the formal introduction of Gandharava Sena's son-in-law to the Council of Ministers, Ratan Singh and Padmavati were left alone. The King and Queen were astute enough to realize that the couple needed time to bond and instructed the palace staff accordingly.

So it was a honeymoon of sorts for the couple. They would swim at a private pool, or take long walks along the beach or in the forest, or sit in the hanging terraces, chatting late into the night. Gradually, Ratan Singh came to know about Padmavati's growing years and comprehended how she had been groomed as the heir-apparent, leading to her highly unusual personality. He grew to appreciate her deeply spiritual side, too.

In turn, Padmavati would listen to the tales from the Mewari's life spent either as a soldier on campaigns against Alauddin's armies or as the Kunwar in Chittor's court, rife with intrigue. Even though he did not speak of it, her perception detected in him the strain of proving his worth as the heir and underneath it all his insecurity of being an adopted son. He spoke of his wives and concubines frankly and assured her that many of these relations were formed to bolster Rawal Samar Singh's political alliances. Padmavati, being a King's daughter, empathized with its logic. Some kind of hope began to form in her heart. After all, Ratan Singh was an attractive man, notwithstanding the scar. In fact, it made him additionally charming, making him appear more like a swashbuckling buccaneer. Besides, his genial manner, courteous behaviour and natural kindness made him extremely likeable. Some days, they visited his foster parents who would be overjoyed, yet a bit flustered, to host the Crown prince and princess. Padmavati loved the way her husband put them completely at ease by simple words of assurance.

The only association of her husband that rankled with Padmavati was that of Raghav Chetna. He still lived with the elderly couple, though it was not what he wanted. He had tried dropping hints that as the bridegroom's companion from Chittor, he should move into the palace inhabited by Ratan Singh and Padmavati, but the Kunwar had ignored them. So, he would buttonhole the princess at every opportunity, using the familiar '*bhojai*' or 'sister-in-law' to address her as if he really was her husband's brother.

Either it was, '*Bhojai*, that is a beautiful necklace. Did Ratan *beero* gift it to you?' Or '*Bhojai*, just turn your face to the left for a moment. I want to catch your profile in this sketch.' He had etched numerous sketches and paintings of Padmavati, some from her actual poses and some from memory. All of them were brilliant, for he was an accomplished artist, but Padmavati found his cloying advances disagreeable. She had also noticed that her husband disliked Chetna's attempts to draw her attention but did not tell him off because he did not want to be rude.

One night, Ratan Singh and Padmavati stood side by side at the rails of the terrace adjoining their bed chamber. The moon hung full and heavy from the inky-blue horizon, its twin reflected in shimmering slices in the sea. Ceaseless rollers were breaking on the rocks. Its silvery glow filled Padmavati with a strange emotion and she began to recite one of her poems; a love story wherein the hungry sea yearns for the moon.

I have been waiting...
Waiting for aeons.
For the beauteous moon to run her cycle
And dip into me...

Dulcet words in her bell-like voice evoked in her young husband a tremendous tenderness that refused to be contained. When she finished and looked up at the man who had become her best friend, he stared down at her, his dark eyes saying more than his lips had ever expressed. It was as if time stood still as he bent to delicately graze a pair of trembling lips that had repeatedly appeared in his dreams. He was taken aback to feel a responsive pressure. But only for a moment; then his lips crushed the velvety flesh with a passion long kept in abeyance.

The next morning, Ratan Singh and Padmavati revelled in their new intimacy. In a gathering, their eyes would seek each other out. They shared smiles only they could decode and existed in a world of their own. They did not notice others giving them knowing looks. Their joy in each other, Padmavati's radiance and Ratan Singh's absent-minded responses during administrative training sessions told their own tale. Their bliss became everyone's rejoicing.

Months went by. Ratan Singh and Padmavati, acknowledged as future rulers, went through rigorous training to assume this office. Their mornings were filled with lessons on kingship, law, diplomacy, war strategy and the like. Afternoons were taken up with combat training; swordsmanship, archery, hand-to-hand combat, battle tactics with horses and elephants. Most enjoyable were the duels that the couple fought with each other. Evenings were pleasant with music and literary discourses.

Some nights, the students would quiz each other on the day's learning.

'Who are the beneficiaries of a ruler's duty?' The princess questioned.

'First and foremost beneficiaries are his subjects, then he serves his country and lastly ensures the continuance of his family line,' chanted Ratan Singh.

'How should a King gain power over his neighbours?' asked the Kunwar of Mewar.

'Through friendly relationships and tactical treaties,' pat came Padmavati's reply.

'How does a country become great...by waging war or ensuring peace?' She quizzed.

'Always by keeping peace, for then trade, inventions, new ideas prosper. In turn that ensures progress of a country. War only brings death and destruction,' Ratan Singh said and then turned thoughtful as he remembered the policies followed in Mewar...fight first, think later.

Studying, training and laughing with his young bride, Ratan Singh enjoyed the carefree amusements of the teens. In fact, as time flew and months went by, his resolve of returning to Chittor began to lose its urgency. Growing up, he had always been involved in the adult chicaneries that ruled the politics of Mewar. His lovely companion made him feel young and he luxuriated in the romance, intimacy and mirth of their alliance. Again and again he postponed the discussion with his bride that he needed to return to his own land. Unknown to the couple, their love for each other had dug deep into their souls spreading roots, leaves and flowers...growing endlessly until their souls really became so intertwined that nobody could gauge where one ended and the other began. Separating the two would be like tearing apart the petals of a lotus flower and so Ratan Singh desisted.

When deemed ready, the young heirs took over the administration of the land guided by the ministers. They were enthusiastic, energetic and innovative. Several new beneficial laws were made for the people. Welfare enterprises took precedence, public wealth was made secure and temple organizational structures improved. The contentment of the Singhas grew, and they loved the pretty picture the glamorous couple made when they appeared amongst their subjects. Gandharava Sena would proudly observe his daughter. She would proffer her opinion whenever Ratan Singh and the ministers seemed stumped for a decision yet was wise enough to never overpower the situation. Gradually the older royals began to relax and make plans for retreats and travel.

The first year of marriage was nearly over. Ladies had begun to slyly tease Padmavati for an heir, but the princess would deflect the queries. After all, how could she reveal that Ratan Singh believed strongly she was too young to take on childbirth?

Autumn was back and the air was balmy. One evening, Padmavati was on the terrace of their bedchamber. She breathed deeply of the sea breeze tangy with salt waiting for Ratan Singh to return from the Council meeting. She gazed at the calm, wrinkled surface of the ocean stretching to the horizon. Though the sky retained light of the day, a translucent moon hung above. Padmavati sighed, thinking, *can anyone be happier than me? Thank you, Mahadev, for showering me with all these gifts. Bless me so that I can care for them well.*

A slight sound made her turn around. It was Ratan Singh. But he had not run to hug her tightly, as he usually did. Puzzled, Padmavati searched her husband's face for an answer. When he finally raised his eyes to hers, she could see they were grave and troubled. 'What is it, my love?' she inquired involuntarily.

'My princess,' Ratan Singh said slowly, 'I have to go to Chittor.'

14

Her narration paused as Uma walked slowly along the ruined wall, one hand gliding over the uneven surface, somewhere crumbling and somewhere overgrown with lichen. Mrinalini's hand also brushed the wall but she hardly paid attention to the rough and smooth intervening touches. Her mind was engrossed with what she had heard. Whether it was in Uma's telling or in the written narrative of the *Wali,* she was so deeply submerged in the exotic romance of Ratan Singh and Padamvati that she found it difficult to break out of its spell to view it coherently.

'Fascinating, isn't it?' Mrinalini softly remarked into quietness of the night.

She felt rather than saw Uma shrug, 'I told you, *bhayeli,* there is nothing to match Padmavati's love story, not even *Dhola-Maru ni Chaupal.*'

'I never imagined Padmavati was such an exceptional woman. Imagine, living so long ago she was a skilled swordswoman, a competent administrator, a sagacious and principled person, a poet, spiritually inclined and to top it all, a beautiful princess from an utopian island,' exclaimed Mrinalini. 'Strange that none of these extraordinary aspects about her have been mentioned in any of the historical documents or archives. In fact, there is nothing concrete there of her origins.'

'It is possible there may have been a conscious effort to erase her origins and undermine her eminence…?' Uma queried softly.

'But why?' Mrinalini demanded.

'Envy, anger and political intrigue; fear that she will become larger than life…she was a woman, remember, living in a world dominated by men? Now do you see why she secretly wrote the *Padma-wali* but kept it hidden from the people surrounding her? She must have been afraid her foes would destroy the truth and delete her reality. She wanted a record of her real life to exist.'

'Tell me,' said the journalist, 'is this story only about the events of her own life?'

'No.' Uma shook her head. 'She has written about other personalities...those who had influenced her or affected the outcomes of her own actions. She even examines her own responses to events and introspects on them.'

'But she could only write from her viewpoint...whether of other people or events, isn't it? How objective would that be?' Mrinalini's logic was breaking through the spell of the Ratan Singh-Padmavati romance.

'What I could gather from reading the *Wali* is that she had made great efforts to be impartial. Besides, one can make out that many of the people close to her had divulged their inner-most thoughts to her, which helped her to write their roles better,' explained Uma. 'And don't forget the dauntless Ginni, her faithful scout. Possibly, when writing about others, Padmavati may have revealed some unpleasant truths.That must also be the reason why she wanted the *Wali* to be excavated from its secret place only when it would be safe.'

'And do you believe it is safe for revelation now?'

'Yes, *bhayeli*. I truly believe the time has come,' came Uma's unequivocal reply.

Unable to suppress her frustration any more, Mrinalini pleaded, 'Uma, please give me the manuscript. I want so much to read it myself. Please, please show me where it is. Take me to the place where you have kept it.'

'I will, *bhayeli*, I will,' Uma pacified her. 'Don't you first want to see where Padmavati lived when she came all the way to Chittor?'

'Yes. Yes. Of course,' said Mrinalini eagerly. 'Are you taking me to her palace? The tour booklet says that her palace was separate from the old royal palace, now referred to as the Rana Kumbha palace.' She looked back the way they had come. Domes, curved and peaked roofs of several half-broken structures gleamed in the moonlight. 'You said that we will go back, later.'

'Yes, my friend,' agreed Uma. 'After Padmavati arrived here, a special palace was built for her. Now, it is called the Padmini palace. *Aavjo.* Let's try and imagine Padmavati's life in the fort of Chittor; a place so contradictory in every aspect to Singhaldweep that it could be in another planet.'

However fast the journalist walked, the young girl was always ahead of her. *She is really a quick one,* thought Mrinalini, taking a couple of long steps to try keep pace with Uma. Responding to her last remark, the journalist mused, 'It must have been so foreign to her. . .coming into this typically cloistered Mewari culture from a liberated society whose ideology was far more sophisticated than the parochial society in an India reeling under the ravages of the Turkish invaders in the early 1300s.'

Uma did not respond. She hurried towards an outcropping of dark shadows mushrooming out of the gloom.

15

Padmavati snuggled into the silken duvet trying to blot out the painful pictures of leaving Singhaldweep. Singhas from all over the island had crowded the beach as the boat was pushed into the waves, carrying Ratan Singh, now the Rawal of Mewar, Padmavati, his queen, Ambika and the ubiquitous Ginni.

It was now a month since Ratan Singh had announced that he had to leave for Chittor. Two messages, both urgent, had led to this decision. One was from the *Mantri* of Chittor informing him of the demise of his father, Rawal Samar Singh and telling him that he had to return to be anointed as the next Rawal. Besides, there was news that Alauddin Khalji had captured Gujarat and was now marching on to Ranthambore. Chittor's turn would come soon and it was imperative that the new Rawal return to defend his kingdom. The other one was a frantic missive from his senior queen, Prabhavati, about rebel Mewari chiefs plotting to take over the Rawaldom in his absence and thus depriving Ratan Singh's teenage son, Kunwar Vir Bhan, of his inheritance.

Ratan Singh had apologetically told his parents-in-law, 'I will return to Singhaldweep, once Mewar is consolidated and strong. In the meanwhile, the Crown Princess will rule this kingdom.'

Gandharava Sena's mouth had turned down at the corners. He had nearly forgotten the discussion with Ratan Singh before the wedding. Besides he had great regard for his son-in-law now and would feel quite lost without him. Champavati's eyes instantly filled with tears.

But before the King and Queen of Singhaldweep could react, their daughter had interjected, 'That cannot be.' As the other three, gathered in the Queen's boudoir for this private conversation, stared at her perplexed, she gently explained, 'I must go with my husband. Those were the vows I took, didn't I? In happiness and in sorrow, in contentment and in strife...I will be beside you, always...'

'No!' declared Ratan Singh, a little harshly. He did not want his exquisite lotus to be pulled by its roots from this lush soil and replanted in the hostile rocks of Mewar. A separation from his princess, though harrowing, was a better option. Her parents were aghast but silent. They had taught her to be dutiful, not realizing that she would apply it first to herself. None of them had considered Padmavati's stubborn adherence to ethical principles.

'I repeat, I do not agree to remaining here while you go. I am sorry to say it but that is my decision,' she said softly, but there was steel in her tone.

Ratan Singh's eyes shot a silent, helpless plea to the royal parents but they were too stunned by the turn of events. Besides, they knew the futility of arguing with their daughter when she was set on her course. Champavati, her worst fears realized, collapsed in grief on the settee while Gandharava Sena looked suddenly old.

Padmavati's heart had gone out to her dear parents. She tried to comfort them all night, while Ratan Singh began to make arrangements for departure. How the royal couple would simultaneously rule Chittor and Singhaldweep, two lands separated by thousands of miles of sea and land needed some thinking. 'But right now, my duty is to go with my husband to Chittor,' she explained over and over again to her grieving parents.

The princess also knew that the beloved Singhas of her land would be devastated to learn of their departure. The next day, she called a public durbar to announce her decision with a promise that she will surely return and soon...maybe in a couple of years. Till then, their King Gandharava Sena would rule over them as he had for so long.

Still, Padmavati's heart was torn into two, leaving her birthplace, her parents and her happy people. All these days, as the ship had cleaved the ocean, riding the swells and dipping into the lows, she had been trying to grow a scab over her aching wound.Through the billowing curtains, the sky was lightening but the gentle rocking of the waves, the creaking of the wooden deck boards below the bed sent a languor coursing through Padmavati's limbs.

By the time she next opened her eyes, the clouds were spiked with pink and gold. Padmavati stretched her bare arms above her head, yawning. Then she sat up, pulling the duvet over her bosom against the chill of the sea breeze. She pulled up her sarong knotting it above her breasts and stepped off the gently rocking bed revealing one long shapely bare leg after another. Balancing herself against the pitch and roll of the ship, she was about to call out for Ambika and her maids. But she swallowed her words when a low thud sounded on the thin wall of the wooden cabin. It came quite close to the closed rear door as if somebody had fallen against it. As Padmavati looked at it curiously, the sound came again. Silently, she pulled an *angavastran* over one shoulder down to her waist. Tying both ends firmly, she covered herself entirely in two layers of cloth. Her eyes went upwards searching the wooden door panels. Sure enough, at a height a little higher than her head and aligned with the moving wall was a dark spot; a little round hole in the door.

Padmavati launched herself bodily towards the door with the hole. It swung open. There was loud yelp and she found herself lying on a solid object that had fallen to the deck of the ship, tangled in the canvas of the lifeboats kept behind the cabin. Padmavati sat astride the grunting, squirming form and looked around. This was the extreme aft of the ship and quite isolated during the half-light of dawn. *No wonder the observer thought it was good time for voyeuristic activities,* she fumed, *or was this an attempt at assassination?* Still sitting on the person and pushing down with her palms so that the she could not be thrown off, she took one hand off and quickly pulled back one corner of the canvas. The face revealed was turned away from her but it made her gasp. In shock, her hands loosened hold and the man whirled on his back.

Padmavati tumbled on the floor but was up on her feet in a trice. 'Raghav Chetna! What are you doing here?' she shouted, angrily.

Belligerence was wiped away from his face, replaced instantly with fear. 'Nothing, *bhojai*. Nothing. . .just taking a walk. . .' The man was shaken and his voice trailed off. He stood up, flinging away the restricting canvas. 'I must be on my way.'

The princess' hand, quick as a striking snake, clutched a handful of his long, loose hair, turning the head awkwardly, tugging his face closer. Snarling at him, she said, 'Taking a walk? Or peeping through a hole into my cabin?'

His eyes shifted uneasily off her angry face. He squealed, 'No *bhojai*. Why should I. . .?'

'Don't you dare call me '*bhojai*', you miserable rat. A sick man like you is no brother to the Rawal.' She let go of his hair with a sudden push. Chetna lost his balance and sprawled on the deck. Looking down at him in disgust, she said, 'Go wherever you can, Chetna. The Rawal will decide whether you will live or die.' Padmavati stepped back through the door and into the midst of her maids and Ambika, who had come running at the noise from the royal cabin. Their mouths were open in astonishment at Chetna's foolish and contemptible perfidy.

Still on his knees, Raghav Chetna put up a hand to brush locks of hair from his eyes and cursed vehemently. His goose was cooked. Despondently he thought, *where can I escape from Rawal Ratan Singh's wrath in a ship sailing in the middle of the vast ocean?* Slowly, he got to his feet and shuffled to a corner of the open deck. He looked down at the swirling grey waters, wondering if he should attempt a jump and a swim. A long dark shape passed by just under the surface and Chetna drew back. *Would he reach land before the sharks got him?*

This was a ship of the royal Singhaldweep navy navigated by a very efficient captain and crew. It was carrying the royal couple, their retinue and endless boxes of wedding gifts showered on the princess and her husband. Ambika was a very significant member of the princess' household. The girls had been close since childhood and were now more like sisters. Ambika could sometimes even anticipate Padmavati's thoughts. There was no way that two countries or even a marriage was going to separate them. Besides, the King and Queen could blindly rely on Ambika's loyalty to Padmavati. In fact, they had requested her to accompany the princess. Ambika was already prepared to do so, though it meant leaving her old mother behind.

Seeing Champavati's trepidation for his niece, Prince Gora Rajsinha, her brother, had also decided to go along with the royal couple to Mewar. With him was his twelve-year-old motherless son, Prince Badal Rajsinha. And of course, Ginni had to be with his soulmate despite the fact they were returning to the terrible, hot land that he had wanted so desperately to leave, for where would Ginni be without his dear friends?

Raghav Chetna was the other inmate of this ship. He was glad he was finally returning home. No longer was he the unsophisticated artist who had first arrived at Singhaldweep. He had become an arrogant palace hanger-on with expensive habits in clothes, jewels and food. At first, after Ratan Singh's marriage, gifts had been showered on him as they had been for Ratan Singh's foster parents. His posture was that of a close relative to the royal son-in-law. And his taste for ornaments, expensive wine, extravagant clothes and even the attention of attractive noble ladies grew manifold. However, he was a witty fellow and used his silver tongue to get his way. He courteously accepted gifts and earnestly returned favours with skilfully-executed portraits of his friends that enhanced their real looks. They had loved these complimentary pictures and Chetna had become popular with the fashionable and wealthy of Singhaldweep. Both Ratan Singh and Padmavati were aware of his deceits but chose to turn a blind eye. His cupidity seemed harmless.

What they were unaware of was Chetna's rapacious interest in Padmavati. He had been mesmerized by her incredible beauty from first sight. Every glimpse of her had tantalized him. Unfortunately, the princess had simply looked through him which irked him as well as whetted his appetite for her. After marrying Ratan Singh, she had behaved politely with him but without warmth. Time and again, he had created sketches and paintings as presents for her. But they were usually returned with a small smile. When he had insisted she keep at least one painting, that exquisitely portrayed her fabled charms, she acquiesced with a polite murmur—and never referred to it again.

To Chetna, her marriage to Ratan Singh was hardly sacred. *After all,* he had thought, *Padmavati is just one of his wives, almost equivalent to a concubine. I, on the other hand, am unmarried. Am I not more eligible?* Despite her coldness, Chetna never gave up hope. In fact, the more she rebuffed his advances, the lustier his fantasies of her grew.

On the ship, her proximity made him nearly crazed with hot lecherous desire. One night, he had been drawn irresistibly to the royal cabin erected for Ratan Singh and Padmavati. It was in the aft of the ship sheltered behind the huge beam of the mast and screened from general view. He could hear low laughter from within. Stepping into the narrow alley between the rear wall of the tent and the ship's rails, he used his knife to make a tiny hole in the wood at the same level as his eyes. It was dark inside, but the murmurs were enough to bring lascivious pictures in his mind. He would return every night when the ship was quiet with only the watch high on the mast shouting out the hours over the roar of the waves. Sometimes, the sounds from the cabin would help Chetna to release the pent up stress brought on by his depraved thoughts.

That night, his lust spent, he had been lying on the floor of the alley overcome with sleep. Before dawn, Chetna had woken to heavy footsteps as Ratan Singh left the cabin to confer with the ship's captain. Land had been sighted the evening before and Ratan Singh was keen to know when they would be close to it. Chetna had sat up. Knowing Padmavati would be alone, an urgent desire to see the object of his lewd dreams tempted him put an eye to the hole. Due to the ship's motion, he had lurched on the wall, banging his head. Before he could recover, the door had flung open. To his dismay, he had misjudged the princess' combative mettle. There was more to her than allurement. Caught by her in the very act, he would now pay with his life for being stupid.

Padmavati completed her toilette with the help of Ambika and her maids. Eating a light meal of fruits, she laughed with Ambika over a joke. The princess was in no hurry to bring the culprit to justice for she knew it could be done any time. The ship was a rat-trap and the rat, Chetna, was caught in it. Eventually, she went out on the deck to join her husband. He was squinting at the horizon through the golden haze of the sunlight dazzling on the leaping breakers. He beamed at her and began to explain that they would be able to make it to land only by evening, which suited his plans.

Ratan Singh was anxious of their safety while journeying overland to Chittor. Sultan Khalji's empire now stretched from the delta of the river Ganga all the way up, spreading across its fertile valley and further. The lands around the

Yamuna and Indus rivers as well as its tributaries in both west and north and encompassing Gujarat in the south west were under his iron fist. According to Prabhavati's last message, he had now entered Mewar and controlled the fort of Ranthambore. Khalji usually left his generals and supporters in charge of his conquered lands as he went about extending his empire further. The regions that they would have to traverse on their land journey to Chittor would be swarming with the Sultan's soldiers and officers who dominated the area. In such conditions the most vulnerable were women who would be picked off the streets if they caught the eye of a Turk. Most women were forced to stay indoors in *purdah*. If women travelled at all, whether Hindu or Muslim, it had to be under the protection of a group of men, well covered from head to toe and hidden away in *dolis* or palanquins.

Aware of the liberties that Padmavati had been used to since childhood, he wanted to discuss with her their travel arrangements. The journey from the mouth of the river Ganga all the way to Chittor would take a few weeks despite repeatedly changing fast horses. He fretted over how he was going to keep her dazzling glamour concealed from the Turkish vultures until they reached the safety of Chittorgarh.

When Padmavati had heard him out, she said, 'Don't worry, my Gem.' She did not address her husband by his name but rather a synonym of his name 'Ratan' meaning precious stone or treasure. 'I will wear those tent-like robes that Indian women wear and cover myself from head to foot.' Relieved, Ratan Singh had let out his breath. He did not want to force his beloved to do anything that she didn't want to. 'Did you think I would go about wrapping only a sarong and flower garlands around myself?' She teased him and watched his eyes light up.

'Personally, I would want you dressed in exactly that or even less,' he bent down to whisper into her ear making her giggle, quite un-princess-like.

Now, Padmavati leaned on the table where a map of Bharatdesh was spread out. She traced her index finger on the route that Ratan Singh had marked out on it with a charcoal. It began at the Ganga delta, went across its basin and then veered off where the Chambal River met the holy waterway. Then the charcoal path cut across directly to Chittorgarh. She brought her finger back to the delta and tapped it twice.

'This is the place where we plan to land this evening?' she asked, thoughtfully.

'Yes. Our ship will anchor at sea and then we will take a boat. I thought it was good idea to come ashore in the darkness,' explained Ratan Singh, not at all taken aback at her questions about the journey they were about to embark on. Most women from his Mewari background would not ask any. Probably because they would not know how to read a map and also due to the fact they had been groomed to follow their husband's bidding unquestioningly. But Padmavati...she was different and Ratan Singh loved her for it.

'What about this river?' Padmavati had moved her finger to the blue line signifying the course of the waterway.

'What about it?' Ratan Singh knit his brows, puzzled.

'Does it have boats on it?'

'Yes. I suppose so,' said her husband, still frowning.

'Why don't we use the river to travel instead of the road? We can sail up the Ganga, then change course into the Chambal River that flows beyond the Sultan's empire. Once we are safely beyond its borders, we will be much closer to Chittorgarh. We can easily ride to it,' Padmavati suggested, adding, 'It will be safer, won't it, from all kinds of human and animal attacks?'

Ratan Singh looked down at the map, his eyes moving along the Ganga and Chambal rivers. He jabbed a forefinger at a spot and said, 'That is the right spot to keep a contingent of soldiers waiting with our horses.

From there, it should take us a little less than four days to reach Chittor.' He looked at his wife, 'What a brilliant plan! With a readymade route on the river, why was I planning a land journey trying to skirt all the trouble spots? My princess, I salute your sagacity.'

'My dearest Gem. Don't make me into an oracle. I was only talking some sense. Travelling the waterway just occurred to me. I am a water-girl, remember?' Padmavati smiled at her husband.

Ratan Singh began rolling up the map, saying, 'Let me discuss with the captain about hiring a suitable river-boat that could wait for us in the delta. When we leave in the evening, all we do is transfer to the boat and begin sailing up the river.'

'Great idea! But before that, there is something that I need to tell you,' said the Princess in a low but serious tone.

Her tone made Ratan Singh's hands stop midway and the map unrolled out instantly. It slipped off the table but he only narrowed his eyes and waited.

Padmavati related to him that morning's incident. Her husband's face grew darker and darker and his eyes stormier at each word she uttered. Finally, he exploded, 'I will have him blinded by hot irons. He will never set eyes on a woman or anything else as long as he lives.' And, he purposefully strode off towards the wheel-house, shouting for the captain. Padmavati picked the map from the floor, rolled it and tucking it under her arm, strolled to the rails to see if she could sight land. Behind her, the decks broke into an uproar as sailors pounded across them searching for the culprit.

16

They had stopped for a break before the climb. It had been a long, hard dusty ride across the highlands and the horses needed rest and water before tackling the steep rocky path. Looming above them were the craggy Aravallis with a section flattened into a plateau. The fort of Chittor was laid out on its escarpments. Roughly oval in shape, it looked like a fat fish. Padmavati put a hand up to shield her eyes from the dazzling afternoon sun and squinted up at her future home.

All the way here, Ratan Singh had been telling her about it. The legend of its origins was quite a romantic tale, attributed to the mythical Mahabharata hero, Bhima. Apparently some yogis had promised to give him the talismanic stone, *paras pathar,* that could turn anything to gold, on the condition that he build a fort over the hill of Chitrakuta over a single night. The mighty Bhima had nearly completed the fort within the stipulated time, but the yogis tricked him by crowing like a cockerel, moments before the final stone was laid. Bhima, believing it was dawn before the fort was complete, struck the ground in the centre of the fort with his foot in frustration. It was such a powerful blow that it created a huge hollow. Water had sprung up from the spot to form a large reservoir in the centre of the fort known as *Bhimlat Kund*.

Observing the fort with a warrior's eye, Padmavati noted how cleverly the plateau had been used as its foundation. *The walls look massive...nearly 180 yards high,* she mused, *and at the top of its highest building, it must be at least 500 feet from the ground. The ramparts would be ideal for watch towers. Of course, no fort is impregnable but this one looks formidable and is an excellent example of defensive architecture.* Though she could not see it from here, Ratan

Singh had told her about the Chittori, a kind of pimple on the southern end of the hill which commanded a view to the east and west of the fort. Any projectile such as hot oils or catapulted stones could easily be launched from the fort walls. With its height even a medium-sized stone thrown down would be a killer for the enemy forces below. *Yet,* Padmavati gave a wry smile, *this citadel had changed hands quite a few times.* The Gehlotes had taken possession of it just a few decades ago during the time of Rawal Jaitra Singh, an ancestor of Ratan Singh's adopted father, Rawal Samir Singh.

While externally the fort looked as rugged as the surrounding Aravallis, her husband had described the beautiful city of palaces, gardens, *havelis* and temples inside. There were numerous tanks, *talabs, kunds, baolis* and lakes. In fact, the water bodies ensured that the garrison in the fort would never run short of water even during a siege. Her husband's enthusiastic narratives always ended not by praising Chittor's beauty but speaking of its fame that rested more on the extraordinary tales of heroism, chivalry and sacrifice of its people. And whenever he uttered these words, his voice would choke with pride and adulation. Padmavati would gaze at him and think, *the history of Singhaldweep has no such heroes or tales to boast of.*

The princess' reflections were broken by a gentle hand on her shoulder. She turned around to face Ratan Singh, who looked splendid in the burnished chain armour of a Mewari soldier. Instead of the helmet, he had tied a gorgeous turban in orange and yellow stripes on his head. Its *sarpech* was a small ostrich feather pinned to the gigantic Singhaldweep sapphire turban pin. Padmavati was looking no less captivating in the garb of a Mewari bride in the auspicious red *lehanga* and *aangi* which is like a long, flowing skirt, and a waist-length jacket. A golden net *choondari* or long scarf spangled with tiny rubies was gathered over her chest, wrapped over her head and tucked into the skirt band. While gem-encrusted ornaments hung from her ears, neck, wrists, waist and ankles and twinkled in the sunlight, what Ratan Singh noted with satisfaction was she was wearing the *borlo,* a large pendant on her forehead and the *bilia,* the ivory bangles on her arms. They were the symbols of a newly-wed Mewari woman. He was a little anxious of their reception when he arrived with his new, foreign bride.

'You are all *banithani,* my princess,' he said with a grin. When his wife wrinkled her nose at him, he added, 'You look so lovely, a perfect Rani of Chittor,' and was rewarded by a sunny smile that made his heart do a little skip and jump. 'Let's go,' he said. A groom knelt beside Padmavati's horse holding out cupped hands. With her husband's supporting hands on her tiny waist, she stepped lightly on the groom's hands and gracefully mounted her steed sitting side saddle. Till now, she had ridden astride and as hard as the men but Ratan Singh had advised her otherwise for her entry into the fort. Ambika and her serving women were also dressed in the traditional Mewari dress. Soon, a tiny procession wound its way slowly up the narrow path leading to Chittor.

Trotting sedately, her jewellery jingling, Padmavati's mind flew back to when she had stepped on this strange land only known to her as Bharatdesh. As the longboat carrying Ratan Singh, Padmavati, Ambika and the serving women grounded on the dark beach after midnight, there was a hullabaloo behind them. The second boat was still halfway between the ship and the shore. It had been carrying some soldiers and Chetna, who Ratan Singh had decided put in chains to travel with them under guard to Chittor where he would be suitably punished. Confused shouts were coming from that direction. All of them looked back and in the dim glow from the ship, they watched the boat capsize. Ratan Singh cursed under his breath. The soldiers in armour and carrying weapons would flounder in the sea; maybe drown. Their party had climbed out and stood on the deserted beach, as the sailors pushed the boat back into the waves and urgently began to row to where the other boat was bobbing upside down. Though it was dark, the sailors managed to save all the drowning soldiers and take them aboard. Only one person had been missing. . .Raghav Chetna. Nobody knew whether he had sunk instantly due to the weight of the chains or if he had swum to the shore. 'Most likely he would have gone to the bottom,' said the captain of the soldiers.

'He deserves worse,' Ratan Singh retorted. 'Let's go on with our plan. I have no tears for him.'

So the small group with the party of soldiers had embarked on the journey up the mighty Ganga in a *bajra,* a wooden houseboat, rowed by six men. For Padmavati, Ambika and the Singha women, this cruise opened up a world of wonders. It was the first time that they had left their small, familiar island and stepped on foreign shores. Besides, Bharatdesh was so different from Singhaldweep. Though, they had been mostly secluded behind closed doors and windows of the three rooms on the barge, they would peep through slits in the windows to view fascinating sights passing by as the houseboat sailed up the river. If they ever ventured up on the roof-top deck for a breath of fresh air on some evenings after being roasted in the heated rooms, they had to be covered from head to foot with faces veiled. But their eyes would dance in every direction behind the lace of the veil trying to take in diverse spectacles.

The land itself was so varied from one region to the other. Sailing up the river, the changing panorama of flora, animals, people and their customs was like a story unfolding. In the thick forests of the delta they saw trees whose roots walked in water. Crocodiles swam alongside their barge and tigers watched them from isolated sand bars. Gaudy birds screeched, instigating Ginni to scold them loudly. Soon the intimidating environment gave away to serene coconut palms leaning on the edge of banks to admire their reflections in the still river waters while urchins waved to them from quiet villages dotting the banks. Further up, human habitation increased; there were clamorous towns and more boats in the river transporting people and goods. As they sailed on, the hurly-burly heightened and traffic became busier. Along with larger towns, temples sprang up on both sides. People bathed at wide steps that ran down into the river. At times, corpses were cremated on the same steps. Night-time saw temples light up with thousands of lamps for their evening *aarti* and prayers. Bobbing around their boat, dark waters twinkled with earthen lamps placed on large leaves and floated by devotees of the holy Ganga. Familiar intonations of religious chants and bells tolling would drift across to their boat making Padmavati homesick for the tranquillity of her Mahadev temple.

Bharatdesh was a chaotic medley, not just of vegetation and fauna, but of assorted languages, dresses, foods and even in the appearance of its people. On their own island one usually saw tall, stately men and women with skin shades of ivory and cream. Here the astonished Singhas observed that people were short, tall, fat, thin with skin colours ranging from dark ebony to corn yellow to pale pink. Some had high cheekbones and narrow eyes. Others had podgy faces with bulbous noses. Still others had thin hatchet-like profiles. And what amazed them most were the sheer numbers; hordes of humanity walked, ran, swam, bathed, rode horses or palanquins, lived in mansions and villas, huts and hovels along the banks of Ganga. Some lived under trees and on the *ghats* of the river, too poor to have a roof over their heads. They were like waves of another river flowing through the land...a human river. Never had either Padmavati or the others seen such a press of crowds before. They were glad to be insulated from its confusing chaos in their barge.

Dark-clothed and armed, horsemen would often stand out among the hordes. Padmavati watched how the rest of the people instantly made way for them. That they were conquerors was quite plain; their arrogance and rude manners proof of their uncultured, wild descent. Most people, whether rich or poor, kept out of their way and sight. It was a relief that their group did not have to confront any of the Turks from the Sultan's army.

If they thought they had seen it all, they were wrong. After a few weeks, they reached a bend that took them up the Yamuna river, a tributary of the Ganga. When the boat spun off the turgid Yamuna into the fast flowing but narrower Chambal, the landscape changed dramatically. By the next day, they were twisting into swirling gorges where the boatmen struggled to keep the barge upright and not crash into the high rocky walls of the cliffs rising on both sides. Sometimes the accompanying soldiers would help the boatmen navigate. Even Ratan Singh lent a hand. Her women murmured prayers but Padmavati enjoyed the thrill of the boat ploughing through the foamy river. Gradually, a couple of days later, the river had widened and waves calmed; the boat sailed placidly. Still bordering the banks, the granite hills and plateaus were dotted here and there with forts perched on their heights.

Padmavati could not but be influenced by her initial sights of Bharatdesh. She was impressed by its vastness, its assorted geography, its heterogeneity and the multiplicity of variance in its traditions and culture. *Certainly, it is a much older country than Singhaldweep; rather, it could even be called ancient*, she had mused. It was with great relief that they were told to throw off the layers of cloth. The women did not need to be shut behind doors. They had exited the borders of the Sultan's empire.

A week on the Chambal and they disembarked at a rocky bay. A group of men dressed in the yellow and orange livery of Chittor awaited them with horses and stallions. They had bowed low to their new Rawal but there was no time for any formalities. The boatmen were paid off in gold and exhorted to keep their lips sealed about their passengers. Then the Rawal, his bride, and their retinue had quickly mounted and nearly flew through the ravines. A day and night of hard riding and they halted at the edge of another variation of this surprising land; an undulating, golden expanse of the Thar desert.

Padmavati stared at all the sand and turning to her husband, asked, 'And where is the ocean?'

Ratan Singh had roared with laughter while his seasoned soldiers cracked a smile through their beards. 'Ocean, my princess?' he asked and went on to remark, 'This is a thirsty land where people die for a few drops of precious water.'

Padmavati had nodded, screwing up her eyes against the glare of the sunlight reflecting from the sand. Ratan Singh had brought the loose edge of her sarong over her head and pulled it over her nose and mouth like a mask, tucking it securely behind her neck. 'Now the flying sand and the heat of the sun will not bother you.'

Her husband spurred his horse, kicking up the loose sand and the company followed. Guests, such as Prince Gora and young Prince Badal rode just behind the Rawal and the *NaiRaniSa,* as the Mewari soldiers had begun calling the Rawal's bride from Singhaldweep. Ambika and her women were in the next row and behind them rode the escort from Chittor. Unerringly, they rode an unmarked path through the desert, halting nights at *serais,* inns that consisted of a rough camp of tents around a bonfire in a small oasis. Padmavati would tumble onto her mattress spread on the warm sands as soon as they reached, too tired to even eat. Only Ginni, who was perched on Ratan Singh's saddle, had been somewhat comfortable during this hard travel. It had taken them three days to reach the base of the Chittorgarh hill. Along the way, Padmavati learnt first-hand the hardships of a life lived among the rocks and sands of Mewar. This awareness threw some light on the inflexible temperament of the average Mewari. Possibly, she had mused, it came about because they are forced to struggle for survival against the inflexible forces of Nature right from birth.

Padmavati was jerked out of her thoughts by a clamour. When they came round the last bend from where the gigantic gates of Chittorgarh were visible, she realized it was the babble of excited and exulting crowds that lined their path on both sides. As the horses pranced through the seven gates between the crowds welcoming the new Rawal, the chanting began. *'Apanon Annadaata aavno! Apanon Annadaata aavno!'* The princess smiled. Obviously these people loved Ratan Singh and it warmed her heart to see this public display of their loyalty. Prince Gora and his son, Badal were also beaming. Such a joyous welcome to the Rawal and his queen filled them delight. Many women touched the ruler's horse and then raised the same hand to their foreheads in genuflection. The princess wondered, *did they give him the status of a god?* But when her horse came abreast, they stared at her silently. Some of faces showed thinly-disguised resentment. When she had passed by, their slogans for the Rawal were renewed. Padmavati felt her heart sink, but her face did not change expression and bravely, she kept her smile on.

As they entered through the *Ram Pol,* rose petals showered them but she knew they were not for her. The procession turned a corner and now the princess noticed a row of men sporting the Rawal's colours of yellow and orange. They were holding back the front row of the crowds. The royal palace was approaching and this was the guard of honour. The massive carved wooden doors of the main palace loomed up ahead. As they began to ascend to it, a tall, muscled dark man in flowing kurta and *zari* waistcoat standing at the doors announced, '*Khabar Raakho! Khabar Raakho!* The Sun of the Hindu Dharma, The Custodian of Ek Linghji, The Rawal of Mewar, Ratan Singh*ji* approaches!'

The Rawal dismounted and turned towards Padmavati's steed. A groom was already kneeling next to it with cupped hands for her to descend. Here, in public glare of his subjects, Ratan Singh could not break tradition to help his wife. He was the Rawal of Chittor and his status was much above everyone; definitely above that of his wife. Within seconds, Padmavati took her position one step behind his left shoulder. Ratan Singh had explained to her earlier the Mewari rituals performed by the women of the groom's home to receive a new bride and she was quick to learn and act. Together they climbed the marble staircase and stood waiting in the colonnaded porch before the open doors. Inside them, decorously veiled women in gay *lehangas* and *choondaris* giggled and elbowed each other to get a glimpse of the *NaiRani* who had pulled her own veil down to her waist. But none of them came forward to receive her. Everyone was waiting.

'Where is the senior *RaniSa*?' growled Ratan Singh, finally. 'Why is she not here to welcome the new *beendni*?'

His irritation sent women scurrying and tittering among themselves. Behind her veil, Padmavati's eyes darted beyond the female figures seeking an authoritarian profile. But nobody's face matched a *Rani's*. A few more minutes ticked by and she could feel her husband's ire mounting. Suddenly, the simpering women parted but instead of the *Rani*, an elderly woman garbed in white hobbled towards them with the help of a cane. Her face was wreathed in smiles. Ratan Singh took a step forward to support her, saying, '*Baaa...*'

Padmavati's head came up...*his mother?* As Ratan Singh bent down to touch his mother's feet, she also moved to do the same. But the old lady raised her hands to stop her, saying, 'No, my child. Don't step inside without the sacred rituals. It is not auspicious.' The princess raised her eyes to look into the kindest face she had ever seen. Wrinkles rearranged themselves into a sweet smile as the lady called out, 'Basanti, bring the *puja thal* and welcome our *beendni*.' Looking up at Ratan Singh's frowning visage she added, in a low voice, 'Prabhavati will not come to perform the rituals. She is fuming in her room. I would have loved to do them myself but being a widow, you know, I am debarred from all propitious activities.'

By then Basanti, wife of a Thakur, had arrived with the silver tray on which all the items of felicity were arranged around a burning, earthen lamp. As she flung rice above the newly-wed couple and smeared turmeric-sandalwood on the foreheads of the groom and bride, the women began to sing traditional nuptial songs. Concluding the rituals, a pot piled with rice grains was placed before Padmavati's feet. *Ba* said, 'Now my child, with the toe of your left foot tip the pot over and step over it. Prosperity will always trail in your footsteps, then.' The princess did as she was told and stepped into her new home.

Her mother-in-law lifted her veil and gasped, 'Oh my Krishna! Is this a real girl or an *apsara* from the *swarglok*?' She held the young princess' face in her palms and kissed her on the forehead saying, 'May the gods bless you with all bliss of a long and joyful married life.' Her remark about the bride's looks initiated a wave of comments as everyone craned to look at this wondrous beauty. But the old lady, helped by a few wives of senior Thakurs and Ranas, led the bride away to Ratan Singh's chambers. Despite knowing of her arrival, no rooms in the palace had been set aside for the *NaiRani,* by the orders of Rani Prabhavati.

Ba, her noblewomen and Ambika tried to make Padmavati comfortable in her husband's rooms, while Ratan Singh paced the floor angrily. He stood at the *jharokas,* frowning at Ginni, who was perched on a branch pecking at a ripe custard apple. Eventually, he exploded banging a fist into an open palm, 'How dare she! How dare she insult the Rawal! I will have her sent home. I don't care if she is the senior Rani.'

Ba replied mildly, 'You know that you can't do that, Ratan. Her father is a powerful Rana of the clan. Just ignore her…it will blow over.'

'No, *Ba*. Prabhavati has become too arrogant. She must know how to kneel to the Rawal.' Ratan Singh's tone was adamant.

'Let it go, *hukum*. She is jealous and that is natural. After all, she is your wife too.' Soft, sensible words from his girl bride were like a cool spray squirted on flames.

Ratan Singh looked at her in surprise. *Just when I think I know her, she reveals another aspect of her personality. She stuns me each time with her perception; her insight. Truly she is a lotus. Each petal I peel back discloses a new gem*. His fiery rage subsided to embers.

His mother looked from her daughter-in-law to her son and smiled gently. *My Ratan has brought home a pearl*, she deduced. A serving maid entered with a tray bearing tall silver glasses of chilled pomegranate juice. She offered the tray to the princess who picked up a glass, gratefully. Her throat was parched in the dry air. About to bring it to her lips, she was startled when Ratan Singh leaped across the room and snatched the glass from her hands. 'Wait! It may be poisoned,' he shouted. Before the shocked eyes of everyone present in the room, he took the glass to his mouth and drank deeply. Swallowing the liquid, he said, 'Let's see if this is just pomegranate.' After a few seconds of stunned silence, he offered the glass back to Padmavati. 'Now you may drink, my princess. I will arrange a taster for you. But never forget to be careful here, always...always.'

Sipping slowly at the blood-red liquid, Padmavati deliberated, *today, I stand at the threshold of my destiny. The purpose of my existence is to win the trust of these people, to be accepted by them so that one day, Chittor and I become one.*

17

'That is preposterous!' exploded Mrinalini.

'Pre...what? What is that word? And why are you angry? Because she was in the danger of being poisoned?' queried Uma coolly.

'No...I mean yes, that too,' Mrinalini said, agitatedly, 'but all of it...all of it.'

Uma halted. And after a moment, asked, 'All of what?'

'Well, Uma, how unfair is it that Padamvati has to undergo a makeover? From a liberated, decisive, confident equal partner in a marriage she must turn into a demure, obedient wife on reaching Chittor. Why should she have to change? Why couldn't Ratan Singh change? Or why couldn't he convince his family to accept his wife as she is?' Mrinalini's brows were knit in indignation.

Uma's words floated out to her, as calm as always. 'Mrinalini *bhayeli*, you forget the times in which *Padma-wali* was written. Singhaldweep was an exception; an island isolated enough to make its own social rules. Though, you must remember that even there the rights given to females had their limitations. But Bharatdesh was under the yoke of the Muslim invader. These were barbarians; there was no humanity in them. Their ways were wild... no education, no liberty, no social niceties for anyone. Everything was dictated by the man who could grab the throne by whichever means. Alauddin Khalji killed his uncle, who had great affection for him, to get the throne and hung on to it only by being a cruel and feared ruler. Women were either playthings or possessions to be kept under lock and key as they were considered symbols of family honour. Whenever the Muslim armies defeated a Hindu king, the women of his family were carried away to the Sultan's harem. There they suffered the ignominy of dishonour and death. Thus the ladies of a defeated king preferred to give up their lives rather than face this torture and that is how *jauhar* began.'

'But Padmavati was different, and Ratan Singh acknowledged that, didn't he?'

'Yes he did. In fact, probably he had this idea that she would be his chief Rani. He wanted her beside him; together they would rule Chittor. But for that it was essential that she be accepted by the people of Chittor. That was the reason he wanted that they see her following the Mewari traditions.'

'But what about Padmavati herself?' Mrinalini asked. 'How could she, an independent girl, bend her will to such disparaging customs as being veiled and walking a step behind her husband?'

'Remember that she accompanied Ratan Singh of her own free will; she was acting according to her ethical values. She firmly believed that as a wife she must be an asset to her husband and his family. Could she fulfil that role by revolting against his family traditions? She was wise enough to understand that the family viewed her as a foreigner and a threat. First she needed to win the family over. Only then could she win Chittor. Once that was accomplished, she would be entitled to change anything she wanted to. Still, all said and done, Padmavati could not change her basic nature. Staying within the bounds of tradition, she continued with her decisive, emancipated ideas and actions. You will see that as her tale unravels.'

Mrinalini was quiet as she reflected on Uma's analysis. Then she said softly, 'And even without knowing her or meeting her, did the princess' enemies hate her enough to want to kill her?'

'Yes. You see, they were afraid of her and what she could accomplish,' came an equally soft rejoinder from Uma.

In the meanwhile, the moonlight shone on a white gate gradually taking shape before the girls. As they came closer, a well-laid out garden was revealed through a pillared gate. There was a board with a name but Mrinalini could not see it in the darkness. They entered. To their left was a long line of symmetrical arches. On the right was a low building commencing with an open area.

'Horses were tethered here,' explained Uma and passed on to a long corridor with rooms on one side. Each room had a curious cup-like window. 'These were apartments for maids,' explained Uma. 'When the royal couple went through, maids would stand at the windows to shower them with flower petals.'

'Nice idea,' commented Mrinalini and looked around in surprise. 'This building is in quite good condition as compared to the others. Why is that so?'

'This is Padmavati's palace,' said Uma, as if that answered Mrinalini's question.

The journalist narrowed her eyes at this strange response but chose not to comment. From the rear, she watched Uma's *dupatta* flutter on her thin shoulders in the night breeze. Then Mrinalini turned her attention to the stone walls and turned her eyes upwards to the domed roof. Other than a wide marble border running along the edge where the wall met the incline of the roof, the walls were embellished quite simply. *Strangely spartan if this was, in fact, the palace of a queen.* Giving voice to her thoughts, Mrinalini said, 'This palace does not look very grand. Why did Padmavati live here? Why did she not live in the main royal palace?'

'Now that is what the next part of the *Padma-wali* is about,' said Uma. Her feet hardly made any sound as she slowly walked to one of the arches overlooking the inner courtyard and a central garden. One hand rested on the shadowy side of the curved wall as she took up the tale again.

18

'What? Do you mean to say that you have built this for me?' Padmavati was unable to take her eyes off the small white building anchored in the middle of the lake. It was a white three-storied structure with *chattris* or pavilions crowning the roof and cradle-like balconies projecting from windows or *jharokhas*. It looked like a toy palace in the centre of the *Chaurasi Deva Sarovar*, which was fed by the waters of the *Bhimlat Sarovar*. Located at the extreme southern part of the *garh* it was guarded by the massive wall running west to east to its north and embankments on its other three sides. Facing them was a set of entrance stairs that dipped into the *sarovar*.

Ratan Singh grinned, 'Your birthday gift had to be different.'

'Different? Nobody ever gave me a floating palace before.' She hugged her husband tightly.

Ratan Singh put his arms around his wife and kissed the top of her head. But the next instant, she gently moved out of his encircling arms and her eyes raked the walls and gardens for unseen spectators. Enough people were already against her. She did not want any gossip about her unseemly behaviour. But all that met her eyes were Ambika and her ladies murmuring at a discreet distance from them. Her husband put an arm around her waist, saying, 'Come, let's go down. Let me give you a better look at your pleasure palace.'

As they went down the steps to a boat tied to a post, Padmavati said softly, 'Why do you indulge me so much? This gift will start another trail of questions on whether you are spending Chittor's wealth on me. I hate it when you are attacked by the council.'

'Don't worry. I can prove this was not paid for out of Chittor's treasury. I have some wealth of my own too, my princess,' he said, helping her into the boat and taking up the oars. Her ladies stood on the edge of the open arched pavilion from where the garden began. They were exclaiming at the beauty of the *Jal Mahal* or lake palace. The boat took hardly a few minutes to reach the stairs leading up from the waters to an arched doorway. Ratan Singh tied the boat to a pole jutting above the lake. He held Padmavati's left hand as she gathered the voluminous embroidered *lehenga* in her other hand and slowly climbed out of the boat and up the few steps to the landing.

Together they entered the *Jal Mahal*; another short flight of stairs and a small corridor widened into a spacious courtyard. Padmavati went ahead and turned left onto a small verandah. On one side was a doorway, through which she stepped into a large room. A long mirror hung on one wall. Feeling a breeze on her cheek, she turned and found a small *jharoka* to the north.

'This is your *shringar kaksha*,' explained Ratan Singh. He pointed to the small opening, 'That is only to cool the room. Otherwise all privacy has been ensured in this room.'

Padmavati smiled, 'You haven't forgotten the incident on the ship with Chetna.'

'How can I? That villain!' exclaimed Ratan Singh and then mused, 'I wonder what happened to him…'

'Forget him.' Padmavati waved a hand dismissively. 'Let's see the other rooms.'

Yes, yes. Come this way.' Ratan Singh enthusiastically led the way across the courtyard to the room opposite, whose door was from the north. On the opposite wall and to the left were two large *jharokas*. Sunlight streamed through them lighting up the room. The west wall was solid.

Padmavati whirled on pointed toes circling the bright room and turned with a wide smile to her husband.

'Do you like this room? I have designed it especially for your meditation. The beams of the rising sun will directly enter this room and I remember you saying that light from the western direction was inauspicious, so that wall does not have a *jharoka*. Do you think you will find this place peaceful enough?'Ratan Singh's face was anxious.

'My love, my Gem! This is a beautiful room. Not only will I meditate here, I think I will spend most of my time in this room. Just standing here, I can feel the beneficial vibes pulsating around me. Thank you for being so thoughtful about my needs.' Padmavati's eyes shone with tears of joy.

Ratan Singh said, 'Wait till you see everything.' Taking her hand, he pulled her towards the staircase that took them to the next level. Through a narrow verandah, they entered a large room directly above the *shringar kaksha*. It had ostentatious *jharokas* on three walls and a small one on the west wall. Cool drafts off the lake's surface wafted into the room while northern light washed it.

Spreading his hands, Ratan Singh said, 'This is the Rani's *shayan kaksha*. No. Actually, this is our room. It will be airy whichever direction the wind may blow. I know how you long for cool sea breezes. Here we can pretend we are back in our fairy-tale palace of Singhaldweep.' He held his wife's hands and looked down at her lovely face, his eyes dark with intense emotion.

'No.' The princess shook her head. 'This is our fairy-tale palace here, at Chittor. We can stay here sequestered from the world.' A slow, utterly beatific smile spread across her husband's face.

Now she tugged at Ratan Singh, eager to see the rest of this magical palace. Behind their bedchamber was a large terrace with gracious *jaalidiwal* facing the north. Upstairs, in the centre of the topmost terrace surrounded by more *jaalidaar* walls was the crown of the palace...a small pavilion with carved pillars. Sitting there, towards the west was the awe inspiring view of the endless rolling plains below the *garh* carved by the Gambhiri river. One could see the horizon curving at 180 degrees.

On the opposite side was the more cloistered view of the lake and gardens with the arched verandah in the foreground. The *kalash* on the dome above the second floor was also in view. Padmavati sat down and for a long time looked across the expanse of fields, trees and shrubs below. 'I love how this *chaatri* towers above the fort walls. From here I can see far, far away…nearly to Singhaldweep.' She whispered the last words to herself.

'Yes, my Princess. I know how this fort smothers you,' Ratan Singh said softly. 'I want you to feel free and that was the reason for this *chattri* above the palace. You can view the world outside this fort from it but the *jaalidiwal* will seclude you from other eyes.'

'Thank you, my precious Gem.' Padmavati stood on her toes and kissed her husband full on the lips. His arms curved around her waist as he pulled her close, his lips grinding hungrily against hers. When they came up for air, she said with a catch in her voice, 'What a way to baptize our love nest!'

'Hardly,' countered Ratan Singh, holding her tighter, 'I know a better way.' He grinned down at her upturned face.

'No…,' Padamvati smiled as she playfully smacked his cheek. 'Don't be naughty. My ladies are just across the *sarovar*.'

She wriggled out of his hold and ran down the stairs. He chased after her shouting, 'I'll catch you.' They looked like children chasing each other through the palace, not a worry creasing their brows. But the reality was quite contrary.

On her first day in Chittorgarh, when Ratan Singh had insisted that she needed a taster; somebody who could be trusted, Padmavati had felt that her husband was over-reacting. She was surprised to see her mother-in-law agree with him. *She had seemed quite pragmatic,* Padmavati had mused. In fact, *Ba* had even suggested a name. . .apparently a woman from among the retainers at Ratan Singh's own family's *haveli*. And until the woman, an elderly widow arrived, Ratan Singh had only allowed her to eat after he had licked at his own finger, dipped into every one of the twenty-odd bowls encircling the large silver plate that arrived three times daily from the palace kitchen. Not a sip of any liquid—even water—could cross her lips without Ratan Singh first taking a gulp of it. It was tiring, especially when he was at his duties and she had to wait to satiate her hunger.

Padmavati had felt all the caution taken with her food was unnecessary. It was true that neither Rani Prabhavati nor any of the other thirteen queens or even the concubines had visited her in Ratan Singh's chambers ever since her arrival but Padmavati was quite sure nobody was trying to poison her. *Ba,* Ratan Singh's mother would come daily to chat with her. Both the women had taken to each other at first sight. *Ba* lovingly called Padmavati, *Banni*. She would walk in with some gift for the young girl, saying. '*Banni,* look at this *bandhni chunri*. The colours will make your complexion glow.' Or 'This used to be Ratan's favourite bowl. During lunch today, give him dessert in this, *Banni*.' Sometimes, the old lady would quietly smoke a *hookah* in the Rawal's chambers and observe Ambika comb out her *banni's* long, thick hair. *Ba's* affectionate words often brought to the princess' mind her own mother and she would give the old lady dazzling smiles to hide her tears.

A week after they had arrived, Ratan Singh decided it was time to put in place the policies and systems that he, as the new Rawal, wanted to introduce. Foremost among them was appointing Padmavati, or the *NaiRani*, as the administrative head of the Council of Mewar. It was, of course, a radical move but the Rawal, a convert of Singhaldweep's egalitarian society believed it was essential for Mewar to support equal status for men and women, if it wanted to progress. Besides, he believed Padmavati's administrative acumen was far superior to his own. His confidence in decisions would solidify once she had thoroughly vetted them as the Council Head.

So one morning the Rawal had walked into the Council chamber followed by Padmavati, demurely veiled. Though puzzled, the Thakurs and Ranas had bowed in respect to the *NaiRani*. Prince Gora Rajsinha, who was also present, had beamed with delight to find his niece given so much honour. After introducing the *NaiRani* and extolling her skills and abilities, Ratan Singh had announced her administrative role. For a confounded moment, there was utter silence. Ratan Singh had looked around defiantly. An elderly Thakur had stood up. Without a word, he turned and walked out of the door of the Council chamber. As the Rawal had stared after him, several men who had served with his father, left the room too.

'What does this mean?' roared Ratan Singh. His uncle-in-law had been dismayed at this show of opposition. Padmavati had glanced at her husband through her veil, a silent appeal for calmness in her gesture.

'It means that the Council does not agree.' The voice belonged to Rana Lakshman Singh, a cousin of his senior wife, Rani Prabhavati. 'Mewar cannot be administered by a woman. Nobody will accept the *NaiRani* as the Council Head. Rawal Ratan Singh, you have been away too long. Have you forgotten that even letting a woman enter the Council chamber brings ill-luck to the realm?'

'That is old wives' tale...a superstition,' the Rawal had declared, his voice rising above the murmurs in the room.

'Call it what you may, *hukum*. We believe in it and we do not support your decision,' the Rana, already annoyed that his sister had been side-lined by the *NaiRani*, had insisted.

It was then that Padmavati had risen to her feet. Bringing her palms together, she bowed deeply and said, 'I thank you, my lords, for welcoming me. You have rejected your Rawal's choice but may I know where my candidature lacks for this post?' Her words had been polite, yet the challenge resounded in them.

'For one,' suavely replied Rana Lakshman Singh, 'you are not a warrior. How can a non-warrior head a council of warriors?'

'What makes you assume she is not a warrior?' retorted Ratan Singh. 'She is a skilled combatant.'

'Oh, is she?' had sneered the tall and thickset Rana. 'Then I challenge her to a sword duel right here, right now. Let's see her skill.'

Amidst sounds of surprise from the gathering, Padmavati's clear voice had rung out. 'I accept your challenge, Rana. I beg you some time to prepare myself,' and she had swept out of the chamber. Ginni came to perch on Ratan Singh's shoulder, saying, 'Let them tie themselves up in their own ropes.' He had cackled as the Rawal smiled.

Inside, everyone began speaking at once. Older men who had left the chamber returned, hearing the noise. Views about this strange incident were being bandied about when Padmavati had returned to the chamber. Other than her husband, Ginni and Prince Gora, nobody had realized it was the princess because her face had been encased in the white metal mask and she was garbed in Singhaldweep's dress of a white dhoti, pantaloons and waistcoat. In her hand she held a naked sword. Ratan Singh had stood up and said, 'The *NaiRani* is ready. Are you prepared to duel with her, Rana?'

The company had stared open-mouthed at the lithe figure with the sword. 'Is that the *NaiRaniSa*?' they whispered. A space was cleared in the centre of the chamber. The opponents facing each other could not be more a study in contrasts. One was a heavy, tall giant and the other was small, slim, wiry. Saluting each other with their swords held up, they had taken two steps back and considered the other. The moment the Rawal had rung a bell, the Rana cut down with a mighty slash wanting to unhand the princess. But she had vanished from the spot. He felt a rush of air to his right. Turning, the Rana had just manged to save his sword arm, as the princess swiped from his right flank. Angry at his miss, he had charged at her, sword held high to smash down, but his opponent had given a leap, holding her feet close to her body and his weapon had smashed harmlessly on the floor. She somersaulted and had landed on her feet like a cat. While he was still trying to regain balance, her sword had plunged in from his unguarded left and slashed his left forearm. Blood trickled out. The Rana had looked down at the cut in surprise. Then he roared, 'How dare she? Don't dance around. Come and fight like a man!'

'Or like a woman,' piped up Ginni.

Padmavati had come up front and locked her sword with the Rana's. She tried to push it to the floor in the classic swordsman's defeat, but the heavier man's weight had given him leverage and he swung it around. Now her sword was under his. He had pushed down hard. She held on, recalling Ratan Singh's training on how to escape this death hold. As the Rana brought his full strength to bear on his sword, the princess had pushed back hard and then suddenly slipped her sword out. In a blink, her sword was back in the hold but now above the Rana's sword pressing down with all her might. Her opponent, unable to respond to the sudden release of pressure on his sword, had lost balance and toppled over. His sword clattered on the wooden floor announcing a definite end to the duel with the winner standing proud, an erect sword held up.

A collective gasp of astonishment had gone up from the chieftains. The Rana picked himself up, his face stormy with rage and his arm bleeding copiously. The princess had sheathed her sword, folded her palms and bending low, bowed in four directions. Then she had spoken in soft, musical tones. 'Thank you, my lords of Mewar, for your patience.' Turning to her husband, she had said, 'I thank you, *hukum,* for offering me the position of the Council Head but it will be better for everyone present if it is given to somebody else. And now, if you will allow me, I beg your leave.' Princess Padmavati, *NaiRani* of Chittor had stepped out of the chamber. Even Ratan Singh's face had registered surprise.

When she recounted the incident to *Ba,* the old lady had agreed that it was the best course she could have taken. Later, she had consoled her indignant son, saying, 'There are more ways to serve the realm than being head of the Council. And as far as you are concerned, who can stop you from taking *Banni's* advice?'

Padmavati had taken the old lady's wise words to heart. From the very next day, she began to visit the villages and bazaars inside the fort. At first, the common people had been wary of the *NaiRani* who was so unlike royalty. She rode a horse through the meadows and orchards, insisted on paying shopkeepers for their wares, paid obeisance at their village temples, drank water at their wells, thought nothing of licking pickles off thick bajra bread inside their dark hovels and playing *guli-danda,* a kind of stick cricket, with their snot-nosed children. But it had taken them a little time and some common sense to realize that her gestures were sincere and soon the villagers opened up to her. They had also noticed the parrot who accompanied her everywhere. Parrots were a good omen...so the *NaiRani* could mean no harm.

As she had mingled with Chittor's commoners, Padmavati became aware of notions, customs and myths that would never have penetrated the palaces. She saw the auspicious rituals of a bringing home a bride and then reducing her to a servant and baby-maker for the family; she observed the stringent caste differences; she participated in festivities for harvest, worship of gods and goddesses and fasts for the welfare of husbands. She gave lessons to the women on health and hygiene. Once, Padmavati had helped with a birthing and enjoyed celebrations when a son was born. However, she did not fail to notice the relief on the face of the mother. She had been shocked to know that after the mother's last delivery, the baby daughter had been drowned.

She loved to sit with the elders, who gathered under the banyan tree in the centre of the village to smoke their *hookahs*. The princess would listen to their tales of sacrifice, heroism and myths connected to Chittor's history. Sometimes she would ask questions and even pose opposing arguments. Though no other women dared to speak in such a manner, the old men had indulged her due to her position. As she became more and more accepted into the village society, she had ventured to speak of her own views.

'*Bavji* has made both man and woman, hasn't He?' The princess would ask the elders.

'Yes.'

'Then why is a boy child welcomed at birth but not a girl child?'

'Girls are a burden on the family. They cost dowry and have to be protected. Any blemish on them is a dishonour to the family,' explained one.

'But only girls take the family to the next generation, don't they? How will your homes run, animals be fed, men of the family get their meals, grain be threshed if you kill all girl babies?' Padmavati had countered.

Wrinkled faces silently shook their heads at each other, meaning, *she is too smart. We can't overturn her arguments in this war of words. Better to keep quiet.*

One day, she had tackled the priest at the village temple who was not permitting a poor widow and her son enter its hallowed precincts.

'Why not?' She had asked.

'They are low caste, *NaiRaniSa,*' reasoned the priest.

'They are as human as you and I, Pandit*ji.* You are literate and well versed in the Vedas. Where has God said that caste must define who enters His home?' Padmavati had argued.

The priest had lowered his head, knowing she was right and grudgingly let the woman and her son inside.

It was slow progress as Padmavati had tried to change the way the people of Chittor thought. She would teach reading and writing to the children; argue with the men on social customs but give them new ideas about irrigation and crop-sowing; learn new recipes from the women and teach them to grow herbs for simple home remedies. It was also a learning curve for the princess because by trying to understand the needs of the common people, she tried to assimilate the unexplored heritage of the Mewaris. These simple villagers became her friends and she had grown closer to them than any of the inmates of the palace other than *Ba* and her husband.

It had taken Padmavati quite some time to get used to wearing the layers of flowing *lehenga* and bodices encrusted with mirrors and embroidery that comprised the traditional Mewari garments. The mirror work would chafe her soft skin especially in the dry heat. Half the mornings would be taken up by Ambika and the maids to complete the princess' toilette as they would pin and mould the elaborate dress, braid her long hair and festoon her with the heavy ornaments that she was expected to wear as a Rani of Chittor.

Sometimes, Ambika would suggest that while they were inside the Rawal's chambers the princess could relax in a soft sarong and jacket. Padmavati would sigh and remember the comforts she used to enjoy back home but then she would sit up and say, 'No Ambika. I married the Rawal for better or worse. This is my home now and I must get used to its traditions…the sooner the better. It is better for all of us that we accept our situation and not pine for what is not.' And in that way she gently reminded Ambika and her maids that she would expect them to follow the Mewari traditions too!

When her women would make faces at meals which had foods quite different from what they ate at home, Padmavati made it point to savour a particular dish, though its spicy flavour would bring water trickling from her eyes and nose. Over time, of course, she came to appreciate the *dal bati churma,* smack her lips over the variety of *kachoris* and go into raptures over *ghewar* and *malpua*.

Nothing had escaped *Ba's* sharp eyes and she noticed the efforts this new bride from foreign lands was making to imbibe Mewari traditions. She was wearing their clothes, eating their food, attending their religious rituals, keeping their fasts and learning their language. She had watched with amazement her involvement with the villagers. Her son would discuss with his bride the happenings of his Council chamber and take her advice on different matters of state. But it was not just *Ba* who was observing her.

One evening, the princess was leaning out of a *jharoka* sniffing at the dampness rising from the grass watered by the palace gardeners. Instinctively, she had felt she was being watched. Turning her head to the left, she saw a figure under the spread of a giant *peepal*. It was man…no, a youth, lean and tall, dressed splendidly. The turban with its gleaming *sarpech* jewel was in the royal Chittor colours of orange and red. Idly, the princess had wondered who he was, but when her eyes moved up to the man's face, she was stunned. He was staring straight at her but that was not what held her eyes. Looks of pure hatred had flashed from those eyes like poisoned arrows! She had knit her brows. *Who is this man? And why does he dislike me so much? I don't remember having seen him before,* the princess contemplated. Turning her head and looking into the room, she had softly called out, 'Ambi! Come here, please.'

Her friend, who had been folding some clothes, instantly appeared beside the princess, saying, 'Yes Princess.'

The princess gestured. 'Who is that man?'

Ambika had glanced and instantly withdrew from the *jharoka* muttering, 'That's the Crown Prince, Kunwar Vir Bhan*ji*, Princess.'

'Oh, is that Vir Bhan? Prabhavati *didi*'s son? But isn't he just sixteen years old? He looks much older,' Padmavati had said, in an interested tone.

'Princess, I don't think you should show yourself at the window. It may be considered indecorous,' Ambika had warned.

Immediately, Padmavati had turned away from the *jharoka,* saying, 'Yes! Yes! Oh why do I keep forgetting the rules?'

Ambika added, 'Yes, he looks much older and already enjoys the repute of a philanderer. He is known to tease women, even those elder to him. He is a spoiled brat, protected by the senior *Rani*.'

'Hmmm...now I understand why he is sending those murderous looks towards me. After all, he is his mother's son...,' Padmavati had tilted her head at Ambika and chuckled.

It was not that Ratan Singh did not do his duty by Rani Prabhavati and his other wives. He ensured they had their own *mahals,* attendants and spending money as before. He visited them to ask after their welfare, yet made it clear to them that he owed them no conjugal duties. He had assured his senior queen that her son, Vir Bhan would remain the Crown Prince as always. But as the days went by, it was obvious who held the Rawal's heart, mind and body in her little hands. It had only made Rani Prabhavati more and more insecure.

She constantly told all those who would listen, 'This witch will take away my royal status. Once she has a child, maybe a son, Vir Bhan will no longer be the Kunwar of Mewar.'

Since Rani Prabhavati happened to be the head of the royal household, the wives and concubines would nod at her lead, even though many of them secretly admired the gorgeous *NaiRani*.

Rani Prabhavati had not once visited Padmavati during the months that she been in the royal palace. But the Rani's spies were spread across all the parts of the palace bringing reports on everything that Ratan Singh's newest wife was doing, whom she was seeing and who visited her. What was frustrating to the senior Rani was that her spies could not enter the private chambers of the Rawal. There *Ba* held sway and only those loyal to her or belonging to her own *haveli* or constituency were allowed to serve. That was the circle of safety inside which *Ba* kept her son and her beloved *Banni*.

One evening, Ambika had brought a weeping girl to Padmavati. She was a Singha girl from the princess' personal retinue. Instantly, Padmavati came forward and holding the girl by her arms, had asked softly, 'Why? What's the matter? Are you hurt?'

'No, Your Highness, but I have had the most frightening experience,' she had said, tearfully.

'Tell everything, Surbhi,' Ambika prompted.

'Your Highness, I had been walking through the outer corridor leading to your chambers, this morning. It is very dark there, even during the day.'

Padmavati had nodded encouragingly.

The girl continued, 'Suddenly, somebody caught my arm and pulled me into an alcove. I know it was a man though I couldn't see the face. He was behind me but his hold was rough. In my ear, he whispered hoarsely, "Will you tell me everything about the *NaiRani*...where she goes, what she speaks, what she and the Rawal do? I will pay you well. Tell me."

I was in terror, Your Highness but I managed to squeak, "No. Never. I will not spy on my princess."

He twisted my arm and when I screamed, he fled warning me that he will hurt me if I tell anybody of this. But...but...Your Highness...I am your subject, not of this Mewar. I...I...cannot betray you.'

'Thank you, Surbhi. Go to your chambers now and rest. Don't worry about the threats. I will protect you.'

At night, when she had spoken of the incident to the Rawal and *Ba*, they reiterated that Padmavati must not leave her chambers unless well-protected by guards. Ratan Singh had spoken of the incident in the Council with an ominous warning that there was going to be an investigation and the culprit will be hanged. Prince Gora had given a contemptuous laugh and remarked, 'Chittor's valiant warriors spy on women? Is this the way Mewar conducts its governance?'

Quite a few faces, among them Rana Lakshman's and Kunwar Vir Bhan's, had glowered at this sneer.

But Padmavati wanted to solve this problem in her own way. She had understood the reasons for Rani Prabhavati's insecurity and wanted to convey to her that there were no grounds for it. She had no intentions of taking away the senior Rani's or her son's rights, and awaited an opportunity to express this to her.

So when dark clouds scudded the sky, lightening flashed but no rain fell to relieve the thick humidity, women in Chittor began to prepare for the Kajri Teej festival. They would pray to Lord Shiva and sing *kajris* to express their pining for their beloved. Padmavati had felt this women's festival would be a suitable occasion to hold out a conciliatory hand to her rival, Rani Prabhavati. Waking before dawn, bathing and dressing, Ambika and the princess had walked down to the senior Rani's chambers followed by maids carrying sweets and fruits. Since they would be fasting until the moon is sighted in the night, women in groups enjoyed a meal before first light to sustain them during the day. Padmavati had wished to share her meal with Prabhavati.

She reached the doors of Prabhavati's chambers, which were guarded by Koki, the Chief Eunuch who managed the royal palace household. Instantly, he had bowed to her, '*NaiRaniSa,* what can I do for you?'

'Please inform *Didi* that I have come to share my Teej meal with her,' requested Padmavati.

'*Hukum,*' nodded Koki, scurrying indoors.

They had heard him repeat the message. Even before he finished speaking, the sharp sound of a slap came to the visitors. 'Get out!' screamed Prabhavati. 'I don't share my meals with dirty foreigners. . .how dare you come here with such stupid things!'

Koki had come hurrying out and fallen down at Padmavati's feet, mumbling, 'I am sorry, *NaiRaniSa.*'

Her face burning with humiliation, Padmavati had said, 'It is not your fault, Koki.' In a loud voice, she addressed the Rani inside. '*Pranam Didi*. I hope to see you at the Ek Linghji's temple this evening for prayers.'

'Go away, you witch!' The Rani had screamed in reply.

Never had the princess confronted such rancour and rage. She turned back to her chambers, a little sad. *At least I tried,* she had thought.

That evening, she had gone with Ambika and her ladies for the ritualistic bath at the *Gomukh Kund*. This was a deep tank that was filled by a rushing mountain spring spouting from the mouth of a rock shaped like a cow's head. It was a practice followed by all royal ladies before attending the evening prayers at the nearby temple of Ek Linghji, the *Isht Devata* of Mewar. As the princess had begun to descend the steep steps into the *Kund*, there was a commotion at the entrance. Padmavati had turned to see Rani Prabhavati emerge from the underground passage that linked the *Kund* to the royal palace. She had been followed by her ladies, Koki and the other palace eunuchs. A large basket of flowers held up by servants had come at the end of the procession.

The princess had climbed back to the platform where the passage opened and bowed to the senior Rani with her palms together respectfully. But Prabhavati had behaved as if the princess was invisible. She had whirled around so that her back was to Padmavati who was still bowing. In a nasal tone, she had given loud instructions to her ladies to remove her ornaments prior to bathing. Padmavati had turned red with mortification. Silently, she began to descend the steps again. Some of the senior Rani's ladies had giggled slyly. Ambika had given the group a couple of murderous looks that quelled their glee and followed her friend. *Gomukh Kund* was enormous and the two groups could easily bathe without intruding upon each other.

Padmavati had hurried in her bathing because she wanted to be out of the place before Prabhavati's group completed their bath. As she came out of the *Kund*, she had noticed the huge basket of flowers guarded by two eunuchs on the top of the steps and idly wondered what it was for. *If it is for the evening prayers, it should be at the temple and not here,* she had thought, climbing the wet stairs. The princess was about to put her foot down on the second step from the top, when she had happened to look down. She had given a loud gasp and instantly withdrawn her foot. Ambika who had been just behind her peered downwards and screamed. 'Snake! Snake!' A thin, black reptile had been coiling and uncoiling on the wide stone step. It was a venomous krait. One bite from it was fatal and Padmavati had been about to step on it!

Ambika's screams had brought Koki running. With a stout stick, he had given a hard blow to the snake's shiny black head that splattered into a mush of flesh and blood. The princess, who had recovered by then, quickly skirted the dead reptile and climbed the last step. She was now safely on the platform. Her ladies had surrounded her and all of them walked up the slope to the temple. They had spoken among themselves agitatedly; how had the reptile had slithered to this area, which was completely paved. There were no trees or snake holes nearby.

'Almost as if somebody had brought the snake here,' Ambika had remarked loudly. Her voice carried down the steps. Prabhavati's ladies had also risen from the *Kund* and were chattering excitedly about the incident. A deathly silence had fallen on everyone at Ambika's words. In one accord, as if the same idea had struck each one at the same time, all eyes had gone to the large basket of flowers. *Had the snake been concealed in the basket? And brought here on purpose? If so, what was the purpose?* The answer had been as clear as crystal. Somebody had wanted to hurt Padmavati and hurt her seriously, even fatally. *Who could be so malicious but her rival, Rani Prabhavati?*

Suddenly, the senior Rani had felt the heat of many pairs of speculative eyes on her. Instantly, she began climbing energetically towards the platform seeking escape through the passage, ordering her entourage to follow her. Padmavati had stared at her retreating back; quite sure that she was the culprit. Yet, when Ambika had beseeched her to tell Ratan Singh about the incident, she refused, explaining, 'I have come here to be accepted as part of the Rawal's family, Ambika. Prabhavati *didi* is my senior. How can I complain about her, or even worse, accuse her?'

Ambika had not been convinced. 'It is a matter of your safety. She tried to kill you.'

'No, my dear friend. We don't know for sure how the krait got there. We have no proof that *Didi* was responsible. Our suspicions may be wrong. And by complaining what will I get? I will only make the Rawal angry and alienate Prabhavati *didi* even more.'

'But she may make another attempt.' Ambika's voice had cracked with fear.

'No, Ambika. What have we learned in our land? If you give love and forgiveness, it will be returned double fold. Don't be afraid, my friend,' Padmavati had said gently.

'But these are not Singhas, Padmavati,' Ambika had cried. 'You cannot trust them. Everyone has told me how spiteful Rani Prabhavati is.'

But the princess would not be swayed.

Nevertheless, incidents such as these have a way of blowing with the hot breeze through the palace. By next morning, it had reached *Ba's* ears and she immediately questioned her *banni,* who gave evasive answers. The astute lady had confirmed it all from the servants who were anyway her people. When the Rawal came for his mid-day meal, it all came tumbling out even as Padmavati had tried to dilute the issue. As expected, Ratan Singh had been furious. He had leaped up from his low stool, his meal half-eaten. Pushing his feet into slippers, he was ready to march to his senior wife's chambers to take her to task.

Exactly then, an attendant had entered to announce that Rani Prabhavati had sent sweets for Rani Padmavati. He bore a message from her saying, "Hopefully Rani Padmavati had not fallen ill from yesterday's shocking incident"

'See, how right I was!' said Padmavati. '*Didi* is so worried that she has sent me this message.' To the attendant, she had said, 'Please bring her gift inside.'

As the servant had gone out, Ratan Singh had sat down heavily in a chair, saying, 'How will I teach this girl not to trust people so easily? My princess, grow up. This is the real world, not a wonder world like Singhaldweep. Here, if your guard slips, other people will grab...' He had stopped speaking, as the minion returned with Prabhavati's attendants bearing a tray piled with delicious sweetmeats. They had placed it on a table beside Padmavati and backed out. Other than *Ba* and the royal couple, only Ambika had remained, hovering uncertainly behind her friend. Padmavati had reached out for one of the tiered *barfis*, when somebody shouted outside the closed doors. Ratan Singh had jumped up and gone to the door. Outside, the colonnaded passage had erupted into a babble of voices and clattering feet. Everyone had run towards the noise. The Rawal had followed them and a path opened up for him to see a woman rolling on the ground in great pain. Suddenly, her body had contorted, arching upwards as if in a nervous spasm. Then it relaxed and fell down on the floor. A thin stream of blood had trickled from the corner of her lips. Death had taken her. It was the widow from the Rawal's village...hired as Padmavati's taster.

Ratan Singh did not have to make many inquiries. The attendant who had been escorting Rani Prabhavati's retainer with the sweetmeats had told the taster to eat one of them according to the rule laid down by the Rawal himself. Within minutes, the poison in the confectionary had worked its way into the bloodstream, so potent had it been. The woman had been assailed by a paralytic attack that choked her to death.

That very evening, Padmavati with her entire household had been moved to an isolated room in a garden in the southern-most part of the *garh*. She could not protest in the face of two assassination bids. The Rawal had already been building a separate residence for the *NaiRani*. Workers had been at it, desilting the *Chaurasi Deva Sarovar* for the past many months and it was nearly complete. Her room, the first night, was part of a set of outhouses set inside a formal garden spread over a wide area adjacent to the *sarovar*. Ratan Singh had wanted to move her household to this palace on Padmavati's birthday. But the two dastardly acts had expedited the move.

Night had fallen before Padmavati had a chance to explore her new home. So it was only next morning that the Rawal offered to take her on a tour. After going through the several outhouses meant for maids and strolling through the beautiful flower gardens, they had climbed to the *chattri* on the third level of the northern verandah, overlooking the *sarovar*. *Koels* were cooing, butterflies fluttering and a peacock danced on a nearby terrace. The stage had been set for his gift. The Rawal had kept the best for the last and had been craving to see the princess' pleasure when he offered her birthday present. And he had not been disappointed. Her ecstasy with the *Jal Mahal*, her lake palace, was beyond words!

19

A golden finger of light touched her face gently, as if hesitant to distract the pilgrim seeking worlds beyond this one. She had been sitting in the classic lotus pose for nearly two hours before the eastern sky had lightened. Her limbs were wholly relaxed, her breathing deep and steady as if she were in the unconscious state of sleep. But her consciousness was sharper than when she was wide awake for she was attempting to journey in realms where awareness is more of the spirit than the body.

She floated freely above her body, which was just a shell sitting in the room. The curious sense of liberation, where time and space were boundless, suffused Padmavati. She tried to fly through space as before, but she could not. She tried again, but something was holding her back. She decided to let go and just experience the beauty of the spirit. She began to rise through the layers of her consciousness. Exhilaration pervaded her as she felt the presence of the Omnipresent Infinity permeating her completely. Ever since she had been able to achieve this state of perfect oneness with the cosmic presence, it had brought her so much bliss that it was always difficult for her to return to the physical existence of this world. But even absorbed in the Divinity, she would feel an intangible urging to return to her physical body. She looked downwards to the thin connecting thread that pulsated luminously and sighed, *here it is enchanting but I have to go back*...Gradually, the illuminated thread grew shorter as Padmavati descended.

A gentle puff skimming the surface of the lake moist with dew of the desert dawn caressed her cheek. Slowly, Padmavati's eyelids lifted and the thick, long lashes curled up. For a time, she gazed at the waves rippling just outside the low *jharoka,* sunbeams playing tag with them. A peacock called raucously and Padmavati stirred. Ginni twittered from the *jharoka* and the princess beckoned. When her friend hopped in, she said, 'Ginni, my dear, will you please take a round of Chittor and bring me the news?'

'Sure,' said Ginni, 'but I thought you could float in space yourself.'

'Yes,' admitted Padmavati, 'I could. But now I can't. I don't know why. Ever since I have come here, I am unable reach that level where I can freely move about. Do it for me, my friend. I want to know what is happening.'

Obligingly, Ginni flew off. Soon he would be back with a variety of news about the villages, palaces and *havelis* of the fort.

Padmavati sat in the quiet room. The palace was still sleeping and it was her time of reflection. The last few months had been idyllic for the royal couple. Waking up to cool mornings in the privacy of the *shayan kaksha,* simple meals to the chirping of birds and dancing peacocks, days filled with duties; the Rawal with his council and the princess with Chittor's people, afternoons occupied with arms practice with sword, spear, mace and archery. Delightful evenings given over to music maestros who performed ragas and raginis vocally or on instruments. Sometimes they spent quiet evenings, too; playing chess with silver chessmen. Nights were only theirs, devoted to their love, binding them together into one entity. Truly rapturous, their fulfilment brought them such blessedness that their serenity spread through the *Jal Mahal*. Despite being so absorbed, Padmavati found time to visit *Ba* and offer veneration to Ek Linghji, another form of her adored Mahadev.

Sometimes, letters would arrive from Singhaldweep. Reading them, the princess and her ladies would be both in tears and laughter, while Ratan Singh would go around looking guilty. He had not forgotten how speedily they had sailed from the island kingdom, leaving them with promises till now unfulfilled. At night, he would tell Padmavati, 'A little more time, my princess. Let me settle the chiefs and we can make a trip back to Singhaldweep.'

Surreptitiously wiping her tears, she would say, 'Did you hear me complain, my Gem?'

One afternoon, Ratan Singh arrived with attendants carrying yet another gift for his beloved wife. When they removed the covers, Padmavati squealed with delight. The Rawal indulgently smiled at her excitement, wondering once again at this unique creature he had married. *Other women would have been as thrilled with gifts of gems, jewels and ornaments as my princess is with my simple gift,* he pondered. Padmavti was whooping with joy as she fingered the white suit of chain armour that her husband had specially got fashioned for her. There was even a matching helmet with a white plume to fit her small head. Instantly she put it on and paraded before the Rawal like a child in a party dress.

Padmavati smiled as she recalled Ratan Singh's amusement at her impromptu modelling.

It was winter and there was a nip in the air, when Padmavati left her meditation chamber. As it was still early, she was attired in a sarong overlaid by a jacket and the contours of her voluptuous yet elegant body were defined by its folds. Her loose hair floating behind her like a black cloud, she glided up the stairs to her *shayan kaksha* to check on her husband but halted in the doorway. She was taken aback to see the covers flung back, and the bed empty. Instead of stepping in, the princess went around to the terrace but drew a blank there. Anxiety making her pant slightly, she ran up the stairs to the roof and sighed. There he was! Silhouetted against the grey sky where clouds still hid the eastern light, Ratan Singh stood inside the *chattri,* scanning the desert, his back to her. Her bare feet made no sound as she tiptoed to him. But her attempts to surprise him were of no avail. Without turning around, he said softly, 'My princess, I was waiting for you.'

'Ummm. . .you are no fun,' pouted Padmavati. 'I wanted to tickle you. . .' She laid her head against his broad back and entwined her arms, bangles clinking, around his chest.

Ratan Singh laughed low in his throat and raising his right arm brought her head forward on his chest. 'Let me show you something that will tickle you.' And he pointed to the desert.

Grey-blue waves in peaks and ebbs covered the sand for miles around vanishing into the distant predawn shadows. On all three sides, as far as the eye could see, the surface of the desert was creased by these blue peaks.

'What! Have you brought the sea to me, my lord?' Padmavati's voice was incredulous. 'Were you not satisfied by building me a lake palace that you ordered the ocean to change its direction and flow to Chittorgarh? Now we are in a fort floating on a blue carpet.'

Ratan Singh once again laughed softly but there was no mirth in it.

'I wish I had the power to make the ocean flow to Chittorgarh, but unfortunately I am only human. My power is limited to mortal struggles,' he said, in a bitter tone and pointed out to the desert. 'That is one such struggle.'

As Padmavati looked up at him inquiringly, he sighed deeply. 'My princess, they are not waves of sea water but rows of tents. The army of Sultan Alauddin Khalji is waiting in them for us to surrender.' At her sharp intake of breath, he added, 'Yes, the Sultan has laid siege to Chittorgarh, the seat of Mewar power.'

Padmavati put both her palms on the *jaali* wall and peered through the fretwork. After observing the tents for a while, she remarked, 'They are not close enough for our archers or to pour down flaming oil, but they stretch away to the horizon.'

'Yes, my love, this is the Sultan's army. It is much larger than all the armies of the Mewari chiefs put together. Fighting it head-on is sure suicide,' replied Ratan Singh.

'I know,' she nodded. 'But why should we worry? We are safe inside our *garh*. The Sultan will have to send for his army's provisions all the way from Delhi. The desert won't give him any food, while...'

'...not Delhi, from cities much closer. Remember how far his Sultanate has spread,' interrupted Ratan Singh.

'Alright,' acquiesced Padmavati. 'But for how long? We are in a much better situation. We have enough water... eighty-four *talabs, kunds* and *baoris.* Even with my little knowledge, I am sure they will suffice for twelve months. You have yourself told me that fifty thousand people can live in this fort for four years without dying of thirst. Harvest is just over and our granaries are full and our watch towers are on alert. Chittorgarh is impregnable, my Gem.'

Ratan Singh held her shoulders and looked down at her face shining with conviction. With the light at his back, Padmavati could not make out the expression in his eyes but from the set lines of his face, she knew he did not share her confidence. Abruptly, he turned away from her muttering, 'So was Ranthambore...' He strode towards the stairs, his saffron *kurta* and *angavastran* billowing in the morning breeze, and vanished from view.

For some time, Padmavati stared at the empty space where her husband had been standing a few moments ago, a peculiar dread rising like dark smoke in her breast. But she forcefully compelled it to go away and went back to her watch post at the *jaali* wall. Activity had begun in the camp below as the sun rose above the horizon. Soldiers were entering and leaving tents, the guards changing duty with shouted passwords. Smoke was rising from some tents probably as the cooks began stoking their *chulaahs* for the morning meal. *So this is the awful army of the terrible Sultan of Delhi*...contemplated the princess from Singhaldweep, *trapping us and our fields down below.*

Thoughtfully, she made her way down to the terrace on the second floor where the couple was served their breakfast. The moment she settled on the low seat, an attendant approached with the princess' preferred morning repast of fresh green coconut water and sweet desert dates. Ambika was supervising the service with gentle glances at the attendants. The princess asked her 'What is there for the Rawal's breakfast?'

'Chila with hot green chutney and pepper fritters,' replied Ambika, 'but...'

Padmavati took a sip of the coconut water and asked, 'But what, Ambi?'

'He has left the palace...,' she replied.

'Left? When?'

'Just now.'

Padmavati sipped at her glass, silently. Her gaze went to a stork standing on one leg visible through *jharoka,* but she did not see it. Ambika noticed a tiny furrow in the smooth fair brow and wondered what was worrying her friend. She would find out later when both were alone during the princess' toilette. The princess hardly touched the sweet dates and left the table in the same reflective mood, calling Ginni. Ambika was still puzzled as she signalled the attendants to clear the dishes.

Downstairs, Padmavati discussed with Ginni how he should divide his time between Chittor and the Sultan's camp. Ginni knew what would be expected of him. All the princess needed to do was to remind Ginni to play his role well, for she would be waiting for his information. Ginni cocked his head to the side and vanished with a glint of green.

Ratan Singh had rushed from the rooftop *chattri* directly to his chambers in the royal palace. Taking just enough time to dress, he sent messages to the Mewari chiefs to assemble for an emergency conference. They were already in the *garh* for the monthly Council meeting. Then he had leaped on his horse to gallop around the flagstone path that circumvented the *garh* to check the sentry towers. *Ba* had hurriedly putting together a *thali* for his morning meal, but he had rushed off without tasting a morsel. In the meanwhile, Ginni had completed his round of the enemy camp. Both reached the Council chamber at the same time, though Ratan Singh did not see Ginni. The bird waited outside the open *jharoka* for the right moment to divulge the knowledge he had already shared with the princess.

Ratan Singh lowered himself on the ornamental chair that served as a kind of throne for the Rawal of Mewar. All around him were gathered the hoary Thakurs and Ranas from Mewari clans, some of them accompanied by their sons. They were anxious, for they were trapped in the besieged Chittorgarh. If the Turkish ruler took the fort, each of them had only a handful of their bodyguards to protect them. They were too agitated to sit down, as they loudly discussed Khalji's siege and how it should be tackled. On one side of Ratan Singh, a little separate from the others, sat Prince Gora Rajsinha, Padmavati's maternal uncle. Raised voices gave disparate modes of dealing with the enemy camping at their gates. Prince Gora was also trying to speak but being a Singha, his soft, courteous words were completely lost in the noise. Ratan Singh knew the only way to handle his unruly lords. . .by raising his own voice above theirs. He bellowed, 'Stop! Quiet!' When the last murmur died down, he went on, 'Prince Gora has something to say. Let's hear him.'

As the Singha prince cleared his throat to speak, a loud comment came clearly across the congregation. 'We don't need foreigners telling us how to manage our affairs.' Instantly, murmurs of assent rose from the rest of the chieftains. Rana Lakshman was the rebel who had insulted the Prince. He was bent on forming an opposition to the young Rawal. The Rawal's insulting comments about Rani Prabhavati, especially after the murder attempts on Padmavati, were still ringing in his ears.

Prince Gora's face fell and he made a move to leave his seat at this stinging indignity. Ratan Singh was outraged and a razor-sharp rebuke was about to fall from his tongue but he bit it back. He needed the loyalty and strength of all the chiefs and their armies to stand against this formidable foe. Besides, he had learnt the lessons of tact very well in Singhaldweep. Calmly, he raised a hand to quell the cries and announced, 'No doubt the clans of Mewar are the bravest in the land. We are lions on the battlefield and will die before we surrender an inch of Chittor.' Then in a softer tone, he said, 'But isn't Mewar not equally famous for its hospitality and *athitisatkar?* We care for our guests with the courtesy they deserve, foreigner or not. Don't we?'

It was a challenge. Heads, many grey with age, bent downwards with shame. It had not been a chivalrous gesture to humiliate a guest from the home of the Rawal's bride. Rana Lakshmana looked around in dismay. Just then Ginni flew in and perched on Ratan Singh's shoulder. Nobody noticed the little bird as it energetically chattered into the Rawal's ear. He had not finished when, the Rawal jumped up in utter amazement, shouting, 'What?!' Ginni squawked at being interrupted and then resumed his monologue. The entire gathering, including Prince Gora, turned as one body to gaze at Ratan Singh.

The Rawal was so shocked that he could not help blurting out Ginni's information. 'The Sultan has laid siege to Chittor because he wants Rani Padmavati!' He spoke as if in a daze while stunned faces stared at him unable to believe their ears.

Prince Gora was the first to recover. Knitting his brows, the dignified gentleman nearly shouted, 'What did you say? What do you mean?'

Ratan Singh sat down and wearily gestured to the chieftains to sit too. Silently, everybody took their seats with expectant eyes on their Rawal. They waited for him to explain his outrageous statement.

'While we were quarrelling about how to vanquish the Sultan, Ginni had winged it to the enemy camp to glean some information about their forces and their plans. He estimates that this is nearly all of the Sultanate's army gathered to besiege us. As we also know, it is returning from its campaign in the South, so these are trained veterans. Ginni could not count the tents for they were in hundreds. He decided a better place for information would be the Sultan's tent. At an opportune moment, he entered the royal tent and hid himself on a roof pole. When the Sultan entered with his generals, he was complaining loudly about how incompetent they were, as they had not been able to find out anything about our defences nor had they been able to get a shepherd or a farmer to show them a hidden path into the fort. Eventually, he ordered them to get out, saying he couldn't spend months waiting for their answers.

Once they had left, the Sultan had called out to somebody waiting outside, "Come in, *Faankar!*" And Ginni nearly fell off his perch as Raghav Chetna entered.'

'What? Who? No!' came several voices from amongst the company.

As the Rawal tried to control his own rage, somebody asked, 'But didn't he drown in the sea?'

'According to Ginni, Chetna didn't look at all like a drowned man; in fact, he seems quite well and happy. He must have come ashore and made it to the Sultan's court. As Ginni watched, the rogue executed a deep *kurnish* to the Sultan, who strolled to one end of the tent and pulled off a cloth covering a painting. The Turk then stuck a pose before the picture and gesturing to it, exclaimed, 'Is she really so beautiful? Is she worth bringing my entire army to lay siege to Chittor when the Mongols are knocking at the gates of Delhi?'

'Oh great Sultan!' snivelled the scoundrel. 'She is even more gorgeous than my portrayal of her. I am only an artist. How can I capture the sun and the moon with my simple brush? *Huzoor*, you will not regret this effort when you set your eyes on her. Then the Sultan...'

Ratan Singh stopped speaking.

'What did the brute say?' demanded a Rana.

With some difficulty, the Rawal resumed speaking, 'I am repeating their words as Ginni has just narrated. You should know exactly what we are facing, even though these vile words burn in my throat...

"*O meri Jaan!*" the powerful Sultan of Bharatdesh laid a hand on his heart and exclaimed, "When will I set my eyes on you? I am already famished and faint for my love of you. Your eyes...your lips...like opium...intoxicating. If this *musavvar* can make me so drunk, what will happen to me when I actually see you..." It seems Alauddin rambled on for a while.'

'And what was Chetna's response?' asked Prince Gora Rajsinha, brows knit.

'He said that she really is a magnificent woman, to which the Sultan's response was to say, "Magnificent? No, no Chetna *Faankar*. She is luscious, sensuous, titillating. Look at her bosom...like two plump pigeons. Oooohhh... if only I could hold them in my hands...ahhhhhh..."'

Ratan Singh's face was red as he repeated these words, but he knew that to impress upon his Ranas and Thakurs the depths of Khalji's depravity, he needed to be fully honest.

The faces surrounding him were dark with anger and a kind of low growling spread amongst the gathering.

'I suppose there's one thing that should make us all smile...Ginni, who had been listening to the Sultan's wet fantasies felt like vomiting, and tried to cough out the disgust that was clogging his throat. He ended up shooting down a jet of spittle on Alauddin's head. The man was so absorbed in his daydreams that he didn't even feel the blob of phlegm land on the cloth skull cap tightly wedged over his balding head. He went on with his fanciful flights, "She is like a delicious feast...I want to eat her up...swallow her whole, Chetna. Ahhhh...when? When? When? Ye Allah! When will your gift reach me?..."

At this point, Ginni says that he had had enough. Still, curiosity made him change position to view whose painting had made the Sultan drool with such lewd fantasies. Imagine his horror when he saw it was a picture of Rani Padmavati! Quickly, he flew back here to relate it all to us.'

Shocked silence reigned in the large hall as the breed of proud Mewari pedigree digested this enormous insult to their lineage. Whatever may be their collective opinion of Rani Padmavati, she had been married to their Rawal by holy, sacred rites. She was the symbol of Mewar's honour. No man, and especially not a Turkish invader, could be allowed the insolence of lusting after her.

'Can a man fall to such depths? We thought we had given our daughter to the Bharatdesh of the Pandavas. Is this the same Bharatdesh?' Speaking his mind clearly, Prince Gora strode out of the room.

His softly-uttered words were sharp enough to cut the Mewaris to the core. '*Fajiti! Fajiti!*' shouted the clan chiefs, responding as uproariously as a turbulent river breaking its dam. Faces contorted by wrath, each one was shouting out his opinion of what should be done to the arrogant, unscrupulous, conceited Turkish dog, Sultan Khalji.

In the midst of the furore sat one silent man, the parrot still perched on his shoulder, gently pecking at his ear. The enormous pain in his heart was clearly visible on his face. *My precious princess...why can't the world leave us alone?* A mist of terrible premonition surrounded Ratan Singh. He was no coward and had, since his youth, fought numerous battles with the Sultan's army but this time he wished he could halt the march of time. Numbly, he stared down a precipice whose bottom was shrouded in darkness.

20

Surreal and silver, lines blurred as they extended to a shimmering reflection in the placid waters. Mrinalini was so entranced by the magical sight that she was struck dumb. Moonlight bounced off the rough ruins behind the white palace, providing a radiant halo to the smooth, pristine walls broken by graceful *jharokas* and crowned by the silhouette of the *chattri.*

Uma quietly leaned against the pillar of an arch of the open pavilion facing the *Chaurasi Deva Sarovar*. Mrinalini tried to remember what the plaque beside the gate said. The journalist recalled reading a name for this enclosure in the tourist booklet. 'Was it *Rani Padmini Palace* or *Rani Padmini Udyaan?*' She wondered aloud.

Uma instantly retorted, 'The fools! Why don't they know the right name for the princess?'

Mrinalini had nodded silently, though it did cross her mind,—*why does this girl take so much umbrage at the name? It's almost like a personal affront!*

Before coming upon this wondrous sight, Mrinalini had wandered through the gardens and the arched facade perched beside the lake engrossed in observing the architectural style. The small maids' rooms beyond the stables adjacent to the corridor were typically random. Possibly their asymmetrical design was due to the fact that most of this fort was built in stages over long periods of time. Especially attractive were the cup-like balconies overlooking the corridor. Uma had walked ahead and after a time when Mrinalini turned around, the girl had vanished.

However, when she came out into a pavilion on the upper level, the girl was standing near a pillar gazing across the rippling *sarovar*. She could not see Uma's face but her relaxed posture suggested she was lost in her thoughts. In fact, she had started when Mrinalini inquired, 'What are you looking at?'

As a response, Uma had pointed to the *sarovar*. Only when Mrinalini came up behind her did she see the ethereal palace that completely took her breath away.

'This *mahal* must be the crowning glory of Chittorgarh,' gushed the captivated Mrinalini when she finally found her voice. 'Nothing, but nothing can compare with the beauty of this lake palace.'

'Yes. This is Padmavati's *Jal Mahal* that I spoke of. Rawal Ratan Singh specially made it for her because she missed her green and blue island so much.' A strange sadness tinged Uma's words.

Mrinalini sighed, 'If ever I had such a passionate lover, I would be ready to do anything for him, even die...'

'That's what she did...,' whispered the air; so softly that Mrinalini was not sure whether it was Uma who spoke or she had imagined hearing it.

Clearing her throat in an attempt to retain some of her objectivity, Mrinalini asked, 'But how did Ratan Singh manage to build such a palace in just a few months after he brought Padmavati to Chittor? After all, there was no technology then for swift construction.'

'That is certainly a question,' replied Uma, unhelpfully.

'So was a structure already existing? I find it difficult to believe that a palace could have been built in so short a time,' insisted the sceptical journalist.

'Well, *bhayeli*, you say that you have read all about the fort, haven't you?'

'Yes. I have,'agreed Mrinalini, adding pompously, 'I always look up all the information before embarking on a project.'

'Tell me then, how long did Maharana Kumbha take to build the nine storeys of Vijay Stambha?' Uma quizzed her.

'Umm...ten years, I think,' answered Mrinalini.

'Yes. One storey each year. Then is it too difficult to believe that a small palace like this one could not be built over a few months?' Uma asked, softly.

'Uhhh...okay,' Mrinalini grudgingly conceded. She did not like being trumped so she changed the topic. 'Is that the *chattri* up there from where she first glimpsed the army of that blackguard, Alauddin? What a cruel, pitiless barbarian he was! Even history records him as a cruel sovereign. Who else but he could think of such a brutal way to secure Padmavati?'

'Yes. He was a monster,' Uma said in a choked voice. 'When he entered Chittor over the bodies of our warriors, he butchered nearly thirty thousand innocent citizens.'

Puzzled, Mrinalini's eyes came back to the girl. *Why is Uma sounding so emotional? Didn't it happen centuries ago? Just a few minutes ago she was quite coolly probing my knowledge of the fort. Really weird, this girl!*

But the journalist did not display her perplexity. Instead, she said, 'I can't get over Raghav Chetna! After all that the Rawals of Chittor had done for him, he betrayed them to Alauddin Khalji to take revenge on the Rawal and Padmavati. What a venomous snake that bites the hand that feeds him! He was so evil-minded that he must have shown the tyrant scurrilous paintings of the princess inciting him to attack Chittor, by making him covet Padmavati. Just because the princess had humiliated him, Chetna did not leave any effort to ensure she suffered extreme indignities. His purpose must have been to make her part of the Sultan's harem and be dishonoured. What a scoundrel! Why didn't Ratan Singh throw him to the sharks on the high seas when he had discovered his crime? He is a good example of the saying that evil should be stamped out immediately. He is the devil incarnate!'

Mrinalini expected a reaction to her furious tirade but Uma only contemplated the *mahal* on the lake silently. She was so still that Mrinalini wondered whether the girl had decided to not go on with the story of the *Padma-wali*. To elicit a response, she said, 'You know, Uma, the way you described Padmavati's spiritual powers brings up a lot of questions. I mean, what I know or have read has told me that it takes a lot of effort and years of meditation for people such as yogis to reach that level of spiritual awareness. How did Padmavati reach it so easily?'

She succeeded in the ploy for the girl responded, saying, 'About this I only know what is written in the *Wali*. How the princess became spiritually aware, whether she had learnt meditation techniques in Singhaldweep or whether she came by it easily or not, I have no idea. Of course, later in Chittor, she found it difficult to traverse the spiritual world and that is recorded by her. But beyond that I don't know much. For the reader, it is a question of belief...and I believe her.'

Silently, Mrinalini observed her slim back, the *dupatta* covering her head puffing up in the slight breeze and thought, *how simple that sounds...it is a question of belief. Eventually...at the end, what else is it?*

Afraid to lose the thread of the tale and an opportunity to get hold of the *Padma-wali*, the journalist explored Uma's intentions by asking, 'Won't you continue? What happened to Rani Padmavati while the siege went on? My historical sources say it went on for eight months.'

No response. The silence between the two women grew longer and heavier. Mrinalini was about provoke her again when Uma heaved a deep sigh. It was almost as if she had to let go of some great sorrow. And she began to speak...

21

The news spread like fire through the fort. 'The Sultan has come!' was on everyone's lips, as the *garh*'s residents began to store up food and water, plan rations for themselves and their animals. Being under siege was not new to them. Right from the 8th century, Chittorgarh had been besieged over and over again, run over and captured by rulers of several dynasties. But tales of Alauddin Khalji's cruelty had spread throughout the Sultanate. He was like a demon with no vestige of humanity left in him.

And this was the latest of his atrocities; attacking Mewar to capture its queen. Kings march on neighbouring kingdoms for many purposes...to expand their boundaries, to secure their own borders, alter a historical error, to avenge a past defeat, or even for religious reasons. But till now no ruler had stooped so low as to covet the wife of another king and attack a kingdom to satisfy his base desires. A kind of terror seized the fort. The bustling bazaars became deserted as families shut themselves in their homes to discuss this strange turn of events and people walked around with sombre faces. Villagers, especially those who had been in touch with the *NaiRani* whispered among themselves, *what kind of man is the Sultan? Is he a man or a blood-sucking vampire? If a ruler has no sensibility towards the dignity of queens and shows no respect for them, what will be the character of the soldiers he leads? They will be like an army of marauding violators. No man, woman or child will be spared from their barbarism.*

The siege continued. Shepherds could not graze their flocks on the tiny *adaos* or grasslands sandwiched between the rocks on the slopes of the plateau. Farmers could not till their lands on the plains. The sowing season came and went. Villagers went about with anxious faces. What will they eat in the year to come without a crop? At the moment, the grain from the stores was being rationed. A few poor vegetables from small plots were the only fresh food available. Custard apples that grew in abundance in the orchards were unripe, hard and inedible. Fodder was being rationed, so cows gave less milk. Scarcity of food was being felt both in the palaces and hovels. Clan chieftains trapped inside were cursing their luck at being in the wrong place at the wrong time. Only water was sufficient. *kunds, sarovars, talabs* and *baories* provided enough water through rainwater catchment to last for months.

Chittor's army went into wartime alertness. Overnight, even before the Sultan's horsemen came up the winding road to the fort, a spot was identified on it. Much before the first gate, between hard rock faces on either side, a place was chosen for a wall shield. Trunks of trees cut down from the slopes were piled up, boulders and rocks between them were cemented by a strong mortar mixture of lime, jaggery, thatch and lentils. It set in a few hours and a fifty feet tall wall spanned across the road leading to the fort. Hardly a few yards from the gigantic *Padam Pol,* it was perfect armour. Cleverly, this massive wall was perforated by small vents through which arrows could be shot by archers at the attackers. Watchtower guards revised their duty roster scheduling shorter observation periods per sentry and for partners to cover any toilet breaks. This was to ensure premium alertness during each sentry duty. They would watch impassively as the invaders employed catapults to sling large boulders towards the fort which bounced off the plateau's rocky walls. The fort sat like an eagle's eyrie far, far above. Some of the more daring shepherd boys would climb the high rock called *Chittori Tila* behind the villages. It was an excellent observation post. This rock had a local name which was *Chota Pol* because agile young boys could use the rock to climb over the ramparts and then climb down to a goat path on the plateau slope. The path ran through rocks, bramble and *kikar* trees to emerge at the bottom of the plateau but it was so well hidden that nobody could even get a hint of it from the bottom. Ginni would listen to all that was being spoken or done inside the fort and faithfully report it back to the princess.

In the meanwhile, Ratan Singh held discussions every day with the clan chieftains. They were an impatient lot. None of them wanted to be part of a personal struggle between the most powerful man in Bharatdesh and Rawal Ratan Singh. Instigated by Lakshman Singh, they saw this siege as a clash of egos. They wanted it to end so that they could safely leave for their homes. Each one had different solutions and most of them were foolhardy. Only one old chief said, 'I think we will win this tussle if we patiently keep within our fort. The Sultan will soon get tired of waiting. After all, how long can the Sultan keep his troops away from Delhi?' But there were no takers for patience. Besides, their *thalis* were becoming more and more empty.

The one person who no longer appeared in court was Prince Gora Rajsinha. Since the day he had been insulted by Lakshman Singh before all the chiefs, he had hardly left the small palace where he and his son Badal resided, adjacent to the royal palace. After the Council meeting, Ratan Singh had visited Padmavati's uncle to ask his forgiveness. The elder man had been courteous but cool. Badal, his thirteen-year-old son was always eager to meet his brother-in-law because he loved horsemanship and discussed all kinds of horsy tales with Ratan Singh. Leaving their palace, the Rawal had gone directly to *Ba*.

She told him, 'You have much more serious problems to attend to than the bruised ego of Prince Gora. Leave these things to time. Focus on how you will manage the clan chiefs during this crisis. This struggle must be seen as Mewar's fight not just Chittor's war. We must keep their morale high. We must have their support. Lakshman Singh is like a snake spreading his poison among them to weaken you. I have heard that he is also spreading false rumours about *Banni* among the villagers.' In fact, *Ba* and Padmavati helped Ratan Singh a great deal by bringing him opinions of the commoners, his subjects and the bazaar gossip. It was true, that dormant rumblings were rife that the Sultan's evil eye fallen on Chittor due to the *NaiRani*.

Every day, Padmavati would sit for hours at the *chattri* of her *mahal*, her eyes scanning the camp below for some sign that the Sultan was leaving. Often Ambika would sit with her. These days, Ratan Singh left soon after the morning meal to confer with his chieftains and returned only for his noon meal. Even while eating, his face would be grave as his thoughts spiralled around the siege. Padmavati had also become quite cheerless, but Ambika noticed that whenever her husband was home, her friend would put on a brave face. She would tease him, joke and generally try to lighten his mood. During meals, Ambika overheard them talking about the tense conditions inside the fort. The princess would offer suggestions and solutions to Ratan Singh.

Dusk was blanketing the plateau with multiple rows of lights blinking from the enemy tents. The Rawal and his wife were on the roof when a shout and bang shook the front doors of the main palace and floated across the *sarovar* to them. Ratan Singh rushed to the side of the roof overlooking the garden. He could see men and women rushing to the gate. Padmavati, in the meanwhile, called down the staircase, 'Ambi, please send a sentry across to find out what the disturbance is about.'

'Yes, Your Highness,' Ambika replied and ran downstairs. She always addressed the princess formally in Ratan Singh's presence.

Within a matter of minutes, she was back. Holding out a stone like a large hen's egg, she said, 'This was thrown at the gate of the palace.'

Confused, the couple stared at her. Ambika held out her other hand with a crumpled piece of cloth. 'The stone was wrapped in this cloth,' she added.

Padmavati snatched the cloth from her and flattened it on the table. Written on it was on it 'Chittor *chod diyo* (Leave Chittor)'. The three of them stared at it for a long time. Then Ratan Singh angrily crumpled the cloth and threw it far from the roof top. It soared lazily like a white bird before floating down to vanish among the rocks. The princess' face blanched. Ambika licked her suddenly-dry lips. Ratan Singh touched his wife's face with gentle fingers and said, 'Forget it. It is somebody crazy.' But he rushed down the stairs and rowed himself across the lake. Padmavati knew that he had gone to meet *Ba* and seek her counsel. She decided to also go later to meet the old lady.

The next afternoon, a shower of pebbles hit the front gate. When the guards ran out, they found some urchins disappearing round the corner. All they could do was shake their fists and shout at the miscreants. What else can you do with children?

Ba had more news for her. '*Banni,* our people are tired of the siege. They are hungry and afraid. Farmers have no work and the devil enters idle minds. Don't hold this against them but they believe if you, Rani Padmavati, had not been in Chittor, Alauddin Khalji would not have come after us.' She was quiet for a while. Then placing a kind hand on the princess' shoulder, she said, 'They are simple people. Lakshman Singh and Kunwar Vir Bhan are inciting them, raising passions against you. He is telling them that this siege is your fault. Obviously, they have begun to blame Ratan for bringing you here and inviting all this trouble.'

'What should I do, *Ba*?' pleaded Padmavati, aghast that her mere presence was putting the people of Chittor against her beloved husband. 'You tell me what to do and I will do it all.'

'Right now, you can do nothing other than be Ratan's solace. Mind you, *Banni,* I don't, for one moment, believe this Turkish upstart has brought his army here *only* to capture you. We have been waiting for Khalji to attack

Chittor since long…much before Ratan even went in search of the ultimate beauty of the world. Possibly, the rascal's greed for you is only an excuse, but Vir Bhan is making the most of it. He wants the people to force their Rawal to give you up. He is afraid your child will snatch the throne from him because his mother is no longer in the Rawal's favour.'

'But that will never happen. Your son is a man of just principles and he will never take away Kunwar Vir Bhan's right from him. In fact, I won't let him,' said Padmavati vehemently.

'He doesn't know that. More importantly, he is being fed these insecurities by his mother. She believes everybody in the world is as ambitious and grasping as she is. Tch! Tch! And she is supposedly from a noble house…,' *Ba* shook her head. '*Banni*, keep yourself away from the eyes of the people for some time. I don't want them to brand you as a symbol of ill-fortune. You have too many enemies. Let me think how we can overcome them.'

Padmavati nodded and took leave of her well-meaning advisor in a sober, pensive mood. For the next few days, she gave herself up to meditation and spirituality to seek answers. Daily, Ginni would bring her news of the harassment and misery of Chittor's subjects. He also heard enough to know that *Ba's* deductions were right. She realized that despite all her good intentions and sincere prayers for Chittor, its people were turning against her. At first, she could not believe it; that those citizens with whom she had mingled and who had given her so much love could hate her this much. She was shocked at the extent of their hostility. They wanted her to leave Chittor! Having always been in receipt of love and loyalty from the people of Singhaldweep, this reality brought her a lot of agony. Not wanting to disturb Ratan Singh's slumber, she would pace the terrace desperately analysing what she could do to stop this wave of antagonism towards her.

Another thought made her blood run cold. *Who can predict how all this will end? Will history remember me as the cause of Chittor's destruction?* She recalled Gandharava Sena's pride in her. *Would he be told that his daughter had destroyed Chittor, the famed seat of Mewari power? My parents would die of shame.* These thoughts kept chasing through her mind until her head ached. Morning would find her sleep-starved and tired. Despite all her meditation, she was unable to find peace and it showed in her pale face.

After a sleepless night, when a couple of chirps floated in softly, though light did not show in the eastern sky, Padmavati asked for horses to be saddled. She felt a vigorous ride in the cool pre-dawn would clear her head. With only Ambika by her side, the friends trotted out under the starry skies down the paved path that ringed the *garh* alongside the ramparts. The night was desolate, punctuated with only echoes of shouted passwords between the guard towers whose lights shone like a row of beacons along the circumference of the fort. The princess instantly began feeling better. She rode astride, her voluminous *lehenga* spread out to cover her legs till the ankles, instead of side-saddle as women, if they rode at all, did in these parts. Ambika did the same as the cloak of darkness lent both privacy and freedom. Soon, Padmavati clasped her heels around her tan-coloured mare and she lunged forward. Ambika spurred her horse to the same speed following just behind. They went past the royal palace, past the still waters of the *Bhimlat Sarovar*, lit up with reflections of the quiet stars. The palaces and temples were left behind as the two riders veered off into a narrow dust path through the custard-apple orchards. Adroitly, they bent their heads to avoid the low-hanging branches whose ghostly fingers reached to grab them. Galloping hard, they left behind the gloom of the orchards and were soon in the wilderness of scrubs and rocks. In the east, the sky was greying and early risers were lighting lamps in clumps of stone huts.

Suddenly, it seemed to Ambika that another thud of hoofs sounded on the grass-grown path. Before she could comprehend it, another rider thundered past her. The loose, trailing end of his turban brushed across her face, blinding her for an instant. When she opened her eyes she saw an unbelievable sight. The new rider was nearly abreast with Padmavati's horse. His hand was raised up in the air. It held a thin, raw-hide whip with double-switches flying in the air with the momentum of the galloping horse. Even as she stared in amazement, it came down on the neck of the princess' mare…once…twice. The horse reared up on its hind legs in pain and fear as the sting of the thongs cut into her skin. Ambika instinctively gave rein to her own horse to close the gap between herself and the princess. In front of her stunned eyes, Padmavati's horse bolted, streaking pell-mell across the fields, heading straight for the *Chittori Tila* which towered ahead. Once there, the horse and the rider could easily topple over and crash on the sheer cliffs beyond the fort walls. Ambika spurred her horse to go faster. Ahead, the third horse was now slowly cantering on the path in front. As she flew past, Ambika's unconscious mind noted the big, white steed and the gleam of the large peacock *sarpech* that shrieked to her: Vir Bhan!

But she had no time to think. She had to reach Padmavati's wild horse…before it took the princess to certain death. She bent low, clutched the sides of her steed and pulled back the reins as they dashed over rough ground, clumps of grass flying up. She could see Padmavati had tilted to one side of the saddle. *Was she falling off? No. It didn't look that way. Thank God. She was riding astride and more in control.* Even riding hard as she could, Ambika was still some distance away when she saw Padmavati's horse slowing. Even as she peered in the haziness of pre-dawn, she observed the princess was once again erect in her saddle as the brown mare cantered to a stop at the base of the *tila*. When she galloped up, Ambika was panting with exertion, and sweat streamed off her horse. Padmavati had dismounted and was speaking to her mare in low tones, obviously calming her. She turned as Ambika slid off her saddle and ran to her friend. Padmavati was holding her bunched-up *chuneri* to the brow as one eye was covered with blood that flowed down her cheek and dripped from her chin.

Ambika screamed, 'Princess, you are hurt!'

Padmavati shook her head. 'It's nothing, Ambi. Ragi, my horse, is more hurt. The tip of the switches caught my eyebrow.' Ambika began to wipe the blood off her face as the princess squinted down the path they had left behind. It was empty. She murmured, 'I wonder who wanted to kill me so badly?'

'It was Vir Bhan,' said Ambika in a hard voice. 'Let's get you back and then we must tell the Rawal.'

'No. We cannot tell the Rawal. He is under too much stress right now. I cannot add to his worries. Maybe this was just an accident.' She turned to Ambika. 'Promise me you won't breathe a word.'

Ambika nodded though she grumbled, 'What about your safety? This was not an accident. I saw everything clearly. It was Vir Bhan, and he whipped your horse deliberately. Certainly, he wanted to kill you.'

'Don't worry, my friend. I will take care of myself. Though this was a foolish way to get rid of me...where was the guarantee that Ragi would be insane enough to fall from the *Chota Pol*?' The princess shrugged. 'Anyway, we should return. I think Ragi is calm now. Help me up.'

Ambika held out cupped hands for her friend to mount. She used a rock as footrest to pull herself to her own saddle, saying, 'We must get your wound tended.'

'Don't fuss, Ambi. I don't want people to know about this incident. We will tell everyone that a branch hit me in the dark,' Padmavati said, as the friends began to trot back towards the palace. The celestial sphere overhead was rosy and in the distance villagers were coming out to milk their cows. They passed by platoons of soldiers on guard duty rotation. Both women had taken care to sit side saddle and pull their veils down to cover their faces. Still, the few passers-by folded their palms and bowed in greeting to the women riders whose bearing hinted at their noble birth and status.

On the ride back, Padmavati was unusually absorbed. *The wound is probably throbbing but from her expression I am sure, something else is churning in that head of hers,* thought Ambika, glancing at her friend from time to time. But she was too anxious to get back quickly and apply her special poultice on the cut before it became infected. After all, that whip was used on animals too...

In the small *Mahal* dressing room, maids crowded in with hot water, bandages and bowls of a sticky green ointment. Padmavati was constantly fidgeting restlessly. Finally, Ambika placed the last bandage and tied it firmly. 'There. That should ease the pain, too,' she said.

Instantly, the princess said, 'If all the nursing is over, I would request all of you to leave, please.' The maids began to clear the room and in a few minutes they had left. Only Ambika remained.

Padmavati got up from the seat and walked over to the small *jharoka*. A single ray of the rising sun had beamed in, dust motes dancing in its wake. It lighted up the girl's face. Despite the bandage on the head and unruly hair, her flawless skin was creamy, her pink lips velvety and her eyes were like dark fluttering bees. Ambika looked at her lovingly and thought, *her real beauty comes from her soul; the goodness glows on her face. How can anybody want to kill her?*

The princess turned towards the room at Ambika's inquiring visage. 'Ambi, I am the Queen of Chittor, aren't I?'

'Yes, Princess. You are.'

'But if I am killed tomorrow, it will be so easy for my enemies to convince the people of Chittor that I never was their queen; that the Rawal picked me up, an ordinary girl who caught his fancy, during his travels and gave me the position of a queen; a position I did not deserve. It will not take much effort to explain how my death has freed them and Chittor from the threat of the Sultan and that my death was actually of benefit to everyone.'

'But,' stuttered Ambika, 'That's not the truth. The Rawal will never...'

'If they let the Rawal live after me...' Padmavati sighed. 'No, Ambi.The aim of my foes is to wipe away my existence from the memory of the people of Chittor. Maybe the way I am mingling with them...the way I talk to them is making them afraid. They don't want me to become popular with the people. You know how they are whipping up anger against me among the populace. Remember the stones! If I die, and they propagate that I was a bad woman and unworthy of my position, after a while people will want to forget me. By and by, I will actually be forgotten and despite being the princess of Singhaldweep and the queen of Chittor, I will have no place in the history of Mewar.'

'No,' exclaimed Ambika, 'That is not right...that is injustice.'

'Exactly, injustice it is. And I will not sit by passively and allow it to happen. I will not let my enemies win.'

Ambika looked at her with wide eyes, waiting for her to continue. But she remained silent. Padmavati turned back to the *jharoka*. Its illumination lent her skin a patina of gold-dust. Her friend ventured hesitantly, '...We have to be alert to danger...'

Padmavati murmured, 'Yes. That too...' Looking away into the distance beyond the window, she spoke loudly and firmly, 'I will write my story. I will write down word by word every detail of my life for people to read after

I am gone. Let people, their children, their grand-children, their great grand-children...generations read my story and judge me. Let them decide if I was worthy...if I was noble enough to be the Queen of Chittor.'

Her words rang in the small room ricocheting against the stone walls. Ambika stared at her, fascinated by the regal figure of a young queen articulating her remarkable vision.

22

It is not an easy task, thought Ambika as she slowly ambled through the afternoon bazaar. Padmavati's project required sheaves of parchments, ink and quills. This was not Singhaldweep where it was common for people to write and so all these objects were readily available. Here, other than the *pundits* and scholars, nobody knew how to read, and writing was a distant dream. In fact, the only other people who would need such tools to use covertly were those involved in wizardry or witchcraft. So shopping for such objects would raise eyebrows. People may even suspect her of evil purposes. Besides, as Ambika was known to be the princess' chief attendant, the suspicions would directly fall on Padmavati. And anger towards those assumed to be dealing with black arts was bellicose here. So the question spinning inside her head was, *how can I get the things without the scrutiny?*

How could Ambika be resourceful but circumspect? She had reached the end of the bazaar and a few steps away was one of the numerous *vatikas* or gardens. She went in and perched on a stone bench under a huge banyan as ideas chased through her head, one after another. Idly, she looked towards the nearest stall which had hung out long trails of brightly-coloured cloth to dry on a line. It was a dyers' shop. As the pieces of cloth fluttered in the breeze like sails of yachts gliding over the seas during the Annual Yacht Race at Singhaldweep, the idea began budding. *What is a parchment? Cloth, right? Well, actually layers of cloth. Why can't it be made at home? Hmmm...And ink? How do we make kohl? From soot, right? And quills? Easy! Pluck feathers from the ducks in our poultry and pare them. Done!*

Excitedly, Ambika went from shop to shop to buy objects that had nothing to do with writing like a bale of rough, white cloth, bottles of glue and bags of earthen lamps. When she arrived at the *Jal Mahal* towing a boat with her precious purchases, Padmavati, who was drying her long tresses on the terrace observed her with amazement. She ran down the stairs, her fingers lightly touching the cut on her forehead which had healed but ached at times. She burst into the dressing room, just as the bale of cloth was hauled inside. When Ambika had waved off the attendants, Padmavati asked her, 'Are we making new covers for the quilts?'

'No, my dear princess. We are going to make parchment.'

'What?'

'Yes. Tell me did you really think we could have brought parchments for writing in this illiterate but mistrustful land? Already they believe you hypnotize men with your beauty, yanking the tyrant Sultan all the way from Delhi. So they throw stones at your palace and tell you to go back. What would they do if they believed you were also practising black magic?' Ambika smiled at the princess.

'I never thought of that, Ambi.'

'You don't have to. What am I here for?' said Ambika.

'But what is all this cloth for?'

'You will see...,' her friend said enigmatically.

All night, a light burned in the small dressing room. Attendants noticed it but nobody dared to disturb Ambika who was behind the locked doors. Next morning, they found a curious article hanging on a line in the ground level lounge. It was a long train of white cloth made by repeatedly stitching lengths of material one after the other, each cut to a width of sixteen inches. The cloth was quite thick and if anybody had bothered to touch it, they would have realized there were several layers of cloth glued together. Though the Mewari attendants wondered what kind of garment it was, they had become used to the strange activities of the Singhas and so after a few comments, they forgot about it.

The desert air dried the material to a crisp and by evening Ambika was folding it into a neat package. She laid it out the next day to prevent any hidden damp spots. In the meanwhile, Ambika lighted rows of earthen lamps in her room. She placed upturned brass bowls on them, so that the soot accumulated in the bowls. After several bowls of soot were collected, she mixed them with a little alcohol, water and fine shavings of soap into a thick mixture, viscous enough to be picked up on the pointed tip of a quill or stiff brush.

Once everything was ready, she called Padmavati to the *shringar kaksha*. The long, hot afternoon was time for siesta for most palace inmates. Padmavati stepped inside and closed the door. Ginni observed his friends from the open *jharoka*. Padmavati watched as Ambika unfolded a long swathe of parchment on the floor and placed several quills and a bowl of ink beside it. 'Here we are, Princess, ready to pen your life story.' She grinned at the princess like a cat who had lapped up a whole bowl of cream.

Padmavati bent down to touch the stiff, light brown parchment. It crackled slightly as if impatient for words to be scratched on it. She fingered the home-made quills and ink.Then she jumped up to enclose her friend in a hug, 'You are a wonder, Ambika! How did you do this?'

The girl chuckled, 'If you have a strong will, it opens paths.'

'So true,' agreed Padmavati. 'Exactly as it happens with me. Still, it must have taken you a lot of pain to arrange for the writing tools. I noticed the parchment you made with your own hands and in such a way that nobody, even here in the *Jal Mahal* knows about it, Ambi. Thank you, dearest friend.'

'Princess, I believe that is the essence of our endeavour. There must not be even a whisper about this project. We have to do it in absolute secrecy.' Ambika's voice was resolute.

'Yes, Ambi. We have to be careful. Too many people have vested interests to erase me and my reality. They are projecting me as a nobody from nowhere who married the Rawal to realize my ruthless ambitions for the throne of Mewar or as a witch with evil powers...whatever serves their end. If people know I am a princess in my own rights and the ruler of a kingdom, my enemies' lies will be revealed. If people know of my royal blood, they will hesitate to protest my presence. That will not serve the ends of my foes. That is the reason they want to get rid of me so that they can grab the throne of Chittor after Rawal Ratan Singh. If they know I am writing my story, I will become a dangerous threat to them. They will definitely want to muzzle me. They will prevent my story from becoming a written factual account. So that after I am gone, my story dies with me. We have to take all precautions or the truth will never reach the right people.'

'Even in the *Jal Mahal,* one never knows who is loyal to us,' Ambika said, 'I think afternoons and nights are the right time to carry on with the writing. Few people are about. But...nights are not a good idea. The Rawal will be with you, so maybe afternoons are the only...'

'Don't worry, Ambika. I will find a way to steal out at night too,' said Padmavati. She rubbed her hands, 'Let's start right now.' She picked up the quill and then stopped. 'What should we call it? Hmmm...I will...call it...my *Padma-wali*. Yes. That's what it will be...*Padma-wali*. What do you say, Ambi, Ginni?'

'It is very suitable, Princess. *Padma-wali, Padmavati's tale*. Perfect!' concurred Ambika. Ginni, her faithful companion, trilled in agreement from the *jharoka*.

So the friends sat down on the cool stone floor. Ambika stretched the parchment tightly on a low desk as Padmavati dipped a quill in the sooty ink and inscribed

'Om', a mystic symbol representing the holy Trinity, on top of the parchment. Both girls closed their eyes for a moment to evoke the blessings of the gods. Padmavati, once again, dipped her quill and took a moment to gather her thoughts.

'Is this going to be only your story, Princess?' interrupted the intrepid Ginni.

'No. Ginni,' replied Padmavati, 'I want to write about everything and everyone around me. I will try to present an objective view but I plan to include my learnings or opinions too.'

'Oh good! We will also be in her *Padma-wali,* Ambika. After all we are the princess' best friends,' cackled Ginni.

'Something like a journal?' asked Ambika.

'I suppose so,' agreed Padmavati. Then she quickly and deftly scratched some words on the parchment. When she sat back, Ambika silently mouthed the words; *I am Rani Padmavati of Chittor, Princess of Singhaldweep. This is the true story of my life. How I came to Chittor, what happened to me in Chittor, how I have come to this moment in my life is written here by my own hand…*

Every night, the friends would shut themselves in the *shringar kaksha.* With one small *jharoka,* they felt it was the safest place in the palace. When the first chirpings sounded, Padmavati would run upstairs to her bedroom and stealthily slip into her bed. Ambika would sprinkle fine sand over the writing on the parchment which had begun to look as if multitudes of black spiders had left marks of their ink-dipped feet all over it. She would fold the parchment carefully and place it under the garments in the huge, wooden chest which stored the princess' dresses from Singhaldweep. Only Ambika had the key to it. The ink and quills would go to her room. Even if anybody discovered them, they would not wonder because Ambika often used lampsoot to highlight her eyes. Besides, Ambika held a privileged position and was above questions.

One night, Padmavati returned to her *shayan kaksha* to discover Ratan Singh sitting up in bed. 'Where have you been?' He demanded.

'I had gone up to the *chattri*...I couldn't sleep,' casually replied the princess and slipped in beside him.

He lay down and putting his arms around her, held her tightly. 'Don't go away without telling me. All kinds of deadly fears rise up to trouble me when you are not with me, my princess.'

'Uhhh....,' she moaned snuggling against his chest. 'I won't...I promise.' Silently, she berated herself for lying to him...but there was no other way.

'Besides don't go up to the *chattri*. What if an arrow from those vile Turks struck you?' He said.

'So far up? They will never reach.'

'No, my love. Don't be so sure. Two nights ago, the villagers complained that they saw a couple of the enemy soldiers swinging a rope at the walls behind the village. They tried to catapult boulders too but they fell harmlessly on the slopes. They are exploring all ways. And...,' he sighed, '...my chieftains are clamouring for action...'

'But why?' asked Padmavati, though she knew the reason. Mewari chiefs knew how to fight bravely but were incapable of any war strategies.

Ratan Singh turned over, murmuring, 'Sleep, my princess. Soon it will be day and the rigours of life will take over.' She rubbed his back slowly trying to unknot the tight, tense muscles. When his breathing deepened, Padmavati soundlessly left the bed. She went to the terrace and woke up Ginni.

'Oooooh...waz...t...matter...,'he mumbled opening one eye.

'Wake up, Ginni,' Padmavati said urgently, 'I want you to go to the enemy camp and get news from there.'

'Now? I'm sleepy. Why don't you float there yourself?'

'Oh Ginni! You know my consciousness is unable to move about freely. Please. Please go now. Before dawn, they will be relaxed and you may hear something useful. Please Ginni, dear.'

'Oh okay...won't even let me sleep,' grumbled Ginni, fluffing up his feathers, ready to spread his wings.

'Thank you, sweet friend. I will wait in the meditation room for you. Come back before others wake up,' instructed the princess.

In about an hour's time, Ginni hopped through the *jharoka* into the dark room where his friend waited anxiously.

'What news?' she asked.

'Dissent! Dissent!' announced Ginni gleefully and went on with the details.

'As I flew over them, the sea of tents loomed up in the darkness, punctured by the dim fires burning beside nodding sentries. I searched for the tents of the commanders. Their views were more important than the foot soldier's; the lowest echelon always cribs...Soon I had spotted one; larger, circular not conical, lit-up and guarded. Inside, two men casually garbed in *shalwar* and flowing long shirts, without armours huddled together. They spoke in whispers and grunts, but I heard them clearly.

"It is becoming impossible...," said one.

"Hungry men are angry men...what can we do?" said the other.

"Food can be arranged but the soldiers have been away from their homes for too long. After the campaign down south, the Sultan brought them here promising them gold and loot to take home. But it has been seven months now. Where is the gold? How long will they stay here among dusty rocks far from home? I fear already some are deserting…"

"But the Sultan will have our heads if this muttering reaches his ears," said the first.

"But my soldiers will revolt any day and cut off my head when I am sleeping. Frankly, I agree with the men. How long can empty promises fill hearts that are missing wives and children?" hoarsely demanded the second.

His companion looked around fearfully and snapped at the speaker. "Are you mad? Shut up. Even listening to this kind of rebellious spittle will have me killed as a traitor. Don't you know the Sultan?"

"I do! I do! But disaster is in the air. A mutiny is about to break and whatever you and I say or don't say, we cannot stop it."

So the time is ripe, Princess, to crush them,' summed up Ginni.

Padmavati smiled. She had heard enough. 'No Ginni, my friend. Any battle, even the one you win, means death and destruction. I have a better idea. We will win this battle without shooting a single arrow or losing one life. I am going to propose a solution which is radical and risky, but your information has given me the assurance that it will work.'

'Ummm…,' hummed Ginni, hopping from one foot to other.

'Don't dance.' She wagged a finger at him. 'I need your help. Listen….' And she told him her idea. 'But you have to convince the Rawal and *Ba* that the enemy is really ready to rebel.'

Ginni nodded his head. 'Your idea is a good one. I will tell them what I have heard. Will you give me the pomegranate that *Ba* saves for your breakfast? She is always shooing me off when I try to pick out some seeds.'

Padmavati laughed. 'Yes, of course, I will. Now I will have to rush and get dressed. There is hardly any time before we leave for the meal with *Ba* and wearing all those clothes and accessories take so much time,' she said, standing up. Flinging over her shoulder a reminder to Ginni, 'Don't forget to come when we are at the *Ba's* palace,' she ran out. Ginni preened, swelling into a small ball. His black, beady eyes danced at the prospect of a pomegranate breakfast and he flew off to look for a juicy worm or two.

Ratan Singh stopped eating when Padmavati announced that she had a suggestion to break the siege. *Ba* put down the ladle she was using to serve them *kari,* a tangy gram-flour curry. All three were sitting on *pidis,* low stools with individual short tables laid out with large silver plates and numerous matching bowls filled with fruits, savouries, spicy fritters and sweets. It was a splendid meal, but all thoughts of food vanished as both listened to this girl-princess, who constantly surprised them with her astute observations.

Before she began speaking, the princess had ensured they were alone. She had sent out the attendants, shut doors and windows and checked behind curtains and under beds for hidden interlopers. Even then, she continued to speak in a low voice. When she finished, Ratan Singh raised a finger for silence. He looked around the room and called out, 'Ginni!' The large ornate mirror on the wall trembled as their parrot-friend stepped out from behind it. He glided down to Ratan Singh's shoulder and nipped gently at his earlobe. 'Did you actually hear the commanders say that the Sultan's soldiers are going to revolt?'

Ginni squawked, 'With my own ears.'

Ratan Singh persisted. 'Ginni, you know more than you let on. You heard the princess' suggestion. Do you think it may work?'

Ginni hopped from one foot to another. Then he flew down to the Padmavati's table. Picking up a couple of red seeds from her plate, he chewed at them with his eyes half-closed. He looked as if he was ruminating over Ratan Singh's question but the princess knew he was relishing the pomegranate. *Ba* only shook her head silently mouthing, 'Greedy parrot!'

The three waited till he swallowed the juicy seeds. Then the parrot opened his eyes and looking directly at the Rawal, said, 'Sultan Khalji is in a bind. He promised his soldiers heaps of gold and treasures they could loot from Chittor once they had entered the fort. But there does not seem even a chance of lifting the siege. His army has been on campaigns for many months now. They are tired and are ready to revolt. If he is given an offer that will let him retain his self-respect, he will take it. And look at us, we are being slowly starved. Our treasury is full of gold but can we eat gold? Why not use it to attain our freedom? But our offer has to be worded carefully. The Sultan must not suspect that our food stores are low and we are desperate. To succeed, we must be careful how we make the offer.'

His elbows resting on the low table, chin in cupped hands, Ratan Singh considered the ploy suggested by Padmavati; a hundred chests of gold coins to break the siege. The Sultan's army could return to Delhi, their pockets jingling with Chittor's wealth. It would spare the powerful ruler an embarrassing mutiny and allow him to boast that he had forced Mewar to pay him. And Chittor would be free.

The Rawal raised his eyes to his mother's face. *Ba* sighed, 'Ginni is right. We can't eat gold but it can buy our freedom. It is a good plan to chase the dog from the door but you have to first appease the jackals within our walls.'

Ratan Singh nodded and then lifted his chin. Looking directly at Padmavati, he said, 'You have always been my oracle. This is the only way to overcome the threat and I will take it despite sure opposition from the clans.' He rose to his feet, the rest of the meal untouched on his table, and opened the doors. Slipping his feet into the embroidered slippers resting outside, he strode determinedly towards the Council chamber.

Inside, the women sat silently, as the attendants moved like shadows clearing the room of untouched dishes. Ginni still perched on Padmavati's plate, digging contentedly at pomegranate seeds.

23

Mrinalini gazed at ribbons of the moon's reflection rippling on the lake as the sound of Uma's voice trailed off. Silence filled the space winding its tentacles around the girls.

Eventually, Uma said, 'You are very quiet.'

Mrinalini's eyes reluctantly moved from the shifting images in the water. She shook her head, muttering, 'I can't get over how cruel people were in those days. Mentally and emotionally torturing a girl, even wanting to kill her simply because they were afraid of her influence.'

'Yes,' agreed Uma. 'Ever since Padmavati stepped into her marital home, she faced opposition, enmity and sheer injustice. Her beauty, her kindness, her wisdom and her husband's love only made people envious. Except Ratan Singh and *Ba*, nobody bothered to understand her needs, her dreams or her desires. And you are right. . .she was a young girl in a complex world trying to adjust to its expectations.'

'But look at her spirit! Nothing cows her down. In the gloom surrounding her, she constantly searches for light. Her optimism is her pennant. It flies high. . .nobody can haul it down. Her spirit is so lofty that it always finds a way through the hurdles to shine brightly. And people around her are drawn to that glorious light emanating like a halo from her. The same light terrifies her foes. Unable to comprehend the source of her strength, they want to douse it. They fear it, so they attack it.'

Uma's voice was slightly hoarse, as if overwhelmed by emotion. She said softly, 'So beautifully, almost like a poem, *bhayeli*, you have said it all. Your words have described so aptly the precious pearl that embodies the essence of Padmavati; her inability to see any evil for her eyes were blinded by divine love. Her enemies believed it would easy to do away with her but she was protected by her very innocence. Until she herself…'

'Your story has enlightened me enormously, Uma,' admitted Mrinalini. 'The historical archives tell us very little about this great Rani of Chittor. It only repeatedly recounts her unparalleled beauty and how a Sultan who ruled over half of India lusted after her and captured Chittor to win her but never obtained her. What I didn't know is how eagerly she wanted to become part of Chittor. But when she was distrusted, plotted against, nearly murdered, she stood up against her foes. It was an ingenious idea to write down her true story and bequeath it to posterity.'

'You are right, *bhayeli.* But to tell the truth, cruelty is not restricted to any period. Even now, people are equally bad, if not worse. It is just that history has still not recorded the events of our times,' quipped Uma.

Thoughtfully, Mrinalini wondered, 'Isn't it strange that she believed so strongly that generations to come will read the *Padma-wali* and thus know about her?'

'Why? What is strange about it?' Uma's tone was really perplexed.

'Well, in those days most people were not literate and more so, the women. How did she guess that in the future time, people will be able to read the written word and she left her story for them to read? How did she envisage the coming time so accurately?' Mrinalini was back to being a reporter. But this time she answered her own query. 'Padmavati was unique. Her impairment was that her thinking was ahead of her times. She was born in the wrong era. The world was not ready for her brilliance.'

'Rightly so, and it became her undoing,' whispered Uma.

'Instead of hailing her naturally enlightened acumen and astuteness, people around her doubted her intentions, were wary of her kindness and blamed her for circumstances beyond her control. So sad…' Mrinalini's voice broke.

Once again a lull intervened as each girl introspected on the appeal of a personality lost in the mists of history yet resurrected to life in the midst of these ancient ruins. Almost, as if she was standing with them, right there, observing the fragments of moon floating below.

Mrinalini shook her head, 'Úma, I want the *Wali*. Now. Now. Give it to me, I can't wait any more.'

'I cannot. It is in a place a little distance away. Until we go there, I can't,' the girl replied calmly.

Mrinalini heaved a deep sigh. Controlling herself, she said, 'Ókay. So when are we going there?'

Uma was silent.

Mrinalini wondered if she had been offended. Dousing her impatience, she asked softly, 'What happened after that? Was Ratan Singh able to take the offer to the Sultan?'

'Oh!' exclaimed Uma instantly, animation kindling in her voice, 'there was a great furore in the court. The chiefs of Mewar wanted to open the gates of the *garh* and sally forth to fight the Turks like the brave-hearts that they were.'

'And die as martyrs so that songs could be composed to their heroic sacrifice!' Words dripping with sarcasm, the journalist sneered, 'Always the problem with Mewar's warriors…all brawn and chivalry but no brains! Why didn't they listen to reason for a change?'

'Hmm…,' agreed Uma, 'Thankfully, Ratan Singh had more faith in his wife's advice than in his clansmen's blind bravado. Padmavati's offer was duly scripted on a silk cloth and a messenger was dispatched with the scroll to enemy camp.'

24

The man went on foot. It was impossible for a horse to go over the wall shield that blocked the road beyond *Ram Pol.* So, under the cover of darkness, he slipped out of the *Chota Pol* behind the village. He spent the night sleeping on a flat rock a little below the *Pol.* When the skies lightened, he cut through the thick undergrowth and even stepped precariously through narrow rocky ledges to reach the main road leading down to the Gambhiri aqueduct. This way he did not reveal the secret path into the *garh* via the *Chota Pol.* He was unarmed, for that would seem less threatening. The Sultanate's forces were barbaric and used their swords more than their tongues. At the least suspicion that this was a trick, they would instantly slit the messenger's throat. And the purpose of the entire endeavour would be lost.

Mewar's chieftains were lined on the ramparts of Chittorgarh peeping through the arrow slits in the walls to observe the messenger's progress and discuss the outcome.

'Do you think it will work?' asked a one, a richly embroidered shawl covering his head and half his face against the morning chill.

'If it doesn't, it is the Rawal's fault. We warned him enough, didn't we?' said another, his handsome face pinched by the breeze.

A portly man pulled his cloak around his thick body and remarked, 'At least we will not have to fight these jackals, if they agree to leave.'

On the *chattri* of the *Jal Mahal,* Padmavati, Ambika and the inmates of her household were also trying to catch a glimpse of what was happening, but the angle was too skewed. They consoled themselves that Ginni was flying alongside the man, though nobody knew about it except his friends. Only *Ba* and Ratan Singh were not to be seen anywhere.

The messenger wore Chittor's livery of red and yellow. Once he was in the open fields, the bright colours flashed amidst the un-furrowed plains, marking his presence. Eventually, when he was a hundred yards from the camp, his path was blocked by the camp sentries. They came running up and in no time he was in a pincer hold with unsheathed swords bristling at him. Squinting down, the viewers could see a dozen soldiers searching through his clothes for weapons and discovering only the scroll. They could see the rough gestures of the enemy asking him about it. The messenger was begging them with folded hands. Finally, the chief of the guards untied the scroll. His eyes scanned the unfamiliar script which he could not read. When the soldiers began to march Chittor's messenger towards the centre of the camp where the Sultan's tent was positioned, the spectators heaved a sigh of relief. Despite all the criticism showered on Ratan Singh, it seemed his clansmen were quite keen to see if the Rawal's ploy would work.

Unseen and hidden, Ginni had already attained a seat inside the Sultan's tent. What he saw there made him gnash his teeth in frustrated anger. The scourge of India sat facing the painting of Princess Padmavati, a cup of wine in hand, while the treacherous Chetna lolled beside him extolling the Queen's virtues yet again. The chief of guards burst into his tent. Chetna's oily recanting broke off abruptly. About to speak, the Chief realized that he had interrupted a private session. Instantly he fell to the ground in a deep *kurnish*. It was well-known that the Sultan could unleash his fury at the least provocation. But grape-juice had brought a mellowness in its wake and Alauddin turned to look at the man scrabbling at his foot. 'Yesss...,' he slurred.

'*O Sikander-i-Saini*, O great King! Chittor has sent a missive,' the Chief uttered in a voice choked with fear, still looking at the ground.

'Chittor?' bellowed the Sultan. 'Who has come? The Queen?' Lascivious eagerness flashed in kohl-ed piggy eyes even as Chetna stared at the Chief, his jaw open in amazement.

'No Sire. It is a mere messenger,' said the hapless man waiting for blows sure to rain on him for not saying what the Sultan wanted to hear.

But Alauddin had been in his cups all night and felt too lethargic to even kick the man. He muttered into his beard, 'A messenger! What do I do with a messenger? Take him to the commanders and let them decide whether he should live or die.' He gestured to Chetna to continue with his sycophantic ranting and turned back to the image of Padmavati smiling at him from the canvas. Disgustedly, Ginni flew out.

'*Ji Huzoor*. As you wish, Sire,' nodded the Chief of Guards and crawled backwards to the tent flaps like a huge scarab beetle. Once outside, he released his pent-up breath and gave one great leap, shouting, 'Eeiyaaah!' So glad he was to have emerged from the Sultan's presence with his head still on his shoulders that he could not help the jubilation which he followed up immediately with a devout, '*Allah-O-Akbar*! Then, suddenly aware that the Sultan's guards were staring at him curiously, he composed himself. He began to walk towards the commanders' tents to inform them of their leader's wishes. Ginni flew over his head.

The *ulema* translated Rawal Ratan Singh's message, written in scholarly Sanskrit, to the five generals, each commanding the two infantry units, the two cavalry units and the single unit of war elephants, respectively. When he finished, the five men stared at each other perplexed. *Was Chittor bribing them to go away?*

'Read it again,' said one. So the *ulema* read it again and translated it verbatim to the commanders. Ginni knew the translation was correct and his beady eyes swung from one face to the other to measure their response.

'Does it say that the Rawal will give us all this gold so that we retreat?' finally asked another commander. Never in their military campaigns for the Sultan, had they come across such a proposal, especially one from the proud Mewaris.

'Yes Sire,' replied the *ulema.*

For the commanders, it was a wonderful solution. By accepting the proposal, they would be able to quell the mutiny and save their face. But there was one unknown factor in the calculation...Sultan Alauddin Khalji! *How would he respond?* Each commander's expression asked that question.

Eventually, one of them said the obvious. 'We won't know the Sultan's mind unless we ask him.' Everyone sighed. Alauddin's mind jumped in unpredictable ways but the cat had to be belled...

As they got to their feet, the guards asked, 'Sire, shall we slice this man's head off?'

'No, no,' said one. 'He has to take Sikander's reply back. Put him in chains until then and bring him to the royal tent.' The trembling messenger, who was only a young boy, was nearly faint with fear. He was sure that these fierce men would kill him.

So a procession led by the five commanders, followed by the *ulema* and trailed by the guards dragging the Mewari boy in chains slowly wound its way through the camp towards the huge royal tent. Ordinary troopers stood still watching this strange activity early in the morning while many left whatever they were doing and followed the group. Ginni flew above their heads, unnoticed.

When the royal guard announced that his commanders wanted to urgently confer with the Sultan, Chetna was taking a break to wet his dry throat with gulps of wine. Alauddin was first and foremost a military leader and he never forgot that. He always gave the highest priority to his military commanders on whom his entire Sultanate's existence depended. So they were immediately granted audience.

All five commanders, the *ulema* and the guards, who pushed Chittor's messenger down to the ground, bowed in a deep *kurnish*. The Sultan barked, 'Rise!' Everyone rose, but stood with eyes lowered to the carpet. Alauddin waved a hand to Chetna who jumped to quickly pull the silken cloth over the painting veiling it from pedestrian eyes. The senior-most commander raised his eyes only when his ruler said, 'Speak!'

'*Sikander-i-Hindustan,* Chittor has sent us a message,' he began.

'I know that. What else should I know?' Patience was not his virtue.

'They are offering us gold...'

That made Alauddin's small eyes drooping with alcoholic drowsiness widen. 'Are they now? Why?'

'In return, we must break camp and raise the siege, Sire.'

'What!' exploded the Sultan and then was silent. He stared at the veiled painting for a full minute while the company in the tent did not even dare breathe. Then he turned to the speaker and said, 'Well!'

The commander, a greybeard, gulped but went on bravely, 'Sire...the soldiers are grumbling...no gold has entered their pockets...they haven't seen home for close to a year now. The siege is not...not going well...' He trailed off, while the other four commanders nodded their agreement.

'Hmmm....,' grunted the Sultan while Ginni perched right over his head, shifted from one foot to the other. 'They will send a hundred chests of gold, you say?'

'That is what the message says, Sire,' said the veteran.

'Alright,' the Sultan said abruptly. 'We agree to Chittor's offer. Add fifty more chests of gold in our counter-offer. When all of it reaches us, Sikander's army will break camp.' He waved his hand. 'Send back my reply to the Rawal of Chittor.'

'*Huzoor*,' bowed the commanders and began to back out while behind them the guards were already about to reverse through the tent flaps with their prisoner. The generals were struggling to look grave. They did not want their faces to betray the joy leaping in their hearts that their irascible despot had agreed to Chittor's offer so easily.

Suddenly, the Sultan bellowed, '*Roko!* Stop!' Chetna jumped and the wine sloshed from his cup. Everyone down the line braked instantly. The guards dragging out the captive lost balance and tumbled all over the poor boy who squealed like a hurt puppy.

The entire company came back to stand like culprits before the seated ruler. When he had their attention, he reprimanded them, 'You are fools! Did you think I would let off these proud Mewaris so easily?'

Obediently, all of them shook their heads; five generals, four guards whose prisoner was anyway lying on the floor weeping fearfully, one *ulema* and Chetna.

'This Hindu pride has to be crushed; crushed under the Turkish heel; crushed to dust.'

Five generals, four guards, one *ulema* and Chetna nodded vigorously.

'They have a made an offer to my army. What have they offered me? Nothing.'

Five generals, four guards, one *ulema* and Chetna shook their heads from side to side.

'I also have my desires; I also have a thirst.'

Five generals, four guards, one *ulema* and Chetna nodded vigorously.

'Take them my offer.'

Five generals, four guards, one *ulema* and Chetna nodded again.

Ginni was immensely enjoying the pantomime being staged below him until Sultan Alauddin Khalji loudly declared 'My army will lift siege only after I see the face of the great Padmini, the Queen of Chittor!'

About to nod, the heads of the five generals, four guards, one *ulema* and Chetna froze in mid-action like marionettes with broken neck springs.

There was complete silence as each face in the tent expressed various degrees of shock. Only the soft weeping of the boy could be heard. One of the guards kicked him viciously which only made him shriek louder. 'Oh, take him away,' roared their ruler. The four guards swung into action dragging the boy out of the tent.

His five generals were still standing before the Sultan, uncertain if they had heard correctly his demand. It was a custom with the Khalji army to carry off wives and daughters of vanquished or killed kings to either add them to his harem or kill them. But this was different. He wanted to see a reigning Rawal's consort's face. His craving was an insult to the Rawal, irreverence to the queen and a radical break from social tradition. It was covetous appetite at its ravenous worst and even his boorish companions were appalled.

'So? What are you waiting for?' Alauddin shouted. The commanders came to their senses and executing deep *kurnishes* bowed out of his presence murmuring, '*Ji huzoor! Ji huzoor!...*' while the *ulema* scuttled out as fast as his short legs would carry him.

Outside, the generals looked at each other's long faces silently. Then one of them shook his head. 'How could he...? After such a humiliating demand, Chittor will withdraw this offer. And we will be left high and dry.' The others made similar noises but they had their orders.

'*Ulema*!' roared one. 'Write down the Sultan's message and give it to this snivelling fool.' To the guards, he said, 'Escort Chittor's messenger with our demands to the border of the camp and kick him back to the *garh*.' Having done their duty, in a mutually dejected mood, the five commanders returned to their tents.

Inside the royal tent, Ginni was furious. He nearly flew down to attack the barbaric, monstrous Sultan with his beak and claws but stopped himself in time. He remembered he was here on Padmavati's behalf and she was waiting for his report. Attacking the Sultan relaxing on the cushions would be suicidal. Instead, he fluffed his feathers and released a stream of gooey shit right on the Sultan's upturned face. Up jumped the man screaming for his body guards to catch the bird who dared to enter his tent and use him as a toilet. Of course, it was impossible for them to grab the quicksilver Ginni, who glided out adroitly. While the guards shouted, he flew up and away from the camp.

Rays of the noon sun had begun to slant across the burning rocks of the Aravallis when a shout went up from a sentry post. An alert soldier had picked out red and yellow flashes moving through the undergrowth. The shout was taken up by the other posts, 'He is back!' By the time the boy, half-dead with fear and gasping for breath, reached the *Pol*, a sizeable reception was awaiting him. The administrative head or *Mantri* of Chittor did not spare a thought for the physical or emotional distress of the messenger. He held out his hand. The boy retrieved the leather scroll from his clothes, placed it on his outstretched hand and collapsed in a heap at his feet. As the mother fell crying on the prostrate figure, the *Mantri* mounted his horse. Sitting on its back, he told the father, 'Come tomorrow to the treasury to collect his reward. Be glad your son was returned alive by the vultures.' And he spurred his steed towards Ratan Singh's palace.

Ginni glided in through the open door of the princess' *shringar kaksha*. Padmavati and Ambika were sitting on the floor. The parchment was spread out and the princess was competently and quickly scratching in letters, words and sentences. Her dexterity in handling these homemade tools had increased considerably but still her fingers could not keep pace with the speed of her thoughts. The instant Ginni settled on the floor beside her, her heart gave a leap and a drop of ink left the nib quill to spread rapidly into an uneven blot in between graceful curlicues of the Brahmi script. But Padmavati did not see it. She put down the quill and sitting back on her haunches, said, 'So?'

Ginni described what had occurred at the camp. For an instant, red clouds of rage swamped the princess as the full force of the affront hit her. Before this, her feelings towards the man who had laid siege to Chittor in the vain hope of attaining her had been ambivalent. She believed he had been misinformed and misled by Raghav Chetna into a foolish action. But hearing his outrageous demand, she was furious. *Who does this Alauddin think he is? Am I a court dancer to be viewed?* She was filled with anger, disgust and hatred for this unknown barbarian. By the time news had reached the *garh* of the messenger's return, Padmavati's natural prudence had cooled her rage. She realized now what a deep insult this arrogant demand was to the Rawal and feelings of guilt washed over her. His chiefs would deride him. They would accuse him of inviting this ignominy; bringing dishonour to Mewar all because he decided to offer the enemy a bribe. They did not know that it was *her* plan, not *his*, that had backfired. She had to do something about it. She had to find a solution. It was her responsibility.

She rushed to *Ba's* palace as had become her habit whenever she was troubled. She found Ratan Singh there. He was dressed for the Council meeting and had come to seek *Ba's* blessings. Padmavati gave him a small, encouraging smile but her heart sank. Guilt stabbed her through and through as she thought, *is he going to open the Sultan's message before the whole council? No, he must not...*

He gave her the charming smile that had always managed to send a thrill through her, saying, 'Your plan has done the trick. The Sultan has sent back a message. So he must have agreed.'

Realising he was still blissfully ignorant of the disaster awaiting him, she asked, 'How do you know?'

He shrugged, 'Otherwise the dead body of our messenger would be hanging upside down for all to see that he had rejected our offer.'

'Hmmm...I see.' She tried to rescue him by suggesting, 'Don't you think you should read the message by yourself first before announcing it to the Council?'

'I could.' He nodded, 'But the entire Council is waiting eagerly to hear the Sultan's message. Besides, I am impatient to tell my chieftains how we were able to win this battle without a single casualty. I must go, my love. I will return soon with the good news.' And he rushed out, not seeing the hand she had raised in vain to stop him.

But *Ba* had noticed her agitation. '*Banni*, come to me,' she said as she sat by the window stitching mirrors on a *choondari*. Padmavati went to sit at her feet. *Ba* kept aside her threads and combed her fingers through the princess' silken tresses. 'Tell me, child. What troubles you so much? I see grey and heavy clouds on your brow.'

Padmavati turned to the gentle old lady and laying her head in her lap burst into tears. They poured like the raging summer storm as the young girl could no longer hold back all her sorrows; her yearning for her parents, longing for her beautiful land, her disappointments in Chittor, the rejections she had suffered, her fear of people who wanted to hurt her, her guilt at being the reason of her husband's humiliation and now, this final insult.

When the princess could cry no more and only wet hiccoughs came up, *Ba* turned up her lovely face, now swollen and red, with gentle fingers. Padmavati could not resist the love and kindness in those old eyes and out tumbled the entire camp episode as seen and heard by Ginni.

Leaves of the huge *peepal* outside the window mirrored the rays of the dipping sun. The reflections formed golden patterns on her face as Padmavati's voice trailed off into silence. The two women gazed out of the window for a long, long time while the sky wrapped itself in pink chiffon, then violet silk and finally purple satin spangled with silver dots. Fireflies began to blink in the bushes when *Ba* softly said, '*Banni,* did you know that the real ruler of Mewar is actually Ek Linghji? The Rawal of Chittor is only the *Dewan* or custodian of Mewar. He administers Mewar and protects its honour in name of Ek Linghji. You are the *NaiRani* of Chittor. Therefore you, too, are co-custodian of Ek Linghji's Mewar.' She was quiet for some moments. Then placing a hand gently on the head of the girl at her feet, she asked, 'Now tell me, *Banni,* what are your thoughts?'

The girl stirred. Never had she felt so helpless. 'All I know, *Ba,* is that I don't want a single drop of Mewari blood to fall for my sake.'

None of the women remarked on the fact that Ratan Singh had not returned as he had promised.

By now, he must surely know. Does he hate me? The younger one quailed at the thought.

Does he blame me for exchanging the innocent joys of an ordinary life with the daily insults of being in the limelight as the Rawal..., wondered the older one.

'What answer will Ratan send back?' sighed his mother.

'Only the obvious one, *Ba*...Alauddin's demand will be met...He will see the face of the Queen of Chittor,' declared Padmavati in a firm voice.

25

Swords waved threateningly as the chiefs of Mewar advanced on the figure seated pensively on the throne. Each one was shouting so loudly at the top of his voice that words collided into an unintelligible cacophony. Still, the Rawal did not raise his head or make a move to escape the hovering blades. He was too deeply sunk in sombre reflections. After one's ears got used to the noise, one realized that the fierce warriors were not abusing their Rawal but the smug Sultan.

With measured steps, Ratan Singh had confidently walked into a crowded Council chamber glad to see all the lords present. Only Prince Gora's seat was empty which had disappointed him. *Finally, my princess will receive the honour she deserves. The moment the Sultan's message is read out, I will inform the Council about the real architect of this offer. They will know how wise my princess is,* he had thought. *It would have been nice for her uncle to hear it, too.*

He had taken his seat on the great carved chair. The murmuring in the room had died away as everybody settled down. 'We are ready to hear the Sultan's message, *Mantriji*,' Ratan Singh had said.

The *Mantri*, his whiskers bristling, pompous with importance had unrolled the leather scroll on which was pinned a parchment. And he had begun to read,

'Rawal Ratan Singh,

Here are my conditions for withdrawing the siege of Chittor.

Send to me

A hundred and....' The chieftains in the room frowned.

'...fifty...' The Rawal frowned.

'...chests of gold coins...'

'What?' Rana Lakshman Singh yelled.

'And the most imperative condition that allows no negotiation is...' The *Mantri's* voice faltered and fell silent. Every pair of eyes was on his face.

Ratan Singh raised his head and said in an impassive voice, 'Read on, *Mantriji.*' The man cleared his throat nervously but remained silent. 'READ ON!' barked the Rawal.

'Umm...Sire!...it has come to our knowledge that the Padmini of Chittor, Queen of Mewar is a noble woman of great allurement and beauty. The Sikander of Hindustan, Sultan Alauddin Khalji wants to offer her a gift. His desire is to reward her with his appreciative presence and the beneficial light of his eyes as he looks upon her angelic face.'

The room exploded and nobody heard the *Mantri's* last words... 'From her fervent admirer, Sikander-i-Saini, Sultan of Hindustan'

The warriors, old and young, leaped to their feet, unsheathed their swords and demanded that the Rawal lead them into battle against this dog of a Sultan who dared to tear apart the dignity of their Queen. That was Mewari blood! Whatever may be their internal differences, one pin-prick to the honour of Mewar and every man was ready to avenge it with his life. And Alauddin's demand cut deeper than the sharp point of a pin.

Hindu tradition ruled that removing the veil of a woman of Mewar in the presence of a strange man was like denuding her. It was the ultimate dishonour not just to her but to her family...to her lineage. In this abhorrent instance, a non-Hindu, a foreigner, a Turk dared to express the desire to look upon the unveiled face of a Mewari Queen!

'A deranged desire!'

'...should only be answered by the sharp edge of our blades against his throat!'

These sentiments and more were flung by the furious chieftains and the clamour was rising uncontrollably until Ratan Singh stood up. Holding up both hands, he shouted, 'Stop! Stop!' It took some time for his voice to be heard but finally the babble dropped. 'I request all of you to go home and think on how we should proceed with this heinous demand. Certainly we have to act, but taking hot-headed decisions will only worsen the situation. Let us meet again tomorrow morning.' Saying this, he turned on his heel and left the chamber.

Ratan Singh was weary. He was a warrior and he knew how to vanquish the enemy facing him. Honour was his strength, but he did not know how to deal with this attack on his dignity. He mounted his horse but did not give direction to it. So his horse trotted down the familiar path and soon the Rawal found himself in front of Padmavati's palace. As the guards came running to take the reins of his steed, he descended and rowed himself to the *Mahal* in the lake where the earthen lamps shimmered softly to the strains of devotional songs or *kirtans* for the evening *aarti* in Ek Linghji's temple.

Instead of going into the *shayan kaksha* to seek out his wife as was his habit, or the terrace where they lounged, he went right up to the *chattri*. He sat facing the dusty plains and the camp of his enemy. His heart was full of despair. When Padmavati was told by her maids that the Rawal was in the Palace, she came up the stairs and found his dark, huddled figure silhouetted against the starry sky. Stealing up behind him on bare feet, she stood there silently for a while. Then she went up to him and whispered, 'You are my life but if you don't even breathe, how will I live?'

He gave no sign that he had heard for some time and when his wife was about to speak again, he suddenly turned and fell at her feet, crying, 'Forgive me, Princess. I have wronged you.'

Padmavati was startled and cried out, '*Hukum*, what are you doing? I am your *ardhangini*; your other half.

We are two hearts in one; two bodies in one. You cannot... must not stoop below my heart.' She raised him up and he leaned against her as tears coursed down his cheeks. She wiped them with her *choondari*, murmuring, 'My precious Gem! Hush! My love...no, no hush...'

In a broken voice, he whispered, 'I chose the incomparable lotus from a bower full of flowers. Promising to gift her the world, I brought her home. But did I keep my promise?'

'Hush, my Gem.' His wife put her fingers against his lips.

But the Rawal could not stem the bleeding of his heart, 'All I brought my beauteous lotus was pain, disrespect and shame...'

'No, no.' Padmavati vigorously shook her head. 'Has a woman even got one measure of the love that you have given me? Has any Mewari wife ever been more eminent in her husband's regard as I have been? Has any woman been the jewel in her husband's crown as I have been in yours? No, my precious Gem. You have given me everything and even more. I don't think anybody has ever received so much.'

Ratan Singh was more in control of his emotions now. He looked down at her fair, upturned face glowing in the darkness like a moon. Again she said, 'Believe me, my sweet. I am supremely happy.'

His dark eyes reflected twin images of her face as he said, 'You will be even more glad to know that tomorrow we sally forth to teach that barbarian Turk a lesson. Tomorrow, we fight.'

'No.' The sound was loud, firm and final. 'No blood will be shed.'

'The time for that is past,' Ratan Singh said. In succinct words, he told her what had passed in the Council chamber, ending with, 'An insult such as this can only be washed off by blood.'

'If it is Mewar's tradition to wash off insults with blood, then it will be my blood, not Mewari blood that will flow.' Padmavati stood tall and erect as she said this.

'I don't understand, Princess. What do you want?' Ratan Singh was frowning.

'This whole idea of bribing the Sultan was my idea. The purpose was to free Chittor from the siege without losing a single life. Right?' She asked.

'Yes, but...'

'The plan misfired. Our enemy is a wily fox. You give him one chicken, he wants the whole coop...besides, I realize what a tyrant he is. He is not concerned about his troops' welfare or that they may revolt. He is selfish and greedy. He only wants his toy.'

'We know all this about him. What is your plan?'

'My plan is simple. Give him what he wants,' said Padmavati simply.

'Give him what he....? But that is foolishness. You have just said it—his demands will never end. Besides, NO...,' Ratan Singh exploded. 'That lecherous Turk will not lay his sinful eyes on your pure face, Princess. I will not tolerate it. I would rather kill him.'

'And die for your intolerance...? That is not wisdom, my Gem,' Padmavati countered.

'Preserving one's dignity is sometimes more important than wisdom, Princess,' pronounced Ratan Singh gravely.

'If you die to preserve your dignity, then of what use is that dignity?' argued Padmavati.

'An honourable death is far better than suffering humiliation,' replied Ratan Singh loftily.

'That is the Mewari way, not my way,' said Padmavati. 'Look for a way to survive, so that....,'

'...so that you live to fight another day...?' interrupted Ratan Singh. Bitterness had crept into his tone.

'...perhaps that day, victory may decide to come over to your side,' finished the Princess.

'Anyway, there is no point in this argument,' declared Ratan Singh. 'Tomorrow, be ready to pray for my victory by smearing my forehead and my sword with the auspicious vermilion. *Ba* will explain the ritual to you.'

In answer, the girl-princess slowly walked over to the low stone balustrade before the *chattri*. She stood there contemplating the steep drop to the sharp, pointed rocks. Ratan Singh came up behind her and observed her set expression. 'What is it, Princess?' he asked, a sudden fear clutching his heart.

'What is the point...? Won't it be better to end it right now, right here?' Padmavati's voice seemed to come from a distance.

'Point...? End? What?' demanded her husband, searching her face. She was silent. 'Princess?' pleaded the Rawal.

'What is the point of my life? If my destiny is to be only a lure that traps men's base desires and eventually becomes the cause of many deaths, isn't it better to eliminate such a foul life as soon as one knows this?' Her voice was low as if she was speaking to herself while her eyes remained focused on the rocks below.

'Princess!' exclaimed her husband. 'How can you say this?' He enclosed her in his arms and carried her bodily to the *chattri* seat. 'How can you even think your life is foul? You are my sun, my moon and my whole world. How can you consider ending such a precious life? You are not responsible for the sins of other men. Don't you dare say that again. Do you have no thought for me?'

'But I will be responsible for men dying if you don't stop all this talk of war. My mind is made up. If there is fighting tomorrow, the first death will be mine. I will no longer speak of it. No, I will do it and when you are not there to save me,' mumbled the girl against his chest, sounding more like a truculent child than a Queen of the realm.

'But, my princess, if we don't fight this ferocious beast, how do we free Chittor?' asked Ratan Singh, frowning into the darkness.

'By giving in to his demands,' replied Padmavati.

'Alright. So we give him the gold, but what about his demand to see your face?' He could not fathom her thoughts.

'So he sees my face. How does that harm me? Or harm you?' reasoned the girl.

'It harms my family honour. It undermines my prestige as the Rawal of Mewar,' said Ratan Singh quietly.

'Do you remember whose honour and safety comes first in your list of duties as the ruler of your land?' It was a quiet question to the Rawal.

'People of my land...my subjects...they come first, always and every time.' Ratan Singh's tone was heavy and flat.

'And who comes last, my Gem?' prompted his wife.

'I, me, mine always comes last,' whispered her husband.

'I don't think we need to discuss this any further,' she decided. 'Let's go to bed, my Gem. You have a long day ahead of you in the Council, tomorrow. And *Ba* and I have a lot of arrangements to make.'

'*Ba*?' Ratan Singh's eyebrows climbed up. 'She knows of this?'

Padmavati smiled.

'And she approves?' The son asked again.

Padmavati smiled again.

26

'No! I don't agree with this,' Mrinalini vehemently declared. 'How could she give in to such an atrocious demand and in so docile a manner? How could she, who was so full of fire, suddenly turn demure and dutiful? It doesn't go with the strength of her personality.' She shook her head.

Uma said slowly, 'Yes, Padmavati was quite strong. But something was eroding her confidence. By then, a feeling of self-reproach was building up inside her. Though she became conscious of it much later, Padmavati had begun blaming herself for all the troubles that had descended on Ratan Singh and Chittor.'

'Oh!' exclaimed Mrinalini, 'Do you mean to say that this unconscious self-guilt was goading her to go through this undignified gesture?'

'Maybe she hoped by letting the boorish Turk look upon her, he could be persuaded to go away. Maybe she thought that by suffering the humiliation, she could save both Ratan Singh and Chittor from further pain. That she did not want any bloodshed to avenge her honour was certainly true.'

'Oh my God! What a Queen!' exclaimed Mrinalini, somewhat understanding the mind of a desperate, young girl torn between self-respect and obligation. 'Look at her courage. She was willing to face social ostracism so as to fulfil her commitments to her people. Truly she is a queen who deserves a mention in our history.'

'Yet,' interjected Uma, 'it was denied to her. That is the reason I am so keen that you should have her manuscript, the *Padma-wali*. With your capabilities you will be able to reveal the truth. Finally inform the world about the real Padmavati.'

Strangely, this time the mention of the epistle did not make the Mrinalini insist on obtaining it. Instead, she said, 'Okay! Okay! Go on with your story, Uma. I can't wait to hear whether Padmavati really indulged the fancy of her lecherous admirer.'

The girls were still standing at the pavilion on the arched facade of the garden. Behind them the wall sported a tarnished mirror and before them the gently flowing waves of the *sarovar* reflected the night sky. Uma raised her face to the stars overhead and murmured something that sounded like, '*Aabh ni aavjo, bhayeli...*'

'What did you say?' queried Mrinalini, knitting her brows. The back of Uma's head only shook from side to side in silent denial. 'Please go on, Uma. Don't stop now; not at this point. What happened?'

'From here, the *Padma-wali* gives quite a detailed picture of the events. I think the princess was able to describe many things without actually being present at the spot mostly due to Ginni. He had become the princess' eyes and ears. He was everywhere...like...those black machines,' She pointed upwards to the ceiling where a mounted camera pointed to the stairs.

'Oh you mean Ginni was like a CCTV camera for Padmavati. He recorded everything that was happening and reported it back to the princess.'

'Something like that...,' agreed Uma.

'Whatever...,' Mrinalini waved her hand, adding, 'Please continue with the story, Uma. I can't bear to wait anymore.'

27

When the hot rays of the sun finally beamed to the earth, Chittorgarh's special day was nearly half done. Residents of the entire fort had been up and about their various tasks since the first hour of the day. While the palace chefs under *Ba's* supervision were toiling at rows of enormous roaring *chulhas* or open cooking stoves, the women and attendants were decorating the presence chambers and dining halls of the royal palace with leaf and flower buntings. They hung up gaudy *torans* and *bandhanwar* worked in mirrors and embroidery to frame all doors and windows. *Bandhej* and *lari*-work scarves wrapped the marble pillars, fluttering gaily in the breeze. Huge wall tapestries displaying war elephants and the emblem of the Rawals of Chittor were spread across the wall behind the main dais. This was where a row of intricately-carved and ivory-inlaid low tables and matching stools awaited the chief guests. In another room, large silver platters or *thalis* were being arranged with vermilion, sandalwood paste, earthen lamps and auspicious rice to welcome the visitors in the true Mewari tradition.

Streets weaving through the fort, the villages and the bazaars wore a festive look with coloured streamers and buntings strung across them. Men, women and children had pulled out their best clothes; men in white with the tails of their bright turbans flowing down their backs, women in their brightest *lehenga-aangi* and *choondari*. The children ran about in gay clothes. They bathed their cattle and anointed them with vermilion.

The chieftains of Mewar were dressed in their finery. Fine brocade *angarakhas* fell to ankles and chests were covered with ropes of gold braids and pearls. A variety of rich *sarpech* glittered from silken turbans; ornamental scabbards were strapped on and formidable moustaches were waxed to upturned tips. Even the noble ladies were caught up in the festive frenzy. They decked themselves with their newest jewels, pearls and gem-encrusted *lehengas,* though they would remain sequestered in the palaces. The soldiers of the Rawal's army were garbed in new livery with gleaming weapons. Horses and elephants were caparisoned with gold-embroidered cloth and displayed jewels on their heads. Horses even wore bracelets on their forelegs. The animals were skittish with excitement. Ginni was everywhere at once, his beady eyes taking in all the sights.

The Rawal was convinced that the Sultan's visit to Chittor must echo the grandeur and formality of royalty calling on royalty. It must be an interaction between peers, between equals. So however uncivilized or unreasonable the other ruler's demands may be, he should be accorded the state honours due to the eminence of his position. He is the *atithi,* the guest and in Mewar, they believed the *atithi* to be akin to God. So he must be welcomed with all the tradition, ceremony and warmth of the famed Mewari hospitality.

The day after he himself had been flummoxed by Padmavati's decision, Ratan Singh had announced it to his Council. It had been like raising a desert storm. The chieftains of the realm had flung metaphorical sand into his face, blinding and deafening him with their furious words. It took a very long time for Ratan Singh to get his own words and logic across. Eventually, they had listened and Ginni had nodded from the open *jharoka*. After the first flush of incredulous indignation had passed, many of them had reflected on the Queen's decision. Here was a young and beautiful woman willing to sacrifice decorum; suffer this indignity to save Chittor from the siege of a demon. She had put Chittor's honour before her own; this was an abstraction easily understood and accepted by the Mewaris. However, Ratan Singh had noted that both Rana Lakshman Singh and Kunwar Vir Bhan had stood aloof when the protests were pouring in. The vultures were hovering…

Once he had the empathy of the chieftains of Mewar, he urged them to withhold their disgust at Alauddin's coarse demands and give him a taste of Mewari courtesy and manners.

'Let us honour him like an Emperor and it might soften his stance towards Chittor. Don't forget he has conquered Ranthambore but left his own son to administer it. He raided Gujarat but has still not annexed it. His Sultanate is now too vast. He is keeping administrators in charge of the remote kingdoms he has conquered. They send him revenues to maintain his armies. If we are able to impress him, I can broach a similar arrangement with Mewar. We send him revenues and in return he leaves us alone. What do you say?'

The Thakurs and Ranas had been quiet. Only Lakshman Singh had remarked, 'So we sell our independence? We auction Mewar's honour?'

'It is called diplomacy, Rana Lakshman. Till now, Mewar has believed only in the glory of martyrdom. We have believed that when the enemy faces us, don't try to talk him out of war. Go headlong into battle and lose hundreds of brave men. Mewar has legions of dead heroes but how do they help our land when a new enemy attacks? Is it not wiser to save lives than lose them? Kingship does not only mean leading men into battle, it also means using tact and diplomacy to avoid war.'

'Wise words,' pronounced one grey-haired chief. Twirling his white whiskers, he asked, 'But will it work?'

'There is no harm in trying, is there? After all, if the new queen is willing to make such a great sacrifice to bring peace, isn't it our duty to make an effort too?' Ratan Singh pleaded.

'Yes. It is our duty,' said several voices. Others joined in. Only Rana Lakshman and his disciple Vir Bhan smirked and left the room.

When the news reached Prince Gora, he had visited the *Jal Mahal* and tried to dissuade Ratan Singh from going ahead with Alauddin's indecorous demand. The Rawal took him to Padmavati. She had explained to her uncle the purpose behind the appeasement. He was not fully convinced and warned them that risks were involved.

'And what of your reputation, my daughter?' He had asked Padmavati.

'My reputation lies in the safety and harmony of my people, Uncle,' she replied passionately. The older man had gone away impressed but apprehensive.

It had taken the villagers one week to break the wall shield preventing entry into the seven *Pols*. It had served them well by keeping the enemy at bay effectively but now they were inviting the enemy into their fort. Finally, piles of debris had been rolled down the slopes and into the ravines lining the road. Water carriers had washed the paved stones clean. The seven *Pols* and the fort walls were gaily bedecked with marigold garlands.

An air of excitement prevailed in the royal palace and all its adjoining buildings. Only Rani Prabhavati's palace remained gloomy and drab. The queen was in a vile temper and even a mention of the happenings outside meant the speaker would be whipped. Keeping windows shut, she lay feigning a headache in her dark bedchamber. As her palace attendants tiptoed around the room, Vir Bhan came striding in. Before they could stop him, he entered his mother's chamber. Nobody heard what mother and son spoke but after he left, Rani Prabhavati had asked for some fruits and *chila* pancakes and demanded that her bathwater be readied.

The only person untouched by all the fervour was the *NaiRani*. Despite a night spent in writing her journal, she rose as usual before light, bathed, meditated and shared a light meal with her husband. Ratan Singh observed her calm demeanour and wondered, *what makes her so undaunted and self-assured?* He asked her, 'Are you not planning to dress in your best jewels and dress?'

She looked up at him, her lovely almond-shaped eyes serene. 'My Gem, you know that jewels, gold or raiments do not interest me. The love you wrap me in is the costliest robe I own and I array myself every day in it. What is so significant about this day that my *shringar*, my ornamentation needs more than your love to adorn me?'

Ratan Singh eyes shone with unshed tears. He could not speak. He picked up her hand, as satiny and delicate as a flower petal, and placed his lips reverentially on it. Padmavati smiled and said, 'Only remember to follow *Ba's* instructions to the letter. The pavilion in the garden has been prepared as she had wanted. Make sure that the barbarian is brought there immediately after noon. Light from the sun is just right then.'

'Yes, my princess,' said Ratan Singh. Her composure had soothed the tensions bubbling up inside him. He stood up and gave her a tiny bow. Grinning boyishly at her, he complained, 'Between the two of you, my wife and my mother ruling my life, I am just a slave.' His wife threw a cushion at him which he caught neatly. Giving her another grin, he went out, as Ambika took the cushion from him.

Left alone, the two girls looked at each other. Ambika raised an eyebrow. 'I can't wait anymore for night to fall and then write everything in the *Wali*,' replied Padmavati to the query, muttering almost to herself, 'Time is running out...,'

Frowning, Ambika came closer to her and whispered fiercely, 'What does that mean? Time? Why is it running out?'

Padmavati only shook her head silently.

'Please Princess, why did you say that? What do you know? Have some tidings come to you during your meditation?' Ambika's voice held a note of apprehension.

In response, Padmavati took her friend's hand and nearly dragged her down to the small dressing room which had now become a place where the girls and Ginni could converse in complete privacy. She shut the door letting shadows play in the room. Ambika frowned in puzzlement looking into her friend's face. 'No, Ambi,' Padmavati shook her head, 'I have not received any messages. It is just that...,' she stopped speaking and turned towards the *jharoka* which let in the latticed sunlight.

'Just what, Princess?' Ambika asked quietly.

'I have this great urgency inside me to complete my story quickly. As if...as if...there is very little time to do so. That's all,' she said, turning back to her friend.

Ambika gave a nervous little laugh. 'You scared me with all your talk of...time running out.'

'But right now, we have time only till noon to write. So...run and get all our things,' she said, giving her friend a push.

Soundlessly, Ambika opened the door and peeped out. *Nobody will question why the princess is shut in her dressing room today,* she thought making her way to her room.

In the meanwhile, Ratan Singh, riding his stallion, trotted along the flag-stoned circular path observing the arrangements, deliberating, *all this is a ruse to lull the enemy. Will it work? Will he agree to my terms?* Unseen by him, Ginni flew from tree to tree following him.

Suddenly, the trumpets sounded a fanfare to warn the reception party that the guests had rounded the corner and were now in plain sight, approaching *Ram Pol.* Winches had rolled down the gates forming a great wooden drawbridge stretched across the wide chasm that formed a natural obstruction when the gates were up. Ratan Singh galloped to *Ram Pol,* where an excited group of bobbing turbans in all the hues of the rainbow could be seen. Quickly, he dismounted, flinging the reins to a groom and went forward, patting the pleats of his turban and rolling the ends of his stiff whiskers upwards.

In full array, the Sikander of Hindustan came towards them prancing on a magnificent pure white Arab horse with trappings of gold and silver. He was a tall splendid figure in purple robes with a long silver undershirt and pants. On his head was a round turban of spangled gold. Peeping from its centre was the peak of the customary Turkish skullcap. An egret feather quivered, clasped on a huge ruby *sarpech*. His dark, hooded eyes looked straight ahead. Beard and whiskers well-groomed, his narrow face looked grave, in fact, the thin long nose with flaring nostrils and unsmiling lips almost made him appear as if he was constantly sneering at the world. Ranged on either side of him on equally impressive steeds were his five generals, only a little less richly and elegantly clad than he was. Accompanying them, to the Rawal's extreme annoyance, was the wily fox, Raghav Chetna. While the first row looked like guests invited to a lavish banquet, behind them stomped a large platoon of cavalry, complete with coats of chain mail jangling, armed to the teeth. Looking at them, Ginni wondered, *was the Sultan coming on a social visit or to war?*

But the Rawal was prepared. He nodded to his soldiers, who instantly formed a double row behind him, their spears crossed. Behind them, more soldiers stepped into formation, their swords bared. Ratan Singh walked up to the Sultan sitting on his horse. Putting his palms together, he bowed low and said, '*Sikander-i-saini*, Sultan of Hindustan, welcome to Chittorgarh. The chieftains of Mewar and I are honoured to have you as our *atithi* and guest today. We are delighted to offer you our *atithi-satkar* and the hospitality of Mewar.' And then he waited, his palms still together.

There was utter silence as everyone, even the generals stared at Alauddin. Eventually, a small smile played on his thin lips. The company present audibly released their collective breath while Ginni executed a hopping dance on his perch above the gates. The Sultan began to dismount, so a groom from the fort ran up to help him and hold the reins. Instantly, the generals also dismounted and threw their reins to the grooms who came up. Of the same height but thinner than the Rawal, Alauddin appraised Ratan Singh from head to toe. Then he gave small laugh that did not reach his eyes. 'If the Rawal of Chittorgarh comes on his feet to welcome me, I should also stand on my own two feet, shouldn't I?' Alauddin's voice was deep and hoarse, as if his throat has been bruised by the wine he drank so copiously.

'*Ji Huzoor, Shehenshah,*' came the instant reply, in unison from the generals and Chetna, while his soldiers bowed their heads silently.

Ginni observed the chieftains of Mewar. *Were they also going to kow-tow to the Sultan?* But they looked to their Rawal. Not at all fazed by this curt response to his courteous words, Ratan Singh stood to the side and made a sweeping gesture with his right hand, indicating his guest precede him. As the Sultan stepped up, the Rawal walked at his elbow. His generals and Chetna fell in behind them. The moment the Sultan's armed guard began to follow, they were stopped by the soldiers of Mewar. Ratan Singh murmured, 'Chittor's gates are open for the Sikander and his generals but the Sultan's army cannot enter the *garh*.'

Alauddin nodded, as if he had expected this. His hand made a cutting gesture behind his back and his soldiers halted outside *Ram Pol*.

Inside the gate awaited an open horse-carriage decorated with strings of marigold. Its double seats were piled with cushions and sausage pillows. A yellow and orange wooden ladder was placed against its side. The Sultan climbed in and settled into the cushions followed by the Rawal of Chittor. Backs covered by brightly embroidered cloth, gaudy tassels hanging from the necks and head dresses worked in gold, the pair of black ponies hitched to the carriage stamped their hoofs. 'Hup-hup,' shouted the livered groom holding their bridles. As the ponies trotted, the carriage wheels rolled and the groom walked alongside. Following it came three more carriages with Alauddin's commanders and Chetna. Behind them came the chieftains of Mewar. In slow motion, the cavalcade proceeded down the inner road lined with Chittor's soldiers in ceremonial attire with bared swords that dipped in salute to the royal personages. Behind them, the Rawal's subjects crowded the ground. As the procession went past, they shouted, 'Sultan *ki Jai*! Chittor *ki Jai*! Victory to the Sultan! Victory to Chittor!' Alauddin was pleased by this ceremonious reception and he dipped his head to the people acknowledging their greetings. At first, the generals smiled. But their attention was soon caught by the guard towers along the ramparts. Being military men, they narrowed their eyes and nodded knowingly to each other, *if only we could have a plan of their fortifications...*

All at once, the eyes of one general fell on Chetna. The blackguard was enjoying his brief stardom in the fort where he used to bow down to even the lowest of the Rawal's officers. The general spoke in a low tone, 'Chetna, why did you not tell us their defence layout till now?'

Chetna, startled out of his smugness, stammered, 'I never noticed it before. Besides they have revised and reinforced the system, I think.'

'Then you will make a sketch of their new defence systems today and bring it to me when we return. It must be true to details and facts,' said the General, giving him an icy stare. Nobody in the Sultan's camp liked the traitor.

Trying to wheedle out of this risky business, Chetna said, 'I? I? But what do I know of military affairs?'

'Enough to sketch the guard towers, the number of soldiers in them, breaches in the ramparts, position of the

Pols, gates, palaces and villages,' growled the General. 'It is an order, Chetna, you viper!'

Chetna was caught between crossed swords. If any of Chittor's chiefs, officers, soldiers even villagers suspected him of spying on the fort defences, he would be put to the sword. On the other hand, the Sultan's general would surely have him killed if he did not obey him or made faulty sketches. He gulped. Patting the bag slung at his waist in which he always carried parchment and charcoal, he muttered, 'As you say, *Janab*.'

Ginni cackled softly hearing this dialogue.

In the carriage, the Sultan turned to the Rawal, 'So when do I see the glorious Padmini you keep hidden in your palace?'

Ratan Singh's blood boiled at the insinuation that his wife was a pretty object that decorated his home, but his face was impassive, as he said in a soothing tone, 'All in good time, *Sikander-i-saini*. First, you must relax, freshen up and partake some Mewari dishes especially concocted for you by the *patranis*. The journey up the mountain must have tired you out.'

Alauddin gave a small laugh. '*Patranis*, eh? *Patranis* have cooked for me?'

Ratan Singh nodded, thinking, *how conceited he is! I must cater to this ego of his to get my way through.* He knew that no Rani would ever cook for a Muslim, regarded as untouchable by the strict traditions of caste followed by the Mewaris. *Ba* had brought together a group of lower-caste villagers and supervised them to prepare the meal. Even the cooking was done outside the palace kitchens, under the custard apple trees. Once the Turks had eaten, the dining hall would be cleansed of their defilement with *gangajal* and cowdung and their dining vessels thrown away.

Nevertheless, when the Sultan's group entered the huge hall scented with flower buntings and incense, they were fully impressed by the veiled ladies singing and circumambulating them with the silver *thalis* and lamps to welcome them. They assumed the women were noblewomen from the Rawal's family. They didn't know they were the common women from the villages as even the palace maids had refused to confront the scourge of Bharatdesh.

Once the *atithi* were seated, the chieftains of Mewar also took their seats. Then began the spectacle as course after course entered the hall, held high on the shoulders of servers. Huge golden plates encircled by matching bowls in various sizes placed before the guests began to fill up with fritters, sauces, curries, mounds long-grained scented rice, a range of roasted and fried breads and endless sweetmeats. There was *dal-bati churma* and *methi-bajra poori, laal-maas* and *mohan-mass, ker sangri* with *bajra roti, gatte ki pulao* and *mewari kadi, aam ki launji* and *boondi raita*. To cool off the sharp, spicy and tangy zing on their tongues there were helpings of *badam ka halwa, dil khushal, churma laddoo, mawa kachori* and *gujia*. Ginni could not restrain himself and snatched a *gujia* that Chetna was about to bite into. He screamed angrily at the bird who sat on a high alcove and gleefully dug into the sweetmeat. Servers plied the *atithi* with more and more coaxing them sweetly to try each dish many times over. The Sultan and his generals, half-starved with the scarcity of rations in the camp, gorged themselves until they were lolling on their cushions unable to eat another morsel. A slight signal from the Rawal and the tables were cleared swiftly and silently. He and the Sultan sat at a special table away from the rest. While the guests belched contentedly chewing *paan* and *supari*, Ratan Singh said softly, 'You can see, my lord, that Chittor lacks for nothing. Mewar is affluent with gold, food and the loyalty of its brave men. The *Sikander-i-saini* is welcome in Chittor whenever he wishes to visit. Mewar will be happy to share her wealth and soldiers with the Delhi Sultanate to ensure peace in the region.' And he held his breath.

'Splotch!' a stream of red *paan* juice made a mess on the white marble floor. Ratan Singh stopped himself from wincing. Alauddin's expression said that as far as he was concerned, it was quite alright to dirty your host's home in this rude manner. As a servant cleaned up the floor, Ratan Singh waited. Finally, through a mouth filled with *paan* the Sultan managed to say, 'We will see. We will see. And now for the Padmini...' Tiny drops of *paan* juice sprayed the Rawal's face. He stood up with a sigh, *I have to go at it slowly.*

'Certainly, my lord,' said the Rawal courteously. 'But only you will have a view of her. Your men have to stay here.'

'Yes. Yes.' Alauddin turned to his generals and said, 'You can amuse yourselves as you like till my work is done and we leave Chittor.'

They stood up and executed deep *kurnishes* and remained bowed until the Sultan left the room with Ratan Singh. Then they rushed outside ensuring Chetna was with them and strolled towards the gardens surrounding the *Bhimlat Sarovar*. The chieftains of Mewar stared at their departing backs in surprise.

For a moment the parrot-mole was confused whom to follow. Then he decided to accompany the rulers.

The royal carriage with the Sultan and the Rawal halted at Padmavati's palace. Guards flung open the gates. Women veiled in gaudy *chuneris* sprinkled them with rose petals as the men entered. But the Sultan was too impatient to pause for the *tilak* ceremony. He strode ahead, his head turning here and there seeking the beauty of his dreams. Ratan Singh ran after him and guided him up the stairs to the pavilion. There, a group of soldiers in Chittor's livery met them. Before he could protest, they bound Alauddin's eyes with a black cloth and guided him to a wide mirror placed high on a wall. The mirror reflected the *Chaurasi Deva Sarovar*. At its uppermost edge, the first step of the *Jal Mahal* rising from the water was visible. A double row of soldiers, their swords bared and held aloft, formed a wall behind him.

'What is this?' roared Alauddin, hearing the clang of swords. 'Is this a trick? Are you taking me captive?'

'No, my lord,' Ratan Singh said in a calm voice. 'As you are aware, the ladies of Mewar do not show their face to any man who is not family. It is a matter of great sacrifice on the part of the Queen of Chittor that she has agreed to unveil her face for you.'

'So...?' angrily asked the Sultan.

'You will see the Queen of Chittor, but only in this mirror. You will see her reflection and with that you must be content,' he explained quietly with a glance at his soldiers.

Alauddin did not like it one bit. His dream had been to see the famed beauty, talk to her and, he believed, to charm her into entering his harem. But surrounded by this small army of Chittor, he had no choice but to agree to this arrangement. So he nodded, swallowing his ire.

Instantly, two soldiers stepped up, one on his right and the other on his left. Their swords came up to his exposed neck, sharp blades held to either side, holding his head erect and facing straight ahead. If his head twisted even slightly to either left or right, the blades would gash his neck. Ratan Singh untied the black cloth from the Sultan's eyes. Alauddin balanced his head carefully and looked into the mirror. Slowly, very slowly, the row of soldiers behind him moved, half to the right and half to the left. The blue waters of the *sarovar* were revealed in the mirror, cool and pure. As Alauddin stared into the reflection, a face appeared.

It was floating above the water, only exposed till the chin. Fair and glowing skin like petals of white lotus, dark eyes fringed by impossibly thick curled-up lashes like fluttering fat black bumblebees, a patrician nose ending in a cupid's bow of rosy pouting lips. Wisps of dark hair framed this alluring face. Alauddin was stunned into silence. *How could a woman be so ethereally bewitching? Is she real?* Still as a statue, he forgot about the swords held to his neck. Mesmerized, he was drowning by the second into a pool of enticement. He could not breathe. He could not tear his eyes away from this tantalizing sight. Eventually, he let out his breath whispering, '*Ye Allah*! I am lost.'

Instantly the curtain of soldiers closed behind him and the magical sight vanished. The blades at his throat loosened. Alauddin turned around, thirsting for another look at the enthralling beauty. But no! There were only rows and rows of soldiers and their swords. The Queen of Chittor was gone.

'My lord, we should leave.' Ratan Singh was at his elbow.

'Can't I see her once more? Only once more?' The Sultan of Hindustan was pleading like a love-sick youth.

'No, my lord. You wanted to view her face, once. It has been done,' said Ratan Singh, gently guiding Alauddin down the stairs and out of the gates to the waiting carriage. As the horses trotted down the road to *Ram Pol*, Ratan Singh began once again, '*Sikander-i-saini,* have you considered my offer of keeping peace between the Delhi Sultanate and Mewar?'

'You are too impatient, Rawal,' snapped Alauddin irritably. 'Let me think about it. Let me consult with my advisors.' Through his head only one thought chased its tail. *I must have her. I must have the Padmini. I must have her...must...must...have her.*

Rattan Singh's heart sank with gloom and utter disappointment. His ploy had not succeeded. *Alauddin is too wily,* he thought angrily.

The carriage reached *Ram Pol* and rolled to a stop just inside the huge gates where the chieftains of Mewar were ranged. Chittor's soldiers were also standing in formation just inside the gates. Outside, the Sultan's armed platoon waited alongside a queue of wooden carts heaped with, boxes of gold fulfilling the additional demands made by the Sultan. The generals and Raghav Chetna were mounted and ready. They looked quite pleased with themselves. The Sultan's horse was being brought to him as both rulers descended from the carriage and walked to the gates. Everybody expected Ratan Singh to say his farewell at that point. But the Rawal felt that his proposal may be considered more seriously if he extended the courtesy by accompanying his *atithi* a little further. So he walked out of the gates at Alauddin's side.

When the pair was about ten yards from the gate and the Sultan's platoon a mere two yards away, Alauddin turned to Ratan Singh and enclosed him in a hug. His hand behind the Rawal's back made a gesture to his soldiers. Instantly, their horses leaped forward and surrounded the two men on the ground. Alauddin released Ratan Singh, whose arms and head were clasped in a pincer hold. The rest of the soldiers aimed their arrows towards *Ram Pol* and the shocked spectators. Ginni emitted loud squawks as Chittor's soldiers rushed forward, but a rain of arrows arrested their charge.

The Rawal of Chittor, Ratan Singh had been captured by the Sultan of Hindustan. As he was bundled onto a horse, hands strapped behind his back and taken away hemmed in by armed soldiers, all he heard were sounds of chaos behind him and men shouting, 'Pull up the bridge.! Shut the gates! Lock *Ram Pol*!' But he didn't hear anyone shouting, 'They are taking our Rawal! We must save him!'

It was as if Chittor had given up on him; as if he had lost Chittor.

28

'We have to save him!' Padmavati jumped up, the quill falling from her fingers and the bowl of ink overturning on the floor. Ambika picked up the parchment just in time, as the ink flowed towards it.

Ginni, who had brought the news, muttered darkly, 'If he is still living...'

'Don't you dare, Ginni! Don't you dare say one ill word for the Rawal,' shouted the princess, her breath coming in gasps. Then she ran out, followed by Ambika, who had the presence of mind to lock the door of the dressing room with the precious journal lying there in full sight.

She rushed after her friend, shouting, 'Princess!' Attendants, servants and guards looked at both women anxiously. News of the disaster had already spread in the fort.

Padmavati stepped into her meditation room and composed herself into the lotus pose, murmuring, 'I must see that he is safe...that he is not hurt.' She closed her eyes to transcend into the spiritual realm. She used to be so adept in journeying from one domain to another that it usually happened in seconds. But nowadays, she had often found her path blocked. That day, when she was so desperate to travel, she could not. She tried several times but could not leave the physical plane which had turned upside down with recent events. Its turmoil affected her mind, which darted here and there seeking escape. Serenity within and mental focus were the two essentials in this art and she could attain neither of them right then.

Tears streaming piteously down her lovely face, the princess looked helplessly at her friends. 'How will I know how my precious Gem is?' she cried. Covering her face with hands, she was shaken by a storm of despair and bitter grief. Ambika's cheeks were wet, too.

'Girls! Girls!' scolded Ginni. 'Have you forgotten me? Now stop crying this minute, Princess. How can you be so weak?' He reminded her. 'Now is the time for which you have been groomed...to be resolute and calm in crisis. Have you forgotten your lessons? You cannot afford to break down.'

Padmavati wiped her face with the back of her hand like a little woebegone girl. 'Hmmm...you are right. It's just that my heart is breaking...I can't imagine the torture my Gem must be suffering. If only I knew his situation... I could be braver,' she said in a small voice. Then stretching a hand to Ginni, she implored, 'Will you go right now and find out?'

'Not until you show me you are as strong as you really are,' said Ginni, firmly.

Wiping her face roughly with her *choondari,* the princess blew out her cheeks and crooked her elbows at the shoulders, saying 'See! I am as strong as Hanuman, the monkey god.' Ginni cackled at her mimicry and even Ambika gave a watery smile. 'Now, please go Ginni. And come back quickly. I won't breathe till you do. GO!'

Ginni swooped through the wide open *jharokas* and soared up in the sky to cross the ramparts, flying across to the enemy camp. Both girls turned from the window and Ambika said, 'You haven't had your lunch. We have been so busy with the journal that I didn't notice how time flew. Let me get you a platter of your favourite *gatte ki khichri.*' Ambika also remembered the locked dressing room and the secret within it. *I must put it away in the chest,* she thought, getting to her feet.

'No, no, Ambi. I can't eat. Nothing will go down my throat. It is blocked with grief.' She shook her head and then muttered, 'All my fault...all my fault.'

'But why, Princess? How is it your fault?' Ambika reasoned with her.

'If only…if only I had not suggested to the Rawal to use this opportunity to wriggle into the Sultan's favour. If only I had not given him the idea to placate the Sultan and save Chittor from his hawkish gaze. If only…I had not inflamed that barbarian's base instincts by revealing myself. I thought I was being very clever by dangling a carrot and then using it to dig a safe hole for us…now look where my arrogance has led me….' Padmavati tears began to flow again.

'No Princess, it was not your fault,' consoled her friend. 'How can one control circumstances? Or change what destiny has decided, and especially anticipate the workings of a beastly mind?'

'Look, Ambi, look where my stupidity has brought me? I have lost the most treasured gift that God gave me, my husband, friend and lover. Is this my destiny?'

'No, no, Princess,' Ambika exclaimed, gathering the broken girl in her arms.

Right then, in glided Ginni. He perched before the two girls and cocked his head. 'Is she crying again?' When Ambika nodded silently, he added, 'Okay. I won't say what I saw….'

Instantly, Padmavati sat up. Kneeling on the carpet and facing Ginni, she said, 'I am not crying. Tell me Ginni, is my Rawal alright?'

'Yes, he is. He is being held prisoner and is surrounded by guards all the time. But he is fine. He is not being tortured. He is allowed to eat proper food and has a comfortable bed. It is just that he is not permitted to leave the tent,' Ginni pronounced.

'Oh thank you, Ginni. Thank you. You have brought me the most wonderful news,' said Padmavati trying to embrace her parrot friend, who slipped out of her hands.

Ginni did not like hugs and embraces like the girls did. It embarrassed him!

'Here is something that the Rawal has given for you.' And from under his wing, Ginni picked out a ring with his beak and offered it to the princess. The diamond on it flashed as he dropped it in Padmavati's open palm.

'His wedding ring! I gave it to him...told him never to take it off,' breathed the princess and slipped it on her thumb.

'He said to tell you that this is proof of his well-being. Besides, one never knows who may force it off his finger... those Turks!' And he spat to show his disgust.

Ambika spoke for the first time, 'I am glad the Rawal is well and safe, but if they have not tortured him or, God forbid, put him to their sword, why are they holding him?'

'Good question,' quipped Ginni as both girls looked at him, expecting more. 'Exactly my question, too. So I explored a bit and heard the generals discussing that capturing the Rawal was trick devised by the Sultan.'

'Trick? Why?' Padmavti put her head to one side. Now that she knew that Ratan Singh was safe, the cogs of her astute mind had begun to turn...questioning, analysing and evaluating the situation.

Ginni observed the girl before him as the last rays of the dying sun formed a golden halo around her. Even despair and grief could not dim her beauty. 'He wants to use the Rawal as bait,' said the bird.

'Bait? For what?'

'Not for what...for whom. You are the catch! He is confident that as long as the Rawal is in his power, you will do anything to free him, even offer yourself to him. He wants to use the power of your love to break you.' Ginni's voice was flat.

For a long time, there was silence in the room. Outside the *jharoka*, birds returning to their nests chirped and chattered loudly. Then Padmavati gave a mirthless laugh. 'We can't disappoint the Sultan of Hindustan, can we now?' She stood up, saying, 'Come friends. We have work to do.'

The girls galloped down the path and Ginni flew overhead. Consultation with *Ba,* the only person she could rely on for support, was essential. Besides, in her own selfish grief, she had forgotten how Ratan Singh's captivity would have affected her. When they reached the palace, they were surprised to find hardly any lamps lit. Padmavati hurried inside. At the door, she met the palace *vaid* and doctor. Her heart leaped up in fear and she asked him, 'Is *Ba* alright?'

He bowed to her, '*Pranam NaiRaniSa,* how can a mother be alright when her son is taken captive? And that too, by the Turks who kill without pity?'

'How ill is she?' asked Padmavati.

'Her heart is in pain. I have given her a concoction of herbs and camphor but she needs stress-free rest. But do you think her grandson will allow it?'

'Kunwar*ji*?'

'Yes. The young man is in her room scolding her and telling her what he thinks of her indulging you. Forgive me, *hukum,* but I cannot bear it when my patients are being hurt. So I am leaving and will return when he goes.' Saying this, the *vaid* rushed down the front stairs.

Telling her friends to wait outside, Padmavati entered *Ba*'s palace cautiously. She did not want to accost the crown prince. She crept down the half-lit passage and reached the doors of the bed chamber. She put a finger on her lips to silence the guards about to greet her and stood outside the half-closed doors. Vir Bhan's loud words and angry tone was clearly audible outside.

'Now that your son is dead, I am the Rawal and I order you not to allow that whore, *NaiRani,* to come to your palace,' he was shouting.

'No, no. My Ratan cannot be dead...' came *Ba's* frail voice.

'Oh yes, he is,' insisted Vir Bhan. Padmavati's fingernails dug into her closed fists in anger at the cruelty with which her grandson was tormenting *Ba. I have to let her know that her son is well and safe,* she told herself. *But I must wait until this idiot leaves.* She looked at the guards but their faces were impassive. Then her attention was drawn back to the situation indoors.

'And I will avenge my father's death. It is all because of that witch he brought back from Singhaldweep. First she separated my father from my mother and me, then she made him disregard all our customs and traditions. She came to the Council and challenged my uncle, Rana Lakshman...imagine! She thinks she can rule Chittor...the silly vamp! And now, after extracting all Chittor's wealth through my father, she gets him killed.'

'No, Vir. You are wrong. *Banni* is not like that at all,' weakly protested his grandmother.

'*Banni*!' He said it as if it were an abuse. 'I will give your *banni* to the Sultan. All this trouble with him is only because he wants my father's whore. Well, let him have her and leave us alone.'

'Vir!' *Ba* was aghast. 'You can't do that. *Banni's* position is like that of your mother's. You can't give her to the Sultan.'

'Yes, I can and I will. I am the Rawal, *Dadi*. I will do what is best for our people. And she is a disaster for Chittor. Now I have to meet my uncle, the Rana. We are holding a meeting with the chieftains of Mewar and decisions will be taken there.' Saying this, he turned on his heel and strode out.

The guards saluted him. Behind them, Padmavati melted into the shadows. When he had mounted his horse and rode away, she entered *Ba's* bedchamber. As her eyes adjusted to the gloom, she saw the old lady groaning on the bed. Her ladies and maids sat around her. They made place for the *NaiRani*. The princess bent down and spoke clearly to the old lady. She wanted her words to be heard by the others who would spread them through the palaces. '*Ba*, I am your *banni* and you believe me, right?'

'Yes, my dear,' *Ba* whispered, her eyes closed in pain.

'I have news that your Ratan is well and safe in the Sultan's camp. Ginni spoke with him and brought me his ring. See, here it is,' said Padmavati.

The old lady opened her eyes slightly. The diamond glinted in the shadowed chamber. Having seen it, she closed her eyes. Taking her folded palms to her forehead, she whispered, 'Thank you, Ek Linghji. Bless my *banni*.'

Padmavati showed the ring to everyone in the room and then rushed out. There was a lot to do and she had received *Ba*'s blessings. Directly, along with Ambika and Ginni, the princess went to the Council Chamber. There was a buzz in the great hall, as the chiefs discussed the situation. As Padmavati and Ambika walked in, dishevelled and veils hastily pulled over their faces, murmurs died down. Everyone stared at the pair, many with mouths open. Padmavati confidently stepped up to dais and announced, 'Ranas and Thakurs of Mewar, I bring you good news. Your Rawal is alive and unhurt. He is prisoner of the Sultan, but well.' All the men looked at each other in puzzlement. Padmavati raised the diamond ring and said, 'This is proof. I have his ring.'

Instantly, there were comments like, 'Yes, yes. That is his ring.' And 'He had it on his finger when the Sultan visited.'

'Now that it is established that he is alive, our duty is to get him back. I have a plan, but I cannot take Chittor's army with me. It is needed here to defend the fort. But I need some soldiers. If I can have a few soldiers from each of your personal bodyguard platoon, my plan to rescue our *Annadaata* will succeed. Will you give me your soldiers to rescue the Rawal?' Padmavati asked.

The chieftains looked at each other. Suddenly, a harsh voice came from the door. 'We don't need you lecturing us about our duties. We know what to do better than you. After all, we are the Mewaris, not you.'

Kunwar Vir Bhan strode in followed by Rana Lakshman Singh. Both came up on the dais, forcing the girls to move to one side of it. Rana Lakshman said, 'Chiefs, we do not know if the *NaiRani* is telling the truth...whether the Rawal is alive or not.'

Instantly, Ginni went into action; flying around the room and calling out. Ambika interpreted his words, 'Ginni says he has seen and spoken to the Rawal in the Sultan's camp. He brought the ring that the Rawal sent *NaiRaniSa*.'

Confusion reigned in the room as the men argued with each other. Some said that the *NaiRani* must be believed while others said that it was all a lie. Rana Lakshman shouted, 'Listen to me, my lords.' All faces turned to him and the murmuring lowered. 'Even if the Rawal is alive, he is a captive. In his absence, his son takes over the Rawal's duties and his decisions must be considered.' He placed a hand on Kunwar Vir Bhan's shoulders, saying, 'No doubt he is young. But we are his advisors and we have the experience. In this case, without knowing the plan, is it right to promise our soldiers to the *NaiRani*? After all she is young, too and a woman. What work do women have with war and soldiers?'

Rana Lakshman's words seemed to resonate more with the warriors in the room, though Padmavati noticed a few stroking their beards...silently and thoughtfully. Ginni landed on her shoulder and whispered, 'Let's go, Princess. We will get no help here.'

Without another word, the girls and Ginni exited into the dark night.

Behind them, they heard somebody laughing and a mocking remark floated out, 'Let's hand the *NaiRani* over to the Sultan and in exchange get our Rawal released'. *Must be Vir Bhan,* thought Padmavati, her ears turning red. As they mounted their horses, she recalled that her uncle, Prince Gora Rajsinha, had not been in the Council. *Where was he?* So, she turned her horse towards his palace.

Hearing hoof-beats on the path, Prince Gora himself, came to the door. Padmavati bent to touch his feet, as did Ambika. Affectionately, her uncle put an arm around both girls and the three went in. Badal, the twelve-year-old cousin of the princess, was polishing the studs of his saddle. He loved horses and insisted on caring for his horse himself. He flung himself on Padmavati, saying, '*Didi, Didi!* Do you have news of Ratan *Bhaisa*? Is he alright?' His anxious queries showed how much he loved his brother-in-law.

Padmavati held him by the shoulders and said, 'Yes, thank God. The Rawal is safe and well, but a captive.' Then she turned to her uncle. '*Mamu,* why were you not at the Council meeting today?'

Prince Gora looked away and muttered, 'I cannot bear the humiliation...sorry, my daughter.'

Padmavati caught both his hands in her own saying, 'No, *Mamu*. Don't apologise to me. I know how much you have sacrificed by coming here so far from our home and staying back to look after me. And...'

'And what, Padmavati?'

'Today, I come to you for your support.'

'You don't need to ask me. It is and has always been yours. Whatever is within my ability...all of it,' the old warrior said.

'And mine too,' piped up Badal.

Padmavati smiled at the boy, whose mother had died at his birth. Then she related everything that had happened ever since Ginni had returned with Ratan Singh's ring from the Sultan's camp. She also told him what she had in mind. Prince Gora listened carefully, asked a few questions and then declared that her plan was fine. The only thing missing were soldiers. The chieftains of Mewar were not willing to spare her even a few of their bodyguards for the forces she would require for this bold endeavour.

'How do we get them?' mused Prince Gora.

Ambika said, 'But Sire, I noticed that when Rana Lakshman was speaking, all the chiefs were not in agreement with him. Many of them know that he is taking advantage of the Rawal's absence to fill the vacuum with his own power, and also that Kunwar Vir Bhan is only a pawn in his game. Did you know that on the first day of the siege, before the exits of the *garh* were sealed, Rana Lakshman had sent his youngest son, Ajay Singh, to the hills of Kailwara? He has some well-laid plans of his own.'

'Yes. I always suspected that Rana Lakshman Singh is not completely loyal to the Rawal. Still, the other chieftains will lean towards power. But tomorrow, let me talk to each one personally,' Prince Gora said.

As they discussed various methods of convincing the Ranas and Thakurs of Mewar, neither the girls nor the Prince noticed that Badal had left the room. Finally, after a simple repast, Padmavati and Ambika left for their palace. It was quite late and clouds hid the moon. Fireflies twinkled in the trees and bushes as they galloped past. The night looked magical, but its beauty was lost on Padmavati, whose mind was chasing after solutions to the possible problems cropping up in her plan.

The girls were going through a deserted stretch when, all of a sudden, two riders appeared on the path. It was a dark patch with orchards on both sides and they could not see the faces of the intruders but their stance was belligerent. Ginni, flying overhead, squawked, 'Careful!'

Immediately, Padmavati slipped out her sword as did Ambika. After Vir Bhan's attack, both ensured they carried their swords when riding out. Holding the blades upright, they thundered towards the horsemen. As they came closer, the waiting riders took a few steps back and raised their swords, too. But their blades seemed to waver. It was clear that the men had not expected a confrontation. In a few moments, Padmavati leading, both girls were abreast of the men, but on either side. They slashed swiftly and brutally downwards at the blades of the men with their swords as they sped past. Then they turned around their horses and came back for a second attack. One rider had lost his blade and was already riding away as fast as he could. The other was standing still, his sword raised, not quite believing that their so-called victims were not running away but coming back for a second strike. By the time, Padmavati charged, he had turned tail and fled. The girls rallied, their horses were sweating and Ginni cackled, 'Good job, girls!'

'At least our regular training has been useful,' laughed Padmavati. Ambika grinned as they wheeled around and galloped towards the palace, their swords still unsheathed and eyes peeled for any more attacks plotted by Rana Lakshman and Vir Bhan. They reached home without further interruptions.

Next morning, Padmavati's entire household woke up to a hullabaloo. 'What's happening?' demanded the princess, 'Has the Sultan laid siege to my palace?'

Ambika came running up the stairs, saying, 'Princess, you must dress and come down to the gate.'

'Why?'

'You will see.'

She helped Padmavati to quickly array herself and pulled the *choondari* forward so that the head was covered but her lovely face remained unveiled. They ran downstairs and were rowed across the *sarovar*. They could hear the jabbering of many voices as they walked up the avenue to the gates. The guards flung the gates open, revealing a mob. Men milled about speaking loudly in the Mewari tongue. Some were in armour. The moment they saw her, all the noise died down and each man placed his palms together and bowed low. Padmavati acknowledged their salute and asked loudly, 'What is the meaning of this? Why are you here?'

One man, whom she recognized as the *Adhiyaksh* or Commander of the Chittor army, came forward and spoke respectfully, 'We are the soldiers of Chittor, *NaiRaniSa*. We have come to offer our services to you. We came to know that you are looking for soldiers to help you rescue our Rawal. So we came, *hukum*.'

His simple words brought tears to the Princess' eyes. She scanned the masses of men backing up the paved road. She could not see the end of the throng. 'But who told you that I was looking for soldiers?'

'I did.' And a grinning Badal stepped out from under the *Adhiyaksh's* elbow.

29

They were walking fast. Uma had set up a rapid pace, quite different from how they had ambled down to Padmavati's palace. All of a sudden, the air around them was charged up. Whether it was the tension from the events Uma had been describing from the *Padmawali* that had spilled into the night or a change in Uma's disposition, Mrinalini could not tell. When the journalist had asked her where they were going, Uma had only replied tersely, 'The royal palace.'

'You mean Rana Kumbha Palace?' the Mrinalini had gasped out as she tried to catch up with the girl.

'Well, it has been called the Rana Kumbha Palace only after Maharana Kumbha's reign. But didn't I tell you that he had built it over the old royal palace? That was the original palace that housed the royalty of Chittor,' she replied.

'Rana Kumbha ruled from 1433 to 1445,' added Mrinalini. 'The reigns were very short then, weren't they? But what is the hurry now, Uma?' The girl didn't answer. So she asked again, 'Uma?'

'...we are late,' muttered the girl.

'Late?' asked Mrinalini, her tone puzzled. 'Late for what? I thought you were telling me a story and I was listening. Is something else happening too?'

'You will see...' Uma said cryptically.

They had reached the inclined ramp to Rana Kumbha Palace. Passing through the wooden doors, Mrinalini stopped inside a large courtyard. As she looked upwards, there were tiers of canopied balconies on the wall in which the door was set.

'Be careful of the rubble underfoot, *bhayeli*,' said Uma, softly walking ahead.

Mrinalini took careful steps and something crunched under her sprinters. 'It all looks so grand even in this ruined state,' she remarked while thinking, *this girl is strange, indeed. A while ago, she was curt and now she is melting with concern...blowing hot and cold...*

'This is the oldest palace. During Padmavati's time everyone...the queens, *Ba*, the Rawal, his relatives, hangers-on, attendants, servants and bodyguards all lived here. It even had stables for horses and elephants,' offered the inscrutable Uma.

'Hmmm...but where are we going now? And what happened next in the story? What was actually Padmavati's plan? You haven't told me anything about it. You only called it 'the plan'. Was the Rawal rescued?' Mrinalini shot off all these queries, sensing Uma was in a better mood now.

'I will tell you all of it. Every story needs a setting... the right setting....' Uma's floated back. Mrinalini went through another arch and there was a flight of steps facing her. She slowly went down into an open space.

Uma's back was to her as Mrinalini approached a huge depression in the centre of a fenced-in area. In the shape of an inverted trapezium, its paved walls sloped downwards on all four sides. Suddenly, she knew what it was. The *Jauhar Kund!* Mrinalini stared into it, stunned. *Is this where so many women had burned themselves?* She felt a tingle pass over her skin. Air began to deplete from her lungs. In a moment she would begin to hyperventilate... somewhat like when she confronted flames, even from a matchstick. Mrinalini opened her mouth to gulp air and tried to control her involuntary reactions.

She looked downwards. The bottom of the pit was lost in darkness. *Yet why can I see smoke spiralling up?...No, no, that's just my imagination. The pyres can't be still burning.* Just then the moon shifted through the clouds and a ray lit up the bottom of the *Kund*. It was filled with dry leaves and other rubbish...quite innocuous, really. *Still, there was something in the air*...raising the hairs on her arms. She swallowed hard. 'This place is giving me goose-bumps. Let's go,' Mrinalini said, turning around and walking back to the steps.

'Yes. This place holds the tears, pain and heartache of hundreds of innocent women...the flower of Mewar. I call it the soul of Chittor,' Uma said softly moving in the opposite direction to another flight of ascending stairs. Her words floated back to Mrinalini, who had to turn around and follow her. 'The *Jauhar Sthal* has three gates. We came in through the western gate and we need to now go through the southern gate.' Panting and breathless, the journalist had just caught up when Uma pointed to a small temple-like structure. Mrinalini noticed, it was capped by three conical roofs.

Uma explained, 'This is the Ek Linghji temple where Padmavati would come to worship.'

'So did the women worship here before immolating themselves in the *Jauhar Kund?'*

'Yes,' replied Uma. 'Women would fast and bathe, dress in their wedding clothes and ornaments, worship at this temple, partake the *prasad* and then walk through the gate to the *Jauhar Sthal*.

Moonlight gleamed on a flight of steps going down from the temple to a wide paved platform below. Mrinalini spied another flight of stairs going further down from the platform to vanish in the darkness below. She heard gentle splashes. The moon peeped out again and the darkness below melted into a large water body circled by high rocky walls.

'Is this another *sarovar*?' She called out to Uma, who was slowly descending.

'This is the *Gomukh Kund*. A mountain spring feeds it falling from a cow's mouth carved on the cliff, there.' She pointed down into the shadows. 'But *bhayeli*, come down and let me show you where Chittor's pride resides.'

Both girls descended to the wide stone platform. On one side it extended to a pavilion.

'You see, on special occasions, the royal ladies would bathe at the *Gomukh Kund* and pray at Ek Linghji's temple,' explained Uma, looking up at the temple above them.

'Oh yes. Like Padmavati did during Teej...'

'Exactly,' said Uma. 'During those times, the royal ladies would come to the *Kund* through an underground tunnel from the royal palace to this place.'

'Oh! Can we see the tunnel here?'

Uma pointed to the pavilion, saying, 'It is inside that, but it is blocked now.'

'Why?'

'Many reasons...'

Mrinalini went behind the girl's back into the small pavilion. On her right she saw a projected wall of stone. Moonlight gleamed on its rough surface. Somebody had etched a large three-pronged *trishul* on it in vermilion. The journalist stared at it. Somehow, the whole place gave her peculiar vibes and she shivered. Strangely, there was a kind of smell in the open pavilion...like the mustiness of a room closed for a long period of time. She shivered again and almost ran out into the night. Absentmindedly, she observed that stars had begun to fade in the sky.

Mrinalini glanced at Uma's back and asked, 'Why did you call this Chittor's pride?'

'You will know soon enough,' came her perplexing reply.

Mrinalini said quietly, 'Will you tell me the rest of the story now?'

'Yes, *bhayeli*.'

30

Flashes of amber, yoke-yellow, crimson, rose-pink and azure appeared like strobes between the grey rocks and spiky-green acacia trees bordering the road trailing down to the enemy camp. These were palanquins or *dolis* of various hues, one after the other, wending their way down. Curtains tightly closed, their hefty bearers chorused a popular song beating rhythm with their measured steps as the palanquins swayed from side to side. At the head of the cavalcade were Prince Gora Rajsinha and little Prince Badal on steeds with gold trappings prancing in little steps. It was exactly like a bridal procession, which it was in many ways. On the roof of one *doli* Ginni sat, swaying gently. Inside it, Padmavati sat in extreme discomfort. She was weighed down by a *lehenga* worked in gold thread and gems. The embroidery on her *choli* pinched and pricked her soft skin. Several heavy necklaces on her throat brought her neck downwards while the head jewel or *rakhdi* of *kundan* and rubies pulled at her hair painfully. A large *nathni* with gems and long *kundan jhumkas* made her nostrils and ears ache.

But her mind was far away. At dawn she had gone to the temple of Ek Linghji above the *Gomukh Kund*. She had sat a long time in prayer before the deity. Pouring milk over the black stone, she had let the old priest smear a vermilion and turmeric *tilak*, a broad vertical band on her forehead. She felt like a warrior seeking the blessings of the God to win a battle. When she came out of the temple, she saw men carrying logs of wood marching towards the *Jauhar Sthal*. Curiously, she followed them and stopped in dismay. The huge hollow pit was already half-filled with short logs, wood chips and hay. A strong scent of sandalwood floated in the air. Beside the *Kund* stood several covered earthen jars of *ghee* or clarified butter. A eunuch in royal livery was supervising the men who tipped their burden into the hollow.

'Why...why...is this *Kund* being filled?' The princess had stammered.

Respectfully bowing to the queen, the eunuch had answered, 'For the *satis, hukum...*'

'*Satis*?' Padmavati was puzzled.

'Yes, *NaiRaniSa*. For the wives of the soldiers killed today,' the eunuch had explained impassively.

For a stunned moment, she had stared at the eunuch's face. Then she had turned away, a terrible guilt flooding her. *Had she given any thought to those who would die for their loyalty to her husband, today? Had she thought of their wives, children, loved ones? No. All her concerns had been for* **her** *husband,* **his** *mother and* **herself***?*

Even now as she swayed, suddenly feeling faint, she wondered if it was ethically correct for her to risk the lives of so many men to rescue the Rawal. *But he was their Rawal, wasn't he? Hadn't his men sworn allegiance to him; to protect him with their lives?* But what about their wives? Their marriage oath stated service to their husbands in all circumstances. *Do these circumstances include death? Apparently, they do. For I can see with my own eyes how the brave wives are readying themselves for the ultimate sacrifice?* Padmavati sighed, *will the men fight better knowing their wives will die honourable deaths for them? I don't know. All I know is...many men will die today and many wives will burn as satis...and all of it because of me. Ek Linghji, am I doing the right thing? Show me the way, my lord...show me the right path...*

Her trance was broken by shouts in rough foreign tongues. She realized that they had reached the outposts of the camp. She heard the loud replies of her uncle, Prince Gora and several hoof beats as the guards surrounded the palanquins. *Oh God! They mustn't look into the dolis.* Then a new voice of authority intervened and the guards trotted away. Once again the swaying began as the bearers shuffled through the dust towards the cluster of tents. But now Padmavati could hear the clip-clopping of the Sultan's cavalry escorting the cavalcade. She took a deep breath and pulled her veil down to her waist. However, it was a gauzy, diaphanous one and the contours of her alluring visage were clearly visible through it. Still, it was hot and suffocating in the veil. *This is the first time that I have played at seduction, Ek Linghji. Please give me the capability to play it well.*

After some twists and turns, the procession halted and she felt her *doli* being gently brought to the ground on its stilts. She waited, hardly breathing. Distant words floated to her but she could not identify the voices. The closely-curtained palanquin built up a kind of humid heat inside and Padmavati felt a trickle of sweat sashaying down her back. Just when she felt she could not bear it anymore, the swish-swish of feet moving through sand was heard outside. She steadied her wildly beating heart as Prince Gora's voice came to her.

'The Queen of Chittor is here, *O Sikander,* and awaiting your pleasure. But she is tired and wishes for some privacy before coming into your presence,' he said in an ingratiating tone.

He is playing his role well, Padmavati told herself. *Soon it will be your turn.*

'Ah!' said a hoarse voice. *The Sultan, that lecher!* At once, the princess identified the speaker.

'Ah!' he said again as though appraising a succulent dish. 'But how do I know it is the Queen and not some maid from the palace. I must not be tricked, you know.'

She could imagine him wagging a finger in her uncle's face. In her sweetest, softest voice, she called out, 'Uncle, to win the trust of the great Emperor of Hindustan, I am willing to put aside my fatigue. You may raise the curtains of my palanquin.'

'Yes, Your Highness,' replied Prince Gora.

She heard the curtain cords being untied and then the silk cloth rustled. Bright sunlight streamed in. Holding her head high despite the weight of her ornaments, Padmavati sat in a classical pose. Knees drawn up, hands, sparkling with rings and bangles, clasped on them demurely. Gems on the nose ring dazzling in the light, the spread-out *lehenga* glittering around her, Padmavati looked every inch the gorgeous queen she was; like an artist's rendition of proud regality.

A shadow fell over her as Alauddin bent to look in. He could not believe that he was finally seeing the object of his delusions and fantasies in flesh and blood. He almost stretched out his forefinger with its long dirty nail to poke her and assure himself that she was a real woman and not some mannequin. But he stopped himself just in time from making such an un-kingly gesture. As his thirsty eyes drank in this wondrous sight, Padmavati turned her head and smiled slowly.

'Ah!' said the Sultan of all Hindustan. His knees turned to water and he staggered a little. His heart leaped so high that it nearly popped out of his mouth. Controlling the passion that rose in his heart, he straightened himself with a hand on his chest, panting a little.

Prince Gora quickly dropped the curtains and said, 'I hope Your Majesty is satisfied.'

The Sultan nodded several times before he could find his voice. 'Yes. Yes. She will be taken to a comfortable tent and I will seek her audience only by noon.'

The Prince bowed. 'But she will need all her palanquins because they carry her raiments. Also, she needs privacy away from the camp...you understand...she is a queen.'

'Yes. Yes, of course,' said the Sultan waving a hand at his generals. 'Set up a tent fitting to her royal status some distance away from the camp. Let her have her palanquins, maids, whatever,' He wanted to give her the world...after all she was a queen and had come to him willingly. She was his treasure and must be kept happy till she submitted to him completely. Besides, now that the Rawal and his beautiful queen were secure in his cage, Chittor was more or less his. What was the harm in showing a little generosity?

Inside the *doli*, the princess held her breath as Prince Gora broached the critical issue. '*Sikandar-i-saini*, your benevolence matches your fame! My queen has one more request which I am sure you will grant. She is giving up her previous husband, the Rawal of Chittor, to become yours forever and ever. But she is a devout Hindu wife. She has to seek his forgiveness in these circumstances. You see, she must take the dust of her husband's feet in the final farewell.' He saw the Sultan's piggy eyes narrow in suspicion and hastily pleaded, 'Or else she may be shut out of *swarglok* or heaven forever...this is a Mewari custom, *O Sikandar*!'

Being a Muslim, the idea of being shut out of heaven due to earthly sins may appeal to the Sultan, the Prince estimated.

'Hmmm...,'considered his unpredictable host. Possibly Padmavati's tantalizing smile had made butterflies flutter in his stomach as he had conjured up the enchanting moments he would spend in her company. He pursued his thin lips and frowned at the Prince. Finally, he declared, 'I cannot refuse a woman of her unique charms. She is a true Padmini. I grant her this desire as a wedding gift....' As the Prince bowed in gratefulness, the Sultan commanded his generals, 'Bring the Rawal to the queen's tent and allow a meeting.' Turning to the curtained palanquin, he bowed in a *kurnish*, saying, 'I shall await your loving presence, my dear.' Beckoning for his steed, he mounted and rode away.

In hardly a couple of hours, a large tent was set up for the queen a few feet away from the camp. Her palanquins were parked behind her tent and out of sight of the other tents. Padmavati and Ambika got ready, as did the others. It was time for the final move. Prince Gora stood at front flap of the tent, peeping out from time to time. A cloud of dust wound through the camp heralding a group of horsemen in a hurry. In a few minutes, the cloud approached their tent. Closer, it turned out to be six guards, armed to the teeth, holding between them the reins of a horse on which Ratan Singh was trussed up like a piece of oxen meat. Leading them was one of Sultan's generals. His face was dark and scowling. He did not like to leave his prized prisoner in the midst of Mewaris, even if most of them were women.

Prince Gora emerged from tent and stood silently as the horses cantered to it. General and guards dismounted, hauling the Rawal down, who instantly kneeled in the dust for his feet were hobbled. Instead of greeting the Prince, the general announced loudly, 'We have brought you the prisoner. You have fifteen minutes for the meeting. We will wait here to escort him back.'The Prince inclined his head with dignity. The general gave a signal and Ratan Singh was dragged brutishly to the tent opening. Leaving him lying on the ground, the soldiers with their leader retreated a few feet away.

Gently, the Prince supported Ratan Singh and both of them managed to limp inside. Instantly, Ambika and Padmavati cut through his ropes as Ginni fluttered overhead. They chafed his ankles and wrists as the princess quickly whispered the plan to him. When he could stand, they slipped his armour over his head. Padmavati had removed much of her ornaments and was also in her white armour as was Ambika. Prince Gora wore his armour too, and all four untied the back flap of the tent and walked out of the tent. It was teeming with the armed soldiers of Chittor who had played the role of palanquin bearers. The palanquins had carried their armour and weapons.

The Rawal mounted Prince Gora's stallion and Padmavati sat behind him. Both held unsheathed swords. Ambika ascended Prince Badal's horse. She tied a bundle of Padmavati's ornaments to the saddle horn and waited for the twelve-year-old Prince Badal to climb up behind him. She also held a bare blade. But Prince Badal refused. He had decided to stay behind with Prince Gora, the *Adhiyaksh* of Chittor's army and all his soldier friends to hold back the Sultan's forces. Padmavati did not like it at all. But the boy-prince Badal insisted that he must fight alongside the forces who had joined this adventure on his calling. She could not disagree with his reasoning but felt uncomfortable putting to risk her young motherless cousin. The *Adhiyaksh* assured her that he would look after both princes.

'Ginni,' called the princess, 'Please stay here and help them.' The parrot nodded obediently though he was not sure how he would help.

Right then, she had no choice; they had to make the dash to the Chittor fort which was a good ten-odd uphill miles away. The two horses and their riders streaked away from behind the tent, trying to cover as much distance as they could before the enemy was alerted. They were still far from the aqueduct over the Gambhiri that led to the road twisting up to Chittorgarh, when a shout went up from the guards waiting to escort the prisoner back.

As they spurred their horses to chase the runaways, Chittor's army stood in their path. The general and six guards were hacked down instantly. By then alarms had been sounded and entire camp was in a furore. Chittor's *Adhiyaksha* shouted, 'To the corrals!' The soldiers rushed to enclosures holding the war steeds. The Sultan's forces reached them around the same time. Without horses, there was no way to overtake the Rawal's rescue party, the *Adhiyaksha* knew. His soldiers jumped over the fences, slashing left and right. Some blades caught terrified, neighing horses and some beheaded the would-be riders. Sand turned crimson, thirstily draining the spilled blood.

Little Prince Badal fought as fiercely as the men around him. He could not bear to injure horses but he attacked the Sultan's soldiers. Using the true edge of his sword, he lunged at them boldly, chopping and cleaving off hands, legs, head and torso. He wielded his blade using all the tactics he had learnt from his hero, Ratan Singh. The soldier next to him fell at his feet, the shaft of an arrow trembling in his chest. Badal looked up to see that enemy archers had surrounded the corral. They were fenced in. The *Adhiyaksha* shouted, 'Stop! Halt!' His soldiers lowered their swords. To the archers, he yelled, 'It is not honourable to kill men who surrender.'

At a command from their officer, the archers lowered their bows and allowed Chittor's soldiers still holding their swords make their way out of the corral. In a few minutes Chittor's warriors were standing hardly an arm's distance from the archers. More importantly, they were inside the range of the bows and so immune to being hit by the arrows. One look from their leader and Chittor's soldiers fell on the archers with swords. Surprised at the attack and with no time to exchange their bows for swords, most of the Sultan's archers fell where they stood. It took time for them to rally but by then the rest of the Sultan's army had rushed from the camp.

The brave band of warriors from Chittorgarh were surrounded and outnumbered immensely. They formed a tight circle around their *Adhiyaksha* and the two princes. Knowing death was imminent, they took the final stand, swords flashing, advancing, turning, whirling to take the front guard. Fighting for their honour, they slashed and hacked, thrust and stabbed furiously, each one killing several foes before giving way under the hail of steel. Eventually, only the Prince Gora and Prince Badal were on their feet, twisting and turning, leaping and parrying a number of swordsmen at a time. But how long could sheer bravery fend off death? First the twelve-year-old boy-prince fell, taking a stab to his heart after laying low at least six foes. Then it was his father's turn to be beheaded. As his empty helmet rolled on the ground, a battle, whose sounds will be heard across centuries, came to a finish. It was a heroic sacrifice for the love for one's land and loyalty to one's leader; a tale for the bards to sing to future warriors.

Some of the Sultan's forces had managed to ride behind the Rawal, Padmavati and Ambika. As the two stallions desperately elongated their paces to outrun the enemy riders, the clang and clash of battle echoed across the sand and rocks. Ratan Singh and Padmavati, bending low over the horse's neck, looked back to see a curtain of dust rising from the far side of the camp. A little visibility showed men in the throes of battle. Padmavati couldn't help thinking, *was this the right way? Leading these men to certain death? My uncle is there. And my little cousin, poor motherless Badal. . .he has hardly begun to live and I have left him to die. . .*

Soon the Sultan's horsemen started gaining on the horse ridden by Ratan Singh and his queen. Padmavati whacked the closest one on her right with her sword and he fell, his leg caught in the stirrup, dragged by his horse. Slicing her sword at the neck of the left rider, she beheaded him. Ratan Singh's legs clasped his horse's belly. It came alongside Ambika's horse and together they splashed over the aqueduct over the Gambhiri.

'Ambika, ride hard,' screamed Padmavati. 'Tell them to lower the *Ram Pol* gates. They must be ready to winch them quickly.'

Ambika bent over her horse's neck to give it headway and surged ahead. The sturdy Indian steeds climbed up the mountain road steadily and confidently. Since the Arabic stallions of the Turks were not so sure-footed on rocky terrain, Chittor's two horses gained ground. Though the enemy riders pushed their horses, it was a slow climb for them. Padmavati looked back constantly, ready to wield her blade. Finally, the seven gates of Chittor were in sight.

They dashed through them while archers shot arrows at the charging enemy. From the ramparts the entire mission had been visible. *Ram Pol* had been lowered for the rescue party to enter but men stood alert at the winches ready to draw the gates up.

Seeing home a few yards away induced extra energy in Chittor's steeds to make the final dash. But the chasers were right behind. As the two horses thundered across, winches began to turn and the massive wooden gates lifted up from the fifteen-foot ravine they spanned. The gates had already risen at an angle when the first enemy horse stepped on it. As the gate continued to rise, the horse lost balance starting to slip. Its eyes rolled up, neighing in panic. Within seconds, the armed rider and horse fell screaming into the deep ravine. The rest of the enemy horsemen came up to the ravine and stopped short. Archers above the gates showered them with deadly arrows. A few toppled off, with arrows sticking out from heads and chests while the rest turned tail and retreated down the road.

The Rawal of Chittor was safe.

31

Thick smoke rose into the twilight. Ornaments jingling, silk lehengas swishing, anklets chiming, the women began to trickle into the *Jauhar Sthal*. They had bathed at the *Gomukh Kund*, offered their prayers at the temple of Ek Linghji and now were ready for the final act. *Thalis* in their hands, with auspicious lamps alight, their faces were calm. Padmavati stood back in the shadows against the wall, Ambika beside her. Through the mist of tears, the double conflagrations were bright red spots dancing before her eyes. One was the pyre on which *Ba's* earthly remains were turning to ashes. Ratan Singh, wrapped in a white cloth, his head shaved, sat before it, still as a stone. At a little distance away, hungry flames leaped out of the *Jauhar Kund*.

Despite the paralysis of grief, Padmavati's mind went back over the hours they had spent at *Ba's* bedside after their dramatic dash into the *garh*. She had been breathing heavily, eyes closed when they had tiptoed in. But as soon as her son bent over her, her lids had fluttered open. 'My Ratan!' she had breathed.

'*Ba*. Here I am. I'm with you,' he had assured her.

'You had been taken...' she had whispered.

'Yes, *Ba*. The Sultan took me but your brave *Banni* brought me back...at great risk to her own life,' he had explained.

'I told you she is a jewel. You've brought me a treasure,' she said, but her voice had been faint. Tears had spilled down Padmavati's cheeks as *Ba* had closed her eyes. But her fingers beckoned from the bed and Ratan Singh pulled her forward.

'Yes, *Ba*,' she had said.

'*Banni,* I leave the honour of Chittor in your hands. Guard it with your life. Do not let even a fragment of Chittor's virtue be besmirched by the hand of a heathen barbarian,' *Ba* had spoken with effort and Padmavati had shaken her head, silently. She had been choking on her grief.

But *Ba,* feeble and ill, was so anxious that she had half-raised herself from the pillow. Holding the princess' soft hands in her bony claws, she kept pleading, 'Promise me. Promise me, *Banni.*'

Gulping down her tears, Padmavati had whispered, 'I promise, *Ba.* I will protect Chittor's honour with my last breath. Now, please rest.'

'Ahh…rest,' the old woman had exhaled…her last breath. Her head had fallen back on the pillow, lifeless. Ratan Singh and Padmavati had kneeled on the ground, breaking into sobs. The rest of the royal household had been kept behind the doors of the bedchamber by *Ba's* orders. Then they had rushed in. Beating their chests and screaming, led by Rani Prabhavati, they had made a mighty show of their grief. Ratan Singh and his wife had quietly left the chamber.

Now the scene played out in the princess' mind over and over again until the crowds chanting around the *Jauhar Kund* distracted her.The women were intoning Vedic marriage mantras. In broken voices, some were singing songs traditionally sung at weddings. They were readying themselves to honour the knot that had tied them in marriage to their husbands by joining them in death. Padmavati's tears dried up as she watched the women in fascination. She contemplated their strong resolve. *Look at their loyalty to their marriage vows! Willingly they embrace this painful death by fire, leaving behind their children and other loved ones just for the sake of their marital promises. This is real courage…in all its rawness. Today, I know that courage has many faces; one of them is the quiet, unsung valour of the women of Mewar.*

As each woman jumped into the crackling flames, the sorrowful cries of their children drowned the singing. As the pungent odour of burning hair and other gases rose with the smoke, spreading a pall over the *Jauhar Sthal,* something changed inside Padmavati. Her heart turned heavy and filled to bursting with the torment of guilt. She cursed herself, *I am the reason their husbands are dead. I am the reason they are immolating themselves. I am the reason the children are orphans. I should be diving into the flames with them.Why am I alive when I am the cause of so many deaths and so much unhappiness?*

Then her glance fell on the white-clad figure sitting beside the flickering embers of his mother's funeral pyre. She could no longer bear it. Padmavati turned to run from the terrible conflict between her beliefs and reality. Ambika called out. The princess was so agitated that she would have run all the way to her palace but for the grooms rushing behind them with the horses. Hardly able to breathe between her wracking sobs, Padmavati mounted her horse and galloped off. On reaching the *Jal Mahal,* she shut herself in her dressing room, feverishly writing in her journal. Only Ambika was in attendance as she filled the parchment with depictions of not just the events but declarations of her own views, insights and reflections. The *Padma-wali* had become a catharsis of sorts for Padmavati. Pouring out her pains, pleasures, perceptions and sensibilities on parchment had brought her deep solace.

Yet, this evening the comfort she sought from her writing would not come. Her remorse was too sharp. Restlessly, she kept the journal aside, telling Ambika, 'I can't write today. Let the parchment, ink, quills remain in my cupboard here. I will continue writing at night. Now I need fresh air...I am choking...something seems stuck in my throat.' Padmavati went up to the *chattri*. Looking towards the enemy camp, she observed it blazing with lights. There was furious activity going on. *The Sultan must be mad with rage at being duped this way,* she mused absent-mindedly. Looking up at the stars appearing in the dusk, she shook her head. Yet the memory of the deaths she had witnessed that day could not be erased; the warriors of Chittor, her uncle and cousin, *Ba,* the widows...

It was the first time that Padmavati had so closely experienced death; the ultimate truth of life. And that day she had felt its pain not once but several times over. Yet, her distress did not stem only from the deep grief of her dear ones dying. Her terrible anguish came from elsewhere. Padmavati looked up at the heavens and cried out, 'O Mahadev! O Ek Linghji! I have wronged my people. I have wronged my parents. I have wronged you. I have acted against all my ethical principles. It is I, and only I, who is responsible for all the deaths today. And I have no excuses to offer. I risked all the lives not for the safety of my people but for my own happiness. I, who keep counselling the Rawal on kingship, failed the test myself. I am a sinner, O Mahadev! What can I do? How can I redeem my sins? How can I find peace from this constant fire in my heart?'

Her tears fell like a tempest, unending and unstoppable. She was bent double on the seat as paroxysms of grief shook her slight form. In a curious coincidence, the grey clouds that had spread their sheath on the sky since morning, melted in empathy. Rain began to pelt down; beating the stone roof rhythmically, steadily increasing in crescendo. Padmavati's body trembled in sorrow, oblivious to the downpour drenching her. It was Ambika who half-dragged her and half-carried her down to her bed chamber. Soothing her with soft words, she bathed her friend, washing away the grit and grime of the day's ordeals. Dressing her in fresh dry clothes, she forced some coconut water down her throat, spoon by spoon.

By the time Ratan Singh returned, Padmavati had calmed down and her inner strength had returned. That night, she held her husband in her arms as he, in turn, was racked with sorrow at his mother's death. Breathing in her husband's body scents, Padmavati thanked the Mahadev many times over for returning her love to her, despite all her own sins.

That night the deluge continued…in torrents. It was unseasonal and unusual…as though the thick smoke of sorrow from the *Jauhar Kund* had risen to the heavens above Chittorgarh to rain down in the tears of the *Satis*. When the watery dawn appeared, another sight…striking terror into the hearts of the soldiers guarding the seven *pols* was revealed. Column after column of war elephants had climbed up through the stormy night to form up before the first gate of the *garh*. Troops of the Sultan's army had hacked down the thickest of the *kikar* trees on the slopes to provide battering rams for the elephant army.

Sentries were shouting from the guard towers. The perimeter of the fort ramparts in between the guard towers was under attack. Something like a mast rigging of a ship had been invented by knotting together lengths of thick strong rope into a rough net of squares. Poor visibility due to heavy rains had been to put to good use by agile climbers among the Turks to clamber up the vertical face of the cliffs. This intrepid advance party had securely hooked at least four such nets on the cliffs. Of course there had been a few casualties who had been crushed to smithereens on the sharp stones below. But it had been worth a chance to enter the precincts of the citadel. Now using hand and foot holds, the soldiers in armour were climbing up. No doubt, the heavy rain, weight of the armour, the height of the plateau cliffs will probably take them all day to actually reach the top of the ramparts. Besides, archers from the guard towers could shoot arrows picking off climbers but projecting rocks would provide protection, too. Eventually and in time it was a strategy that would help the enemy to enter the fort.

News of the enemy's game plan arrived when the Rawal and his wife were trying to force some food down their throats next morning. Without a word, Ratan Singh heard out the messenger. Then he remarked softly, 'This was expected. Tell them, I am on my way.'

For a second, he sat in grim silence. Then he turned to Padmavati, 'This is the end of the road, my princess.'

'Why do you say that?' cried Padmavati, though she knew well the reasons.

'You know, my love, hardly any of Chittor's army is left. We have just enough forces to man the guard towers...'

'But the chieftains of Mewar? They will help...each has his bodyguard intact...'

'How many will support me and how many are Rana Lakshman's men, I don't know. Of course, nobody can refuse to fight the enemy at our gates. I will make one last attempt,' Ratan Singh declared.

'Last attempt? What do you have in mind?' Padmavati said softly. 'Are you planning to parley with the Sultan, once again?'

Ratan Singh sighed. Then he spoke forcefully, 'No, my princess, the time for parley is over. I have tried to walk every path that leads to peace. But the Khalji does not want peace. Now only one way is left to me...the honourable way...the Mewari way. We must throw the gates open, take the final stand to defend Chittorgarh to our last breath.'

'But that is sheer suicide,' his wife gasped.

'Our honour is all that is left to us, my Princess. Mewar is known all over Bharatdesh for her valour. We have Ek Linghji's blessings. Mewar has never chosen conflict with her neighbours but when war has been thrust upon us, our men and women have proved their lives belong to Chittor. We will give up our blood and breath before we let the enemy cross the threshold of Chittor.'

Padmavati looked up at her husband, so tall, so handsome, so passionate. Once more she fell in love with the man standing before her whose voice rang out reiterating the glorious traditions of Mewar. Almost to herself, she murmured, 'So many have already died...if all of you embrace the immortality of a warrior's death, how will Chittor survive, my Gem?'

'Remember our lessons, my princess?' queried the Rawal. 'Kings exist as long as they reign over a kingdom. Without a kingdom, there is no king. Without Chittor, I am no longer a Rawal. If Chittor goes into the hands of the enemy, it better be over my dead body,' he said softly.

Ratan Singh stood up and cupped Padmavati's exquisite face in his large hands. 'Now listen carefully to what I have to say. I have made arrangements for you to travel to Singhaldweep. Koki, the Chief Eunuch, has my orders to guide you and Ambika down the *Chota Pol* path. Once you reach the bottom, the three of you will hide in the thickets till darkness. Then with Koki, both of you will ride into the mountains to my ancestral *haveli*. Rest there for a few days while Koki arranges for a ship to take you home.'

'Home? What home are you talking about? My home is here...with you, my Gem,' Padmavati twisted her face out of his hands and moved away. 'I will go nowhere.'

'This is not the time to be adamant, Princess. This is the time to use one's wits and you have lots of that,' Ratan Singh pleaded. Padmavati shook her head. 'Do not argue,' He said harshly, nearly scolding his beloved wife for the first time. 'Do as I say.There is no time. I have to go...my soldiers wait for my orders.'

Padmavati turned to her husband. Her large dark eyes glittered with unshed tears. 'I have taken the vow to be your *ardhangini*; to be with you in happiness and sorrow. Allow me to redeem my vow, today. My duty is to be beside you. If this is the end, let me fight shoulder to shoulder with you, my Gem. Our forces are depleted. If you let me join you, one more sword will be added to your strength. Let me go with you, my Gem. Together, we will defend Chittor,' she pleaded.

Two quick strides and Ratan Singh looked into the lovely face that was turned up to him beseechingly. Slowly, he brought his lips down to hers. It was a long, unending kiss. Against her lips, he whispered, 'I can't, Princess. You are too precious.' Releasing her, he turned on his heel and left.

Padmavati's hands remained outstretched. Her large eyes above it were dark with pain. Ambika waited for a few minutes and then whispered, 'Princess?'

Her trance broke. Padmavati picked up her *lehenga* with both hands and ran down the stairs. Ambika knew the princess had gone to the *shringar kaksha.* When she reached the small room, the princess was on the floor unfolding the stiff cloth on the desk. Ambika held it flat, while Padmavati hurriedly scratched letters, words and sentences on it. *What will be the end of this story?* Ambika wondered silently, watching her friend frantically writing away. Finally, the princess came to the last page. Here the text ended...with a flourish of Padmavati's signature.

Looking up at her friend, the princess said, 'Ambi, I knew this would be the end of my story and so I have written it here. This journal, my life's story, the *Padmawali* I leave in your care. You have to see that it remains safe till it can be revealed; till the time is right. Until that right moment, it must be concealed. Only you and I must know this secret.'

Ambika stared down at the parchment, nonplussed. Suddenly, a tremendous boom resounded through the noisy rush of water falling from the heavens. Both the women looked up. *What was that?* Confused shouts came from behind the closed door. 'The war elephants! They are hammering at the gates. They are breaking down *Ram Pol.*'

Ambika couldn't help thinking, *here we are in grave danger and the princess is only concerned with her journal!* But the habit of unquestioning obedience made her take the proffered parchment.

Once again, the princess stressed, 'Promise me, you will do as I say. Promise me, Ambi. This is your last duty to me. Give me your word, Ambi.' Her voice rose in urgency.

'Of course, Princess, but now...'

Padmavati cut her off, 'Run...go and hide it in your room, now. Then—then go and find out if the chieftains are going to march with the Rawal or not.'

Ginni perched on his shoulder, Ratan Singh had gone to his Council Chamber, which, as he had expected, was crowded with the agitated chieftains. Rana Lakshman Singh was exhorting them to support Kunwar Vir Bhan but some of them were arguing with him. When Ratan Singh entered, the assemblage fell silent. Their eyes followed him as he climbed the dais. He spoke quietly but firmly, 'War only leads to killing and destruction. Therefore it has been my constant endeavour to avoid it. I have always believed in peace and keeping Mewar secure through friendly treaties with neighbouring kings.'

'But Rawal, this is not a neighbouring king. This is a conqueror and a barbarian. He has defiled the honour of a queen,' quietly reminded an elderly lord.

'I agree,' sighed the Rawal. 'Still, I tried, but this arrogant Sultan does not believe in peace. He has left us no choice but to take up arms against him.' There was only an instant of silence and then the hall echoed with shouts of encouragement. 'Tell me, O Chieftains of Mewar, who will go with me to defend the honour of Chittor?'

Most of the men shook raised fists saying, 'I will. I will.' Only a few chiefs loyal to Rana Lakshman Singh and Vir Bhan glanced at the pair. Unable to put up a protest against a fight for the honour of Mewar, their hands went up. Taking their lead, slowly the remaining hands went up too.

Another tremendous boom reverberated through the *garh*. All heads turned to the sound. 'The Sultan's war elephants are battering the gates. If we don't go out and take the enemy, they will break *Ram Pol* down and enter Chittor,' warned Ratan Singh.

'Then what are we waiting for?' shouted Rana Lakshman, attempting to make up his earlier lack of enthusiasm. 'Let's go and muster our troops. We will meet at the *Ram Pol* within half hour.' Saying this, he ran out of the room followed by Vir Bhan. The rest of the chieftains rushed after him. Only the Rawal was left in the Council chamber. Looking upwards, he silently asked *Ba* to bless him. Then he rode out into the pouring rain towards the armoury. He never saw Ambika concealed behind a curtain. She slipped away to relay to the princess that the chiefs of Mewar were backing their Rawal with their full might.

The booms of the battering rams were sounding steadily now, as they had been for the past thirty minutes.

Just within the *Ram Pol,* an army consisting of the mounted bodyguards of all the Mewari chiefs and the few remaining platoons of Chittor's foot soldiers had taken up their positions. Many of horses sported long, black cloth snouts. The Sultan's war elephants were trained to hold swords in their trunks and cut down the adversary's horses and riders. Black snouts attached to the horses' noses like trunks would deceive the enemy elephants into believing that the horses were baby elephants! It was known that war elephants did not attack horses wearing snouts.

Naked swords aloft, spears waving, moustaches bristling, fierce eyes under metal helmets, chain armour clinking, the defending troops looked quite substantial. More so, their leaders exhorted them with spirited words. Their task was to defend Chittor and the men responded with fervent shouts. No doubt it was a magnificent display of the renowned Mewari bravado and raw courage but when ranged against the formidable army of the Turks, would their determined mettle suffice? Only the passing of the next few hours would tell the tale.

One could hardly hear one's own voice amidst the ear-splitting blows shaking the massive gates. Ratan Singh leaped up the stairs in the twin gate towers to access the wide ledge above the gates. It was lined with rows of archers positioned on the notches of the gates, bows strung and arrows ready to fly. Peeping from a slit, the Rawal waited until the first row of four elephants approached the gates, tree trunks aimed. Then he shouted, 'Let go!'

Intent on their targets, arrows arched towards the animals. Some of them pierced the eyes of the elephants. Others picked out their *mahouts*. Screeching in pain, the wounded elephants threw down the tree trunks. Blind and rudderless they ran hither and thither careening into the elephants behind them or stamping on the soldiers who were advancing under the protective guard of their massive bodies. Then the second row of elephants was hit. So were the next rows. It was complete chaos. Enemy soldiers and horsemen were so busy, getting out of the way of the pain-crazed elephants that they did not notice the gates being winched down.

Chittor's troops surged across gate-bridge and hacked down the confused flanks of the adversary forces. By the time they could rally, a great deal of damage had already been done. But the army of the Sultanate was a disciplined one, trained on campaigns across the length and breadth of the country. Commanders shouted orders, prodded men with their own swords and cut off the panicked retreat. Eventually, the cavalry and infantry battalions wheeled around and took on the Mewari troops. Mounted men with spears pointed bore down on opponent horsemen. They clashed mightily with shields and armour ringing. Soon the narrow road was filled with cursing warriors, neighing horses and screeching elephants. Men fought furiously, often trampling over the injured or dead, headless or limbless or those with spears jutting out of their bodies. Unhorsed warriors and foot soldiers engaged in combat with swords and daggers. Mewari archers from high vantage positions on the fort ramparts rained down showers of deadly arrows.

Rawal Ratan Singh was in the centre of the fray. He had jumped off when his horse had been slashed down. As his sword thrust and parried in the horde of fighters, he would often fight two opponents at the same time. The other chieftains and their troops, old and young, fought just as courageously. Rana Lakshman, despite his devious polity, was a fearsome figure in battle. Most enemy soldiers avoided the burly figure as he hacked expertly with his blade. Ratan Singh realized the enemy was being pushed back. After all, a different indomitability comes forth when one is defending one's own hearth and home. He yelled at the Mewaris around him, 'Hold ground! Move forward! Cut down the Turks!'

At one moment, he spied his son, young Kunwar Vir Bhan fiercely fighting Raghav Chetna. Usually one to avoid fights, the wily artist must have been forced to don armour and accompany the Sultan's forces.

'Good for you, Vir!' shouted his father. The teenager held the hilt with both hands and gave one mighty downward slash. His sword crashed on Chetna's head. The man collapsed; never again would he plot and deceive! Vir grinned at his father, not noticing Chetna's place had been taken up by a group of enemy soldiers. Suddenly, five men had encircled the young Kunwar. Seeing him beleaguered, Ratan Singh roared, 'Hold on, Vir! I'm coming across.' But his way was cut off by a huge Turk intent on swinging a mace at his head. By the time he slew the man and leaped over his body, his son was already on his knees. His legs had been smashed but he was still wielding his sword; still facing the enemy. Ratan Singh could only watch in horror as a heavy sword cleaved his son's head in two. The heir to Chittor's Rawaldom fell in a pool of blood. Ratan Singh, his father, was not allowed to shed even a single tear as he had to stave off the enemy immediately pouncing on him.

Bravely holding ground and fighting ferociously, many of Chittor's fine leaders were cut down. After all, the Turks were many and the Mewaris few; the dead of the Sultan's army were constantly being replaced by fresh troops while Mewar's army had no back up other than the archers who could not replace cavalry or infantry losses. Slowly inexorably, the Mewaris began to fall back, retreating towards the still-open *Ram Pol.*

Fierce combat was now taking place nearly at the gates that bridged the wide ravine. Suddenly, Ratan Singh saw a bobbing white helmet plume. It seemed familiar. He turned his head towards it, risking a nick on his cheek. Sure enough, the plume was attached to the white helmet he had gifted Padmavati along with the silver-white chain armour. *Was she here? In the thick of this battle? Why? Why did she not obey me? Why are her ideals dearer than my words to her?* A chain of thoughts sped through his head while he slashed and stabbed at the enemy. Despite the foe at his heels, he began to sidestep towards the area where he had seen her sword boldly rising and falling. For a millisecond, he saw her in action, a veritable amazon, her wiry figure leaping above the opponent's thrusts. Faithful Ambika, herself in chain armour was fighting beside her friend.

Ratan Singh got behind the princess. Shouting at Ambika to follow him, he put an arm around his wife's waist and bodily picked her up. Padmavati screamed. She flung her arms and legs vigorously, struggling to free herself, unable to see the face of the person who had captured her. Ratan Singh ran inside *Ram Pol* and deposited the princess on the ground inside. He ordered Ambika to keep her there and roared at the gatekeepers to wind up the gates. As the huge winch began to turn, he ran out into the battleground. By the time, Padmavati recovered and tried to return to the conflict, the gates were already half-closed.

Unable to join the fight, the princess ran up the tower to the archers' ledge. Ambika anxiously followed her. Just as the princess passed one of the notches, an arrow stuck the archer on the neck and he fell at her feet. Another arrow zipped in. . .right into the fleshy part of her arm. Pulling it out with a grimace, Padmavati picked up the bow and the quiver from the dead archer. Fixing an arrow, she took aim and almost instantly spied the opponent bowman. Letting loose a spate of quick shots, she hit her mark. Then she looked downwards and could not look away.

In dismay, she looked upon Ratan Singh in a savage battle with one of Sultan's commanders. The Turk was gigantic and towered over the Rawal. As she watched her husband use all his strength and skill to contend with the man's height and heft, she wished she could have gone to his help. She fixed an arrow to the bow but dared not pull off a shot for fear of hitting the Rawal. He was using all the tricks in the book, but the Sultan's giant general was gaining the upper hand. Ratan Singh was tiring; the brutal combat of hours was taking its toll on him. In terror, Padmavati saw the giant deal him a mighty blow on his shoulder rendering his left arm useless and hanging. Her husband went on fighting with his sword-arm. As he executed a feint with his sword, Ratan Singh was forced to bend a knee. Exactly then, another enemy soldier on horseback behind the Rawal, sliced downwards. Horrified, disbelieving, Padmavati saw her husband's head topple from the neck, roll over and over until it came to rest by the sandal of an ordinary soldier.

The Rawal of Chittor was dead.

Padmavati felt a bolt of pain flash across her own neck. Unbearable agony blazed through her body forcing from her lips a name she had never uttered during her husband's lifetime. It burst out in a mighty scream, 'RAATAANNN...'

Her shriek resounded above the din of the raging conflict. Its intense pain reverberated across the stones of Chittorgarh. Faithful Aravalli cliffs echoed its ringing tones, 'RAATAANNN! RAATAAAnnn! RAataannn!' For that one instant, the world stopped spinning; the sun paused in its path; even Time was compelled to stand still. Padmavati's lacerating wail was so piercing that it seemed to engrave her husband's name in every element of nature and in all human hearts. It was an articulation of unendurable anguish by a woman whose very breath had been snatched away cruelly. It would not go unmarked or unnoticed by eternity.

Like a lotus whose stem has been snapped, Padmavati collapsed in a heap at Ambika's feet. 'Help me!' cried her friend, trying to lift the princess. At that instant, Koki, the stalwart Chief Eunuch, appeared at her elbow. Together, they carried the unconscious girl down the stairs. Koki laid her across his own horse and holding its bridle, directed it to Padmavati's palace.

It's over, thought Ambika, hurrying behind the horse, *I must get the princess away.*

The moment she was gently put on her bed, Padmavati opened her eyes. She struggled to sit up though Ambika pushed her down gently. 'No, no,' she said frantically. 'I have to get dressed.'

'Dressed? Princess, the enemy is at the gates. We have to leave Chittor. We must go back to Singhaldweep. The fort is not safe for you. We have to go,' Ambika declared.

'Go? Go from my home?' The princess shook her head. 'I will go nowhere, Ambi. Now be quick. Don't argue. Help me to dress...in my bridal *lehenga* and ornaments. As my Gem would say, I must be all *banithani* when I meet him.'A small smile played on Padmavati's lips but did not reach her dazed eyes.

'No, Princess.' It was a shocked, confounded cry from the heart of her childhood friend.

'Yes, Ambi, yes. Now go. I have promised *Ba* that Chittor's honour will remain intact. The war is lost. The Sultan's troops will enter the *garh* soon. As you say, there is little time. Tell Koki to come here at once.' The princess pushed Ambika. 'Hurry.'

Ambika went out to find Koki hovering in the terrace. 'We have to take her away, whether she wills it or not,' she told Koki.

'We can't,' replied Koki sombrely. 'The enemy soldiers have discovered the *Chota Pol* path. They have begun to climb. Our escape is cut off.'

'Nooo...,' Ambika covered her face. Then she remembered Padmavati's order. '*NaiRaniSa* wants to speak to you.'

Koki immediately slipped into the *shayan kaksha* bowing. '*Hukum?*'

To Padmavati's query, he replied, 'The fire in the *Jauhar Kund* went out last night, *hukum*.'

'Then light it again,' she commanded.

'That is not possible. The *Kund* is filled with water. It is not covered and everything is wet,' he replied.

'So is there no place which is covered and can be used for this purpose?'

'I don't think so.'

'But the women of Chittor must be saved from the Sultan's army. This will not be for only *satis*. It has to be for all the women,' declared the princess.

'I understand, *hukum*,' said the Chief Eunuch impassively.

'What does the Rani Prabhavati say?'

'*RaniSa* came through the passage from the old palace to inspect the *Jauhar Kund* but when she saw it filled with water to the brim, she went back without saying anything,' informed Koki.

'The passage! That is covered, isn't it?' exclaimed Padmavati.

'Yes, *hukum*. But it is a closed area...'

'And...and I remember about halfway inside it there is a large natural cavern. Doesn't it have a high roof?' asked the princess.

'Umm...yes,' agreed the Eunuch.

'Take my command to Rawal Vir Bhan...,' she began to say.

'Princess, the Kunwar fell in battle at the *RamPol*,' Ambika reminded her.

'Then it is my command that you must obey.' As Koki nodded, she went on, 'A platform must be erected in the cavern and it must be heaped with all that is required for a pyre. Go. Do it. Tell all the women in the royal palace and in the villages to prepare for *jauhar* in an hour's time. Inform the priests that the ceremony must be conducted with all haste. I will be there, soon.' All of a sudden, the stricken wife had become the royal queen.

Koki bowed and scuttled off.

The New Queen had decided. There was much to do and he had only one hour.

Ambika hovered near the princess as all the women completed the worship of Ek Linghji in the temple above the *Gomukh Kund*. She held the silver platter holding the *prasad* and the sacred drink. Padmavati drank the whey with basil but left the sweets untouched. Her face was pale, yet nobody looked as gorgeous and radiant as the princess among the glittering and crimson-clad women. She was garbed in the splendid *lehenga* and jacket that she worn when she had first entered Chittor. Her long tresses that

Ratan Singh had loved to run his fingers through were braided and piled high under her embroidered veil. From head to toe, she gleamed with ornaments. Ambika saw Rani Prabhavati shooting furious glances at the princess. *Even now the Rani cannot let go of her envy and hostility,* thought Ambika. *Will she carry it to the next world?* Pushing the woman out of her mind, she whispered into the princess' ear, 'I am coming with you.'

Padmavati smiled at a lady and whispered back, 'No, you are not. You will not even enter the passage. You promised me you will do your duty.'

'Don't leave me behind, princess. I have been with you, always,' pleaded her friend.

'Not this time, Ambi,' said Padmavati firmly. 'I have given you a responsibility, remember?'

'What if the Turks kill me?' Ambika tried another tack.

'You will find a way out. You always do. You have to, Ambi.'

'How will I live without you, Princess? Not a day have I spent in all my life without your presence. How will I live in a tomorrow that won't have you?'Ambika whispered in a choked voice.

'Ambi, tomorrow is new day; a new life; a new strife. Good bye, my sweet friend.' Quickly hugging the disconsolate girl, Padmavati hurried to take her place in the queue led by Rani Prabhavati.

Ambika was suddenly swept aside as the rest of the women joined the line singing wedding songs of joy. There were women and girls of all ages but not everyone was singing. Some young girls looked frightened. Some had tears spilling down their beautiful cholis. Many mothers were hugging and caressing their young sons who were going to be left behind. Some fathers were holding their baby girls to their chests, unable to let them go to their death. Many mothers clasped their little girls' hands tightly lest they run away to escape this terrible fate. However, most of the widows had calm faces…probably effects of the marijuana in the sacred drink and thoughts of joining their husbands in the next world.

I must go with them, too, thought Ambika, desperately running up the queue, pushing through until she was as close as she could get to the princess. The long train of women began to move towards the entrance of the underground passage. She shuffled along keeping her eyes on her friend. She hardly saw the men lining the path, openly grieving for their loved ones going to their deaths. She was hardly aware of the fetid air inside the tunnel. Her eyes were focused on the shining figure walking at the head of the queue. Some of the women stumbled and fell in the melee. Women who were nearest them lifted them up.

A little distance inside the passageway, a rough, wooden platform came into view surrounded by logs of sandalwood, wood chips and bundles of hay heaped high. A group of priests were chanting verses from the Vedas and pouring ladles of *ghee* on the pyre. She saw the senior queen, Rani Prabhavati halt at the foot of the ladder to the platform. The senior queen hesitated. Padmavati slipped past the queen to ascend the ladder with quick, firm steps. *Why is she in such a hurry?* Ambika thought, dismayed.

When Padmavati had settled down in the centre of the pyre in her usual lotus pose, Ambika crept up to the base of the platform to plead with joined palms again, 'Please Princess, please. Let me come with you. Don't leave me behind.' Padmavati did not even look at her.

Ambika saw a fluttering in the lap of the princess. It was Ginni nestling with his soulmate. *How unfair!* Ambika exclaimed silently, *Ginni has the right to go with her but not I!*

Ambika was so intent on supplicating the princess, that she did not notice when the chanting had ended.

Suddenly in a whoosh, flames rose like a fierce orange column right in front of her. Ambika felt its sizzling hot breath on her face and hands. Pain ripped through her. Her hair and skin burned. Screams erupted in the cave. Ginni's shrieks were almost human. Women jumped off the pyre and were engulfed in flames. Children ran around like small torches. The priests rushed to the cave opening to escape the inferno. Ambika was caught up in the crazy scramble. Crushed in between the bunch of frightened priests, she was swept out by the panicked group through the narrow tunnel. Half fainting and burned badly, she had collapsed on the platform above the *Gomukh Kund*. Thus she was saved the painful sight of the explosion that took Padmavati to blessed oblivion.

32

Uma's voice faded into silence. A notion floated through Mrinalini's head: *this is no story. All of it has actually occurred.* When Uma was describing the *jauhar,* the journalist had begun to feel the familiar symptoms of her phobia. She was choking, her skin pricking with stings of flames and the hairs on her arms were rising. As if the inferno was roaring before her, she could smell roasting flesh. Desperately, she tried to control her reactions, telling herself it was only her natural loathing for fire that was bringing on these weird sensations. She tried to shake them off but they wouldn't go. She opened her mouth to gulp in some cool pre-dawn air to clear her head. *Why did it taste acrid?*

The silhouettes of the foliage clinging to the rock-face of the *Gomukh Kund* were being etched against the grey eastern sky. The girls were still on the stone platform above the natural tank. A few feet away was the pavilion sheltering the blocked tunnel. Uma stood quietly with her face turned towards pavilion. Her head was cocked as if she was listening to something. Her last rendition had been so graphic that the air was tingling with its horrors.

Trying to inject some normalcy into the situation and to revive herself, Mrinalini cleared her throat. 'Fantastic!' Her voice sounded quavering even to her own ears. She tried again, 'Fantastic tale, Uma! So Ginni and Padmavati died...and Ambika? What happened to her?'

'Oh Ambika was so badly burned that her very ugliness saved her from the depredations of the Sultan's soldiers. They took her as a servant to their camp. After some months, she was able to escape to Singhaldweep. It was she who took Padmavati's heroic tale to her sorrowing parents and the Singhas,' replied Uma in a low voice.

'And she must have left the *Padma-wali* behind because you found it, right?' Mrinalini wanted to tie up all the threads neatly.

Uma did not reply and the journalist realized her question did not warrant one. She tried to make up her gaffe by asserting, 'I don't think any queen has had such an eventful life. I understand now how she has become a cult around these parts. But I can't fathom why all historical records of her times whether of Khusro or any other do not mention her. The first time the world comes to know about this fascinating queen is from an epic in Awadhi by a Sufi poet. Strange! After your tale, I wonder...I am tempted to believe you. Was she deliberately expulsed from history?'

'Maybe...' murmured Uma in a low voice.

She seems tired. After all she had been speaking continuously for most of the night, thought Mrinalini. Wanting to distract her own mind from a peculiar distress that weighed down like a stone on her heart, she continued speaking, 'Her devotion to Chittor, her sacrifices, her diplomatic strategies...all prove her ability at statecraft. Possibly she would have made a better Rawal than Ratan Singh.'

'Ratan Singh followed her advice even when it went against his own judgement, but it did not bring peace to Chittor,' pointed out Uma in a dull tone.

'That is because her ideas were way ahead of her times and were not understood by either by the chieftains of Mewar or by that savage boor, Alauddin. She was born too early and that was her tragedy,' analysed the journalist, 'And now for her journal...Show me where it is, Uma.'

The girl stirred as if she had been woken from a dream. 'The *Padma-wali*...?'

'Yes. You said, after you finished the tale, you would take me to the place where you had hidden it....' Mrinalini's words trailed off as a sudden thought pierced her like a sharp nail. Her years of news reporting had caught the false note in this narrative. Agitated, she turned to Uma with raised hands, saying, 'Just a sec! Just a sec! Hold on!'

One of her hands went to her forehead unconsciously rubbing at it. Mrinalini was trying to erase the ridiculous irrational sensations she had been feeling a few moments back. They were clouding her usual clarity and logic. With half a mind, she noted that Uma had not responded to her sudden outcry. More focused on extracting the truth, she carried on, 'You have been describing in every detail the battle for Chittor and the events that followed it, though you said yourself that the writing of the *Wali* ended before the Mewari soldiers rode out. The battle itself...or, or... let's take the preparation for the *jauhar* in the underground cave...there,' she pointed to the vermilion-smeared stone wall. 'You spoke about specific things, such as Padmavati's dress, the varied reactions of the women and...and so much more. All of this could not have been written in the *Padma-wali*! How did *you* know that the princess drank the basil whey but did not touch the sweetmeats unless... unless...', she was finding it difficult to articulate the weird idea forming in her mind, '...unless you actually saw it? Or somebody who saw it, told you about it.'

Uma was mute as if she had not heard a word.

Mrinalini felt she had been too harsh in her urgency to get to the truth. So she used a softer tone. 'Let's go back to how it really happened. Padmavati gave the journal to Ambika to hide before she went to the battle where Ratan Singh was killed. She came back to the palace and commanded the Koki the Eunuch to prepare for the *jauhar* in the underground cave. So...that means after she left her palace for the battle, returned and proceeded for the *jauhar*, Padmavati had not written anything more in the journal. So everything that you have narrated over the last half an hour has been your own recital and not from the *Padma-wali*.Then how...how do you know who ordered the *jauhar* and how it was conducted? Only somebody who was actually present in the place would know so many minute details. How do you know? Were you there?'

'Yes.'

'What?' The journalist was sure she could not have heard right.

'Yes,' said Uma, louder now.

In two steps, Mrinalini reached the girl. Holding one of her thin arms, she roughly turned Uma around to face her...and recoiled! Choking back a scream, Mrinalini stared at the face...no, a mask...charred skin peeling off in chunks and hanging down to show bright pink flesh. Eyes that were dark, deep hollows with no eyebrows, a nose that was a black triangular hole. She had no hair, only a bald, charred, seared pate stretching upwards from a terrifyingly hideous face half-covered by the translucent dupatta. Lipless, the mouth moved...whispering to the petrified journalist, 'Don't you know that there is no difference between Uma and Ambika? They are one and the same. ***I*** am Uma and ***I*** am Ambika.'

Mrinalini froze.

The girl held up a hand...claw-like...thin roasted bones that were fingers and asked, 'Why do you constantly ask for the *Padma-wali?* It is yours. It is with you, not me.' Then she came close and whispered into Mrinalini's ear, who reared back in shock. The creature's hollow eyes glittered as she asserted, 'Now my work is done. My promise is fulfilled. I can hear them call me and I must go.'

Even as Mrinalini's eyes widened with disbelief, a strong gust of wind swept down from the cliffs. From inside the pavilion came a tremendous rumble. The stone wall blocking the underground passage burst open. Hissing and spluttering, a tongue of fire leaped out of the tunnel cavity. Mrinalini trembled as flames encircled Uma like huge python lapping her up like a hungry monster. *Now*

Uma, Ambika or whatever that pathetic creature was, will finally be at peace. This was Mrinalini's last thought, as she slowly crumpled to the floor.

It was nearly seven am and morning light was washing the vault of the *Kund*, when the old caretaker discovered the girl. She was lying alone and unconscious on the platform before the pavilion of the blocked passage. He called out for help. Gardeners, who watered the lawns at first light, came running. They were about to lift the inert body of the girl, when Mrinalini opened her eyes. She sat up by herself and seemed quite fine.

'I am alright,' she assured the puzzled men, sipping water from a glass they had offered her. 'I will take care of myself, thank you, *bhaya*.'

Seemingly dismissed quite peremptorily, the men nodded and went away muttering about 'modern girls who don't listen to warnings…'

Mrinalini looked around herself to see whether she was really quite alone. She glanced at the pavilion. The stone wall blocking the passage was intact. Bright sunlight and the twittering of birds made her wonder, *did I dream everything? And Uma?* Gradually, she became aware that the load previously weighing her down was gone. Mrinalini realized her entire being was suffused with an astonishing tranquility.

She leaned forward and picked up her backpack from the stone floor. Then her hand slowed. Somehow, the bag seemed heavier. She put her other hand inside and felt around. *Something rough and stiff…what is it?* She slid it out and slowly turned it over and over. A yellowed parchment scribbled across in black spidery calligraphy in a strange script. It was folded many times into a flat square. *Was it the Padma-wali?* Mrinalini's hands caressed it. . .*at last. . .Padmavati's real story. . .*She looked around and carefully slipped it back into the bag.

Exactly at that instance, like a flash, she recalled. . . Uma's stunning last words whispered in her ear. Before vanishing, the apparition had hissed, 'Both Mrinalini and Padmavati mean the lotus maiden. You are she, aren't you? I knew it was you from the first moment I saw you. Did you take me for a fool, Princess?'

Glossary

Mewari

Aacho	good
Aabh ni aavjo, bhayeli...	Come down from the sky, friend
Aajyo	request to come
Anndatta	Provider of food
Avajo	request to come
Ba	Mother
badam ka halwa, dil khushal, churma laddoo, mawa kachori and gujia	traditional sweets and sweet dishes
Badhera	ancestors
badhni chunri	scarf with tie and dye patterns
balyo	boy(called with love)
bandhanwar	traditional door hangings
Bandhej	clothes in tie and dye patterns
banithani	ladies properly dressed with appropriate makeup and ornaments
Banni	Bride (loving address)
Bavji	God, Deity
beendni	bride
beero	brother
Bhaisa	Brother
Bhojai	brother's wife
bilia	ivory bangles
borlo	ornament worn by ladies on forehead
chattris	dome-shaped pavilions
chod diyo	leave
choondari	traditional long head scarf made with bandhej patterns,
chuneri	scarf to cover women's head

chunnadi.	printed scarf to cover women's head
Ek Linghji	Deity, another incarnation of Lord Shiva
Ek Linghji ki Jai	Victory to Ek Linghji
Fajiti	Insult
Garh	fort
Gatta Ka Sabzi, chila, dal-bati churma, methi-bajra poori, laal-maasm mohan-mass, ker sangri, bajra roti, gatte ki pulao, mewari kadi, aam ki launji, boondi raita.	traditional festive foods of Mewar
Hukum	a term of respect used to refer to any elder Rajput while replying
jaalidiwaal	fretwork wall
Jai	Victory
Jal Mahal	Lake palace
Jauhar	Hindu custom of mass self-immolation by women
Jauhar Sthaal	location of mass self-immolation
Jharoka	overhanging enclosed balcony used in architecture of Rajasthan
kalash	pot, pitcher
Khabar Raakho	Pay attention
Khamaghani	Hello, greetings many times over
Kund	a tank or small reservoir
kundan	gemstone jewellery
kundan jhumkas	genstone chandelier earrings
Kunwar	prince
lari	tie and dye pattern in stripes
lehenga-aangi	traditional long skirt and blouse worn by Rajathani women
lehengas	traditional long skirt worn by Rajasthani women
Maro Bapji	My father

Mharo dhaani	My village
Murkis	ornament worn by males in the ear in the shape of a ring
NaiRaniSa	New Queen (with respect)
Nathni	nose ring
paan	betel leaf
Phad	a style of religious scroll painting and folk painting, practised in Rajasthan
Pol	gate
rakhdi	ornament worn by women on the forehead
Rangro	alternate name of rajputs
Rawal	title of the ruler of Mewar
sarpech	turban pin
Sati	self-immolation by wife on husband's death
shayan kaksha	bed chamber
talabs,kunds, baolis	types of water bodies
tilak	coloured spot or mark worn by Hindus, esp on the forehead
torans	decorative door hanging

Hindi/Urdu

aatma	soul, spirit
Adhiyaksh	Commander, Man-in-charge
Allah-O-Akbar	Allah is Great
angavastran	a white piece of cloth or stole, worn by Hindu men draped over the shoulders.
apsara	heavenly nymph
ardhangini	better half
atithi	guest
atithi-satkar	hospitality
bajra	houseboat
barfi	sweetmeat of milk
chulhas	open ovens

dhotis	A garment worn by male Hindus, consisting of a piece of material tied around the waist and extending to cover most of the legs.
Dewan	custodian
dolis	palanquins
Dupatta	a long scarf worn by women
Faankar	artist
gangajal	water of the holy Ganga River
ghee	clarified butter
haveli.	villa
hookah	hubble-bubble
Huzoor	an Indian of high rank, or a title of respect for such a person
Ishta Devata	cherished divinity
Jagran	Awakening
Janab	Sire
Kajal	kohl
Kameez	long tunic worn by women
kirtans	songs in praise of God
kurnish	deep bow of salutation
kurta	long tunic worn by men/women
mahal	palace
meri Jaan	My love
mahouts	elephant drivers
Mamu	uncle who is mother's brother
Mantri	Minister
mela	fair
musavvar	painting
Namaste	Hello, Greetings
Padminis, Chitarinis, Hastinis, Sankhinis	categories on women according to the Vedas
paras pathar	philospher's stone
Parivar	family
Patranis	Royal queens
prasad	holy offerings

puja thal	platter with auspicious items meant for ritual devotion
purdah	sequestered
salwar	loose pyjamas worn by women
sarovar	lake
shalwar	loose pyjamas worn by Turkish men
Shehenshah,	King of Kings
shringar kaksha	dressing room
Sikander-i-Hindustan	Conqueror of Hindustan
swarglok	heaven
trishul	trident and holy symbol of Hinduism
ulema	Arabic for learned scholar
vaid	doctor
vatikas	gardens
yogi	religious guru
zari	embroidery with gold and silver threads

Singha

agasthi malaya	a necklace of agate stones
Dimithi	domed earings
Ira Handa	circular hair ornaments
karapati	choker
mala hatha	seven gold necklaces enjoined
nalalpatiya	head ornament with a piece along the middle that ended in a large lotus pendant on her forehead
paddakam	pendant
paalaka	chain made of gold beads
pethi maala	seventh necklace of the mala hatha
Poruwa	Weddng platform
seli valalu	broad gold bangles

References

Print

The Many Lives of a Rajput Queen, Historic Pasts in India c.1500-1900 by Ramya Sreenivasan. Pub: University of Washington Press

Rani Padmini, The Heroine of Chittor by BK Karkra. Pub: Rupa Publications India Private Ltd

Padmini Charitra Chaupai by Poet Labdodaya Krit. Pub: Sadool Rajasthani Research Institute, Bikaner

Online

https://archive.org/details/padumawatiofmali00maliuoft

http://www.speakingtree.in/allslides/true-story-of-rani-padmini-chittor-place-of-jauhar-haunted

http://www.davishunter.com/home/place/Chittorgarh

http://www.chittorgarh.com/tourism_at_chittorgarh.asp

https://kambohmag.wordpress.com/2011/09/26/history-of-kamboh-kamboj-kamboja-etc

http://www.jairajputana.com/2012/12/gora-badal-story-in-hindi_19.html

http://hattai.page.tl/Marwari-Dictionary.htm

Visits

City Palace Museum, Udaipur

Fort at Chittorgarh

National Mission for Manuscripts

Acknowledgements

Right at the outset, I would like to declare that *Padmavati* is a work of fiction.

Enthralled by the persona of this famous queen right from my schooldays, I always wanted to write about her. Imagine my surprise when I began to delve into her historical background and found hardly any authenticated facts. Other than literary works over the last few centuries, initiated by the epic, *Padmavat* written by a Sufi poet, Malik Mohammed Jayasi in Awadhi in the CE 1540, there was no real empirical data on her. So I had no choice but to rely on my own imagination to depict the charisma of this enlightened, fearless, accomplished and heroic queen. While I did get a few recorded dates and figures about Alauddin Khalji and Rawal Ratan Singh of Chittor, their personalities are largely sketched from my impressions of their times and historical events. Descriptions of Chittorgarh and its history are, of course, factual and garnered from my visit to the monument.

Nevertheless, the tale of *Padmavati* would not have seen the light of day without the roles played by certain people in its creation.

My heartfelt thanks go to Bhaswar Mukherjee, Kena Shree, Anahita Lee and Shefali Martins who have given me great deal of their precious time and proficiency to peruse and validate my rendition.

Without Kunal Nachane's astute editorial skills, the telling would never have acquired the polish it definitely needed and I am utterly grateful to him for it.

I cannot but appreciate the infinite patience with which my family, Satchit, Shayan, Priyatna, Kaushik and Stavya have tolerated my crabbiness as well as helped me in my research while I struggled to bring *Padmavati* to life.

Last but not the least; my deep gratitude goes to my publisher, Dipankar Mukherjee and the *Readomania* team for the opportunity to resurrect through my book the eminent personage of this great Queen of Chittor.

About the Author

Sutapa Basu is a best-selling, award-winning author as well as an educationist, poet, columnist, translator and a writing coach. Her historical novel, *The Curse of Nader Shah* won the Best Fiction Award by AutHer Awards, 2019 instituted by JK Papers and *The Times of India*. She is the 2016 First Prize winner of *The Times of India's* Write India Campaign for Amish Tripathi while her debut, a psychological thriller, *Dangle* was nominated for the Anupam Kher Award for Best Debut English Novel in 2017. In March 2021, she received an award for Excellence in Publishing by the Public Diplomacy Forum. He nonfiction book, *The Birth Of My Nation* has been nominated for Best Young Adult Literature by Valley Of Words Book Awards, 2023.

Her best-selling historical fiction is *Padmavati, The Queen Tells Her Own Story* published in 2017. Her second historical fiction initiated the Invader Series with *The Legend of Genghis Khan* published in 2018 and continued with *The Curse of Nader Shah* published in 2019. Two of e-anthologies of short stories were published in 2020. In 2021, a cosy-mystery adventure, *The Cursed Inheritance* and an English translation of the iconic Bengali *Thakurmar Jhuli* titled *Princesses, Monsters and Magical Creatures* were released. In 2022, *The Birth Of My Nation, Tracing India's Nationhood,* a non-fiction historical narrative for young readers was launched. The next book of historical heroines, *Parvati Bai, The Forgotten Witness of the Battle of Panipat* was released in 2023. In 2024, another YA thriller, *Murder in the Jungle,* was published by Niyogi Books.

Her short stories have appeared in anthologies, *Crossed & Knotted, Defiant Dreams, When They Spoke* and *Write India Stories*. Her poems have been published in *Muse India,*

Kaafiyana, The Dawn Beyond Waste and *The Remnants of Loss.* Her children's tales and poems appear in several K-12 educational textbooks.

Sutapa coaches children, school faculty and aspiring authors at *Sutapa's Studio.* She is a podcaster with *The Sutapa Basu Show* podcast and runs a live chat show *Bistro Buzz Conversations with Sutapa Basu* that hosts unique people.

Find out more about her, watch her videos and read her blogs, stories, poems and writing techniques on her website sutapabasu.com & Readomania.com.

Other Books By Sutapa Basu

HISTORICAL NOVEL

THRILLER

NONFICTION

TRANSLATION

ANTHOLOGY

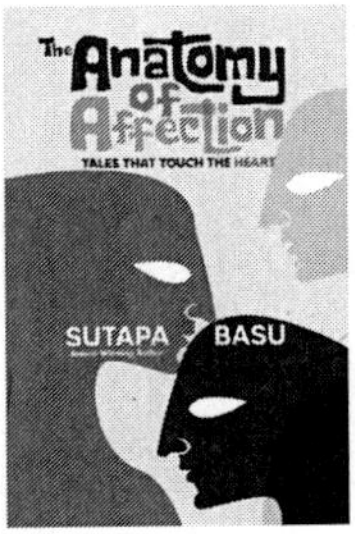

Readomania

Readomania exists to nurture, curate, and bring to you content you love. We are a publishing house that takes pride in encouraging talent, new or old, and provide a wonderful platform for awesome stories.

We make this possible in multiple ways.

The first as an independent publishing house. Readomania boasts of multiple imprints across various categories—fiction, nonfiction, children, to name a few. An eclectic mix of content for its readers, when you read a Readomania title, you enter a world that's yours, supported by unique and quality narratives.

The second, as an online publishing platform for writers—a place to share stories, poems, opinions, travelogues, a way to explore your creative talent. Available as premium, as well as free-to-read content across multiple genres, the reader is spoilt for choice.

Join us in this journey, as we explore, develop, and present stories to our readers and audiences. Welcome to the world of Readomania, get ready to craft stories that enrich lives.

You can visit us at: www.readomania.com